THE KNIGHT BEFORE CHRISTMAS

Bronwyn narrowed her gaze and smiled icily. "I may have been one of many women who felt a fleeting desire to kiss you, but you will never have to worry about me being one of them again."

Catching her chin between his thumb and forefinger, Ranulf turned her head so that he could read her eyes. And there, reflecting in the darkening cobalt depths, was the truth. She wanted him, and her feelings were just as strange and startling to her as his were to him.

"I don't believe you, angel. I think you wanted to kiss me and desire to do so again."

Then his mouth came down on hers before she could even think of resisting.

Bronwyn heard a sound and realized it was coming from her. His lips held her spellbound and the light touch of his fingertips was transporting her into a realm where all realities and concerns drifted away.

"More . . ." she heard herself beg just before his mouth again sought hers in another kiss . . .

Books by Michele Sinclair

THE HIGHLANDER'S BRIDE

TO WED A HIGHLANDER

DESIRING THE HIGHLANDER

THE CHRISTMAS KNIGHT

Published by Kensington Publishing Corporation

The
CHRISTMAS
KNIGHT

MICHELE SINCLAIR

ZEBRA BOOKS
KENSINGTON PUBLISHING CORP.
http://www.kensingtonbooks.com

ZEBRA BOOKS are published by

Kensington Publishing Corp.
119 West 40th Street
New York, NY 10018

All Kensington titles, imprints and distributed lines are available at special quantity discounts for bulk purchases for sales promotion, premiums, fund-raising, educational or institutional use.

Special book excerpts or customized printings can also be created to fit specific needs. For details, write or phone the office of the Kensington Special Sales Manager: Kensington Publishing Corp., 119 West 40th Street, New York, NY 10018. Attn. Special Sales Department. Phone: 1-800-221-2647.

Zebra and the Z logo Reg. U.S. Pat. & TM Off.

ISBN-13: 978-1-4201-0855-2
ISBN-10: 1-4201-0855-7

First Printing: October 2010
10 9 8 7 6 5 4 3 2 1

Printed in the United States of America

To John,
who gave me invaluable insight into
the world of single-sighted vision,
and his wife, Jessica,
who shared a little bit of their life,
revealing the spouse's side of their love story

Prologue

Wide spacious ships with single mast sails were the primary means of traveling short distances. Ships transporting large quantities of goods drifted slowly at the speed of approximately a knot per hour. The distance between Fécamp, Normandy, the closest port to Rouen, the capital of the Duchy of Normandy, and Southampton, England, which served as the primary port for Winchester, the medieval capital of England, was nearly 130 miles, or approximately five days by sea in good weather. Travel by land depended upon horses, type and condition of the terrain, and the quantity and size of goods being transported. Journeying from Westminster to the wilderness of Cumbria crossed more than 275 miles and typically took nearly two weeks, but the trip could be made in less than five days if one traveled very light and by horse.

Deadeye.

That's what they called the man Laon had been chasing since spring. And it was appropriate. For the famed dark-haired knight refused to wear a patch. How he lost his left eye was a mystery, and if anyone did know, they were not saying. Rather all the mumbling aboard the ship was about Laon and how he had found—more like unwillingly caught—the only man who had refused to become a lord.

The small fleet of ships had been traveling to England for two days and the seas had been exactly as expected this time of year—unwelcoming. The weather continued to fight their northwesterly course, dramatically slowing their voyage with fierce wind, creating uncomfortably large white-capped waves that constantly slapped at the wooden oak planks of the Viking-designed cog.

Laon studied the lone imposing figure standing by the ship's side, staring at the rolling sea. The newly titled, reluctant lord was impervious to the enormous swells that made nearly everyone else on board seek the ship's rail for temporary relief. Only today had Laon felt well enough to study the battle-beaten knight and prepare some kind of defense or explanation. But he could fabricate not a one, for Laon regretted nothing he had done. The difficult man had left him little choice. A new lord was needed, and Ranulf de Gunnar—whether he wished it or not—was the only viable Anscombe heir.

Laon did not expect to be pardoned for his actions, but he did hope for understanding. Loyalty between a man and a king was important, even necessary, but the loyalty exchanged between a knight and his liege could mean the difference between life and death. Especially in Cumbria, the remote hills of northwestern England.

So when the previous Lord Anscombe had lain dying, needing someone to find his elusive nephew and ensure he assumed his responsibility, Laon had gone, never imagining Anscombe's heir, a favored commander of England's new king, would be so hard to find . . . or to persuade. And in the end, Laon couldn't.

So he had resorted to shrewd means to not only find, but bind the solemn knight to a life the man had made clear he did not want.

Sir Ranulf de Gunnar was the next in line to the Anscombe title and forfeiting that right would be ruinous for an already struggling people. The resulting vacuum would tempt not only northern marauders determined to steal and plunder whenever prosperity became possible, but those enemies who lived close by, waiting for a chance to gain even more land and power.

A voice cried out by the ship's mast and a young boy dressed in several layers of rags to keep warm rushed across the deck carrying what appeared to be a heavy coil of rope. Unable to see in front of him, the lad collided into the large knight's back and would have fallen if it had not been for Ranulf's quick reflexes and accurate timing. He gently righted the cringing boy, who avoided looking at him before taking off again.

Laon fought the urge to move back into the shadows as Ranulf turned to scan the forecastle. His single umber-colored eye quickly inspected the activity of the bow. The evidence of the eye's missing mate was hidden beneath a closed, flaccid lid, concealing the empty wound. Most probably thought the injury was the result of an unlucky encounter with a sword, but only someone familiar with the fiery depths of hell would recognize the probable cause behind the mottled scar disfiguring the left brow and cheek. Laon was one of those few.

Moving back into the shadows, Laon attempted to covertly study his new liege lord. But as if the man understood just what Laon intended, the hard figure returned his gaze to the sea so that his back was once again all that was visible. He had given no evidence in his expression that he was aware of Laon's scrutiny, but Laon was certain nonetheless that the newly titled lord was fully cognizant of who was around him and what they were doing. A skill he had employed shrewdly in Normandy.

Finding him had been difficult, but eventually achievable. Speaking with Ranulf, however, had proved near impossible. He moved from one battle to another, attending the duke's court for only brief periods of time before setting out for a new location, training field, or battle. At first, Laon had believed it to be just bad timing causing him always to be where the elusive knight was not. But when it became obvious Deadeye was cleverly and intentionally avoiding him—and would continue to—Laon realized the truth. Ranulf was well aware of his cousin's death and he had no intention of accepting the Anscombe title or the responsibility.

So Laon had done what his new lord no doubt considered underhanded, devious, and far from honorable . . . but it had worked. And now there would be consequences for using such tactics. Just what those were, however, Laon was having difficulty discerning.

Ranulf de Gunnar was far from young and had long mastered the ability to appear disconnected from all that was around him. It was not surprising. If one survived the wounds caused by a fire, the experience did more than just damage the skin, it changed a person inside. The pain of recovery either broke their spirit or made them stronger. That the new lord was made of the latter was obvious, but whether he had become wiser or bitter was impossible to distinguish from afar.

The wind caught the collar of Ranulf's tunic and flipped it up, slapping him on the side of his face. He pivoted and flicked it aside. His expression remained what it had been since the inception of the voyage. No anger, no remorse, no self-pity . . . no warmth. Emotions were not something the man displayed. His nickname "Deadeye" led one to believe hatred and wrath marked his life's path, but Laon suspected there was much more to the one-eyed knight than the outward shell revealed. Long-distance observation would divulge nothing more than what Laon already knew, leaving only one way to determine the makeup of Cumbria's future.

He must talk to him.

Ranulf ignored the old knight who had single-handedly ripped his simple, but livable life away and replaced it with one only a fool would want. His previous life may not have been pleasant, but as a prized commander to the duke of Normandy, who in a few days would be crowned the king of England, it had been very lucrative and—most important—isolated from the general populace.

The old man advanced another step and shifted his stance to counter the movement of the ship. He was standing on Ranulf's left just outside of his limited range of vision, but that didn't mean Ranulf could not hear where the aged knight was and just what he was doing. Ranulf had learned to perpetuate the myth of full sight with an acute sense of hearing, which let him know exactly where the old man stood. Close, but far enough away to step out of reach if Ranulf decided to physically assault him, and yet, just near enough for conversation. Something the old man obviously hoped Ranulf would initiate.

If the scheming knight had been anyone else, Ranulf might have been inclined to talk, if only just to order him away. But he was no longer naïve to the lengths the old man would go to achieve his desires. Few men had the audacity—let alone foresight—to seek out the duke and duchess of Normandy and convince them of their cause. And yet, Sir Laon le Breton had displayed a surprising amount of audacity by doing just that. Of course, fortuitous timing had helped. Henry had just learned of King Stephen's untimely death and his rightful succession to the throne, making the stability of England—especially in the remote areas of the country—of high importance. Having loyal noblemen overseeing distant regions would be critical to securing Henry's reign. So Ranulf had been ordered north to his new home, his new title, and his new responsibilities . . . his own feelings on the matter noted, but ignored.

"Mind if I join you?" The deep and even voice boomed across the short distance, cutting through the wind.

Ranulf fought the urge to look at the man and continued staring at the rolling sea. The knight's commanding tone had been unexpected and had almost caused Ranulf to react instinctively in a deferential manner. Almost. Instead, it served as a reminder that the old man was far more than he appeared. "Better than staring at me."

"So you did see me."

"Studying your hard-earned prize from afar? Yes, I knew. I make it a point to know where my enemies are," Ranulf replied, keeping his focus on the afternoon horizon. Detachment, not animosity, laced his tone.

Quiet followed and Ranulf wondered how long the battle-wearied knight was going to blatantly continue to assess him, when Laon deliberately walked around so that he stood on Ranulf's right, and in his line of vision. Damn man was far too observant.

Ranulf shifted his jaw but remained silent, hoping Laon would take the hint. Unfortunately he did not.

"Now you can study me," Laon offered coolly, "although I believe you have already been doing so for some time. And though you call me your enemy, you do not really consider me to be so. Otherwise, I would be dead."

Ranulf fell to temptation and stole a side glance at the bold, candid man, who had just surprised him . . . again. Shoulder-length brownish-gray hair was thicker than it appeared at a distance and blew straight behind him as he faced the wind. Unusual slate blue eyes were enhanced by his pale complexion, which possessed the pasty look of someone who did not enjoy traveling by ship. But aside from the knight's pallid skin tone, the man projected a commanding presence. They were of similar height and body build, except Laon was naturally leaner. Ranulf suspected the sinewy muscular form belied the old knight's true strength.

Sir Laon le Breton might no longer have been practiced at wielding a weapon, but Ranulf was on his guard nonetheless. The man dominated his surroundings by controlling both conversations and situations. No wonder the duke had taken a liking to him. Another time and circumstance, so would have Ranulf, but the knight needed to understand that today he was manipulating no one. "You may not be an enemy, but you are certainly someone I don't trust," Ranulf clarified.

Laon shrugged his chin and nodded his head. The man was brutally candid, but Laon had a message of his own. "Unfortunate for you then that I am also your one and only noteworthy vassal, my lord."

Ranulf closed his eyes and took a deep breath before exhaling. He was still not used to hearing the title in reference to him. Learning of Lord Anscombe's death—a distant cousin he had never met—and discovering that his father and elder brother were no longer among the living had been too recent to fully digest. In that one moment, his life, his future had changed. And Sir Laon le Breton had ensured it was a future Ranulf was forced to embrace. In doing so, the old knight had uprooted Ranulf's comfortable life—and he wasn't ready to forget that just yet.

"Keep your fealty. I have my men."

"From what I have learned, the majority of your men won't arrive until spring. Until then you have the support of what? A couple dozen soldiers? While they are no doubt able men, I question if any of them will be very helpful in running Hunswick Castle. Have they—have *you*—ever had to deal with questions about candle making? Or determined what to do when the dovecote is raided by five-year-old mischievous little boys?" The old man smiled as if he knew Ranulf's weakness. "Perhaps the fealty of an old, interfering knight somewhat knowledgeable about such things would not be so useless."

Now that Laon had moved to his right side, Ranulf could see him patiently waiting for a response. Ranulf was unwilling to give him one. Instead, he clinched his jaw, refusing to agree or disagree. Giving up, Laon shrugged unperturbed and turned to face the sea. "You are far too young to be so severe and serious."

"I'm a serious man," Ranulf replied, forcing his voice to remain level and devoid of any prideful anger at the man who dared to criticize him.

"Maybe, but wearing a perpetually solemn expression does not necessarily make a man wise. Nor does it qualify him as a leader." The tone was light, conversational, but the subject matter hinted at the gravity to which the old knight felt.

Ranulf turned to blatantly reassess his newly acquired, yet unwanted mentor. This time it was Laon who looked out to the sea and ignored him. Ranulf could feel his pride churning, twisting inside him in a way he had not experienced in years when he realized that was exactly the old menace's aim. The man was intentionally trying to provoke him, not to arouse anger, but to gain something else—he wanted to understand just whom he was going to serve. "Have you decided upon my character, or do you need more time?" Ranulf challenged.

Laon's misty blue gaze surveyed the rolling waves for several seconds before he turned to reply, this time his demeanor and expression solemn. "Your temperament is obvious for the world to see." He paused for a moment as if he were trying to decide whether he should refrain from further explanation or continue. The latter was chosen. "You are neither kind nor giving, and your manner can best be described as impersonal. When you do engage, you are rather gruff, although I wonder how much of that is habit or intentional. However, you are fair and respectful, even to those you know little or not at all," Laon finished, pointing at the young deckhand Ranulf had assisted earlier.

Ranulf discerned no animosity in the comment reflected back. Such frankness, and from a virtual stranger, was most unusual and yet it was also refreshing. The exchange and its tone almost resembled that of a father-son conversation, the kind Ranulf always coveted but never received.

The old knight had actually *looked* at him when he spoke. Even some of his own men typically preferred to converse to his profile rather than face-to-face. There were many ways to disguise discomfort and over the past decade Ranulf no longer considered it an insult. But he wasn't prepared for a stranger to speak to him and address him as if he were a whole man and not the damaged figure he knew he appeared to be. As a consequence, Ranulf found himself responding to the sincere request with atypical candor. "Your perception is correct. I am what you describe."

"Which one? The gruff fool or the fair wise man?" Laon inquired, simultaneously releasing a half smile.

Ranulf cocked his right brow. It had been a long time since he had done any self-examination, and last time he had, the conclusion had been unsettling. "I do not know myself. I probably have the capacity to be either . . . depending on the conversation."

"Fair answer. I think I might like you yet, my lord." The half smile morphed into a full grin.

Ranulf stared incredulously at the older gentleman. In principle the knight was his vassal, and as such, his demeanor should be submissive, if not reverent. Instead, the old man emitted a presence of one who expected and deserved respect. And surprisingly, Ranulf was beginning to. "I see now how you persuaded the duke to your cause."

"Ah, I didn't sway him, but his wife . . . our new queen is incredibly lovely and quite perceptive."

Ranulf chuckled and shook his head. He couldn't help it. He only wished he could have been there to witness the encounter. "Yes, she is a much better choice of ally. She's powerful, not to mention influential. It is a shame neither of you realized that you were damning a lot of people by forcing this title upon me."

"Your predecessor didn't think so when he bade me to find you and neither did the king."

"My *predecessor* didn't know me. My elder brother was the one groomed since birth for the role of Lord Anscombe. Not me. War was what I was made for.

I belong on a battlefield. Trust me, that is where your people will wish I had remained."

Laon shook his head. "You are no tyrant." Then suddenly realizing what Ranulf meant, he stopped and asked, "Because of your missing eye? Its absence doesn't bother me. Nor will it bother anyone else at Hunswick. What you will bring weighs of far more importance."

Ranulf clinched his jaw and then forced it to relax, resuming a detached expression. "Either you are blinded by sight or by naïveté. Either way, it is not I who'll be disappointed. I told Henry, and now I'm telling you. Be satisfied that I am going. Don't be hopeful."

Ranulf emerged from the ship's innards. His horse was faring, but like the rest of the living, Pertinax would be far happier once they reached the solid grounds of England. Ranulf scanned the back of the deck, saw the man he was looking for, and expressed a small smile before meandering through the maze of crates and barrels tied down to the wood planks. "Can you see the horizon from there?"

"I can and you're right," Laon answered, keeping his eyes focused on the water. "It does help, but I'm old and not made for sea travel. Like war, it's a young man's passion, and at eight and twenty, you should now be wishing for more."

Ranulf took a deep breath and exhaled slowly as he took a giant step up onto the rear platform. The philosophical tenor of the old man's comment announced that he intended once again to challenge Ranulf's perception of himself and the world. Whether

Laon was trying to prepare him for his new responsibilities or convince him that he would be a good lord, Ranulf could not discern. Regardless, the attempts so far had been unsuccessful. But Ranulf secretly had to admit, their discussions over the past few days were some of the most engaging and frank ones he had had in some time. Maybe that was why he constantly found himself drawn to the man and yet rebelling against the very words Laon had to say.

Ranulf looked down at his unpredictable companion, who was sitting on one of the stacked crates, in view of the sea's undulating horizon and yet out of the way of the water's freezing spray. "I'm learning that a man has only so much control over his destiny. I doubt even Henry would disagree."

Laon took a deep breath and then, after a few seconds, exhaled. "I do find it curious your consistent reference to our new king as Henry or the duke."

"He's not the king yet."

"True, but King Stephen is dead and the coronation will take place soon after our arrival. Very few continue to refer to him as the duke, and with the exception of Her Grace . . . and you, no one calls him by his name."

It was a gentle reminder that the duke's status had changed, and consequently, he should no longer be referred to so familiarly. The old man was right, but it would still be a hard habit to break. "I have known *King Henry* for many years, more than most realize. We have a"—Ranulf paused for a moment as if to decide just what to say and settled on—"unique history."

"But you are now a noble and he is a monarch. Your relationship must change."

"It did. The moment he thrust my desires aside and bade me north."

"He must have believed you would be a good leader to convince you to go."

Ranulf's mouth transformed into a firm, unyielding line. "I am loyal to Henry, but that does not mean I am blind to his . . . personality traits. The man is cunning and intelligent, but he is far from generous and only a half-wit would think him benevolent. He had his own reasons for 'convincing' me, as you put it, to assume my latest role."

"And they were not for the good of his people?"

"Not exactly. More like I am to bring and keep the peace. And if that helps those that live there, then good, but more importantly, Henry seeks stability . . . and William a throne." England had been suffering from a civil war for almost nineteen years and its people were longing for a strong government. Most of the English noblemen would support Henry, but altruistic peace was not what the new king sought. His brother also desired a throne and Henry intended to give him Ireland, and to do that, he needed his armies free, not fighting to maintain his sovereignty.

Laon twitched his mouth and after a moment agreed. "Making William lord of a conquered Ireland would occupy him, at least for a while. Of course, the king will need to get the newly elected Pope Adrian to agree."

"Henry will get the blessing. The Pope's English born and quite aware of who the duke is and just what power he wields."

"It seems you have a great understanding of just

what the king seeks and why. Does such understanding extend to yourself?"

"I know myself well enough," Ranulf clipped, instantly regretting the rash response.

"Then just what power do you yield, Lord Anscombe?" Laon asked, turning to look Ranulf directly in the eye. "More importantly, just what do you intend to do with your authority?"

There they were. The first of today's several probing questions. Looking inwardly and analyzing one's own psyche was not a pastime Ranulf indulged in and he did not intend to start now. "Besides get some sleep?" Ranulf quipped back.

A bushy gray brow popped up. "Should I ask?"

"Not if you want answers."

Laon issued Ranulf a slight shrug, indicating he wouldn't press the issue, but was still interested in understanding the truth behind Ranulf's attempt at a jest. Instead, Laon returned to the original point he had been trying to make. "So the king wants a peacemaker, and I and your people desire a fair leader who will guide and aid them when times are tough, which have been many of late. But what do you want?"

Ranulf did not respond because he was not sure of his answer. To return to his life? That wouldn't be fair to his men, and in truth, fighting was not fulfilling work, it was numbing. Ranulf was a good commander, some even claimed he was one of the best, but the feeling of reward and accomplishment with victory had long left him.

Laon waited for either an answer or an impulsive remark, but getting neither, he pushed on, refusing to allow Ranulf avoid the point he was trying to make. He gestured toward Ranulf's missing eye and said, "You survived an injury that changed your perceptions, of both the world and those you encounter. You have felt life's injustice and, for years, used your pain and anger to wield a sword in battle. Now you have the chance *and the power* to change people's lives. You just need to decide what you are going to do. And remember, even doing nothing has consequences."

"Why do you care?"

"Because four of those lives belong to myself and my three daughters." Laon stood up, gave a brief nod of respect, and then disappeared into the rooms hidden beneath the platform. Ranulf stayed where he was, staring blankly out at the stormy sea.

Laon was right. By accepting the title, benefits, and responsibilities of being Lord Anscombe, he had assumed a position of power. And he had considered it from everyone else's viewpoint, but his own. His men needed a home, his king wanted peace, the people whom he was to oversee needed a protector, but just what did *he* want to do with all that came with being a noble? For it mattered no longer that he didn't want the power. He had it.

And just like the old man said, he could choose action or no action—but either would mean change.

The next morning began similarly to the others. Ranulf rose, ate enough stale bread and mead to steady his stomach, and then went to see about the keeping of his horse. He entered the stable area and the large black destrier swung his head around in welcome. In doing so, Pertinax revealed another visitor. Sir Laon le Breton. Yesterday, the old man had finally stopped trying to pry into Ranulf's conscience and motivations, talking instead about himself, his family, and life in northwest England.

Ranulf approached Pertinax just as the boat unexpectedly lurched, causing him to take a quick couple of balancing steps. Laon, still unable to compensate for any sudden rise and fall of the ship, tumbled into the large horse, which snorted a loud and very cross whinny.

Laon steadied himself and huffed, "Your horse is quite unhappy."

"He likes the sea even less than you."

"Doubtful, but I am surprised you brought him. I would have thought the king would have supplied you with a dozen horses if you but asked."

Ranulf arched the brow over his good eye. Laon was unusually cross today. "Maybe, but Pertinax knows me."

Laon's mouth formed a brief "oh" before closing. Over the past few days, he had begun to grasp the impact of losing one's eye. Limited sight was not just a learning curve to be overcome and surpassed, but an impediment with daily repercussions Ranulf experienced in almost all actions, conversations, and activities. Without two eyes in which to pinpoint exact distance, reaching out to take what was offered or pour some ale into a mug was not as straightforward as Laon had initially perceived. After years of compensating for his injury, Ranulf could easily make those around him forget that these were indeed challenges he addressed every day. And his horse Pertinax was one of those supports enabling him to smoothly interact with the world.

"You're right. I should have realized just what your horse means to you," Laon grunted, rubbing his face vigorously with his hands. "I shamelessly blame lack of sleep for my thoughtless remark. I can finally keep my food down, but I like my bed to be firm and unmoving. My tired state is something you are quite familiar with, I suspect."

Ranulf ground his teeth together and followed Laon back up on deck where, when not raining, they spent their mornings. Details of his sleep, or lack of it, Ranulf had been careful to keep to himself. No one, not even he, would be comfortable following the orders of a man who never slumbered more than a handful of hours a night. Almost all men could function tired, but after a while irrationality set in and emotional control eroded away. Each man had his limit, and Ranulf used to wonder when he would reach his. But it had been years since he had enjoyed more than four hours of sleep at a time, and even then he rarely went into a deep unconscious state. He wasn't plagued by nightmares, just the inability to be at complete ease. To be vulnerable.

"Is that one of your men?" Laon asked, pointing to a young man with muscular arms built from months, if not years, of swinging a sword.

Ranulf twitched his jaw. "I did not think them obvious."

"They aren't, but too many times have I seen one of them glance your way, not in curiosity, but with desire for direction. That makes about two dozen on board, unless you have more traveling on the other ships making their way to England," Laon remarked with a sigh of disappointment.

"You hoped for more?"

Laon hesitated. He had trapped himself and to deny otherwise would make all their previous conversations meaningless. "I had. Most of your neighbors, at least the English ones, will respect your assumption of Hunswick Castle, the waters of Basellmere, and its surrounding valley, but your closest neighbor I fear will not be one of them."

"Don't worry about my men, or lack of them. The ones you see could handle three times their number in battle, but almost a hundred more will be arriving in the spring."

"A *hundred*?" Laon gasped. He had known more soldiers would be coming, but he had never dreamed the knight had so many loyal followers. "Good Lord, you will bring Hunswick to its ruin, not its glory."

"My men seek peace, nor war. Most have families and are eager to become farmers, raise children, and live long lives."

"They are married, then."

"A good many. Why? Do you worry there is not enough land to support my men and their families?"

Laon shook his head. "Quite the contrary. The north still suffers from King William's deadly campaigns to end the region of its Anglo-Danish independence and replace it with a Norman allegiance. After decades of sparse population, Cumbria needs more people. There is rich soil and its mountains are laden with ample coal, copper, tin—even iron."

"Then why does fear hide in those blue depths of yours, Laon? Do you think if my men become farmers, they won't respond to a military threat?"

"I do not fear for myself, but my daughters."

"I will protect them from the evils of the world."

"The evils of the world they have seen and felt. The evils of men, however . . ."

Ranulf finally grasped Laon's concern, but his previous comment gave him pause. *The evils of the world they have seen and felt . . .*? Ranulf found it hard to believe the old man would allow any harm to even come near his daughters. He wondered just what Laon had meant. "You have spoken very little of them."

"You have asked even less," Laon countered simply as he moved to get out of several deckhands' way. The breeze had shifted slightly and they were adjusting the large mast as best they could to ensure nature's force was captured. Too many times in the past few days had the wind turned south, forcing them to bring down the sail until a northern gust returned.

Ranulf walked over to a less busy part of the ship and leaned against a stack of crates, temporarily piled high to provide more maneuvering room on the deck. Laon was right. Ranulf had not asked about his daughters. He had inquired about Hunswick, Laon's keep, the lands, the region, the weather . . . everything but the three things the wizened knight prized the most. "So tell me about your eldest daughter. I assume you will say she is blond, blue-eyed, and beautiful beyond compare."

"Ranulf, you are far too cynical."

"You have said so before. So speak. Tell me of your temptresses and how their beauty can ensnare my men with a mere glimpse."

"And for that last sarcastic remark, I shall describe them in detail, and maybe someday you, too, will have daughters and understand the fear that lurks in my aged heart."

And so Ranulf listened as Laon spoke of each one. As it turned out, he had been wrong about their appearance, for if Laon's description of them held even slight accuracy, not a one was blond and only the eldest possessed the same deep blue eyes of her father.

"Bronwyn is very much like myself, in both looks and temperament."

"Then she likes to command and manipulate those around her," Ranulf interjected to prove he was listening.

Laon sent him a slicing glance before answering. "Aye, and if you think me stubborn and relentless, you will rediscover the meaning if you and my eldest daughter ever disagree upon something. And prepare to lose, for even if you are right, she will wear you down until you find yourself acquiescing on the one point you swore never to concede," Laon cackled, obviously recalling one or two times in which she had bested him. Then his voice changed. "But I thank the Lord for her steadfastness and prudence. With my absence, I suspect all have been looking to her for guidance, and they were right to do so," he breathed softly. "Though no man would want her, she is strong in spirit and in mind and the only person I would trust to ensure her sisters are safe and well."

"Which one is Eydthe?"

"My middle child. She is small, but don't let that deceive you when you meet her. She inherited her Scottish grandmother's temper as well as her dark red hair. Of all of my daughters, her mind is the sharpest, but so is her tongue. It is my youngest, Lily, that I worry about the most when it comes to your men," Laon sighed. "She is the spitting image of her mother. Tall and slender with long dark raven hair and gray eyes, she snatches the soul of every man who looks upon her."

And as if he could read Ranulf's mind, he added, "And her disposition is just as sweet. She sees only the good things in life and, as a consequence, brings joy wherever she goes."

Ranulf conscientiously fought to refrain from showing his true reaction—nausea. He had no doubt that Laon believed every word he spoke, but beautiful, kind, understanding, and smart? He had yet to see such a combination and he had encountered many, many women at court. Either Laon's daughters were not half the beauties he claimed them to be or they were far from the sweet creatures he described. Such women did not exist.

"As far as your eye patch . . ."

Ranulf blinked and tried to recall just how and when Laon had changed the subject. "I don't wear one."

"I noticed and I have also seen how it affects those around you."

Ranulf felt a coldness enter his veins he hadn't felt in days. He had been a fool to believe Laon indifferent to his injury, uncaring of appearances. The time had come, as it always did, when curiosity could no longer be ignored and questions would be asked. "Your meaning?"

"A simple exchange, my lord. You wish to ignore a topic and I wish to discuss it. I should have brought it up before, but was hoping you would."

Ranulf clenched his jaw. "I don't talk about my eye because there is nothing to discuss. It is gone and I am not going to wear a horrid piece of leather to make those around me comfortable." *Including your daughters*, he added to himself.

They, like the rest of the world, would have to get used to him or, even better yet, stay away from Hunswick Castle altogether. They had a home and there was no reason the four of them ever had to meet. "Eye patches," Ranulf huffed. "Damn things are a nuisance. In order to keep them from slipping, they have to be so tight a headache is inevitable. And trust me, they are not the secret to making those around me feel at ease," Ranulf added, repeating the rationale he had spouted for years to the duke and his men.

"Good reasons, though I doubt one of them is the real motive behind your refusal." Laon paused long enough for Ranulf to counter. When it became obvious that silence was going to be his only response, Laon went ahead and answered the looming unasked question. "I think you use people's reactions as a test . . . And it is unfair."

Unfair! The man had no idea what the word meant. He possessed his limbs and all his senses. He had a beautiful life, friends, and family. Ranulf neither sought nor wanted pity, for life could have issued a much harsher sentence to be endured, but neither did he need the scorn and antipathy that came from people's unreasonable fear. And if boldly displaying his injury kept people away, the better. "A test that you might have prematurely passed," Ranulf gritted out.

"Your eye did not matter to me then nor does it

now," Laon declared, ignoring the tension growing in his friend, "then again, I have seen bad injuries, disfiguring ones like yours. Most, especially the coddled women and men of court, have not. I have watched you, my lord, and have concluded that you are uncomfortable with your limitations and therefore desire to make others just as uncomfortable. You drive people away just so you don't have to watch them squirm, shrink in fear, or just stare outright. You do it to protect yourself."

"What do you want from me?" Ranulf growled. He steeled his face from emotion, clamping his mouth and gritting his teeth, but it belied the truth. He had been flung back in time, to the day, to the very hour, that changed what he was to those around him.

"I just want you to be honest with yourself, my lord. Until then you won't be free of your past and neither will those who are around you."

Ranulf shot Laon a penetrating look. He wasn't ready to consider the nagging man's comments or admit the truth to them. "I think, knight, we have conversed enough for one trip. And since you will want to go directly home upon our arrival and I will be staying for the coronation, it may be some time before we will have the opportunity to speak again. Until then, Sir le Breton," Ranulf finished and, then with a quick nod, pivoted to walk away.

Riggers were swinging above and Ranulf ducked to avoid the massive ropes that were falling to the deck as they were adjusting the sails once again. A warning shout bellowed from behind him, echoed by several loud rebukes to move. Ranulf whipped around to search for the danger and issue a warning of his own for addressing him in such a way when he realized he wasn't the one being shouted at.

The solid beam used to manipulate the sail had come loose from the cordage holding it in place. Every available seaman had been called and was working feverishly to secure the spar. Even riggers had left their positions, leaving lines unsecured in the wind.

Ranulf was about to continue his march back to his cabin when he spied one of the free lines tossing precariously close to a young deckhand no more than eleven or twelve at the ship's edge. Ranulf hollered at him, but the aspiring seaman was struggling to push back heavy crates that had fallen and were getting drenched by the crashing waves against the rail. The boat swayed and a rope with a large heavy iron hook flew up in the air and was about to crush the boy as gravity pulled it back down. Ranulf reacted. He dove, sliding across the wet deck, yanking the slender form out of the hook's deadly path just in time. Their bodies slammed into a stack of crates. The top box wobbled for a moment and then crashed down on the other side.

Ranulf let go a sigh of relief and eased his grip on the boy, who was himself visibly trembling, realizing just how close to death he had come. Ranulf patted his arm as blood began flowing within it again and stood up just as another wave crashed over the side, soaking his clothes. Grabbing the hem of his wool tunic, he twisted the dark red material and wrung out the freezing seawater, knowing the activity was fruitless. He would have to change and quickly before he became chilled.

He was about to return to his cabin when out of

habit, he glanced to his left to see what others would have registered in their peripheral vision. The men, who had been steadying the spar, were now gathered around the spot where the top crate had actually fallen.

He had escaped death, but someone else had not been so fortunate.

One of the men looked up and glanced his way. Ranulf, seeing the stricken expression, suddenly knew who had been standing on the other side.

Forcing his limbs to move, Ranulf staggered around the cluster of men to see Laon lying on his back with shards of broken wood around him. The old man was struggling for breath. He was not dead, but would be soon.

Loss was never easy, but the old knight's would be especially difficult to handle. Ranulf had friends; some he trusted with his life. One was already in England, waiting for his arrival. Ranulf had been looking forward to introducing Laon to Tyr, eager to hear their blunt exchange. But it was not to be. Ranulf knew he would never meet another who would dare to be not just candid, but honest on topics no one ever ventured.

Kneeling, Ranulf raised Laon's head and clutched his hand. The dying knight squeezed as pain ripped through him. "I'm here, Laon."

The old man opened his eyes and rasped, "Promise me, Ranulf, promise me you'll marry her."

"I'll take care of them. This I promise. All your daughters will be safe. I swear it on my life."

Laon squeezed Ranulf's fingers as he clung to life. "I need you to promise me you will marry her."

"Marry who?"

"Lily, the youngest," Laon gasped. "She is so lovely and so young. She will learn to love you and make you a good wife as my Aline was to me."

Ranulf instinctively let go and tried to release his hand from Laon's grip. He had no intentions of marrying anyone and a dying request was not going to change his mind. "I made you a promise, Laon. I cannot do more."

But the fading knight was not appeased. He reached out and seized Ranulf's wet tunic, giving him the choice to either forcibly remove the dying man's grip or come closer. "You don't understand. Marriage is the only way you can protect them all from—" And the rest was drowned out by gruesome coughs that accompanied internal bleeding.

Ranulf struggled to understand why Laon believed only marriage could protect his daughters and said so, but his fading friend refused to release his painful hold on life. "Family. Must be family. Do this one thing for me . . . and . . . for yourself. Be my son. Marry her . . . marry my Lily."

Agony coursed through Laon's face and every man around him knew that Ranulf held the manner of the old, admired knight's passing in his hands. "I'll marry her, Laon. Your family will be safe, and if that is what needs to be done, then it will be done. I promise."

Calmed by the vow, Laon closed his eyes and gave a brief nod. A second later, his hand dropped to the deck as he exhaled his final breath.

Never before had guilt or pressure swayed Ranulf's decisions, and although it might have appeared otherwise to those men who heard the exchange, neither emotion drove his promise. Ranulf doubted few could understand the real reason he had agreed, but in those last few seconds, Laon was not just a man, a vassal, or even a friend. He was a father, and to Laon, Ranulf was a son. Such requests could never be denied and so Ranulf had agreed.

He just hoped that the duke saw reason and would refuse to allow the match. Because Ranulf was *not* going to get married, and he was damn sure not going to be snared for life to a shallow creature the world doted on because of her beauty.

Chapter One

Though crowned in October after King Stephen's death, Henry II wasn't coronated the king of England until December 19, 1154, in the Westminster Abbey. Appearing at his coronation dressed in a doublet and short Angevin cloak earned him his immortal nickname "Curtmantle." Eleven years his senior, his wife, Eleanor of Aquitaine, was absent from the event due to being heavily pregnant with their second son, Henry III, causing her own coronation to be postponed for four years, taking place in December 1158 at Worcester Cathedral. Marrying Eleanor, a power and influential figure, made Henry the largest landowner in France, including King Louis VII, his longtime rival and Eleanor's first husband.

Bronwyn reached back to close the small cottage door behind her and sighed regretfully as the warm sun beat down on her face. She had put on her heaviest bliaut and now was uncomfortably hot with only herself to blame. Minimizing castle staff had meant she and her sisters had to share an already overworked chambermaid. So to help, they all agreed to assume additional responsibilities, including taking their clothes to the laundress and bringing them back, something about which Bronwyn had been frightfully negligent. Today she was paying the price.

It wouldn't have been so bad if the warm wind that blew through the wooded hills was what a December breeze should be, chilly or even cool. Never had a fall lasted so long or a winter arrived so late. If the weather continued its rebellious mood, the bonfires during this year's Twelfthtide would have to be drearily small, maybe even nonexistent; otherwise everyone attending the festivities would be roasted alive.

Bronwyn picked up her pace and joined her two younger sisters just in time for another squabble to begin.

"If your sheer presence has such miraculous healing abilities, Lily, then you should have stayed. For until Tomas is well, his daughters won't be coming back to Hunswick and I am telling you right now, that abusing poor Charity and having *her* continue with *your* chores needs to stop." Edythe paused and waited for affirmation, but Bronwyn remained mum. She had stopped playing the role of peacemaker long ago, for it never worked.

Realizing that her older sister was not going to lend any support, Edythe proceeded with her censure. "Besides, everyone knows that Tomas will continue to feel poorly until just after Father Morrell finishes his lengthy Christmas sermon. Very soon afterward there will be a miracle recovery in full— *whether you're there or not.*"

Lily's gray eyes flashed. "No wonder Father Morrell doesn't visit more often. Why should he with you around to lecture everyone? And you need not be so smug, Edythe. *No one* fails to come to Hunswick for Twelfthtide, even if they are ill. You're just jealous I was able to cheer Tomas's spirits when you could not." Lily jutted out her chin in a challenging way, knowing Edythe would rise to the bait.

"I'm glad you cheered someone then because your mournful moods of late have been near intolerable," Edythe replied as she sauntered haughtily past her sister.

Lily ran to catch up, her dark hair bouncing behind her. "That's unfair, Edythe!" she cried, not denying the truth of the barb. "Father *would* have taken me to London. And you know it. My one chance to see a king be crowned," she moaned, "and I'm here. Can you imagine the celebration that followed? It is probably happening right now. The dresses, the food, and the men! Eligible, wealthy lords, and barons and knights everywhere!"

"Good Lord, you love to be dramatic," Edythe snorted, her bright blue eyes sparkling with condescension. "And you are incredibly naïve if you think Father would have allowed you to go to Westminster. You would have made a nuisance out of yourself with all your flirtations and silly little giggles. It's repulsive how you act around every two-legged mammal with a beard."

"But it works," Lily returned with a large smile she knew would aggravate her sister. "You should try it,

Edythe. God gave you everything needed to capture a man's eye, but then you open your mouth and drive anyone interested in you my way. If you could just learn to keep quiet."

"Amazing, Lily, for that's *my* advice to *you*. And as far as driving men away, first there would have to *be* someone to repel. Not one man of marrying age or eligibility has visited since Father left, and secondly, if a man can be so easily intimidated, I wouldn't want him for a dinner companion, let alone a husband."

Lily rolled her eyes, their light shadowy color made only more piercing by her fair skin and dark hair. "You don't intimidate, Edythe. You insult."

"And you, Lily, think anything that isn't dripping with flattery and praise is an insult. Father, Bronwyn, and I have protected you far too long from the realities of the world and soon you will have to pay the price."

Lily blinked her eyes in an effort to look bored. "There you go again. When have you ever protected me from anything?"

Edythe yawned and Bronwyn almost joined her. The argument had evolved into a standard battle between the two strong-willed personalities. The conversation would progress as they all did, with either Bronwyn intervening or them sniping at each other for hours until one accidentally pricked more than just pride.

Edythe opened her mouth and Bronwyn shot her a "you know better than to pull me into one of your petty squabbles" glance. Edythe closed her lips and shrugged, finally deciding that she had had enough of arguing with her little sister.

Bronwyn fought back a sigh of relief and lifted

her dark gold hair off her neck to allow the slight breeze coming off the hills to cool her skin. She had washed her hair earlier that morning, and when they had left to make their visits, her semidamp locks had kept her cool and comfortable. Now she longed for a knitted snood to hold the unruly wavy mass up and off her back.

"Why do we fight so much these days, Bronwyn?" Lily asked.

Because you both are scared, Bronwyn thought. "You and Edythe see and live life in different ways. You perceive things as they could be and Edythe as they are. I, on the other hand," she sighed, "seem to want to hold on to the past and keep things as they once were."

Bronwyn knew her voice had grown melancholy at the end. If she continued walking with them, they would grow suspicious of her quiet behavior and pummel her with questions until they discovered what was troubling her. "There's my favorite tree, and with Father gone and all the preparations for Twelfthtide, I have abandoned it for too long. Please tell Constance I will be back before dinner so she won't worry."

Edythe paused to stare at the huge, leafless alder. Its dense branches stretched outward in all directions in a tangled mass. Her face took on a brief look of bewilderment. "I think I'm the only one in this family who isn't prone to fanciful indulgences," she murmured and then waved good-bye as she headed back to Hunswick.

Lily leaned forward and gave Bronwyn a quick peck on the cheek. "Enjoy your walk. Edythe and I will see that nothing is amiss until your return." And before Bronwyn could reply, Lily spun around and dashed out of site, as if she were still a child on an exciting mission.

Bronwyn leaned back against the callused bark and looked east, toward Torrens, the hill she had named as a child after one of her father's dogs. When she had needed a companion the most, Torrens had been there. For every tear, every painful step, frightening moment, or period of loneliness, that shaggy gray wolfhound had been at her side.

Sitting on top of the hill was her childhood home, Syndlear. Constructed early during the Saxon rule, the large tower keep had been the area's focal point for years. Situated high on the crest of Torrens, it possessed a great vantage of the valley and the hills beyond, giving the owner forewarning of oncoming enemies. It looked to be much closer than it was, but a skilled rider who knew the terrain could travel from the valley below to the elevated keep in a half day.

To her right, was Bassellmere, one of the most exquisite lakes in Cumbria. The mountains surrounding it reached into the sky and both were reflected off its deep, dark rippling waters. With woodlands blanketing the surrounding foothills, Bronwyn could not imagine a place that could touch Bassellmere's beauty. Ahead was Hunswick Castle, one of the first to be transformed from wood to stone in northern England. Its odd shape and incomplete curtain walls and towers kept it from being of any note or true protection, but Bronwyn didn't care. To her, Hunswick was home.

Unfortunately, it belonged to someone else.

Bronwyn took a deep breath and exhaled as the

sad feeling that had been creeping upon her took hold. The sweet smell of witch hazel was in the air. The odor-filled flower had been her mother's favorite. Memories of her loss suddenly flooded Bronwyn and she began to hum the verse her mother had sung by her bedside hour after hour, day after day as they lay together, clinging for life. The simple haunting melody had helped her endure life's most painful events and Bronwyn knew deep down that soon she and her sisters would be mourning the loss of their father.

He should have been back by now. His last communication had been weeks ago with the joyful news he was returning. But he never arrived and Bronwyn knew deep down that something had happened.

Her sisters refused to acknowledge what was in their hearts, but Bronwyn had learned the hard way to face life with no pretenses. If their father had been injured, a message would have been delivered by now. Only bad news took so long to arrive.

"Still trying to sing that haunting little tune, angel?"

Bronwyn froze. The voice was deep and smooth and dripping with male charm. The last time she had heard it, it had belonged to a child turning into a man. The pitch had been slightly higher and with unexpected and humiliating croaks that caused him to grow angry and lash out at those around. Her heart started beating faster at the unwanted memory. Why now? Why had Luc Craven decided to break his banishment now?

"I told you last time we saw each other to never call me 'angel' again." Because of him, she hated the endearment—even from her own family.

Luc faked a bristle and stepped into her view. "I thought you might have changed your mind. I am not the boy you once knew."

He was right. Last time she had seen Luc Craven, he had been a skinny weak boy with bright white hair, a sharp pointed nose, and overly long limbs. Someone with whom she had been carefree. They had played together almost daily when they were children. He had always been possessive and willful, trying to dictate everything they did or said. Most of the time she had gone along with his wishes, but oftentimes she had done the opposite just for fun. Then one day the fun had abruptly ended and he had been forced to leave and never come back.

Recent rumors that had crossed the short distance between their households had not done Luc justice. She had heard him called handsome, and Bronwyn could not deny that he was indeed very good-looking. Shoulder-length golden hair, sky blue eyes framed in dark lashes, and a granite jaw that matched the rest of his hard, muscular body were indeed attributes most women would consider appealing. But those women were not from Cumbria . . . and they did not know Luc. For those who were familiar with him didn't see a handsome man, but a cruel one, without compassion or remorse. And looking into the bright crystal blue eyes staring at her, Bronwyn knew Luc Craven had not changed even a little bit in the past ten years.

"I have not changed my mind, Luc. About the nickname or about you."

Instantly, Luc's face hardened and Bronwyn felt the hair on the back of her neck rise. He took a step closer, and outstretched one arm against the tree as he bent over her. "I am a baron now, angel. A man to be respected and obeyed."

His mouth came toward her and Bronwyn turned her head away so his lips grazed only her cheek. "It has been a long time since we last spoke," she hissed, "but do not think that I have changed so greatly. I took no orders from you then, and I will not now. Especially not here. We are on Anscombe land and you have no power here."

The scowl on Luc's face transformed into a broad, genuine smile. "Maybe not now, but soon, angel. Soon."

"Not soon, Luc. Never. My father found the new lord of Bassellmere and Hunswick. He is coming."

"Maybe he is, but not your father."

Bronwyn's deep misty blue eyes searched Luc's face and saw only cruel sincerity staring back at her. "No," she whispered.

With his free hand, Luc grabbed a lock of her light brown hair and caressed it with his fingers. "Yes, angel. And that makes you mine."

Bronwyn's eyes flashed and she pushed as hard as she could against his chest in an effort to get him to move back. But it was like beating solid, immovable rock. "But King Stephen. My father. Lord Anscombe . . ."

"All dead."

"But the king promised . . ."

"That was ten years ago, angel. A long time to be harboring such ill feelings. After my father died this summer, I journeyed to see King Stephen. He was most willing to forgive the innocent transgressions of a young boy in love."

Bronwyn felt all the rage, all the betrayal, from

those years ago surge in her veins. "You didn't intend love. You intended rape."

Unexpected, Luc threw back his head and laughed. Bronwyn tried to duck under his arm, but he caught her elbow just in time and squeezed. "King Stephen didn't remember it that way and thought it a wise idea to mend the feud between our families. I was given leave to choose any of Sir Laon le Breton's unwed daughters after the New Year, and *I want you.*"

"You can't have me," Bronwyn snarled. "My father . . ."

"Ah, yes. His absence was the reason I have not announced my claim sooner, but now that he is dead, I see no reason to delay any longer. You are mine, Lady Bronwyn. You always have been and always will be. I'm done waiting. As your husband, I can make your life enjoyable or a living hell."

He let go and Bronwyn reached into the slit of her bliaut and felt the cool metal against her fingertips. She gripped the hilt and hissed, "I will never marry you and you cannot make me."

"But I can and I will have you willingly or else I will take one of your sisters."

Cold fear swept through her as she realized what Luc meant and how far he would go. "You don't want me, you want Syndlear."

Luc cackled and the sick sound echoed all around them. "Angel, you still don't understand. I want *both* and much, much more."

Bronwyn felt his cool, long fingers close around the back of her head, bringing her mouth to his. She twisted with all her might and again sought the dagger nestled in her bliaut. Pulling it free, she was just about to press the tip into his skin when a deadly arrow appeared from nowhere and lodged itself into the bark of the alder right between her and Luc's heads.

Startled, Luc pushed Bronwyn away and ducked for cover. Determining it was a single stray, he straightened to his full height and grabbed the errant weapon, wrenching it free from the tree's grasp. He tossed it at Bronwyn and said, "Be sure to tell the new lord that his poachers better stay clear of Torrens and Syndlear."

Luc sauntered to his horse, grabbed his reins, and mounted. He edged the animal next to her side, but Bronwyn refused to step back. He would not make her cringe in fear. "That's what I've always loved about you, angel, you never were as weak as everyone thought you to be. Until Epiphany, my lady. At the end of Twelfthtide, we shall wed and you will finally realize that I am the only man for you."

Bronwyn stared unswervingly at Luc as he disappeared into a thicket of evergreens. She was still clutching the small heavy spear in one hand and her dagger in the other, both weapons of death. Her unusual proficiency in the latter was little known beyond her father and the late Lord Anscombe. Both men had thought that wise, believing the fewer who knew of Luc's attempted assault, the better.

They had done everything they could to keep him away, even seeking the king's interference. And King Stephen, being easily manipulated with his attention on preserving his throne from an ever-warring aunt and cousin, had ordered Luc to be banished from Cumbria. Luc's father had been furious, but had obeyed for he knew Laon had powerful allies. But that had not been enough to pacify her father. So Bronwyn had been taught the art of killing, and learned to wield and throw a blade with extreme accuracy. But she had never used it against the living, and as she discovered today, having the ability to kill someone and doing so were two vastly different things. There had to be another way to avoid a lifetime of hell.

Giving herself a little shake, Bronwyn looked down at her hand and realized it was not a wayward hunter's arrow she was holding, but a bolt. The short, heavy weapon had come from a powerful steel crossbow used by only highly skilled arbalesters.

Bronwyn looked up and studied the direction from which the arrow had come. The distance across the clearing would have challenged her best archers, making Bronwyn suspect its owner had not missed, but had hit his intended target. Whoever had shot the arrow was good. Very good. The dense collection of bushes she had been studying suddenly moved. Bronwyn rushed to investigate, but it was too late. She pushed back the prickly branches and evergreen leaves just in time to see someone disappearing on a massive black horse heading away from Hunswick and Syndlear. He was riding fast and with a large metal crossbow thumping on his mount's hind end.

Whoever he was, he did not come from anywhere near Bassellmere or Hunswick. Another day, another time, she might have stayed long enough to find out just who had saved her.

Ranulf gripped Pertinax's reins and let the horse do most of the work. The combat advantages of single-eye vision were limited to one—archery. The loss of his left eye made targeting an object easier. He didn't have to worry about ignoring the secondary image one sees when aiming. On the other hand, the disadvantages of missing an eye were numerous and the ability to ride at a gallop across unknown, mountainous terrain was one of them. On any other horse, he would have been significantly more cautious. As it was, Ranulf aimed Pertinax back to camp, urged the pace into a gallop, and then began to berate himself for being every kind of fool.

That morning he had left his men under the leadership of his best friend to ride ahead and explore the lands that were to become his new home. And to think.

His original plan of persuading King Henry II to dismiss Laon's dying request had failed miserably. The king had not only *refused* to dismiss the idea of marriage, but he had eagerly endorsed it. And to ensure that Lady Lillabet was made aware of her father's wishes and the king's support, Henry had dispatched two riders to ride ahead and deliver the news, forcing Ranulf to immediately begin his own journey north to not just a new home and unsolicited responsibilities, but an unwanted bride-to-be. For days now, he had been clinging to one hope— Laon's youngest daughter would simply refuse to marry him.

He had not realized just how close he was to his new home until he had ridden by an abandoned stone keep earlier that morning. Isolated on top of a bluff, the tower and the surrounding wooden buildings had looked structurally sound, needing only a thorough cleaning and restocking of supplies.

At the time, Ranulf had not suspected the tower to be Syndlear, home of Sir Laon, and pressed forward. But an hour later, the castle it guarded came into view. It was nestled against a lake at the mountain's valley and Ranulf knew he had reached his destination.

As Laon had described, the castle's unique layout was unmistakable once seen. Unlike Syndlear, which was a small, but orderly estate, Hunswick Castle was haphazardly sprawled along the shoreline. The mountainous terrain dictated some of the unusual design, which at a distance resembled a leather water bag being squeezed in the middle.

Along one side the lake buffered a multitude of buildings, including one that appeared large enough to be a Great Hall. Along the other side of the odd-shaped castle was an average-size gatehouse separating two towers. The one located closest to the Hall was of significant size and the other, situated on the other side of the bailey, was round but otherwise unremarkable. What was noteworthy was the stone curtain wall that connected the three structures ended there and did not encompass the whole of the castle. A feeble wooden frame continued behind the stable and other buildings where the wall stopped, and no protection at all was provided along the lakeside. The castle was totally dependent upon being forewarned.

Ranulf had ridden down to the lake to let Pertinax drink and rest and had just been about to mount and return to camp when he had overheard low moans on the other side of the thicket. Rising, he grabbed his crossbow and pushed the spiny branches aside ready to shoot if it was an animal on the attack. But he found instead a tall woman . . . who appeared to be singing.

Her husky voice had not been meant for caroling, and while it was by no means good, there was a haunting quality to it that kept Ranulf where he was. Neither drawing him in closer, or letting him leave. He wasn't near enough to make out the words, but he could see her clearly.

Far from a traditional beauty, she was tall for a woman, with untamed brownish-blond hair falling far past her shoulders down to the middle of her back. The simple dark blue bliaut with its gentle scoop neckline gave the barest hint of the cleavage it hid but did nothing to disguise the willowy figure it covered. A single gold amulet rested in the graceful hollow of her throat.

A light breeze came across the clearing and caught her curls. She looked up so that her face could take full advantage of the refreshing treat and she paused. Her large dark eyes were looking directly at him, as if she had sensed his presence. Pale, her delicate oval face possessed high cheekbones, apricot-colored skin, and a generous mouth that neither smiled nor frowned. She looked like a misbegotten angel, the kind he tended to dream up naked whenever his physical need for companionship surfaced. To him, she embodied natural beauty, the kind few women—even beautiful ones—possessed and therefore made her all the more alluring.

Then she shifted her jaw.

The movement was slight, and from across the clearing, he had almost missed it. The simple twitch was not extraordinary except that it was identical to the one Sir Laon le Breton performed whenever he had been mentally chewing on something. Ranulf wasn't staring at a village maiden; she was Laon's eldest daughter, Bronwyn.

Ranulf grimaced and raked his hand across his head, recalling Laon's description of his firstborn. The man had been blind. Yes, she was tall and her hair might be of a similar color, but *resembled him*? Laon had intimated his eldest daughter was plain, if not homely, saying outright that no man would ever desire her for a wife.

Ranulf glanced back across the clearing. She was singing again, her raspy voice still not on key, but haunting all the same. It had been three years since he had been with a woman and she was creating the most lustful thoughts his mind had conjured in all that time. Tonight was going to be uncomfortable, for Laon's daughter was stirring within him the need that had been building every day of those years.

He needed to leave quickly before she saw him, before she looked upon the disfigured face of Dead-eye de Gunnar.

But again he was stopped. This time by a man. Large, with a rugged face and thick, long blond hair styled in the way of many English nobles, he resembled what every lady of the court coveted. And the nearness of his body to Lady Bronwyn's made it clear the two were very well acquainted, proving once again all beautiful things were tainted.

A cold frisson rippled on the surface of Ranulf's skin and he turned around to get his horse and ride away. He had just hooked the crossbow to his saddle when a sharp, unpleasant cackle pierced his ears. Grimacing, Ranulf returned to the hedge and glanced once more at the couple on the other side. This time he could see Bronwyn's face. While he could not make out what they were saying, her expression and posture had been that of an angry, cornered cat, knowing she was comparatively weak, but fighting back anyway. The exchange was not welcomed but loathed.

Ranulf took a deep breath and debated his options, but when he saw the man roughly snatch her back into control after she tried unsuccessfully to get away, Ranulf's decision was made. Immediately, he returned for his bow and was prepping the bolt when he saw the man lunge for her mouth. She responded with violent twists in an effort to become free. Ranulf ignored his emotional response and aimed. The arrow flew, narrowly missing the man's scalp, but he had felt it. The imposing figure immediately let go and cowered for several seconds, waiting for more arrows to follow. Ranulf prepped another, this time with flesh as his target, but eased his grip a second later when he saw the man move to leave.

Ranulf should have escaped as well, but he had remained motionless, stilled by Bronwyn's reaction, which was not as he had expected. Tears had not fallen nor had she collapsed in fright. Instead, anger had consumed her stance and her jaw began to twitch back and forth. She was planning revenge and Ranulf longed to know just what she had in mind.

He had been so consumed with interest he hadn't realized her gaze had left the thicket from where the man had disappeared and was now on Ranulf's arrow. She gently touched the heavy tip and then looked up as if she knew he was still there. Then, gathering her skirts, she started to march toward where he stood. If he hadn't moved when he did, his first encounter with Laon's eldest daughter would have happened much, much sooner than he had planned.

The next time he saw Lady Bronwyn, he intended to be prepared . . . and under full control.

At the knock on the door, Bronwyn sucked in her breath and steadied herself before exhaling. She had known this moment was coming since her return and had delayed it for as long as possible. Coming in late and missing dinner begged for questions, but sequestering herself had only ensured a sisterly inquisition. One to which she still didn't know the answers.

How does one reveal a father's death, a baron's threats, and a new lord's arrival? All of these Bronwyn had been mulling and considering since her encounter with Luc Craven, but no matter how she looked at the situation, there could be only one response.

Bronwyn slid the drawbar up and opened the door. Lily suppressed a sniffle and darted inside. Edythe, with arms crossed, slowly sauntered in after her. Both had been crying. Hard. Somehow they had found out what had happened. Had Luc rode to Hunswick after they had parted? Had someone seen their encounter and raced back with the news?

Edythe moved toward the middle of the three chairs that formed an arch in front of the hearth. Though each of them had been given their own rooms above the Great Hall by the previous Lord

Anscombe, they all gravitated toward Bronwyn's before bed each night or when something happened. The rooms had once been the bedchambers and day rooms of the late Lord Anscombe, but he had declared them too loud and had moved into the Tower Keep as soon as it had been completed. After that the rooms had become Bronwyn's and her sisters' whenever they visited. And when Lord Anscombe became sick, those visits changed into stays, each becoming longer than the last. Now, after living at Hunswick every day for a year, the castle felt more like home to Bronwyn than Syndlear. Maybe it always had.

Edythe waited until Bronwyn took her traditional seat before speaking. "Father is dead," she stated without preamble.

Lily curled up into a ball on the chair and started to sob. Bronwyn sat immobile. "How . . . how do you know?"

Edythe's sapphire eyes darted to Bronwyn's, her forehead puckering. "What do you mean . . . how? The king's messenger told us."

Bronwyn leaned forward in her seat. "What messenger?"

Lily sniffled and looked at Bronwyn, puzzled. "The one from the king about Father."

"You know?" Bronwyn choked, her mind buzzing with confusion. *A messenger*, Edythe had said. *That* was how Luc had found out about her father. The herald must have traveled across Luc's lands and had either intentionally or unintentionally disclosed the information.

Lily nodded and then buried her head back into her skirt, her bawling renewed. Bronwyn slid off her chair and went to embrace her younger sister. "It will be fine. I promise. I will make it better. You will see," she cooed, but Lily would have none of it.

"How?" Lily demanded, brushing Bronwyn's hands away. "Just how are you going to fix this? And you, Edythe, are you happy now? You thought I too unaware of life's cruelty. Well, *my* being forced to *marry* will certainly end that!"

Lily's short tirade startled Bronwyn. Much had obviously happened this afternoon to her sisters as well as her and none of it good. Before they all emotionally collapsed with grief, they had best start communicating—not shouting.

"Lily, sit up in your chair, and for the next half hour, neither you nor Edythe is to bicker with the other." Both sisters blinked and then complied. It was rare that Bronwyn used an authoritative tone with them, but they knew better than to argue, regardless of the circumstances.

Bronwyn paced for a second in front of the fire and then stopped. "All of us are upset, but until we understand just what problems we are facing and what we are going to do, we need to remain calm, and if possible, refrain from hysterics." She waited until Lily nodded before continuing. "Now, I need to know exactly what happened this afternoon before I returned."

"But you know!" Lily exclaimed.

"I know about Father's death," Bronwyn crisply countered, wishing Lily had some ability to control her emotions. But it was like asking the rain to fall everywhere but a single spot. Futile. "I am unaware of your being forced into marriage."

Lily opened her mouth and then raised her hand

to bite her knuckle. Edythe, seeing her sister's distress, explained, "The messenger came and told us that Father had died in an accident while at sea. But his dying wish was that Lily would marry the next Lord Anscombe. The king agreed and sent him north and he is due to arrive tomorrow."

"Tomorrow?" Bronwyn whispered.

"Yes! Tomorrow!" Lily wailed. "The messenger called him *Deadeye*! He is due to arrive tomorrow and by night's end I will be his wife. Bronwyn, I can't! They say he looks like the walking dead, never sleeps, and cannot die."

Bronwyn held up her hand. "Just what nonsense are you spewing?"

Edythe blinked. "Didn't you speak to the herald?"

Bronwyn shook her head. "I never saw him. I learned about Father from Baron Craven."

"Baron Craven?" Edythe repeated, puzzled. "I thought he died several months ago."

"He did. I was referring to his son, Luc."

Edythe rose to her feet and shook her head. "But he's not allowed . . . he's . . . he's forbidden to come on this side of Torrens. Father said we were protected . . ." Her voice died as she realized the full implications of her father's death.

"With Father gone, Luc is determined to marry one of us and take over Syndlear. I am the one he wants, most likely to have his revenge for what I did."

Now Edythe was outraged. "But you can't! Not to him!"

Lily shook her head, confused. "I didn't even know Baron Craven had a son. How is that?"

Bronwyn bit her bottom lip, wishing she never had to reveal the past. "When I was thirteen, Luc attacked me and would have been successful in . . . hurting me if Father had not arrived in time. Luc was banished from Cumbria, but it seems he was pardoned by King Stephen before his death and was given the king's blessing that one of us would become his wife in the New Year if Father didn't object. And with Father gone, Baron Craven plans to marry me and gain control of Syndlear, thereby crippling the defense of Hunswick and the authority of the new Lord Anscombe."

"The New Year!" Edythe exclaimed. "But that's less than a fortnight away."

"I have until Epiphany to prepare."

Edythe stared her sister in the eye. "You cannot marry him. He was a vicious boy and such a person does not change with time."

"He is still cruel," Bronwyn murmured, her thoughts flashing back to that afternoon, "and you are correct. I won't marry him. And neither will you marry the new lord, Lily. While I don't agree with your fantastical reasons to be reluctant to such a match, I think it abhorrent to force a woman into matrimony. If Father really did desire this, he was only trying to protect us. I intend to do the same, but with far less permanent entanglements."

"We will do anything," Edythe encouraged.

"Including leaving for Scotland?"

Both sisters jumped to their feet and the barrage of questions began. "In winter?"

"But where? When?"

"How will we know where to go?"

"Who will take us?"

Bronwyn waved for them to sit down again and calm themselves. "We will depart on Christmas Day."

"But Twelfthtide!" both Edythe and Lily cried out simultaneously. "We would miss all the festivities! What about Saint Stephen's Day and—"

"We need to leave as soon as possible and Christmas is the first time when people's attentions will be elsewhere for a long enough period for us to leave without being noticed. And once out of the Hills, those who we encounter will assume we are traveling toward festivities. Rivalries will be placed on temporary truce making travel safer."

"It cannot be another time? Later? Perhaps after Childermas?"

Bronwyn shook her head. "The risk is too great. By the time Luc discovers our disappearance, we should be in Scotland and on our way to Perth, where our cousins live. Then in the spring we will go north into the Highlands to see for ourselves just where our mother grew up."

"But what about the new lord? He and I are supposed to marry tomorrow!"

"I doubt that. But if that is true, then you will stall him, Lily," Bronwyn answered quietly. "You are good at dealing with men. Tell him you need more time to be accustomed to the idea. If Father encouraged the union, he cannot be a pitiless man. I have no doubt that he would respect your wishes for at least a few days and that is all we need."

Edythe bit her bottom lip. "I assume Jeb and Aimon will be our guides."

Bronwyn nodded. She had always loved the now old Highlanders who had served as bodyguards to her and her sisters when they were children. Jeb had lost his wife to illness years ago and old faithful Aimon had never married, considering the three of them his surrogate family. "I haven't asked yet, but they would not refuse. To deliver us safely into Scotland if need be was Grandmother's sole purpose in sending them to live with us."

Lily plopped back down in her chair and twiddled her fingers. "I wonder what kind of men we might encounter in Scotland. Perhaps the reason we have not found our anyone in England is because they have been waiting for us up north."

Bronwyn gave in to the compulsion to roll her eyes. Leave it to Lily to twist a situation into something positive—and related to love. "You will find admirers wherever you go. And you, too, Edythe, will be adored by many," Bronwyn added with confidence as she rose and went to the door, indicating that tonight's chat was over.

Edythe shook her head. "Lily desires not a man, but an impossibility. A person just cannot be responsible and spontaneous at the same time."

"Well, you drive all your men away with your seriousness," Lily countered, looking to Bronwyn for support as she strolled up to the door.

Sighing, Bronwyn leaned against the jamb and picked up a lock of Lily's dark hair. "You, Lily, need to find a way to mature without losing your optimism, and Edythe, you set a standard so high and can be so critical of those who do not meet it."

Edythe opened her mouth and then closed it as she joined Lily at the door. "And what about you?" she demanded. "And don't say you are alone because you lack beauty, for you could be quite pretty if you tried wearing something other than dreary colors and keeping your hair in a net all the time."

"Unfair, because you know that I could do as you

ask, change my clothes and hair, but it wouldn't matter. The kind of man I want doesn't want me," Bronwyn uttered matter-of-factly, making shooing motions to get them to leave.

Edythe and Lily finally capitulated and she was alone again. She loved her sisters. They were incredibly different. When Lily laughed, Edythe was serious, carefree versus introspective. They were alike in only one respect: They were both undeniably beautiful. And for Bronwyn, their beauty was both a blessing and a curse. Any man who had ever shown remotely any interest in her always ended up gravitating toward one of her youngest sisters. Through them she had been able to see men for who they really were. They had saved her from making many a mistake in her younger days when she still believed someone was coming . . . someone who would love her and only her.

Someone who would be her hero.

Someone like the ghost who had come to her rescue that very afternoon.

Chapter Two

Also known as Christmastide or the Twelve Days of Christmas, Twelfthtide is the twelve-day period celebrated by Christians beginning the day after Christmas, December 26, to the Feast of Epiphany on January 6. Because days and nights were counted separately, the night celebrations began on Christmas Night and lasted until January 5 when they culminated on Twelfth Night. Most scholars agree the festive season dates back before the Early Middle Ages, but it is commonly accepted that by the fifth century, the celebration of Christmas had spread throughout the whole of the East and the West. During the season, many major holy days are celebrated and though the order and inclusion of festivals has changed over the years, the overall meaning of the season has not.

Bronwyn scooped up her hairbrush, comb, and the two knitted snoods lying on the chest and placed them with her other items on the bed. There lay everything she possessed and even that was too much to pack and bring on such short notice.

Being forced out of her home perhaps should have been expected, but Bronwyn had not been prepared to be summarily shoved out the door within hours of the new lord's arrival. And not even by the lord himself! He had compelled poor Constance to make his cowardly demands and explain that their presence—hers and her sisters'—was highly unwelcome and akin to trespassing. Bronwyn suspected that Constance, their childhood nursemaid, who was also a noted village gossip, relayed the message to vacate a bit more dramatically than the new lord intended, but it didn't matter. Lord Anscombe had arrived and with a temper.

The door cracked open and Bronwyn spied Constance's short frame and frizzy gray hair pop in the opening. "Are my sisters packing?" Bronwyn asked as she began folding the clothes on the bed.

"Aye, they are. I'm telling you, milady, that man will not be borne by many of us. Ordering you out of your own home—"

"It's not my home, Constance. It never was."

"But you have the people's allegiance, and if he thinks he will gain our support by treating the three of you thus . . . well, I'm glad to be leaving."

Bronwyn paused and looked at the plump older woman whom she had known as a child and through her worst days. "You need to stay, Constance, and so do the others. My sisters and I do not need much and it would be a shame for anyone to miss celebrating

Twelfthtide. The new lord and his men will need support, and you are beholden to him. Not me."

Constance scoffed. "The man brought no more than two dozen men with him and not a farmer, a woman, or a child. All hardened soldiers like himself. Nothing that would help replenish what they take and eat."

"Then," Bronwyn began with a mischievous smile, "I think a strict adherence to Advent should be followed. Father Morrell will be quite pleased when he arrives to deliver his Christmas sermon."

"But we never fasted bef—" Constance stopped in midsentence. Her jaw dropped for a moment before it closed into a devious smile that matched Bronwyn's. "Aye, milady. His lordship will soon realize he should have kept you running the place. Henson is too old to be a steward and doesn't know half of what goes on around here."

"That is because we have been protecting him, just as the new lord should." Bronwyn finished folding her last gown and looked up. "In fact, Constance, I intend to tell him myself. Please relay to Lord Anscombe that I and my sisters will leave without incident, but we wish to be introduced first— that to dismiss a vassal in such a way is beyond rude and would not make for good relations."

Constance turned, grimaced, and with a sound akin to a growl, said, "I'll do it, but I doubt he'll see you. He's a scarred one. And not just on the outside."

The door closed and almost immediately it opened again. Bronwyn didn't have to turn around to know who it was. Angry fast-paced chatter proved her sisters had either finished their packing or were refusing to continue. "Are you done? I want to leave within the hour."

Edythe nodded. Lily sulked. "It's not fair we can only bring two satchels. I cannot decide on what to take and what to leave. It is easy enough for the both of you, you each prefer to limit your wardrobes, but I love my gowns. How am I ever to choose?"

"You would have had to do so in a few days anyway when we left for Scotland," Edythe clucked.

Not wanting to hear another argument, Bronwyn gave Edythe a look and said, "Don't worry, Lily. I'll have Constance pack the rest of your gowns and send them to Syndlear in the next day or two. Just make sure you have the most important item."

Lily nodded heartily. "Mother's tapestry was packed first, and *that* is why I have so little room," she said, her scorn directed at Edythe before she moved to one of the two large windows on the far wall of the bedchamber. "Is that him?" Lily asked, her voice full of captivated interest.

"Who?" Edythe questioned, grabbing Bronwyn's hand as she moved to the window to see what caught Lily's rapt attention.

Below were several new men, all soldiers, but two of them stood out. Both held themselves differently as if born for leadership. One was tall and muscular, with shoulder-length reddish-brown hair. He was talking and suddenly laughed, revealing deep dimples that changed his moderately good-looking face into one that was undeniably attractive.

"Oh, he is nothing like I thought he would be," Lily hummed, clearly fascinated. "He looks so strong and capable and friendly."

Bronwyn agreed, but her description of the overly

large figure would not have ended there. He had a pleasant face, but there was much more to the man. A hardness that held absolutely no flexibility. The tall soldier was not to be trifled with.

His companion, on the other hand, was harder to discern. He was shorter, though only marginally so, and his broad back was much harder and more powerfully built. He sat with an eerie stillness to him, as if every movement, even a small one, was controlled and had a purpose. Bronwyn shivered and was about to resume her packing when he turned slightly so that she could make out part of his profile. It conveyed strength—brute strength—for there was no softness in his mouth or facial expression. His dark hair was thin and cut very short, which helped to disguise how it had started balding in the middle. Then she saw the Phrygian cap with its pointed tip clutched in his grasp. Just the idea of him wearing such an absurd item removed the tension that had been building studying him and she almost laughed aloud.

"Men shouldn't be so pretty," Edythe commented, staring at the taller, more handsome of the two. "They are either dull witted or possess an air of arrogance that is even more tiresome. And he . . . I don't know. He smiles too easily and not with his eyes."

"Oh, you're wrong," Lily sighed in disagreement. "Maybe I was mistaken about not getting married. I would be able to protect you from Luc and—"

Bronwyn cut her off. "The new lord could not extend such protection to all of us. And do not be swayed by a pretty face."

"Hmm," Lily sighed absentmindedly and gave Edythe a light elbow to the side. "Well, you have to admit he is intriguing."

Edythe kept silent. She was intrigued, but not for the same reasons as her sister. The man was indeed handsome, but Edythe recognized something else. His mouth. He smiled without smiling. An aura of latent power surrounded him, and just as if to prove her point, one of the stable boys swaggered up to him and made a remark. What was said was unknown, but it caused the tall soldier to whip out his sword faster than Edythe had ever seen anyone move and slice it through the air, stopping just in time before he took Ansel's head off.

Everything in the courtyard stopped, and the stable boy, visibly shaken, immediately started talking quickly, his face one of contrition. Eventually, the sword was put away and both men disappeared toward the stables. Until then, everyone had been holding their breath.

"What are we going to do?" Lily wailed as she threw herself into her hearth chair. "We cannot leave Hunswick to him! He's a monster! He nearly chopped off Ansel's head."

"I doubt that very much," Bronwyn argued. "Ansel can be very contrary and is known for being combative. He probably said something that more than deserved such a reaction. I don't think you will have to worry about the new lord ruining Hunswick."

"Well, then you can be me and stall for time, for I want nothing to do with him or his violence."

"I?" Bronwyn asked, confused. "You want *me* to pretend to be *you*? It would never work."

Bronwyn knew she was far from plain, but compared to her sisters, she was also far from beautiful. Edythe's vibrant red coloring and her petite stature drew men to her side . . . that is, until they discovered her sarcastic, cutting wit, which often focused on making them feel like idiots. But even Edythe found it hard to compete with her raven-haired younger sister, whose glittering pale gray eyes all men gravitated toward.

Bronwyn was about to point out the impossibility of the farce when Edythe plopped down into one of the chairs and said, "Actually, Lily's idea is not a bad one. The new lord doesn't know what she looks like and you are much more likely to stay calm if his temper rises once more."

Latching on to the notion, Lily nodded her head enthusiastically. "That's right! Edythe is right! Oh, please, Bronwyn, be me. It would only be for this morning until we leave for Syndlear and then in a few days we will be gone. Who could it hurt?"

Bronwyn licked her lips, searching for a reason to say no. Lying—even pretending—was not something Bronwyn had ever done well and did not relish the idea. "But if his lordship saw you, he would immediately know he had been deceived."

"Then we will all wear wimples," Edythe countered.

Bronwyn issued her a "you're not helping" look, to which Edythe just shrugged. But her sister was right. Wearing the highly uncomfortable white headdress, which went around the head and under the chin, left only the mouth, nose, and eyes visible. The contraption would considerably reduce anyone's ability to distinguish one of them from another, especially at a distance.

Bronwyn glanced back down at the courtyard and watched Constance leave the stables, angrily shaking her head as she sauntered toward the kitchen. The woman was incredibly loyal to Bronwyn and her sisters, and if anyone slighted them, the old nursemaid felt personally insulted. The new lord had obviously denied the request of an audience and Constance was going to her place of solace. The kitchens. The best source for gossip and food, both she believed to be equal remedies for unhappiness.

Leaving her would be hard, but Constance would refuse to stay at Hunswick if she knew their plans, even though it would be at a great personal expense to her. Bronwyn had known for some time that her old nursemaid and one of the nearby widower farmers had grown quite close of late. During her marrying years, Constance had focused so much on Bronwyn and her mother and their recovery that she had ignored any male interest or her own desires for a family. Children may no longer be possible, but Bronwyn would not deny her friend a chance at love and happiness. No, Constance had to stay.

Bronwyn was about to turn away from the window when she spied the new lord and his companion casually stroll across the courtyard, this time facing her as they made their way to the gatehouse. She could now see both men clearly, though still at somewhat of a distance.

The overly tall one was speaking but it was the other man who had her full attention. There was something about him, how he walked, how he paused when looking around, every movement impossibly controlled, how he scrutinized those who darted by him, his air of command, of self-assurance that only came from experience and mutual respect. Lily was wrong. *He* was the man who had assumed possession of Hunswick.

Without a doubt, Bronwyn knew she was looking

at Deadeye de Gunnar, the new Lord Anscombe of Bassellmere.

Bronwyn leaned against the window frame, silently studying him as he made his way to the gatehouse. But just before he entered, he stopped and looked at the Great Hall, directly to the upper bedchamber windows it housed. One eye was closed, but the other was open and had caught her gaze, refusing to let it go. Her heart stammered and yet she could not look away. His face was a cold mask, hiding every emotion, and yet she knew exactly what he was thinking. He wanted the three of them gone, but especially her.

Then, a second later, he was out of sight. Bronwyn blinked and tried to gather her thoughts. Her pulse was only just starting to slow from its instantaneous reaction to him. He both excited and repelled her.

Constance had been right. The new Lord Anscombe was scarred and not just on the outside. Something Bronwyn understood better than anyone and just how it could change a person. Deadeye de Gunnar was not cruel, just unforgiving. He was no ordinary man and around him she would have to be careful. It was a good thing she and her sisters were leaving and even better that he had denied her request for an audience.

"I think you are right, Edythe," Bronwyn mused as she moved away from the window and started to rummage through her things lying on the bed. Pulling out a white muslin mortarboard with an attached long thin veil, she grimaced and continued, "We should all wear our wimples. It would be best if we left quickly, quietly, and unseen."

"And if he calls for me?" Lily whispered beseechingly.

"Then I shall be you," Bronwyn confirmed. "I think you are right. The new Lord Anscombe is not one to be handled with flirtatious remarks."

The last comment was made more to herself, but Edythe was too quick to let it lie. "And how do you think the new master of Hunswick *should* be handled?"

"At a distance," Bronwyn answered. *And without any compassion,* she added to herself. From experience, she knew that sympathy was the last thing a person like him would want.

"You're a stubborn, damn fool, Ranulf," Tyr Dequhar huffed as he retreated back to the stables, leaving his best friend to discuss escort arrangements with his soldiers at the gatehouse. It was obvious Ranulf was not going to change his mind about evicting the three women—including his bride-to-be—from their home and without so much as a hello.

Tyr had known Ranulf for almost five years and was one of the very few who knew him well, but Tyr would never say fully. He doubted Ranulf ever let anyone know him completely. Then again, Tyr felt the same about keeping his own privacy and had found that Ranulf was one of the minority who respected that. Still, it was hard to keep silent about Ranulf's unexpected decision to order the three women away and right before the holiday season.

Ranulf's decision had not been out of character, and yet Tyr had been surprised at the vehemence behind it. Ranulf had not even been willing to listen to alternative ideas or even hear the old woman complete her request for an audience. And when

Tyr had made a veiled attempt to ask Ranulf about his reasons, his friend had been gruff, almost severe, stating that once Laon's daughters saw him, they wouldn't want to stay. He was doing them a favor.

Tyr had heard Ranulf's justification, he just didn't believe it. His longtime comrade was not insecure and Tyr could not recall a single instance of his friend being concerned if someone was uncomfortable around him. Not his soldiers, other commanders, ladies of the court—not even the queen.

When Tyr had first met Ranulf, he had believed the scarred commander's detachment to be a front, that Ranulf was secretly bothered by people's reactions to him, for no one could be that emotionally remote. But after watching Ranulf's cold demeanor for years, Tyr had come to actually believe it. Ranulf didn't care . . . and yet, whether he wanted to admit it or not, he was compelled to protect these women, even if it was from himself. The man was acting like a fool, and if his friend was standing in front of him, Tyr would probably say so again.

Ranulf stood mute for several seconds after Tyr left. If the insult had come from anyone else, he would have struck him, but he and Tyr had fought and led large numbers of men in several victorious battles. They both had accumulated sizable fortunes. Ranulf had let his build unknowing what else to do with it, but Tyr's wealth had mysteriously disappeared.

Most believed that he wasted it on women, clothes, and drink, but Ranulf was never one of them. Whatever his seemingly playful and flirtatious friend was doing with his money, it was not unconscious or without forethought. Tyr's riches had gone somewhere, but Ranulf knew better than to ask where or why. Tyr very rarely revealed anything about himself, and what Ranulf had learned about his friend came from deduction.

Tyr was Scottish and Ranulf suspected a Highlander due to his fluent use of Gaelic. He was also educated, making him from either wealth or a prominent family—most likely both. And while he was not nearly as lecherous rumors made him to be, Tyr was quite comely and consequently, could—and did—enjoy the ladies. But not a one would ever land his friend in any type of commitment. Tyr Dequhar was the only man Ranulf knew who was even more against the idea of marriage than himself. And the reasons why were a mystery.

Secrets, however, did not bother Ranulf. Every man had them. If he didn't, then he was either still a boy and had not lived long enough to accumulate them, or was a braggart who could not be trusted to keep them. And besides, Ranulf had several of his own. His most recent, he had almost unwittingly exposed.

He hadn't meant to stare at Bronwyn. But her dark penetrating eyes prevented him from looking away. Even at a distance they seemed to be able to peer behind his mask and see inside his soul. She wanted answers, reasons, the truth. He had forced himself to break their connection, glad she couldn't see the details of what he really looked like. And based upon his latest actions and methods of evicting her, his angel would probably only view him as the devil.

Today's encounter solidified his resolve. Until he

was in full control of himself and once again uncaring of how others saw or reacted to him, Ranulf had no intention of meeting Lady Bronwyn or her sisters. And if last night's inability to sleep was an indicator, it might be a long while before that time came.

A short, burly man with curly red-brown hair and matching beard entered the darkened room in the gatehouse. "They're ready to leave, my lord."

Ranulf waved Magnus over to where he stood in the dimly lit gatehouse. "Tristan, Gowan, Ansel, and Drake are going with you. One of you is to return at least every two days until I say otherwise. For now, you are in charge of the women's welfare and I will hold you responsible if anything happens to them." Ranulf held out his arm and Magnus clutched it. "If all is ready, depart and ride swiftly. By sundown they should be back and safe where they belong."

If Magnus was nervous with the responsibility, he did not show it. With a sharp nod, he turned and left to see that his lord's orders were obeyed. Ranulf followed him but stopped just inside the doorframe to scan for Bronwyn. His line of sight, however, was hampered by carts laden with food and provisions and those who were returning to their responsibilities at Syndlear. The small exiting group had become quite large.

Tyr, who had remained out of sight since their last encounter, popped into view and sauntered over with a grin he knew would aggravate Ranulf. "You can thank me later."

Ranulf gestured to the mass starting to make

their way out of the castle gates. "You're responsible for this?"

"It looks like more are leaving than there are. The women needed a few families to help them or did you think that they should also do without servants, ladies' maids, or even a cook? I could just see Magnus tackling the job."

Ranulf grimaced. He had forgotten that Syndlear had been abandoned. "Where are they?"

"The women? Your future bride? Gone. They were the first to leave. So, you can finally escape this gatehouse."

Ranulf's brows popped up in a high arch of denial. "Listen, friend," Tyr continued, "I won't pry into why you care about what these women think, but don't ask me to pretend that that's not the reason behind this nonsense."

Ranulf eyed his friend for a few seconds and then decided against refuting what was the unfortunate truth. "And just what would you have me do? Force them to be in my presence day after day?"

Tyr did nothing to hide his exasperation. "Not all women are like those of court, Ranulf."

"No, but I still have a responsibility to protect Laon's daughters, even if it is from me. It is better they should leave and save them the trouble of pretending not to be offended. Meanwhile, do me a favor and go make sure that Drake knows to stay in the back and help with the slower in the group."

"Where're you going?"

Ranulf shrugged and headed toward the round tower. "You know so much. You figure it out."

Ranulf arrived at the tower steps and was about to enter when the frizzy-haired old woman who had practically sneered at him when he had refused an audience stepped into his path. "You don't want to be doing that, my lord."

"I could say the same for you," Ranulf warned.

Constance held his gaze for several seconds and then moved aside, but she didn't do so quietly. "Men like you have too much pride and for that you'll pay a price." She pointed to the stairwell. "If you enter this tower, I promise that you will have wished you spent just a few minutes with my mistress to learn about this place."

Her direct stare held no shock, pity, or revulsion at his missing eye. If anything, the woman was quite indignant at his behavior to her mistress and was openly letting him know so. Ranulf found himself surprised by her reaction and consequently, was more abrupt with his reply than he attended. "You're one of their maids, are you not? Then why are you still here? Leave and tend to their needs. There is no one left who needs your advice or assistance."

Constance refused to be intimidated. "Oh, you are very wrong, my lord. There is you. Then again, maybe you're right about me leaving. I never did have the patience for fools."

Less than a second later she was gone with the insult still hanging in the air. Ranulf considered chasing her down, but he suspected that just might be what she wanted. Besides, he wanted to watch the group—and Bronwyn—as they left. So he entered the structure and began to climb. The stone stairwell wound in a tight corkscrew up four floors to the roof. He didn't know who lived in the tower as he had not seen anyone enter or leave the structure since his arrival. He had glimpsed a few large items at the bottom in the shadows, but they appeared untouched for some time.

Ranulf pushed open the latched ceiling door and climbed up onto the tower roof. Leaning against the battlements, he surveyed Hunswick.

Located in the woodsier portion of Cumbria, the castle and the lake behind it were surrounded by trees. This made local game plentiful, but farms more distant, enemies invisible, and a strong defense difficult. At least the key defense structures had been converted to stone. But the castle had been originally built around a village and therefore was not laid out for protection, but for improved living. The place had several niceties, such as a chapel, a dovecote, and several wooden lean-tos so that villagers could just come and live practically in the lap of their lord.

The people of Hunswick were far from numerous, unlike some large castles where one could hardly move around the yard without tripping over some child, person, or object. Here there was ample room in the spacious bailey, perfect for the upcoming Twelfthtide festivities.

Ranulf had never really participated in the merriment that made up the season, but he suspected that these women did and that their people looked forward to each day's events. For a second, he felt a brief pang of guilt that he was making them move when it was obvious all the revelry would be at Hunswick. Then he remembered how people had reacted the handful of times he had participated in the holiday and his resolve once again grew firm.

They and I will be better off if they are in their own home and not mine, he promised himself.

* * *

Bronwyn pushed aside a low-lying branch as she moved through one of the thickets outside Hunswick. Giving her reins a light tug to the right, she nudged her horse out of the group's way before pausing to yank off the uncomfortable headdress.

"Stopping?" Edythe asked, halting her own progress.

Bronwyn gave her head a shake. "Just for a minute or two. Never could stand these things," she said, tossing her wimple into the satchel hanging off her horse's right hindquarters. "Go ahead. I'll catch up in a while. I want to make sure everyone is doing well."

Edythe looked back at Hunswick and shrugged. She had always preferred Syndlear to Hunswick and was glad to be going back to her childhood home. She didn't have the memories Bronwyn had of the place or Lily's aspirations of going somewhere new and exciting. She gave Bronwyn a wave and squeezed her lower legs until the horse loped off out of sight.

Glad to be alone, Bronwyn reached up to massage her scalp and untangle the dark gold out-of-control waves as best she could with her fingers. The morning sun was almost overhead, proving only a half hour had passed since they had vacated Hunswick. Besides the one or two nearby villagers that had made clear their disapproval of the situation, no one had approached them or caught up to them, requesting their return. And judging by the stone-faced soldier who had paused on the other side of the clearing waiting for her to continue, no one was going to be coming.

She wasn't surprised. Whatever his reasons, the man she suspected to be the new Lord Anscombe was not someone who appeared to be indecisive or who made a habit of changing his mind. Normally, she liked an unwavering firmness of character in a person, and found it to be an unfortunately rare quality in several leaders—the previous king for one. Today, however, the unyielding decision had cost her the one place she had ever felt safe and at peace.

Bronwyn gave herself a mental shake, reminding herself that the new lord had not taken anything from her that she was not just about to relinquish in a few days and in fact had done her a favor. She was about to urge her horse to rejoin the group when a loud yelp followed by several half curses broke the silence. A second later a bedraggled Constance came into view. Leaves were in her hair and her short legs were squeezing the horse she was riding so hard it forced her plump body forward on the saddle, making her off balance. To compensate for the unsteady feeling, the old nursemaid had a tight grip on the horse's mane with one hand and, with the other, clutched the leather reins so firmly that the poor animal could hardly turn its head or make adjustments to avoid most of the thick foliage on the path.

"Damn man, forcing me to do this," Constance hissed. "And you, too," she aimed at the horse. "Remember that I found a way on top of you and I won't be getting off until I'm ready."

"Well, I hope that is soon," Bronwyn chuckled, causing the old woman's head to snap around with such force she almost fell off. "Whatever are you doing, Constance? I thought you would want to stay with that new farmer you've been so keen on."

Once the horse had stopped, Constance released the mane clutched in her palm and smoothed back her own crazed strays, which were now glued to the sweat on her forehead. "Oh, he can live without me for a few days," she replied, trying valiantly to sound calm and serene and not the harried picture she presented. "Wasn't so sure if you could, though. No one knows you like I, so I came to see after you myself."

Bronwyn cocked a single brow and crossed her arms, mocking her. "Really? On a horse?" she asked, knowing how much her nursemaid hated riding.

"Obviously on a horse. How else could I catch up to you? And don't look at me that way, I can ride. I haven't fallen off once."

"That's because you're riding Merry and she is too tolerant and too old to buck you off despite your grip and your seat," Bronwyn chided, ignoring the old woman's confusion as she looked down at her saddle. "Constance, you hate riding so don't ask me to believe you are here by choice. I know you. If you truly thought I needed help, you would have perched yourself on one of the carts before it left. So get down off that poor animal and tell me exactly what really prompted this supposedly selfless stunt."

Constance grunted and slid off the gentle horse's back. She moved several steps away, took a deep breath, and released it, visibly showing a decrease in tension. "I had about as much choice in leaving as you did. Someone must have told the new master what I was to you three, so after I warned him about the North Tower, he ordered me upon this beast and bade me to catch up to you. The man shouldn't be called Deadeye but Dead Fool."

Bronwyn saw from the corner of her eye that the soldier still quietly and patiently waiting to resume their journey had heard the insult and was visibly shocked. "Constance, maybe you shouldn't speak that way at least until the new lord and his friends have come to know you and appreciate your sense of . . . humor."

The old woman glanced at the soldier Bronwyn had indicated and let go a loud, impertinent snort. "Worried for me, are you? You should be worried for that arrogant goose," Constance instructed as she waved her arm back at the castle. "I told him not to climb that deathtrap of a tower, but he ignored me and ordered me here. I saw him standing atop looking over the battlements just as I left the gatehouse, damn fool. Even called him that and it didn't make a bit of difference."

Instantly the world around Bronwyn stopped and she was back in time. Screams filled the air and the thick smoke made it impossible to see. She could taste the dust filling her lungs and she couldn't breathe. The North Tower had killed five that day, including her mother. And it would happen again.

She had to go back.

"You," Bronwyn shouted toward Drake, still in shock after hearing Constance's blatant and irreverent references to Ranulf, "catch up to the others and tell them that I will be joining them later." Her voice rang out, authoritative and in command, leaving no room for discussion or disagreement. She then swung her horse around and urged it into a gallop in the direction of Hunswick.

Drake had been unprepared for the sudden change in Bronwyn's demeanor from one of a gentle noblewoman to someone obviously well versed and comfortable in exercising power.

Seeing the confounded look on the young soldier's

face, Constance offered some advice. "You can try and follow, but you'll never catch her. And even if you did, you would then have to explain just why you thought her welfare more important than that of her sisters, which trust me, you don't want to have to defend. So if I were you, I would do as instructed and see to the safety of the group. For one thing is for certain, that doesn't include her ladyship anymore." Then she marched over to her horse, made a quick silent prayer, and struggled back onto the mare's back, cursing all the while.

When she saw the dark pacing figure on top of the North Tower, Bronwyn's heart stopped. She had been right. Deadeye de Gunnar was not the tall soldier but the brawny one, and he was oblivious to the deathtrap upon which he stood. The North Tower had been the last structure built and solely by nonmasons. As a result, the fir chosen for the floor beams had been cut too early. By the time the stone walls were complete and the floors installed, no one had realized how decomposed the beams had become.

She gave the reins a sharp yank and her horse immediately came to a halt a few feet away from the tower's plinth. She threw her head back and stared at the menacing man glaring at her from above.

She had hoped her mere arrival would cause him to come down and rant at her for returning, but the new lord instead stood immobile, holding her gaze either unknowing or unbelieving of the danger he was in. "Get down from that tower now," Bronwyn commanded.

Any other time, any other place or situation, she would have been conciliatory in her request. But this was a demand, and after months of running Hunswick, she had become accustomed to being obeyed when she used a certain tone of voice.

For a second, Ranulf wondered if he was having a waking nightmare. His angel had returned without warning, riding up to just below where he stood, and stared at him, seeing every flaw, every scar, every hideous feature that caused women to shrink away. But not her. She just held his gaze, unflinching, and then *ordered* him off his *own* tower. The woman was impossible. And she needed to leave. "This is no longer your home, my lady."

"You think that is why I came back? For Hunswick? I'm here to save your *life*."

Her dark eyes were glittering with anger and her waist-length curly hair had so many corkscrew tendrils that it bordered on unruly. Her raised chin made clear that she would not shrink from a challenge and the rigidity of her back caused the scooped neck of her bliaut to emphasize the swell of her breasts. He had never seen anything lovelier.

Ranulf took a firm grip on his resolve. He had to stay calm and rational if he had a chance of convincing her that it was she who would be yielding and not he. He had more to lose. "I don't care why you've returned. But you *will* be leaving, either on your own power or by one of my men's."

Bronwyn shuddered at the dangerous softness in his voice. His lordship actually meant to haul her physically off his property. Well, he needed to learn that he wasn't the only one who could be stubborn. And no one could be as mulish as she, especially when she was in the right. "We can discuss your meaningless *threats* after you stop acting like a fool and *get off that tower*."

Ranulf closed his eyes in acute frustration. Any temptation to do her bidding just vanished. His angel may be beautiful, but she was also a sprite . . . with claws. "I don't think so," he said with as much disinterest he could muster, hoping that it would aggravate her. Seeing her annoyed expression, he smiled. "It's a fine place up here and the weather is quite comfortable. I might just stay here all night, and *as lord of this castle*, I guess I can . . . *foolish* or not."

Ranulf resumed his pacing. He didn't know why he was engaging in an argument with her. It was totally out of character. But what did she expect riding in, regal and self-confident, her dark gold hair flowing in the breeze, and then staring at him, undaunted, almost as if she didn't see what couldn't be missed.

With each step, small snapping sounds echoed in her ears. Bronwyn wanted to run up there and throttle him. Four stories above her, he wasn't close, but neither was he far. She could make out every feature. Slicing across his brow and a fraction of his cheekbone, the deep scar—part burn, part laceration—was noticeable, but not horrific. His left eye was clearly gone, causing his mottled eyelid to remain closed. It would have looked like he was winking at her except for his other eye. Gold-tinged, encircled by black, it was cold. The man was unmistakably angry. But then, so was she. The new lord was acting like a stubborn ass.

"You narrow-minded man. These people need a

leader, not someone full of misplaced pride who has yet to come to terms with the unfairness of life. Go back to Normandy and sulk some more, *but get off that tower.*" Bronwyn heard the sharp intake of breaths behind her, but refused to turn around or give up. She was creating a spectacle, and in any other circumstance, she would be mortified. But if it drove him down, it would be worth it.

Ranulf stopped in midstride and crossed his arms, accentuating his muscular build. No longer did he need to wonder if she could see him. She saw not only his injury, but much more. The pain it still caused him and suddenly he felt weak in her eyes. "You like to order men around, don't you? Test their manhood? It didn't work yesterday in the forest and it won't today. I am not a man to be provoked, and my lady, you are trying my patience."

The shock coursing through Bronwyn was evident. He was the one. Her rescuer, her hero, the one she had wished to meet, the one she had thought bold, daring, and courageous had not been one of his soldiers, but Deadeye de Gunnar himself. How many times did she need to learn this lesson? Chivalrous heroes did not exist. The world no longer made them. There were none to be found. The last two were her father and Lord Anscombe and they were both gone.

"You, my lord," Bronwyn said through gritted teeth, "are far from the nobleman who previously ruled this castle and these lands. You are nothing but a mercenary with a title."

Her lips were drawn tight and hot, furious tears burned her eyes. It suddenly occurred to Ranulf that his angel felt real fury and it unnerved him.

Women did not attach strong emotions to him, and
for a flitting moment, he longed for her to smile at
him instead. He wondered what it would be like to
have her feel, not anger, and certainly not compassion, but real desire for him. The idea was overwhelming . . . and maddening.

"I never claimed to be a nobleman!" Ranulf bellowed.

Bronwyn cringed. Until now, he had kept his
voice menacing, but low and controlled. His out-
burst had been startling. "Don't shout at me!" she
instinctively hollered back.

"Why? You've been shouting at me!" he returned.
Ranulf honestly didn't know what was going on. He
never yelled. Then again, no one confronted and
countered him either.

Bronwyn opened and closed her mouth twice
before she realized just what she was doing and how
idiotic she must appear. Another loud crack rang
out. The beam sustaining his weight would last not
much longer. "What am I going to do?" she muttered to herself and was about to direct her horse to
the gatehouse when a deep chuckle startled her.

"I can't wait to find out."

Bronwyn's whipped her head around, spying the
tall good-looking soldier she had seen earlier. With
tousled, shoulder-length red-brown hair, he was
much more handsome up close, especially as he was
smiling and flashing his dimples. Another time, she
might have admired them a little longer, but her
mind was consumed with only one man—the most
frustrating, stubborn one of her acquaintance.

She urged her horse toward the grinning giant
and then pointed toward the tower. "You're his

friend, are you not? I saw you together earlier and you were anything but subservient. I assume you are not one of his soldiers, but someone he trusts. Someone he will listen to."

Both of Tyr's brows arched in surprise. He cast a glance toward Ranulf and almost started chuckling again. His always composed friend was staring at them and he was anything but unruffled. "I have never known Ranulf to heed anyone's counsel but his own, but aye, I am his friend."

"Then do something!" Bronwyn hissed.

Tyr's hazel eyes suddenly grew wide with mocking interest. "Like what?"

"Like . . . what?" Bronwyn stammered, wondering if the man was stupid or just intentionally aggravating. "Unless you want to see your friend dead, convince him that he needs to get off that tower immediately."

Tyr's face broke into a huge grin. He couldn't help it. The woman was outrageous. She was also the answer to every question that he had been having concerning his friend's baffling behavior the past two days. This wild beauty had Ranulf in knots and it was no wonder. One didn't encounter women with soft curvaceous bodies, flashing blue eyes, and wisps of sun-kissed hair very often in court or in the battlefield. Ranulf had obviously seen her yesterday and had not been prepared. *That* was why she and her sisters had been forced to leave so quickly. Ranulf didn't want to see her. More to the point—he didn't want her to see *him.*

"If you want him to get down, then leave."

"I cannot leave, whoever you are, until I know that

the new lord is safe and able to assume his role and lead these people."

"My name is Tyr. Tyr Dequhar."

Bronwyn narrowed her gaze just slightly. She could have sworn that he had been about to embellish his name significantly with a title, but had just stopped himself in time. As to why, she would have to discover another time. "Then, Tyr, would you help me?"

"He's made it clear that as long as you are here, he's not coming down. So why do you stay? I think my friend intrigues you far more than he ignites your ire."

"And you find that amusing."

Tyr nodded, his infectious grin growing only larger. "If you knew Ranulf better, you would know why."

Bronwyn swallowed and her eyes grew misty. "I only know that the North Tower kills. It took my mother and it will take your friend."

Ranulf stared at the couple below. He watched Tyr assess his angel and knew when his friend deemed someone attractive. Something was said and Ranulf watched as Tyr's expression changed from one of amusement to rapt attention. Tyr reached out and took her hand in his, not out of desire, but genuine concern. Hot, bitter jealousy twisted inside Ranulf. Bronwyn had been entrusted to him, and him alone.

Ranulf pivoted and stomped toward the stairs. If she wanted him down, to see him face-to-face, Lady Bronwyn le Breton had just gotten her wish. But before he could take the first descending step, a sudden sharp explosive noise filled the air.

* * *

Bronwyn raced toward the gatehouse and into the courtyard. Once inside, she jumped off her horse and ran to the tower. It had happened again.

Her mother had been on the ground floor, helping to look for something buried in all the stored items, when the first floor had given way. She had died instantly, crushed from the debris. This time, the top two floors had collapsed. In horror she had watched Ranulf disappear as a thunderous sound of wood breaking and coming to a crashing halt echoed in the valley.

No one could have survived the fall.

Bronwyn approached the tower, coughing, waving her hands in a futile attempt to clear the air of dust. Like before, the massive stone walls remained erect, but inside the structure was chaos and devastation. Shouts were coming from everywhere as people started dashing inside to search for the new lord's body. Bronwyn couldn't move. She just stood transfixed in shocked horror.

A strong firm grip encircled her upper arm and pulled. "My lady. You need to leave. It's not safe here."

Bronwyn blinked. "It was my fault. I should have left. He didn't come down because I had to stay. To see him. He saved me and I just wanted . . ." Tears formed and fell.

Then she saw him. Ranulf was lying near the top of the tower on the stairs that had been built into the stone structure. Bronwyn wrenched free of Tyr's grasp and leapt up the stairs before he could stop her.

Ranulf felt cool fingertips stroking his cheek and decided he was dreaming. His angel had returned and was whispering softly into his ear and he longed to know what she was saying. As consciousness took hold, he realized they were words of fear and remorse and he knew then that it was not a dream, but a nightmare, and if he were to open his eyes, his angel would be there, looking at him . . . with pity.

Ranulf reached out with his working arm and snatched her wrist. "Don't look at me," he hissed. His confidence had already taken a hit when she dared to argue with him. No one did that. No one.

"Shh. Don't try to move."

Ranulf tried once again to push her away, but his arm wouldn't cooperate. His shoulder hurt, but that pain was negligible compared to the one in his head. "Leave me," he pleaded. Never had he begged before, but he could hear it in his voice, imploring her to go.

Soft lips caressed his right ear. "Please, my lord. Let me save you as you saved me."

Ranulf opened his eyes and tried to lift his head. Intense pain shot through his temple and the world started spinning around him, making him very nauseous. He had already made a complete idiot of himself. She was tending to his shoulder as if he were an unskilled soldier with his first wound and unaccustomed to dealing with pain. He was *not* going to add vomiting to the day's events.

Her fingers reached the edge of his tunic and were about to pull back the opening to further examine the wound when he reached up and stopped her. "Don't. Get someone else. Anyone else."

Bronwyn was about to argue when comprehension sank in. She should have realized that such a severe burn injury would not be localized to just his face. The man neither wanted nor would get sympathy from her because of his past wounds.

Everyone had nightmares, and he obviously was stilling dealing with his.

"Why? I'm not afraid. Are you?"

Ranulf recognized a challenge when one was issued, but he could not recall the last time someone had made such a direct one. He held her gaze for a long moment. "Only of you, angel."

"Don't call me that."

"Why? You look like one."

"Then the fall has made you delusional, and the sooner we get you off these stairs and remove the wood lodged in your shoulder, the better."

Hearing that he was not on the ground and that they were about to move him, Ranulf was in the process of saying "no" when someone jerked up his shoulders and head, causing the world to grow dark.

Ranulf's last thought was that Tyr and the old lady had been right. He really was a fool.

Ranulf awoke to the smell of flowers and the tantalizing scent of woman. Once again he had the unfamiliar sensation of being caressed. This time the feeling of fingers ran softly across his forehead and into his hair again and again, completely overwhelming his other senses, including the painful banging in his head that matched the beat of his pulse. He concentrated on the gentle ministrations and listened to the raspy tones of his angel issuing instructions. Her low, sultry voice did not carry the songbird qualities heard so often in court, but it was soft, clear, and possessed a dangerous quality that could awaken his once-dead heart.

Ranulf held his breath. The silky sounds had

changed from sultry tones to playful ones . . . and they were chiding him.

"You're smiling, my lord," Bronwyn whispered into his ear so that no one else could hear. "Not the large type of grin your friend wears so easily, but enough for me to know that you are awake."

Ranulf blinked his one working eye and saw the face of his angel peering down at him. Her hair had been haphazardly pulled back in a loose braid that at any minute threatened to fall apart. The angry midnight eyes he had witnessed from afar were not nearly as dark as he had originally believed. Lined with concern, they were a deep misty blue, the color of the sea after a storm. He could see no pity or fear in the overly large pools. Only one other pair of blue eyes had ever looked at him that way. Sir Laon le Breton's, her father.

Ranulf discovered not long after his injury that only a certain type of woman would be attracted to his bed. Tyr and a few others had tried to convince him otherwise, and usually it was a mercenary heart he held in his arms, attempting to woo him for his money. But there were a few times, when the woman he held looked back at him with such cold detachment it made him feel only lonelier and less of a man. Three years ago after a highly unpleasant encounter, he decided to forgo female companionship altogether, and until today he had never been tempted to change his mind.

Ranulf could not remember ever wanting any woman more. But indifference from her would be a soul killer. He suspected that if he should try, she might indulge him in a kiss, but he didn't want her pity or her compassion. He desired something else.

Something so rare that he had not once encountered it in the last decade. He needed Bronwyn le Breton to see him as a man.

A knock on the door pulled Bronwyn away from his side. Perturbed by her sudden absence, Ranulf shifted slightly to see the old nursemaid followed by Tyr enter the room. Unable to stop himself in time, he groaned. Bronwyn immediately flew back to his side, but Ranulf could see his tall friend arch a brow inquisitively and flash him a knowing grin as he crossed his arms. Tyr had seen him injured—and more seriously—too many times to believe that pain was behind Ranulf's grimace. His friend recognized Ranulf's desire to be alone and apparently was enjoying himself too much to care.

Bronwyn licked her lips, drawing his attention back to her. "When the floor fell, part of one of the beams broke off and lodged itself in your shoulder. I managed to take it out and slow the bleeding, but I am going to have to sew the wound shut and treat it. I'm afraid it will be very painful."

Ranulf watched as she bit her bottom lip, worried at the agony she was about to inflict on him. But all he could think about was how he wanted to pull her mouth down to his and discover just what heaven tasted like.

"Do you need me to get you something to bite down on?"

Behind her, Ranulf could see Tyr cover his mouth and fight to keep from laughing aloud. The damn man was enjoying this too much.

Bronwyn poked him. "Do you?"

Ranulf blinked and refocused on what she was asking. "Do I what?" he groused.

Bronwyn issued him a scathing look, but the nursemaid was not consoled. "Maybe he isn't right in the head," Constance muttered, standing over him. "Do you know your own name, my lord?"

Ranulf scowled at the interfering old woman and said, "Ranulf to my friends, Lord Anscombe to my people, and Deadeye to everyone else. You choose."

The response from both women was immediate. The one from the nursemaid was as he intended. After shooting him a withering look, the wild, gray-haired woman spun around out of his sight. Bronwyn's expression, once tender and concern-filled, had transformed into one of exasperation. "It's not his head that you should be worried about, Constance. After years of dealing with my sisters, I thought you would recognize obstinacy at the expense of pride," she purred lightheartedly, giving him a wink.

Ranulf almost choked as a result. Unprepared, he started coughing, and for the first time, the pain in his shoulder rivaled the one in his head. Her anger had been stimulating and her compassion disarming, but he wasn't sure he could handle this playful side of her without completely embarrassing himself.

"Stop moving," Bronwyn ordered, "else you'll start bleeding all over again and this time it will be on your own bed. Constance, would you go to my room and bring the black bag and a needle? And Tyr," she said, keeping her focus on Ranulf and his shoulder, "take yourself out of here. Your friend does not need your type of support right now. Come back when silent smirks and dampened laughter will be welcomed."

Unrestrained laughter filled the room. "Damn,

Ranulf, the women you meet and order away. Perhaps it is I who should have been enlisting you for female help all these years," Tyr teased and then ducked out of the room before Ranulf could retaliate.

Constance followed, leaving Ranulf and Bronwyn alone. He suddenly felt uneasy. "Where am I?"

Bronwyn stood, walked over to a large chest, and pulled out several old, worn linen shirts that could only have belonged to his cousin, the late Lord Anscombe. She grabbed one sleeve and started ripping. "We are in the Tower Keep of Hunswick and this is the bedchamber of the previous Lord Anscombe. Now, it is yours." She pointed to the double doors across from her and to his left. "There is your day room."

Ranulf studied her as she ripped each garment into wide strips. "And you are the daughter of Sir Laon le Breton, my single vassal."

"My father is dead. I would have thought you had heard."

Her voice had trembled and Ranulf felt a wave of guilt overcome him. "I did and I'm sorry, angel."

Bronwyn stopped abruptly and captured his gaze. "Don't call me that."

Ranulf mentally scolded himself. The epithet had just slipped out, but her reaction to it had been severe and it had not been due to his being too personal. "Then what should I call you?"

Bronwyn licked her lips and swallowed. Then after several seconds, she took a deep breath and said faintly, "Lillabet, my lord."

Ranulf fought to keep his face immobile. He had not met Laon's youngest daughter, but he knew one thing for certain. The woman in front of him was not his betrothed. Why would Bronwyn say she was?

She was clearly far from comfortable with the idea of lying, but yet she had still willingly entered its treacherous domain. Ranulf was tempted to expose her falsehood, but decided not to at the last moment. Bronwyn was shaking, just slightly, as if she was nervous. Practicing deceit was completely unnatural for her. She didn't like it. Ranulf wondered why she felt the need to lie now, with him and about her identity. The surest way not to discover the truth was to confront her. Still, he couldn't call her by a name that wasn't her own. "You don't look like a Lillabet."

Bronwyn finished ripping the linen shirt and gathered all the torn pieces into a pile. "And just what do I look like?"

"I told you. An angel, and until you give me a good reason not to call you that, I believe I shall continue."

Bronwyn clamped her jaw tight. In truth, she was relieved. She had no intentions of staying for any length of time, but being called Lillabet would be a constant reminder of just who he was . . . and for whom he was intended.

A single loud knock boomed, and without waiting for an invitation, Constance marched in and handed Bronwyn a bowl, a black bag, and a needle and thread. "He won't like it."

"Thank you, Constance," Bronwyn said casually, taking the items. "You don't have to stay. But could you ask someone to send up some yarrow tea?"

Constance gave a brief nod and headed for the door. Just as she was about to step through, she looked back and gave Ranulf a contemptuous look.

"If you need me, I'll be in the kitchens. And you," Constance directed to Ranulf, "lord or not, you hit her and there'll be hell to pay."

Hearing the threat, Ranulf tried to sit up and was about to order Constance back in to explain herself when Bronwyn pushed his shoulder down to keep him prone. "Just what did she mean by that? Why would I hit you?"

"Are you hurt anywhere else that I don't know about?"

"Answer my question!"

"If you can't tell me, I can always check," Bronwyn said with a teasing smile as she reached out to pull back his already ripped shirt and reveal some more of his chest.

Ranulf clutched her wrist. Falling hadn't felt good, and he knew he was bruised. Just how bad he wasn't sure, but he didn't want her to find out either. "I thought maidens were not supposed to see a man."

Bronwyn's smile deepened into laughter and she moved to mix some of the contents in the black bag with the water in the bowl. "And just how do you know me to be a maiden?"

Ranulf blatantly raked his gaze over her once and then returned to meet her eyes. "I would know."

Bronwyn scraped the edge of the bowl. "Mmm. You ever been married?"

"No," Ranulf muttered as he watched her spread the nasty olive green-and-brown paste on a strip of cloth.

"Someone claimed your heart?"

"No," came his sharp reply. Suddenly, he realized why she was pretending to be Lillabet. She was doing it to protect her sister . . . from him. Bronwyn wasn't different. She was like the rest, just a little better at hiding it. "I've been busy doing other things with my life and haven't the time or inclination to spend energy wooing a silly female."

Only the disappearance of her smile indicated that Bronwyn had heard him and the bitterness in his voice. Picking up the needle and the cloth, she came to sit down beside him. "First I am going to sew that wound up. It is going to hurt. Normally I would give you some ale, but it might not be wise with an impending fever."

Her playful banter in both expression and tone had vanished. His harsh words were the cause and it bothered him. "I don't have a fever," he countered, reminding himself that she was duplicitous not only in nature but in identity.

"Not yet, maybe, but with this wound, you *will* have one." Bronwyn reached out to pull back the opening to his shirt and hesitated when his hand covered hers. "Do you need some wood to bite down on?"

"Do you?" he demanded, knowing that a deep puncture wound could be unsightly, but nothing compared to the burned scarred flesh that surrounded it.

"No, my lord. I'm not afraid, and I promise, I have seen worse."

The seriousness behind her words could not be faked and Ranulf released his grip, understanding at last just why this woman could be so unperturbed with his appearance. He had been drenched in the obvious since the moment Bronwyn had first looked at him with her steadfast gaze, seeing his mottled skin and missing eye. She had to have seen something—something far worse than his injuries—to be so unaffected. And if that was true, the sight had to have been grisly, far too grisly for a lady.

Freed, Bronwyn bent over him and started cutting away the material around his flesh. "Once I'm done here, I'll apply that poultice, which I warn you, can be very painful, but it will help with the bleeding and accelerate healing. Unless the fever takes too strong of a hold, you will live."

Ranulf shook his head. "I don't get fevers."

"We'll see," Bronwyn murmured as she dipped a clean cloth into some water and started to cleanse the wound. Then she picked up the needle and asked, "Are you ready?"

"I'm fine."

"Well, don't worry about Constance if you do hit me. There's a good chance you will and I won't hold it against you. I'll know it was just the pain."

Ranulf's mouth twisted with pride. "I've been injured before and I've managed not to hit anyone."

"If you say so," Bronwyn replied.

Ranulf felt the painful pierce of being stabbed and let go a grunt. Ashamed she should see him so weak, he closed his eyes and counted each sharp prick and pull. After twelve, she tied off the string and sliced the end off with a dagger.

Then, a minute later, white hot agony seared his skin and wound. Ranulf fought from crying out but his hand instinctively reached out for hers and squeezed. His grasp had to have hurt and yet she held on and he didn't feel so alone. Her father had made him feel that same way. "I'm so sorry, angel. I tried everything to save him. I didn't know . . ."

"Shhh, whatever happened, no one blames you."

"Angel . . ."

Bronwyn felt him suddenly relax and knew he was unconscious once again.

Chapter Three

The Advent Fast, also known as the Nativity Fast or Philip's Fast for Eastern Christian religions, is a period of abstinence that is observed from the day following the Feast of Saint Philip the Apostle (November 14) to December 24, but dates and time frames vary depending upon culture and religion. It ends with the Mass of the Vigil starting in the late afternoon or early evening hours of December 24. The fast prohibits meat, chicken, milk, cheese, butter, and many other animal products and therefore was the primary motivation for the festal consumption of food during the medieval Christmas. Because the fast lasted four weeks, medieval cooks came up with a variety of ways to evade restrictions, such as making mock cheese out of almond milk and fish to taste like meat. Some people even included an ordinary goose to their menu, stating it was born from the barnacles of a tree that grew near water and therefore being not

*a true land animal. Of course, the host and the cook
had to in honest faith believe an actual Barnacle
Goose was being served.*

Bronwyn sat on the small bench and drummed
her fingers silently against the windowsill as she
looked out at the vacant, dark courtyard lit only by
the faint moonlight shining from above. It would be
a few more hours until the bailey became alive with
activity once again. She wondered how her sisters
were faring and hoped they would understand why
she had decided to stay. Tyr had promised to send
word at daybreak as to what had happened, and
while Edythe would see the situation pragmatically,
Lily would not. She would either believe the whole
thing terribly romantic or just the opposite, unbear-
ably oppressive. Either way, Bronwyn prayed they
both continued to stay away from Hunswick.

Sighing, she turned from the window and squatted down by the hearth to throw another log into
the fire. With the unusually warm weather, the fire
was not necessary, but winter would reappear any-
time now and it was always easier to add a log than
create a fire from new. Rising again, Bronwyn wished
she had something to do besides wait. She had
cleaned the few garments that had been brought up
with Ranulf's things and even mended a couple of
them, something she hated, but it was better than
boredom. Patience was one fruit of the spirit of
which she possessed very little.

The Tower Keep was a large rectangular structure
situated at an angle from the Great Hall, making up
in sheer size what it lacked in height. Disliking stairs
and small rooms, the previous Lord Anscombe had

designed each floor to have the space of nearly two towers. The moment the building had been completed, he had vacated the rooms above the Great Hall and taken the solar for his bedchambers. Only after he had become ill had Bronwyn ever entered the room, and after his death, she had thrown away all the rushes and closed its doors, letting dust overtake all that it housed.

Cleaning the room had been much more of a chore than she had anticipated. Constance had come in for a little while to help, but Bronwyn could see the old woman was tiring herself out and unnecessarily. The activity was a godsend, for watching and waiting for the fever to take hold of Ranulf was torture. Even now, she could see the slow rise and fall of his chest, defying all that she knew about wounds. Only once had he moved in an effort to turn over. He had winced and stopped, but the action had not roused him.

The room, though large, was sparsely furnished and, consequently, simple to clean. Rectangular in shape, it was divided into two areas. On one end was a great bed built on a massive wooden frame with a feather mattress covered with sheets, quilts, and pillows. The bed was curtained with linen hangings, but Bronwyn had pulled them back, tying them off so that she could watch Ranulf from anywhere in the room.

On either side of the bed were two small tables, one for his lordship, which also held a basin and pitcher of water, and one for the future Lady Anscombe, which was bare except for the candle Bronwyn had placed there earlier.

Across the room was a stone hearth, and though

not elaborate, it was of ample size to heat the space. Two large, padded chairs that were originally meant for the Great Hall were placed to one side of the fireplace. In between them sat a small square table Bronwyn suspected typically supported a mug of ale, based upon the ringed stains on its surface and the previous Lord Anscombe's fondness for drink.

Along one long wall were two tall windows, each with narrow padded seats that provided an excellent view of the courtyard and the setting sun. In between the windows sat a large chest standing on four feet that doubled as a sitting area for visitors. The opposite wall had three doors. One overly large door near the middle opened into the lord's day room. Next to it was the garderobe and the one closest to the far end led out to the hall and the stairwell. Between them hung tapestries of the Cumbrian Hills and the waters of Bassellmere with a mist settling on the valley, designed and created by Bronwyn's own mother.

Feeling warmer, Bronwyn sat down on the large beaver rug in front of the hearth. Earlier, while cleaning, she had put four woolen blankets too worn for the lord's bed underneath it for padding, creating her favorite sitting spot. But its comfort was short-lived. She was going mad with the silence.

With her sisters about, there was never a time where she could just sit peacefully. Whenever she had tried, they would always interrupt, wondering what was the matter, or assume the timing was perfect to relate a story or problem or wish. Now that she was alone with only her thoughts, it was too quiet.

Bronwyn chuckled at the realization. Standing back up, she pulled one of the hearth chairs to the side of the bed, but instead of sitting on it, she sank onto the mattress next to Ranulf's unwounded arm. She leaned over to kiss his forehead—to check for fever—and as his lordship had predicted, his skin was still cool to the touch. She pulled back and saw that he was dreaming again, but not a good one. His forehead was puckered and his jaw was rigid, giving the impression of being disturbed or angered. *Probably dreaming about me*, she mused.

She reached out and traced his square jaw, which was now stubbly with dark growth that was soft and inviting. "Why do some men shave and others do not? Does it hurt?" she pondered aloud. "Maybe more would if they looked like you."

Bronwyn knew she should step away, but instead let her fingers travel upward across his cheekbone. She could feel the heat of his skin pouring into her hands and she craved more.

He had paled considerably under his tanned complexion and his harsh angular features seemed softer while he slept. His forehead was not high like her father's, but neither was it too low, so that he looked like he was constantly questioning things. He didn't look to be very old, not even ten years her senior. His short tousled hair created a boyish appearance while his face and body looked like he had been a man for many years. Along the forehead were creases, deep lines that ran into old scars indicating he had faced many difficulties in his life, and not just physical.

"You, my lord," she declared softly as she stroked his cheek, "despite all the rumor and rhetoric are rather ordinary-looking." But he wasn't ordinary. There was something in him, an aura of latent power that had struck her when they had argued, the sort of strength that would have enabled him to survive when other, lesser men would have given up and died.

Her fingertips played at the edge of his hair and finally gave in to the temptation to dive in and caress the dark brown locks. "Why do you keep it so short? For ease?" Bronwyn raked her fingers through his hair once more. "Mmm, whatever the reason, I like it."

Then she let her fingers slide down his nose. "Amazingly straight," she sighed and then moved her thumb across his lips. The act raised gooseflesh on her arms, causing her to shiver as she contemplated exploring the one place she had dared yet to go. Not because of its appearance, but because of its familiarity.

"What happened, I wonder," Bronwyn murmured as she followed the scar from the middle of his forehead down the left side, over the empty socket, and across the top of his cheek to his ear. "You were burned a long time ago, but this was not caused just by fire. Did something fall on you?" Whatever it was had seared his skin at the moment of impact.

"Your face," she continued as she let her hand skim down his neck to his uncovered chest, enabling easy access to redress the wound, "does not prepare one for everything else." Ranulf was attractive to look at, but his body was incredible.

Bronwyn had been around men all her life and both intentionally and accidentally had spied on them in her youth. But never had she seen anything to compare with Ranulf. His sheer presence spoke of authority and command. Even when he slept.

"I wonder if you realize just how imposing you are

to everyone, including your men. But I doubt they follow you from intimidation. Respect drives their loyalty. How do I know this?" she asked herself, pretending it was he who posed the question. "Well, despite your treatment of me, which you must admit was quite repugnant for a knight, I doubt your friend Tyr is easily unsettled. He seems to be one who makes his own decisions. So there must be something to you for him to follow you north."

Bronwyn let her hand stray down his arm, enjoying the feel of his thick and padded muscles. Caressing his wrist and then the fingers that lay across his stomach, she traced the ridged strength, wondering how it would feel to be pulled against them if he held her in his arms.

Ranulf's face twitched, wincing, and Bronwyn snatched back her hand, reprimanding herself for being so naïve. No, the new Lord Anscombe didn't possess a classically handsome face, but it did not matter. His presence was compelling with a vital power that pulled her toward him. "And I'm the strong one," she whispered, "I'm glad my sister will never meet you. It would only make it harder to leave."

Standing up, Bronwyn stretched. She had been talking for nearly an hour before her mind caught up with what she was saying . . . and doing. Embarrassed, she moved away from the bed, glad that no one but her knew of her brazen words and exploration. Needing something to preoccupy her mind until he either awoke or was overcome with fever, she decided that his day room could also be cleaned. At least there she wouldn't be staring at him.

* * *

Upon wakening, two overpowering sensations had assailed Ranulf simultaneously. The pain in his shoulder was far from negligible, but it could be ignored. The warm pressure of soft lips against his forehead, however, had seized all rational thought. All he could do was hold his breath and refuse to move, to do anything that might disrupt the dream. His angel was kissing him. Then too soon, cool air replaced the tender touch.

The dream was not a new one. But none had ever felt so real. Ranulf was on the verge of visually dismissing the possibility when a fingertip lightly started to outline his face, and again he had to fight back the urge to see if it really was his angel. A soft low voice joined the caress, clearly unaware that he was now conscious.

He was not dreaming. This was real. His angel was there, with him, still blissfully uncaring of the wounds the rest of the world found so horrendous.

Ranulf knew he should say something, but he was riveted by her touch, her nearness, and his mind wouldn't let him do anything to prematurely end the fleeting taste of heaven. All he could do was lie there, basking in her female ministrations, listening to the sound of her voice. It was melodic, neither deep nor high-pitched. And when dropped low, it took on a husky sound that would have been incredibly arousing. But then he realized she was talking about him.

Ask any man if he wanted to know what truly went through a woman's mind and he would quickly reply "yes." But ask him again and make him think through his answer and what it would mean . . . and he would ardently say no. Every man Ranulf knew—

even King Henry II—questioned his masculine appeal. Ranulf never questioned his, he knew. Some women could get past the scars and even tolerate conversation and his company, but being intimate with a man who looked at them with one eye and one sunken eyelid deformed by flame was at best uncomfortable, for most frightening, and some even referred to him as a walking corpse.

So when his angel first began musing over his appearance, he had held his breath, praying she would remain silent and keep her thoughts to herself.

Then she had called him rather ordinary.

Nothing in the past twelve years had prepared him for such an assessment. *Ordinary! Was Bronwyn blind?* But she obviously wasn't, for she continued with her appraisal. She studied all his facial features, caressing them, driving him wild. Even his scars. She had traced them, wondering aloud at their cause and coming frighteningly close to guessing correctly. Then her hand had slid lower.

Never had Ranulf endured anything more torturous in his life and all he could do was force himself to breathe and do absolutely nothing to halt this sweet version of hell. It was the most dishonorable thing he had ever done, letting her speak private thoughts aloud, believing him unaware. Still, if he had to do it all over again, he would again remain mum.

Never had a woman touched him like that. Those he had paid for their services had refused to feel his scars, avoiding them. Just the thought of being with one of those harlots after being sincerely caressed by Bronwyn caused him to wince.

Instantly, her touch was gone and he cursed his

lack of control. He was about to reveal his conscious state when he realized she hadn't withdrawn altogether. Bronwyn was whispering in his ear, weaving a new spell over him.

Then it all stopped. As if she suddenly realized she was pouring out her most personal thoughts and decided against it.

A second later, he heard a chair scrape and a door open. Hearing movement in another room, Ranulf forced himself to crack his good eye and confirm he was alone. As he suspected, the door had not quite closed but remained ajar enough to see through. By the shadows playing on the far wall, it led into a spacious setting that could only be the lord's day room.

Now, fully awake and able to think somewhat sensibly, Ranulf realized his body was talking to him, and had been for a while. Rising, he quietly exited to the privy located just outside the room, glad to encounter no one in the hall. He returned moments later and lay back down on the bed, surprised at how weak he was. Bronwyn was still in the day room. He could not see what she was doing, but she was singing the same melancholy melody he had heard the first day he had spied her in the woods.

Sinking back against the pillows, he surveyed the room, surprised how comfortable he found his new bedchambers. He had never met his second cousin, but their tastes in décor were similar. Neither sparse nor excessive. Plenty of room, with large throw rugs and a bed that was exceptionally comfortable.

A splash of water in a bowl in the other room caught his attention and Ranulf mulled over her departing comments for they made no sense. The stuff about him was shocking, almost unbelievable, but the comment about her sister being forced to leave against her will was disturbing. It was as if Bronwyn thought she and her sisters were to be prisoners at Syndlear. *And why shouldn't they feel that way?* he scolded himself. *Wasn't it your words ordering them away from Hunswick until you said otherwise?* Damn. That was something he would have to rectify when he "awoke."

Ranulf was just considering how he should "awaken" and confront Bronwyn about her true identity, when he heard another splash of water followed by an effort-filled grunt, as if she were working on something. Then, she let go a half gasp, half female screech that could only be interpreted one way—Bronwyn had encountered something she deemed disgusting.

Ranulf closed his eyes. She was cleaning. Why was she, a lady, doing a servant's work? The moment he figured out how to stop "sleeping," he would fix that, too. His angel was not going to do the work of a chambermaid, or any other servant.

As if she could hear his thoughts and agreed with his sentiments, he heard the chair beside him scrape and she plopped down into it with a sigh.

"Well, my lord, I am done," she said with a yawn. "What about the rushes? Stop complaining and be more appreciative that the place is now free of dust. Continue to argue with me and I just might find the foulest-smelling ones in the castle and bring them in here."

Ranulf lay still in shock, glad his eyes were closed. It was hard enough not to break out into laughter. The woman was pretending to have a conversation with him and not just any conversation—an argument, of all things. Could it be possible that she had found their boisterous bickering as stimulating as he had?

"Hmm," she whispered, moving closer to him. "Are you having a good dream this time? I hope so." She touched the tip of his nose and then dragged her finger down across his lips to his chin. "I think this is the first time I've seen you smile. You should do it more often. It's quite disarming. So much so that I just might add some hellebores to your rushes that my mother had planted around Hunswick. Its winter blooms smell wonderful and I am sure all the women you bring in here will appreciate my thoughtfulness."

What the hell? Ranulf screamed to himself. He had been really enjoying her imaginative conversation until she suddenly mentioned other women in his bed. Did Bronwyn really believe it even possible? But before he could calm his thoughts, she began spouting off a still crazier idea.

"It's too bad that I can't be one of them, or at least have the chance to try. If you only knew how long I've been waiting for . . ." She paused. Waiting for her to complete her thought was torture. "Someone like you. I just wished you had not arrived too late."

If Ranulf had been standing near a wall, there was a good chance he might have banged his head against it. He was the type of man she had been waiting for . . . but he was too late? Did she still think he was going to die?

Ranulf was beginning to wonder if Bronwyn spoke to make sense, or just to talk. Lord, maybe she was one of those people who had to talk all the time, who needed noise around them. Maybe that was what her father had meant when he implied no man would have her. Who would want a woman with a highly evolved imaginary life and who regularly conducted conversations with herself, pretending others were engaged?

She tapped his arm and then stood up to move away from him. "I'm sorry about the teasing. With two ever-present sisters, it's not often I'm alone with only my thoughts."

Ranulf felt the air rush out of his chest in relief. With the exception of her desire to deceive him about her identity, his angel was still perfect.

"I used to hear my father talk to my mother after she had passed when he was worried about his people, about Hunswick, even Lord Anscombe. I never was inspired to do the same until now. I guess it's easier when you have someone to talk to, even if they can't hear."

Ranulf understood more than he wanted to. He had often felt the need to not just talk, but explode. But to whom? The kinds of things he wanted to say no one would understand, so he had kept them bottled up. Bronwyn had obviously done the same. Why she chose now, and him, he didn't know, but it made him feel more of the hero everyone professed him to be than he ever did on the battleground.

"These people . . . they are proud and hardworking, but most of all they are loyal to those they respect. Treat them well and the home you have always looked for will be here. It was for me."

Ranulf's mind reeled. Just like her father. Seeing into him, analyzing things about himself that he had intentionally ignored, and making assumptions . . . all uncomfortably close to accurate.

"Ranulf . . ." His name rolled off her lips and he debated if now was the time to "wake" and have her say it again, to his face. Then, with a hush whisper, she stroked his hair. "Don't look for me when I leave. I have an idea of how obstinate you are. And while I have longed for the company of a strong, opinionated man, I do not need a protector. Do not let your honor interfere with your duty to these people. And yes, you are very honorable. I can see it in the eyes of every one of your men. Still, I would have liked to have known you better."

No longer could he lie in silence. Bronwyn's once veiled hints of leaving were sounding more and more definitive and less like she was departing just for Syndlear. He was debating just how he should "wake" and confront her when a knock on the door interrupted his chance.

He felt her rise as the door squeaked open. The smell of food entered the room, and based on the growing sounds outside, morning had arrived.

"I'll stay with him and let you get some rest."

Ranulf's heart stopped. It was the old nursemaid. If Bronwyn agreed, this farce was going to come to an immediate and abrupt end.

"No, Constance, I'm fine. I need to be here. I couldn't rest, and if I were anywhere else, I would be driving everyone insane."

A snort. "You look tired, my lady."

"And that is because I am tired," Bronwyn replied with a touch of mockery. "The food will help. Besides, I see Ackart in the courtyard, clearly looking for you. I couldn't deny you time with your man."

Another snort followed by a shuffle. Ranulf swallowed his mirth. Could that old woman be embarrassed? He considered cracking his eyelid to see, but knew the chances of Bronwyn catching him were too great.

"He's not my man," Constance countered unconvincingly. "He's a widower that's all and we can . . . well, he and I find it easy to talk to each other."

Bronwyn must have been giving her a look of skepticism because the pudgy woman shuffled toward his supposedly unconscious form and examined the compress on his shoulder. "He's healing."

"And without fever."

"He was right about that, huh?"

"So far."

Another snort. "If he were to fever, he would have by now. But he hasn't woken up?"

"Not yet."

"Then his head got hurt worse than we thought. Just what we need. A dull-witted lord," Constance mused. "At least he doesn't seem menacing anymore."

Just wait, old woman, and you will learn just how menacing this dull-witted lord can be, Ranulf promised.

"I'll remind you of those words when he starts to bellow again, and for his sake, when he does, at least pretend to be scared. I suspect I gave his pride a wallop yesterday arguing with him like that. I don't think he's used to it."

Damn! Had he whispered his thoughts aloud?

The loud sounds of someone smacking their lips reached his ears. He didn't need to see Constance's look of disbelief. He could hear it. "Maybe," he heard her say, "but I doubt it. That man was born the arrogant sort. It was how he survived whatever hell he lived through, but . . . he does have an unusual quality about him. Something about the face . . ."

"Good-bye, Constance. Tell Ackart hello for me."

Ranulf fought back a sigh. Pretending to be asleep and lying still was exhausting . . . and torturous. Bronwyn must have set the tray on the table next to him for the smell of food filled the air. Once again, he had to choose. End this special once-in-a-lifetime opportunity or continue with the farce and starve. It was an easy choice.

Minutes later he was rewarded.

"Constance is right, there is something about you, but it's not your face. You have a secret weapon, so secret that even you don't know about it. But you could get every woman at Hunswick to leap to your bidding if you ever chose to use it."

Ranulf waited, but she said nothing more. He could hear chewing and he realized that unless he revealed the fact that he had been spying on her, he would never know to what she was referring.

The touch of her fingers against his lips ripped him back from his own thoughts to her. They smelled of meat and he was tempted to lick them.

"Just how many women have you kissed? Dozens? Hundreds? Would your kiss feel like any other man's?"

Ranulf couldn't move now even if he wanted to. Part of him wanted to scream that all kisses were not universal. That should he ever have the chance—or the courage—to taste her, it would not be like any other. He didn't have to experience it to know.

Ranulf's self-control, which had been under attack since the moment he awoke, was near gone. One more word, one more touch, and the urge to pull her down into his arms would be too strong to deny.

But there wasn't another word or touch.

Silence filled the room and Ranulf could no longer determine where Bronwyn was or what she was doing. He hadn't heard her move or the door open. If he had to guess, she was still sitting beside him. He waited, listening, and finally he heard the deep intake of breath and the slow exhale. She was asleep.

Ranulf opened his eye to look around and shifted his uninjured arm so that it barely brushed Bronwyn's hand. She moaned and unconsciously readjusted her arms on the bed so that she could rest against them. In doing so, her hair was released from its knot and fell scattered around her head, causing the sweet smell of roses to drift over him.

For the first time since he saw her, he was able just to stare and be captivated by her beauty. She had fallen asleep sitting in a chair but was bent over at the waist to rest her head on her intertwined arms now lying on his mattress. Unable to stop himself, Ranulf lifted his hand and softly began stroking her hair, praying she would not waken and force him to stop. Instead, she instinctively moved closer to him, seeking the affectionate touch in her sleep. And just like she did to him, he offered a caress, first across her temple and then down her cheek. After a few minutes, he paused and once again she moved closer, curling around his arm so that with the exception of her legs, she was lying next to him.

Ranulf knew he was dreaming and that his next move would make everything a nightmare, but the reward was worth the risk. And with a light tug, he lifted her by the waist and pulled her completely onto the bed next to him. But the nightmare didn't come. Instead, heaven continued as she buried her head against his chest, purring in satisfaction.

Oh, he was living a fantasy and he hoped never to wake up. Life had abandoned him twelve years ago, but if it hadn't, this was how the world was supposed to be, supposed to feel.

Ranulf knew he should waken her. Hell, he should have gotten up and left for he was more than able to. At the very least, he should have demanded some answers, starting with the truth as to who she was.

But he simply did not want to.

Until two days ago, he had merely existed. Then he had glimpsed an angel . . . and tonight his angel had noticed him. And in that instant he had come alive and he needed to feel alive for as long as possible . . . for as long as she was willing.

And despite his desire and intentions to do otherwise, for the first time in several years, Ranulf slept soundly.

The smell of food filled the air, stirring Ranulf from his slumber. He inhaled and instinctively tried to stretch his stiff limbs. Sharp pain seized his left shoulder and he frowned, trying to remember just where he was and how he had been injured. He lifted his right arm and vigorously rubbed his scalp, recollection sluggishly returning. He usually was alert immediately upon awakening, almost as if he were conscious even when asleep. But this time was different. He had truly been out, completely unaware of everyone and everything.

He glanced around the room and a shapely figure

with long honey-kissed hair was at the door. His angel. Instantly, memories returned. Ranulf glanced at the window. No light came in; instead, the firelight reflected off the smooth panes. He had slept through the entire morning and afternoon, only to stir when everyone was about to retire for the night.

"You are incredibly kind, Tory," Bronwyn said in hushed tones, pointing at the small table between the two hearth chairs. Sometime earlier she had awoken, realized her folly, and moved the chair back to its original, and safe, place. "Managing Constance can be a chore, but I assure you that making her your friend is well worth the effort."

"It was no effort at all, my lady," the young soldier gushed. Even in the dim light, his blush was obvious from across the room. "I'm just sorry that I couldn't bring you dinner until so late. Is there anything else I can get you? Water? Ale?"

Bronwyn beamed him a disarming smile and shook her head. She had not meant to tease and entrance with the simple action, but regardless, the spell it had woven had captivated Tory.

Ranulf lifted himself on his good elbow and stared pointedly at the young man. A second later, Tory caught his lord's eye and saw the ruthless possessiveness haunting its amber depths. He swallowed. "Good to see you awake, sir, I mean, my lord," he stammered and headed directly toward the door.

Bronwyn immediately spun around, her mouth open in both shock and delight. Then, remembering Tory, she rushed to the door, clasped the soldier's arm to stop him, and said, "Thank you. Tell Tyr his lordship finally awoke and will be ready for visitors in the morning. Have a good night."

Ranulf, who had instantly felt his blood heat seeing the physical connection, was able to reclaim some semblance of calm when he realized they were now alone again, and with no expected interruptions. He pushed himself into a sitting position and looked over at the hearth. Bronwyn was standing there, staring at him, looking perplexed.

"Still angry with me, are you, my lord?" she asked.

At first, Ranulf was confused. Then understanding dawned on him. He was scowling. Worse, he was declaring his emotional thoughts through expression, something he had learned long ago never to do. What was happening to him?

Ranulf raked his fingers through his hair again. "No. I'm not angry, just starving," he groused, hoping she would believe him.

Bronwyn cocked her head to one side and shifted her chin in deliberation. Then with a shrug of her shoulders, she pivoted toward the table and poured a hot beverage into a mug. She walked over to him and handed him the cup. "It's yarrow tea and should help with the pain and fever."

"I told you that I don't get fevers." His voice was cold and exact. He swallowed some of the bitter solution and coughed, shoving the mug back into her hands. She placed the pewter cup on the bedside table and moved toward the door as if she was about to leave.

"Come here." It was a command, not a request, driven by fear.

Hours before she had reached out to him, desired him enough to touch him sensually. There had been no ploy in the action for some personal gain, and as a result, he wanted her more than he could recall wanting anything his entire life. It didn't matter that nothing would come of it. Nor did it matter that she was pretending to be someone else and he was letting her.

He had been a starving man who had never known a good meal, but after sampling a morsel, his hunger for her would only grow and drive him mad till satiated.

She needed to stay.

Bronwyn met his unswerving gaze with one of her own. "First tell me why."

Because he wanted to talk with her, wanted to spend time with her, wanted to pretend for just a little while that he was like every other man and that she enjoyed his company. Ranulf grimaced. The truth left him too vulnerable. "Because I intend to eat and not as an invalid, angel. So would you please come here and bring me my shirt."

Bronwyn plucked his shirt off the chest and threw it at him. "Don't call me that."

"What . . . *angel*?" He paused but she said nothing. "What do you want me to call you? Lily?" he asked, choking on the false name. She paled considerably and he knew she was not happy with the idea either. "You don't look like a flower, but an angel, a wild, untamed gift from heaven. So, *angel*, come here."

Bronwyn eyed him suspiciously. He had that authoritative sound to his voice again, but she doubted she would win a war of wills this time. Too much of his pride was at stake. She walked up next to the bed. "You may call me *my lady*, my lord. Now, will you tell me why it is necessary that I stay?"

"I intend to get dressed and eat and you are going to help me."

Bronwyn jumped back. "I will not!"

"You will. I'm starving and it's your fault," Ranulf groused, remembering the smell of food as her fingers slipped across his lips.

"My fault!" she exclaimed. "You were asleep!"

Ranulf started a retort and bit it back just in time.

Seeing a moment of weakness, Bronwyn pounced. "Now lie back down and stop fussing. You need to save your strength."

Ranulf swung his legs defiantly off the edge of the bed. "If I am weak, woman, it's because of lack of food."

Bronwyn huffed with frustration. "Then you can eat in bed. I'll make you a plate and—"

"And the day I eat in bed I better be dying. Food leaves crumbs. That brings bugs and I happen to hate sharing my bed with anyone." Bronwyn's face suddenly turned ashen with mortification and Ranulf mentally berated himself for his thoughtlessness. He had been trying to think of a reason for refusing and that was the first that came to mind. Ranulf lifted his arm to try and don the argumentative garment, but his left shoulder would not obey. "Now will you help me put on my shirt?" he bellowed, exasperated and more than a little embarrassed.

Bronwyn shook her head, her blue eyes large with apprehension. "I absolutely refuse to touch you."

Anger flashed in his good eye and in its wake left a coldness that gave her chills. Whatever she had just said instantly changed his mood and the tenor of their quarrel. "Yes, you will, woman," he gritted out. "I am starving and have already skipped one meal listening to you babble about your desires, but I refuse to miss another."

Bronwyn stood motionless for several long seconds. This morning . . . her rambling . . . Ranulf had not been asleep. He had been awake. Listening to her nonsensical chatter about kissing him. She almost faltered but pride took over.

Narrowing her eyes, she marched over, snatched his shirt from his grasp, and yanked it over his head, uncaring of the pain she was causing him. Then brazenly, she placed her hand on his chest and caressed it sensually, intending to teach him a lesson. "It's too bad, my lord," she purred, "that you are too weak and vulnerable to satisfy me."

Ranulf grabbed her wrist and wrenched it from his skin. He pulled her closer so that she stood in between his legs, her face near his. "And just what was it you desired?"

Bronwyn licked her lips and Ranulf realized it was not his humiliation she sought, but to salvage some pride from her own. With his free arm, he reached up to pull on the shirt gathered around his neck. "Angel, I am getting up, and if the only thing I have on are my underclothes . . . so be it."

He was calling her "angel" again.

Bronwyn reached out and stopped his hand with her own. "Fine." She gathered the sleeve and held it so that he could stick one arm in and then worked with him to get his wounded arm dressed.

He was both right and wrong about undressing him. It had been her, but at the time he was just someone hurt who needed help. Dressing him, on the other hand, was a sensual experience that was unnerving her core. Large, strong, and beautifully well proportioned, the powerful lines of his torso etched and highlighted his every muscle as she lowered the shirt over his body. By the time Bronwyn was done, she was shaking.

Ranulf studied her reaction, knowing that was why he had been so emphatic about her dressing him. He could have dressed without her, more painfully, but he had managed to don clothes before with more severe injuries. He had needed to know the truth. She had seen the scars on his face, but compared to the ones on his upper chest, they were mere scratches. And now he knew. His angel was like the rest. Trembling and unable to handle it.

Finished, Bronwyn returned to the dinner tray, poured herself some water in a mug, and promptly emptied it, unable to disguise her quivering hand. Seeing his look of disappointment bolstered Bronwyn. "Well, I'm sorry you find me an inadequate nursemaid, but how do you expect me to react? I've never been in the presence of a nearly naked man before."

"Angel, you got me undressed. I think your morality can survive putting clothes back on my body."

"That . . . that was different. You weren't, well, you weren't a *man* then."

Could he have been wrong? That the fear he saw in her eyes wasn't from his scars, but of a woman who was unknowing of a man? Did she really see him as such?

Invigorated, Ranulf laced his shirt and rose, refusing to continue acting or looking like an invalid to her. Fact was he hadn't felt as far from an invalid in a long time.

Bronwyn stared at the opening in his shirt. Crisp

brown hair peaked out at the neckline, a reminder of the muscular chest beneath. Ranulf let go a short cackle. At the sound, her eyes snapped to his, and seeing his mocking expression, she spun around and grabbed the poker to stoke the fire.

She needed to leave and let him eat. He obviously could move around on his own and pretending he needed her assistance was only prolonging her inevitable departure to Syndlear. So why was she finding it so hard to do so? She didn't like him. He was interesting and something about him stirred her physically, but they couldn't stop fighting. That was it! They argued. No one disagreed with her or challenged her; even her sisters just capitulated to her decisions. Deadeye de Gunnar was stimulating.

Bronwyn took a deep breath and exhaled, relieved to understand why she felt pulled toward a man whom she barely knew or got along with. She should leave and would, but if she did so now, it would be akin to running away. After he ate, she would check his dressing and then depart to her own quarters and in the morning head for Syndlear.

"What the . . ." Ranulf barked behind her. "Where's the meat? The butter?"

Bronwyn smiled. It was going to be a hard few days for everyone at Hunswick, suddenly observing Advent, but it might inspire the new residents to not just enjoy the fruits of everyone's labor, but appreciate and contribute.

Turning around, Bronwyn pasted on what she hoped to be an incredulous look and said, "During Advent Fast? Now, my lord, you wouldn't want others to think you a heathen."

Ranulf picked up the mug, sniffed the tea with

disdain, and put it back down before flopping into one of the two hearth chairs. "I know a hell of a lot more about the topic than you. And I could care less about the opinion of others."

"I doubt that," Bronwyn murmured, just loud enough for him to hear, "on either point."

Ranulf leaned forward and grabbed the plate of fish and potatoes. He took several bites and waved his fork around the platter. "The Church calls for their followers to *celebrate* the season of Advent the four weeks before Christmas, which is nonsense because I know of no one who rejoices in the idea of starvation and . . . abstinence."

Bronwyn's heartbeat suddenly doubled its pace and she had to fight to remain looking relaxed and unaffected. "I believe humility is a large purpose behind the fast."

"And control," Ranulf replied with a grunt. "If I kept such an absurd custom, I and my men would have starved many a year."

Arrogant man. It didn't help that she also felt similarly on the matter and had many a row with Father Morrell on the ritual. "And your pride keeps you from doing anything absurd, I suppose."

Ranulf eyed Bronwyn suspiciously. Their banter was the equivalent of foreplay, except he seemed to be the only one suppressing excitement. His angel just sat unperturbed and serene . . . almost too composed. "It helps. Just as the meat you ate last night. I smelled it on your fingers."

Bronwyn felt her teeth grind as she shifted her clenched jaw. "As Advent is only required on three days of the week, I guess I was fortunate that I was able to consume the last of the lamb before Twelfthtide."

"Making me unfortunate. But what about the exemption of children, the elderly, and the *infirm*?"

The man was acting smug and causing her to react defensively. Bronwyn leaned over to pour herself some hot cider and then settled back in the hearth chair, slowly sipping the sweet drink. She glanced at him and then licked her lips and asked, "Oh, are you infirm?"

Without blinking, Ranulf purred, "It depends."

Bronwyn succumbed to a shiver and looked away. She was playing with fire and needed to stop. "I suppose we could hunt for some barnacle geese. That should suffice for meat and still make Father Morrell happy."

Ranulf wanted to rejoice. She *was* affected by their conversation just as much as he. "Who's Father Morrell?"

"The priest assigned to Cumbria. Normally we only see him two or three times a year, but since Lord Anscombe died and Father left, he has visited more often and made it clear that he would be celebrating Twelfthtide at Hunswick this year."

Ranulf let go a scoff and filled his plate again. "I never understood why people thought a man of the cloth was the best choice to watch over young women. Celibacy is something very few men could or want to endure. Too many priests join the Church not due to a love of God, but from necessity, which does not come with a lot of restraint."

Swinging her legs up underneath her, Bronwyn settled back and studied him overtly. Then after a few minutes, she leaned on the arm of the chair and after a second of hesitation asked, "Just how long did you study to become a clergyman?"

Ranulf stopped in midbite and remained unmoving for at least a half-dozen seconds before resuming his consumption of the rest of the fish. He had been preparing himself for "the" question, the one that everyone—especially more brazen women—asked when they got the opportunity. How did you get your scars? Do they hurt? Will they ever go away? He had his sharp retort all prepared, but once again she had proved herself different than most women.

"How did you know I studied?"

"Obvious," Bronwyn answered, giving him a slow, enigmatic smile. "How many soldiers do you know who could recite the driving forces behind men entering the priesthood? I can see you studying, but actually becoming a priest? I confess that image escapes me."

Ranulf grimaced as he immediately felt himself tighten. He drew in a long breath and forced himself to remain seated. "I did study. But it seems I am not alone. Been preparing for an abbey?"

Bronwyn coughed, nearly spewing the cider she had been sipping. "Me? No," she returned sharply. "As for studying, I have not had the opportunity or the skill, for I cannot read. Lord Anscombe was the one—I'm sorry, I keep referring to your predecessor by your—"

Ranulf raised his hand, interrupting her. "It doesn't bother me in the least. I never aspired to the title, and to be honest I, too, think of my dead cousin as Lord Anscombe and will for some time."

"He was a kind man and spent hours talking to me and my sisters about conquerors, lands of faraway, and the battles his cousin had survived."

"Another cousin of mine?"

Bronwyn nodded. "By marriage. He's related to Helga, the mother of your infant cousin who would have inherited the title by lineage if you had not agreed."

"I doubt it," Ranulf mumbled as he stretched out his legs in front of him. It was odd just how comfortable he felt with her, relaxing in just an overly long shirt and his underdrawers. "The duke is not quite that open-minded. I think he expects more from his noblemen than what a mere babe can provide."

She quirked an eyebrow questioningly. "The duke?"

"I mean the king," Ranulf replied with a shrug. "Hard habit to break."

"Maybe, but I think you're wrong about the king's unwillingness to have a babe inherit the title, not when he is also the cousin of a Danish king. It was his uncle who died in the first crusade, and it was stories of his heroism that I was speaking of."

"How do you know so much about my family?"

In spite of herself, Bronwyn was unable to suppress a giggle. "How do you know so little?"

At the sound of her laughter, a great shudder of need wracked through him and Ranulf fought to remain in control. He would do nothing to end this. His angel was enjoying his company, not fighting with him, not wishing to be anywhere else. Such a moment was not rare in his experience but nonexistent and he would not do anything to mar this time together. Soon enough he would have to confront her about her lack of honesty and her true identity, terminating whatever strange camaraderie they were sharing. But he was not inclined to hasten the ending tonight.

"Fine then," he grinned back at her, picking up an apple, "tell me what you *think* you know about my family."

Bronwyn nearly melted at the sight of his smile and gripped the chair to remain upright. Instinctively she grinned back, hoping it hid her true feelings of turmoil. *Oh I really should leave,* she thought to herself, but knew even as the words played through her mind she wouldn't. Not until he asked her to.

"Well, your cousin was one of three children, but his twin sisters died at birth so he was raised an only son. He married, but unfortunately he and Lady Anscombe did not produce an heir before her death. So the title was to be passed down to the next in line. His father had a sister and a brother—your grandfather. Your grandfather had only one child, your father, who in return had two."

"My brother and I. My father and then Hodur were to be the next in line to the title. My father was quite pleased with the idea and raised my brother accordingly."

"I was told Hodur died."

Ranulf nodded. "Last year. He was traveling from France and his boat sank."

Bronwyn flinched slightly at the cold brittleness in Ranulf's voice. He wanted to appear and sound unaffected by the event, but something about his reaction made her realize that he felt just the opposite. His brother's death had taken him by surprise and had hurt him deeply. She could understand that. Her father's death continued to seem unreal, and part of her still expected him to ride into Hunswick and make her feel safe once again. "Were you close?"

Ranulf took a deep breath. "Not as siblings, but we respected each other. We never really talked about his inheritance."

"I . . . uh . . ." Bronwyn stammered, wondering how anyone could be so distant from one's own immediate family, and then she laughed. "I just realized how often I wished for my sisters and me to be less close."

"No, you don't," Ranulf countered, his voice low and serious. "Your life would have been much sadder without them. My father was a sheriff, strict and demanding, and he expected both his sons to put their mark on the world. My brother was to get the title and that meant—"

"You were to study and join the priesthood," Bronwyn finished.

"You're right. I wouldn't have joined. I believe in God, but neither as a tyrant or as a benevolent spirit, and I never subscribed to ritual as being necessary for one's belief. But it did give me the opportunity to study and expand my knowledge and . . . learn of other possibilities. Then that option was gone and I became what I am today." He paused and stared at the eaten fruit in his hand. "How do you still have apples?" he asked just before he tossed the core into the fire.

"The weather was strange this year. Spring and summer came late, so instead of October, they ripened in November. There are only a few left and we are hoping they last until Twelfthtide," Bronwyn replied, not deceived by the change of topic.

Ranulf hadn't mentioned his scars, but she suspected the story of how he got them began exactly where his childhood account had stopped. And she was glad he had ended it. Divulging secrets had a way of compelling one into disclosing some of one's own, and she wasn't about to reveal hers.

"I don't think I've talked so much in months, and you need to rest. I would say to prevent a fever, but I am beginning to believe you. Have you ever had one?"

"Not that I can remember."

Bronwyn glanced at the mottled skin around his sunken eyelid and found that hard to believe, but then again, anyone injured as he had been should have died. Just the idea of never meeting him, that someone else would be assuming responsibility of Hunswick, was unthinkable. Ranulf may not be smooth and soft spoken, but kindness lurked in his heart. Suddenly the urge to kiss him again took hold and she shivered.

"If you are cold, put on another log."

The room was far from chilly. Soon, the unusually tepid weather would be gone and the hearths would need to be fully lit, but since Bronwyn didn't want to explain why she shivered, she rose and did as he suggested.

Ranulf knew when she was about to turn around and make some excuse to leave. He didn't want her to go. He wished that *she* wanted to stay, that she would trust him. Because after tonight, he was convinced that the reason behind her pretending to be Lily was not an obvious one.

"Do you believe in keeping secrets?"

Bronwyn stared at the orange and yellow flames, wondering why the topic had suddenly come up. "I do," she answered before turning around to face him.

"Lies bring pain."

"Eventually, yes."

Ranulf used his good arm and pushed himself to a standing position. "Are you keeping secrets, angel?"

"Large ones, my lord."

"You do not seem comfortable with the concept of hiding the truth."

"I'm not," she agreed, crossing her arms. "Secrets make me very uncomfortable, but that doesn't mean I can't keep them if they are necessary."

"Then let me tell you mine," he said, hoping it might make her comfortable enough to trust him.

"No. I don't want the responsibility."

Ranulf held her gaze for a long time. He prided himself on knowing people, but Bronwyn was nothing like everyone else. She was more like . . . him. And if he were to keep a secret—someone else's secret—it would only be for a scant few and only for one reason.

"Who do you need to protect?"

Bronwyn clutched her already crossed arms. Her back stiffened and she lifted her chin as if meeting a challenge. "My sisters, these people. For the past several months, they have turned to me for direction, help, and answers, and I will not let anyone . . . or any circumstance make them unhappy. Can you understand that?"

Ranulf strolled slowly toward her and cupped her cheek. "But what if the secret causes harm? Or places another in a position they are forever bound to?"

"I would never keep a promise that inflicted pain on another."

A tear fell. Ranulf wiped it away with his thumb. "I

guess all that remains is deciding just when harm takes place then? When are those affected by dishonesty damaged by it?"

"I only just met you . . ."

"Some secrets grow with time and may become too large of a burden for you to bear alone." Her eyes grew large and Ranulf felt an enormous pull to lean down and kiss her. Forcing himself to retract his hand, he took a step back and put some distance between them. "I cannot explain it, angel, but know that I am not open with even those I know well. I do not talk idly or very often find myself at ease, but I am with you. I hope in the future no secrets will be between us."

Bronwyn didn't know how to tell him that it wasn't possible. Fate had brought him into her life too late.

"Until then, will you stay?" he asked, pulling off his shirt before lying back down. "Will you talk to me? My head hurts and your voice calms me."

Bronwyn swallowed and moved to push her chair back to the side of his bed. Ranulf was affecting her in ways she couldn't fight. He was right. Something was growing between them, but it wasn't real. It was based on a lie, and by staying, all she was doing was delaying the inevitable.

Early in her youth, just as she was turning into a woman, she had learned the painful lesson of how important beauty was to a man. Her sisters had that pure, untouched allure that she would never possess. Only Luc had ever offered to marry her, but that was because he coveted power over anything else. And in the end, even he would have sought his pleasures outside of her bed. Ranulf would be no different, but right now she didn't care.

She would stay because she wanted to and for now . . . so did he.

Ranulf waited until she fell asleep once again on the edge of his bed. Slowly, he persuaded her unconscious form to once again join him by his side. The self-inflicted unhurried process had been akin to that of torture, but the reward was far sweeter.

He knew this would happen the moment he asked her to stay and his angel agreed. And he suspected so did she. Why she wanted to lie next to him was a mystery, but he had no doubts to the motivation behind his own reasons. He had wanted to know what it would be like to hold her next to him and believe she wanted to be there.

Tomorrow was soon enough for the truth. He would confront her and release them both from the farce she was playing.

Then he would discover if this moment of bliss could become much, much more.

In the distance, a figure hidden in the shadows studied the night activity of Hunswick. The castle was no longer as vulnerable as it once had been, for guards now roamed the curtain walls and manned the tower battlements. But not many. A half-dozen at the most. Skilled most likely, but not enough to overpower his mercenary group. It has cost him the majority of the wealth his father had left him to fund his army, but the money would be replaced once he possessed what should have been his years ago.

Only one person stood in his way. Ranulf de Gunnar. The man had accepted the title, which went against every rumor of being possible, and now the infamous Deadeye was a lord. And if the news was true, he had also been promised the hand of Laon's youngest daughter. It mattered little. He didn't have Syndlear or Lady Bronwyn, both prizes far more valuable and ones no one but he had ever appreciated.

When he was told of the forced departure of all three women, Luc had wondered if Deadeye's injuries had affected not just his face, but his manhood. Why else would he order all of them to Syndlear with minimal protection? Then again, the position and the responsibility had been thrust upon him. Perhaps the new lord was hoping someone would relieve him of his burden. Luc had no problems in doing just that.

Tomorrow he would ride to Syndlear and visit Bronwyn. He had promised to stay away until Epiphany, but promises to one's intended were meant to be broken. And maybe, after meeting the disfigured Lord Anscombe, Lady Bronwyn would be more receptive to his proposal.

Either way, she would be his. As would Syndlear, and eventually . . . Hunswick.

Chapter Four

To help create the festive mood and atmosphere, decorations were a significant part of the Twelfthtide celebrations during the Middle Ages. Using greenery, such as holly, ivy, and other evergreens to ornament homes, dinner tables, dining halls, etc., dates back to the Roman era and was documented as having occurred in London as early as the twelfth century. But the highlight of medieval Twelfthtide festivities was the food, where a variety of meats, sweets, and drinks were served. A boar's head—not a roast turkey, which became popular later—was a favorite to be served along with roasted swans, peacocks, goose, venison, rabbit, duck, and an enormous range of fowl and poultry. Complementing these were an assortment of breads and cheeses, mince pies, gingerbreads, plum porridge, and several other desserts, all to be washed down with spiced wines and specially made

ales. No wonder these feasts lasted so long and were
so anticipated!

Bronwyn arched her back and stretched her free
arm over her head. Yawning, she smiled as the last
remnants of her dream danced by. Mentally, she
strained to capture the last threads, but all that remained was the feeling of being warm and safe,
something she hadn't felt since her father had left.

Sighing, Bronwyn shifted to sit up and immediately froze, realizing just why she had felt so comfortable. Every muscle in her body had gone rock solid
as memories of last night flooded into her awareness. She *knew* she should have left.

Once again, she had crawled onto the bed in her
sleep. Except, she wasn't lying demurely on one side
as she had before. This time she was nestled into
Ranulf's side and sprawled all over the man, with
both an arm and a leg stretched over his torso
and thigh.

Ranulf inhaled deeply and let go a long breath,
indicating he was still asleep. Bronwyn let go a sigh
of relief. Thankfully, like the last time, he had slept
through her lapse in modest behavior. She forced
her body to relax enough for her to slip off, grateful that she had at least once again remained above
the covers and not burrowed underneath them.

Unnerved by her own behavior, Bronwyn poured
some water into the basin on the small table next to
the bed and splashed the cool liquid on her face.
Dabbing her cheeks dry, she glanced back at the
still sleeping form.

Guilt, or at the very least shame, should have consumed her, but only a strange sense of giddiness

bubbled inside, as if she were a young girl who had just been given her first kiss. Even last night, she had not acted like herself. Instead of listening to the conversation, she had engaged in it. Her reaction to him was silly, probably heightened by the fact that he was doubly forbidden, by both Luc and Lily. In a few days, she would be gone and have unlimited time to explore just why Ranulf de Gunnar affected her so, but for right now, what would it hurt to continue pretending that he was the man of her dreams and she was the woman of his?

Taking a deep breath, Bronwyn smoothed out the wrinkles of her bliaut as best she could and settled back into the chair beside the bed, trying to appear as if she had been there all night. But it did not matter. Ranulf remained asleep, his chest slowly rising and falling in a rhythmic fashion. He still looked pale, but no agitation crept into his expression as one might see if fever had taken hold.

As was her habit, she leaned over, kissed his temple, and verified the coolness of his skin. The powder she had used helped to seal the wound and accelerate healing, but it did not prevent fevers. And Ranulf should have gotten at least a mild one after the injury he received. She could now understand how others found his healing abilities strange, even scary. People often found those different or unusual from themselves as frightening creatures to be avoided. Which was another reason why she needed to leave. She knew too well the pain of someone's irrational fear.

Bronwyn's face was just a few inches above his when she stopped her descent back into the chair and wondered what he would do if he knew the truth about her. *Would you be like the others?* she asked herself, biting her bottom lip while staring at his mouth. *At least with them, I had the chance to experience the pleasure of a kiss before they walked away.*

Then the compulsion to kiss him became too strong, and just before her lips touched his, she whispered, "Who could it hurt? No one need know."

Ranulf had felt both the sweetest of pleasures and the most intense pains when Bronwyn awoke and pressed her body even more acutely against his. Intensely aware of every welcomed, blissful touch, he had told himself that she didn't know, that his angel would never willingly come to him, touch him, hold him in such a way. And he had been proven right. The moment she became aware of where she was and her position, she had pulled away, slipping from his side as gently, but as quickly, as possible.

While she had washed her face, he had taken several deep breaths, steadied his breathing, and fought to regain his control. But the moment her lips touched his, it had vanished.

The feel of her mouth sent sparks flying through his body. It had been a long time since someone had kissed him like this. Too long. Perhaps never. Instead of ending his curiosity, it had awakened a dark possessive desire for more.

Overwhelmed with a physical need unlike he'd ever known, Ranulf freed his uninjured arm and buried his hand into the intricate twists of her chestnut curls. In doing so, he pulled her closer and slid his tongue over her lips, encouraging them to part and let him taste inside. For a moment, Bronwyn hesitated and then innocently tasted him in return, revealing that he was the first to teach her the pleasures of being a woman in a man's arms.

Whispering to himself . . . *go slowly . . . slowly*, he let his tongue glide in and out, relishing her sweet flavor, teaching her just how to truly be kissed by a man. Following his lead, her pulse quickened as her tongue danced with his and she instinctively moved closer, fitting her body sinuously against his. She sighed, throaty and low, telling him without words that he was affecting her just as much as she was arousing him. His angel really was in his arms, meant for him.

Ranulf breathed in her scent and let his fingers roam her curves, wishing it was not wool or linen he touched, but her skin. He wanted to awaken desires and passions inside her that would drown out any other thought in mind.

Ranulf had kissed and *been* kissed before, but not like this. Not with honesty and genuine desire and passion. Her tentative offers were growing with urgency and a hot tide was rising steadily between them. He was stunned by his need for her and soon—very soon—he would not be able to deny himself—or her—what they wanted. Reluctantly, he pulled away and rested his forehead against hers as he caught his breath.

A piece of his soul had slipped from him and, without choice or question, buried itself inside her. He had found his soul mate at last.

"Angel, open your eyes."
Bronwyn moaned and leaned into the hard frame,

pressing her cheek against the warmth, wanting the feel of his arms around her once more.

"Angel, open your eyes."

Bronwyn blinked under the compelling tone. Reality overwhelmed her senses as she realized she was half sitting on the bed, half lying on Ranulf's chest after what could only be described as a passionate encounter. She had dreamt about such kisses and had heard Constance's warning about passion and how easily she could fall prey to a man's overtures, but it was *she* who had kissed *him*. Or had she?

Maybe at the beginning she initiated the embrace, but she had intended it to be quick, just long enough to settle her curiosity. But at that point, her kiss ended and Ranulf's began. He had suddenly become the aggressor—and she had welcomed it. Never had she imagined tasting a man in such a way and enjoying it.

"Look at me, angel."

The husky possessiveness in his tone compelled her to do his bidding. His gaze locked with hers, and swirling in the deep amber depths she saw barely leashed desire that matched her own.

Bronwyn's hand flew to her lips. She pushed against his chest and jumped off the bed almost simultaneously. Spinning around, she went to the window and looked down below. The morning sun was bright in the sky, and activity filled the courtyard.

The guilt she had not felt before was now hitting her full force. She could still feel his lips pressed against hers. Nothing she had ever said or done in her life had prepared her for such an experience. She felt heavy and light at the same time. Shame consumed her, but more than anything else, she wanted him to kiss her again. In those few short moments, he had made her feel beautiful, wanted, and someone worthy of being desired.

Ranulf stared at her immobile back and tried to compose himself. It had just been a kiss, but his body was reacting violently to the need it had aroused. Never had any woman kissed him with such raw need, passion, and open desire. He had heard youths speak of the earth shaking during their first coupling and always believed them to be seriously overembellishing a simple act. He was far from inexperienced, but if he had to describe what had just transpired between him and Bronwyn—"earthshaking" would be the word.

Suddenly, the prospect of marrying did not seem like such a burden. He would free Lily from her obligation to him as soon as possible and make good on his promise to Laon by making Bronwyn his bride. In doing so, he would honor the principle behind the vow and satisfy Henry at the same time. Granted, it wouldn't be in the way his king had ordered, but when he explained the situation, Henry would understand and support the union. Of this, Ranulf was certain.

Excited by the idea and, for the first time, his future, Ranulf laughed and teased Bronwyn, hoping that she would now own to her true identity. "You need not feel nervous or ashamed. It is normal to be curious what it would be like to kiss your soon-to-be husband."

His simple comment and joyful, expectant attitude shook Bronwyn out of her shock. What had she been thinking? Had she forgotten just who he thought she was? No wonder Ranulf had kissed her. He had thought her to be Lillabet, his intended. And if he ever did chance to encounter her sister, he would realize his folly just as every man had before him.

Bronwyn pulled together the last bits and pieces of her pride and marched to the door, yanking it open. "You are incorrect, my lord. I feel neither nervous nor ashamed. I have been kissed before and have no doubt I will enjoy the experience again by many other men. And as for the reasons I returned your embrace, they were far more interesting than that of just plain curiosity."

Ranulf stared at the beams supporting the floor above and tried to reconcile his thoughts. He wanted an explanation . . . and an admission. Maybe it wasn't shame or nervousness that made Bronwyn flee—for flee was exactly what she had done. Her words had been delivered calmly, but the tightness in her jaw belied them. So if it wasn't fear or embarrassment, then it had to have been pride spurring her abrupt departure . . . and her parting words. At least, it better have been, because whether Bronwyn knew it or not, he was the *last* man she would ever know or touch.

Still, pride didn't explain why she had kissed him. And if not curiosity, then what? Pity was impossible not to recognize. She had *wanted* to kiss him. But like him, she just hadn't expected the intensity of their embrace and it had rattled her. So why then was his gut telling him that the embrace itself was not behind her defensive posture, but something else altogether?

Footsteps echoed in the hallway and Ranulf felt his heart rate double. Then came a sharp rap at the door just before it creaked open. The curt knock gave the intruder away and the hopeful tension coursing through Ranulf instantly dissipated. He slumped his wrist across his forehead and resumed counting the boards making up the ceiling.

Tyr poked his head around the large door and, seeing Ranulf awake, stepped inside. "Well, it's good to know that my best friend is so moved by my visit."

"Come inside and shut the door."

Tyr pushed the heavy door back into the jamb and then meandered toward Ranulf. Grabbing the back of the chair Bronwyn had been sitting in, he pulled it farther away from the bed and sank onto the padded seat. He then stretched out, propped his feet on top of the coverlet, and crossed them at the ankles while intertwining his fingers behind his head. "I was going to ask why you've decided to play the invalid for so long, but after I encountered the disheveled but still heavenly creature leaving your tower . . . well, I commend you, Ranulf. I thought you had foresworn women. Now I realize you were just persevering until you met a true beauty and not one of those shallow types lurking about court."

"Nothing happened."

"Uh, her tousled hair says differently, friend."

Ranulf whipped the coverlet off his legs and stood up. Grabbing the shirt he had tossed aside the night before, he pulled it on with a grunt as he was forced to stretch his left shoulder to slip his arm down the sleeve. "Nothing happened," he repeated, this time more emphatically.

He then moved toward the chest by the window and yanked it open. Bending over, he shuffled the contents around, cursing. Most of his stuff had been placed inside—belts, caps, hose, even extra drawers, but no clothes. "Where the hell would she have put them?"

Tyr amused himself for a few more minutes before interrupting his friend's torment. "Try the garderobe."

"Garderobe?"

Tyr pushed back from his stretched position and marched over to the door that led to the small chamber holding all of Ranulf's tunics, shirts, and other garments. "Aye," Tyr answered, swinging it open, intentionally accentuating his Scottish accent. "You live in a castle now, not on the field, and noblemen like you have those kinds of things. It's a convenience. One of the ones I actually miss."

Ranulf grimaced. His Highland friend rarely revealed anything about himself, but he would never question Tyr about his past, just as Tyr would never question him.

Stepping inside, Ranulf saw the same tunic he had been wearing when the tower collapsed. It was clean and the holes were mended. Next to it were three linen shirts, each with their hems resewn. Pointing at the repaired garments, he asked, "Who messed with my clothes? And when?"

Tyr shrugged and moved to sit back down. "I believe the same woman who's at risk for being ruined, despite the fact that *nothing happened.*"

Grabbing a very dark blue, almost black surcoat

rimmed in gold, Ranulf turned around as he slipped the hole of the tunic over his head. "Explain yourself."

"You understood me," Tyr replied, deliberately adding a light singsong tone to his voice. "I'm just pointing out that if you still don't intend to marry the woman, then it might be best to have someone else be in here when she tends to your *life-threatening* wound."

Ranulf didn't miss the sarcasm. Both knew that he had survived worse injuries and without a nurse-maid. "I don't need a chaperone."

"Well, Lady Lillabet sure does, especially if you bound out of here, acting like your injury was only a scratch. No one will believe she needed to monitor you day and *night*. Someone has to look out for her reputation before the tongues begin to swag."

Ranulf gave Tyr a pointed stare and then marched back to the chest to grab what he needed to finish dressing.

Tyr ignored Ranulf's silent rebuff. "So are you going to tell me what is going on?" Using his chin, he pointed to the chaotic state of the coverlet and sheets. "And I cannot remember you spending as much time in bed in two weeks as you have the past two days since I've known you."

His friend was right and it rankled that he didn't have a quick answer to shut him up. "Damn it. If you must know, I was fully dressed and spent several hours eating dinner last night in *that* chair."

Ranulf marched into his day room. Tyr gave a quick side glance at last night's dishes still on the table before following him into the larger meeting space. "Uh-huh. If you say so. Listen, I don't blame you. If I was engaged to Lady Lillabet, I just might stay in bed all day, too."

"She's not Lillabet," Ranulf groaned, leaning against his knuckles on the large round table located in the middle of the room.

For the first time, Tyr looked confused and not sure of the facts. "But I called her by that name and she responded . . ."

Ranulf shook his head. "She's pretending to be Lillabet, either at her sister's instigation or in order to protect her from me."

Tyr rubbed his chin in thought and then shrugged his shoulders in semi-agreement. "Hmm. Well, I don't know about protecting her sister, but the woman has been doing a damn good job of protecting you. Do you know she refused to let anyone in? She didn't want to agitate you when you needed to save your strength," Tyr chuckled, unable to hide his mirth. "I swear those were her words. God knows you know they aren't mine. So, if she isn't Lillabet, then which of Laon's daughters is she?"

"I'm fairly certain she's the eldest. Bronwyn."

Tyr strolled toward one of the two large arched windows and leaned against the stone wall, looking down at the courtyard below. "Bronwyn," he hummed possessively. "Hmmm. I like it. I liked her, too. She has fight. Don't meet too many women with spirit."

Ranulf tightened his fists as he listened to Tyr roll Bronwyn's name in his mouth, appreciating her other qualities and not just her beauty. Ranulf had always regarded jealousy as a ridiculous reaction that could not be justified. And he had been right. Nothing was more absurd than wishing only he could recognize and savor the qualities in Bronwyn that made her special, unique . . . his angel. Yet that was how he felt.

Tyr had been studying his friend's reaction from the corner of his eye. He had known Ranulf for years and considered him his best friend, and for the most part, they shared a frank and honest relationship. Each felt the other was more of a brother than their own siblings, explaining why Tyr had felt not only comfortable in pricking Ranulf's jealousy, but justified in doing so. In truth, he just wanted his friend to be happy, but he doubted if Ranulf—or any of them who had made war a career—knew any longer what that meant.

He had hoped after seeing Bronwyn's tousled state that she and Ranulf had redirected their explosive interplay to something far more entertaining. Anyone who had heard their impassioned and very vocal fight just before the tower collapsed knew something remarkable was happening. Tyr could not recollect a time he'd heard Ranulf argue with anyone. Either he didn't care enough or he made it clear that disagreement was not an option. And from what Tyr overheard around the castle, her ladyship had a similar leadership style. She typically found a way to ensure all were satisfied, but once she made a decision, that was it. So after witnessing her tender ministrations on the heels of their verbal conflict, Tyr had believed his friend incredibly lucky to be engaged to someone whom he could connect emotionally with on so many levels. But to learn that she was not Lillabet . . . but the sister.

Tyr wanted to help his friend, but first he needed to know if he should. "I thought you were engaged to the prettiest of the three."

"Supposedly," Ranulf answered simply. Once again possessive anger flashed in his dark expression.

Tyr almost laughed out loud. This was almost too easy.

Ranulf was the most detached, unemotional person Tyr had ever come across. The man never gave away his emotional state, whether elation, anger, stress, or fear. But jealousy over a woman? That was apparently an emotion Ranulf had yet to conquer. And it might just be the trigger to get him to act before he closed himself off to the first chance he had at real peace and—if Bronwyn felt even remotely similar—happiness.

Tyr decided to fan the spark before it blew itself out under Ranulf's untutored hand. "I had been planning to leave and return to London in time for the Twelfthtide festivities, but since seeing some of the attractions Hunswick has to offer, I've changed my mind. I think I might stick around here and get to know Laon's daughters a little better."

Ranulf fought the urge to pound his fist into the table as another wave of jealousy crashed into him. Whatever spell Bronwyn had woven over him was not diminishing with her absence. If anything, his desire for her was growing. "I thought you'd sworn off marriage," Ranulf growled.

"Who said anything about marriage?" Tyr snapped back. "I just know that when a younger sister gets married, the older one might like some company and Bronwyn is one damn fine-looking woman."

"Leave her alone, Tyr."

The possessive growl in Ranulf's voice was unmistakable and undeniable. Tyr swung around abruptly and faced his friend from across the table. "I knew it!"

"Just what do you think you know?"

"Something happened between you two," Tyr answered, pointing at him. "No man—not even you—can spend day and night with a woman that beautiful and not at least try to kiss her. Did you?"

"None of your business."

Tyr let go a long low whistle. "So not only did you, but you enjoyed it. Enough to still be bothered. I'm kind of wishing it had been me up there instead."

Ranulf moved toward the door. "I think your first inclinations about leaving Hunswick were good ones. Tell the queen I said hello."

Tyr shook his head and leaned back against the table, crossing his arms. "I've changed my mind. Ranulf de Gunnar, the man who wanted no woman, suddenly has two. I'm staying."

"Not if I send you away."

Tyr smiled and waved his hand toward the window and the mountains beyond. "You can't. Unfortunately you need me. You've got activity on the hill. That's what I was originally coming to see you about."

Ranulf pushed the day room door closed. "Tell me."

"You're seriously outnumbered. There are at least four dozen men out there."

"What about Syndlear? Bronwyn's sisters are up there."

Tyr nodded but said with assurance, "For right now they are safe, but I had Tory send a couple more men up there just in case. I would have asked you, but I wasn't allowed to agitate . . ."

Ranulf cut him off with a warning look. "Mercenaries

or trained soldiers?" he questioned, diverting Tyr back to his earlier comment.

"Definitely mercenaries. Most of them look young and barely trained. Only a few could provide any type of challenge. The dozen men you have with you should be more than enough to handle any trouble."

Ranulf stared at the unlit hearth, thinking. "I need to get out there."

"Wait. Once Tory ensures Syndlear and the women are protected, he's going to do some scouting. I expect him back sometime late this afternoon or evening with a better report on just who and why men are on your land."

Ranulf let go a grunt and nodded in agreement. "What else did you learn?"

"Not much. The castle is fairly structurally sound. With the exception of a couple of spots on some roofs, the rest of the place was in overall good condition. Even that tower is stable. The stone walls are safe enough, it's just that they used rotted beams to secure the floors. Other than that, you are a lucky lord."

"Lucky?" Ranulf grunted. "How so?"

"Once I knew that you were fine and only playing invalid, I decided to play lord. Most of your tenants are friendly enough and all seem earnest, but the numbers are small here and not enough to support a place the size of Hunswick. Some actually voiced anticipation for the families and the rest of your men due in the spring. These people are warm, happy, and welcoming," Tyr said, pointing down at the courtyard below. "Hence, you are one lucky lord. I just hope you appreciate it."

Ranulf moved to stand by Tyr and looked at the people lingering around in the bailey. A second later Bronwyn exited one of the buildings and headed across the yard toward the Great Hall. All along the way people stopped her and asked questions. "They shouldn't be talking to her," he whispered under his breath, but Tyr heard him.

"I'll talk to the steward and have the questions come to you. You are the lord now, and your people should respect you as such."

Ranulf nodded, but it wasn't because he agreed with Tyr. Bronwyn looked tired. Didn't people see they were asking too much of her? She had been carrying the weight of this place too long.

The time for playing sick was over.

Bronwyn slipped into her room after being accosted by dozens of villagers and servants asking about their new lord, preparations for Twelfthtide, the evening meal, tallow for the candles, and a multitude of other topics. She had considered sending them directly to Ranulf, but she thought it might be better to give him another day to heal before the entire village pounced upon him. Besides, she doubted very few of their questions were ones he was accustomed to answering. So she gave instructions regarding the evening meal, explained where to start building the additional bonfires and just what crates and carts should be moved to make room. If Ranulf became angry at her imposition, he would not have to worry about her doing it again. She would soon be gone and all the decisions would be his.

Three days. That was all she had left of her current life.

Closing the door to her bedchambers, Bronwyn

spied the bath she had asked for nearly an hour ago situated by the hearth. She immediately began untying and yanking off her clothes. She knelt by the overly large wooden tub and ran her fingers through the water, avoiding the sharp piece of exposed metal binding the slats together. The water was no longer hot, but still warm and inviting.

Sinking into the soothing liquid, she felt her body relax. Her mind drifted to Ranulf and what he was doing . . . if he was thinking about her. She squeezed her eyes and slipped beneath the surface, chiding herself for being so consumed with someone she didn't know and never would. She popped back up and took a deep breath, slicking her hair back off her head. The dip didn't work. He was still on her mind, just as he had been since the moment she had left his side.

It was that kiss . . . she had been kissed before, but not like that. Not anything remotely like that.

She stretched her arm and grabbed the cleanser for her hair, verifying the rose water was nearby. The cook let Constance create the gritty substance every other Tuesday, mixing a wild concoction of grains, vines, and barley. The smell, while not horrible, was unique and far from feminine. However, it did help soften her wild curls and wasn't bad if followed by rose water.

Bronwyn poured some of the cleanser in her hand and began to scrub her scalp. Just the simple action reminded her of Ranulf's fingers and how they delved in to hold her close. Bronwyn moaned and grabbed the scented basin of water to pour it over her head. Why would a man she barely knew affect her so?

The problem was, she did know him. Not in any way she could make someone understand, for she suspected few took the time to see beyond the hardened exterior—but she had.

Ranulf aggravated her, but it had been some time since someone had challenged her reasons and decisions on anything. He had also comforted and teased her as if they had known each other all their lives. And though peace and tranquility were far from what she felt when around him, he made her feel safe and comfortable, as if no one could hurt her. That he wouldn't allow it. She didn't want to give it up, but she had to. Safe was a dangerous thing to feel for it was an illusion. Ranulf couldn't protect her from Luc. Not from a king's decree.

A distinctive knock interrupted her thoughts and Bronwyn issued a quick prayer of thanks before telling Constance it was fine to enter. If anyone could shift her focus to other things, the curmudgeon of a nursemaid could.

The familiar short, rotund figure wobbled in with a determined stride carrying in some clean laundry. "Seems your disappearance this afternoon upset our new lord."

Bronwyn lifted up her arms and crossed them on the edge of the tub. "My disappearance?"

"Your walkabout. I told him that you took one alone every afternoon somewheres around the lake, but that didn't appease him at all. I've seen many a man angry in my life, but I can wait a spell before seeing it again from that one."

"He didn't hurt anyone, did he?"

"Hurt? The man didn't yell, but that kind doesn't have to in order to get his point across," Constance said with a hint of warning as she started to spread the garments across Bronwyn's bed. "I think it was our *lack* of concern that made him most upset. He was baffled that no one was with you or knew your exact whereabouts. Seems you made an impression on the new lord. Are you sure that's wise?"

Bronwyn remained mum. Constance was too observant of human nature and she was already sniffing out the possibility that more had occurred than just nursing between her and Ranulf. Unfortunately, more had.

"Then again, maybe it's the new lord who's been making the impressions," Constance prodded.

Bronwyn was immediately suspicious. She had never known Constance to be indirect when she had something to say. "Not really. He was unconscious nearly the whole time."

"What about when you and he ate by the hearth? I was the one who picked up the tray," Constance revealed, hinting of her level knowledge.

Probably volunteered just to snoop, Bronwyn thought to herself as she let go a sigh. Out of everyone, Constance knew her longest and best in the world and therefore felt justified as a self-appointed guardian. There was no way she was going to just take a hint and let it drop. Sighing, Bronwyn dipped her shoulders down into the now lukewarm water one last time. "If you must know, he is unbelievably aggravating. He refused to eat in bed and even made me help him dress."

There, that should keep Constance quiet.

"I guess if you take a man's shirt off, you can help him put it back on," Constance countered with a shrug.

"Did I forget to mention stubborn, aloof, and unsocial?" *And loyal, kind, and generous*, Bronwyn added to herself.

"You like him."

"You're mad."

"I'm not the only one who thinks so. There was a lot of talk in the kitchens."

Bronwyn stared at her toes pressing the cloth padding on the other end of the tub. She was losing the argument. "Go back to your cohorts and stop trying to see things that are not there. Trust me. The new lord doesn't like secrets, and in case you and everyone else forgot, he thinks I'm Lily."

"I didn't and we've been keeping your secret. And in case *you* forgot, deceit is not something that you're very good at," Constance huffed. Gathering Bronwyn's soiled gown to take down to the laundress, she pointed at the garments she laid out on the bed. "That's all there is for you to wear. The rest of your things went to Syndlear."

"Thank you, Constance. Tell Ackart I said hello," Bronwyn managed to get out just before the door closed.

She spied the door as she compelled her body to get up out of the water. Constance was a servant, but the woman considered her and her sisters as daughters, and if she felt her opinion had not been heard, she was not above barging back in and speaking her peace.

Bronwyn grabbed a nearby cloth and began to dab her body dry. Constance was right to worry. Her attraction to Ranulf had been instant. Even angry, pacing back and forth on top of the tower, his well-muscled body had moved with an easy grace, both effortless and assured. Then when he looked down, her heart had lurched. There was a lean dark presence to him that could be felt even at a distance. And yet, when the wind ruffled the short waves of his dark hair, it wasn't authority and command she saw, but a man who knew what it was like to stand on the precipice of hell and survive. He was a kindred spirit.

Even when they argued, she had felt it. He was someone with whom she could be herself. But she hadn't been prepared for the overwhelming need to physically touch and be touched by him. That she couldn't explain. Never had a man affected her sensibilities, but to deny Ranulf could was naïve.

He entranced her. Hell, he simply had to look at her and she was captivated. And every encounter, every argument, every single thing that had happened between them seemed only to make her long for him more. She had only one choice. Lock herself away. She would stay in her room until dawn and then ride to Syndlear. In three days, Ranulf de Gunnar would be a problem no more.

Jerking the large cloth around her, Bronwyn shoved the end just over her left breast to keep it from falling. Smells were coming from the kitchens and she was hungry. If she was going to sneak down and get some food and drink before the crowd arrived, she would have to hurry.

Reaching over the tub to get her brush beside the empty basin of rose water, Bronwyn felt the sharp pain of exposed metal tearing flesh. Yanking her arm back, she examined the wound located on the soft inner flesh of her left upper forearm. To treat it meant calling for help and then people—more specifically her self-appointed overseer—would hover around her for the next few days. And the closer it got to Christmas, the less she needed to be watched.

To keep blood from dripping everywhere, she pressed her arm against the cloth wrapped around her body and looked for something to bandage the wound. Spying her mending bag sitting by the bed, she pulled out a long strip of fabric and bound the cut as best she could alone. It wasn't great, but at least blood was no longer running down her arm.

She moved to get dressed and a wave of momentary apprehension swept through her as she realized what clothes Constance had laid out. The vibrant jeweled gown was made from a rich deep blue silk. Bolts of blue, green, and silver material had been sent by her father several months ago, soon after he arrived in the Byzantine-influenced Normandy. The pearl trim along the dark hem and sleeves was far from simple, but it didn't qualify as ornate either. Coupled with a soft, somewhat sheer off-white chainse underneath, the ensemble was incredibly beautiful. And it was not hers.

Bronwyn felt trapped. She needed *her* clothes. She preferred them. Quiet unexciting colors enabled her to blend into the background. Lillabet liked to stand out and catch every man's eye. Not her.

Bronwyn considered calling for Constance and demanding another gown, but immediately dismissed the idea. The meddlesome woman would see her arm and demand explanations. Then it occurred to Bronwyn that since she didn't intend on seeing anyone, it really mattered very little as to what she put on.

Bronwyn fingered the elaborate, gathered sleeve of the cream-colored chainse and then slipped it over her head. Next, she donned the bliaut and secured the loose gold belt over her hips. With the gown's low neckline and with the diaphanous nature of the chainse, Bronwyn felt a flash of wantonness surge through her and she wondered just what Ranulf would think or do if he saw her.

Vanquishing the thought, she grabbed her brush and sat down by the fire, repeating long hard strokes as her hair dried. She wouldn't describe her wayward locks as curly, but the tight waves could create a wild look if she didn't tame them through regular brushing.

A whiff of fresh-baked bread entered the room and Bronwyn's stomach growled in response. Food for the evening's meal was being brought into the Great Hall.

Bronwyn fingered her now barely damp locks and decided she didn't have time to finish drying and styling them before everyone would arrive. Besides her arm hurt and braiding the heavy locks would only further aggravate the wound.

Bronwyn quickly yanked on her slippers and snuck down the back staircase leading into the Great Hall. Slowly, she nudged open the door and peeked inside.

Hunswick's Great Hall would never be considered large, but Bronwyn couldn't imagine one that was lovelier. To her immediate left were weapons attached in decorative patterns to the wall. Across from her at the other narrow end of the rectangular-shaped room were the buttery and a covered passage that connected the Hall directly to the kitchens. Along the long wall to her right were six arched-shaped stained glass windows and placed majestically in the middle of them were the main doors, carved by one of Hunswick's own villagers. The old man had been unable to walk, but his ability with wood had been a rare gift.

Opposite the windows was an enormous hearth circled with six padded chairs that matched the two in the solar. She and her sisters used to sit in those chairs and talk for hours with her father and their friend, Lord Anscombe. For the past few months, the three on the right had remained empty, but despite their vacancy, everyone understood they were not to be removed.

Bronwyn glanced around. Usually only a few tables were set up in the Hall, but several more had been added using temporary trestles, no doubt to support the new lord and his men. The sky was not yet dark, but all the rushlights were lit, both those on wall brackets and those impaled on iron candelabras. But with the exception of a couple of servants going back and forth between the buttery and the kitchens to bring in food before everyone arrived, the Hall was empty.

Bronwyn slipped into the room and headed toward the first table, hoping the fare would not be as sparse as it had been last night. Regardless, she intended to take what she could and return immediately to her room.

She was just passing the hearth chairs when a hand snuck out and grasped her right arm. The grip was strong, firm, and while not painful, there was no give in the clasp. She knew without looking who it was, the one person she had both longed for and not wanted to see.

Was fate telling her something? Or was it just cruel? She suspected the latter.

Ranulf had been slumped down in one of the hearth chairs, studying the flicker of the flames, when he heard the light squeak of a door opening. He had assumed it was Tyr who had earlier contrived a reason to leave the Hall due to Ranulf's foul mood. Shifting just enough to verify his friend's return, Ranulf instead had glimpsed the very person behind his agitation—Bronwyn.

His mood had been rotten since she had left him that morning, her departing comments haunting him. *I've been kissed before and will be again. My reasons for returning your embrace are far more interesting than that of just curiosity.* The comfounding declaration had gripped his thoughts, just as she had intended. Still he could not stop wondering, just what could those reasons be?

He had assumed Bronwyn hoped he would seek her out and ask just that, but when he finally had ventured out of his solar, he had learned she was gone! And no one knew where or when she would return. The whole castle was oblivious to her recent attack and therefore had no reason to interfere with her daily jaunts. And Bronwyn, he was learning, was extraordinarily stubborn, and was no doubt walking alone just to prove to herself that she could, despite the potential danger. He knew, because it would be something he would do.

Ranulf had been about to mount Pertinax and go find Bronwyn when he had been told of her return. So he had ventured into the Hall and waited for her to seek him out. And while he waited, he dealt with people, each who had mundane questions, most of which he could not answer. But not one villager had shied away from him. No one had looked at him strangely or even seemed to care in the slightest about his eye or his scars. Just like Bronwyn.

Though he would never admit it to anyone, he missed her.

His whole life, even before his accident, he had coveted his privacy. But for reasons he could not fathom, the entire day had felt incredibly lonely without her around. So when he saw Bronwyn step slowly into the Hall and glance around, looking beautiful, almost unearthly, so many emotions hit him at one time that he had sat frozen, staring, unable to move or speak.

She had bathed and was wearing a deep blue gown that obviously did not belong to her. Instead of loosely draping over her frame as did her other bliaut, this one hugged every curve of her body, hinting at the treasures beneath. It had been made for someone of her height, but of a slighter build. No doubt one of her sisters. Yet it was not the dress, but her hair, that truly captivated him. Falling off her shoulders in waves of dark gold, it framed her oval face and, if possible, made her storm-colored eyes seem even larger and more beautiful.

Ranulf sat riveted, unable to look anywhere else as a wave of possession hit him so hard that it almost caused him to jump up and order her back to her room, jealous that others might see and take pleasure in her beauty. He had never been one to share and he wasn't about to share Bronwyn. Ever. She was his. She had been his since the moment she had

kissed him, maybe since the moment she had first
looked at him and did not look away.

Having sight with only his right eye created a
large expanse of nothing to his left. Yet everything
in his life—from fighting to just pouring a mug of
ale—required him to respond as if he still could see
with the precision of two eyes. It had been difficult
to learn, but over the years, his other senses filled in
many of the gaps. One of them was knowing exactly
where something—or someone—was when they were
near. Reaching out for Bronwyn's arm had been instinctive. So was his reaction.

Back and forth his thumb caressed the soft skin.
It was like silk. He found himself struggling not to
pull her down onto his lap and discover if her whole
body could be just as delicate and intoxicating as
that of her wrist.

He glanced up and saw apprehension reflecting
back in her deep blue depths. It had been a long
time since he had kissed a woman—really kissed
her—as he had that morning. Maybe he was delud-
ing himself. At the time he had believed Bronwyn to
be affected by his touch, but in truth, he had no
basis to believe in his sexual prowess. Only her response. And she *had* responded in his arms. Hell,
she had initiated the embrace, something he still
didn't understand.

Her stormy eyes pierced his with unspoken
questions, so he asked one of his own. "Why?"

Bronwyn swallowed. His thumb was drawing small
circles on her wrist, making it very difficult to think,
let alone speak. The hypnotic caress was tender,
sensual . . . almost possessive. Forcing herself to

speak, Bronwyn returned the question. "Why what, my lord?"

She watched him look away and stare absent-mindedly at the fire, but he refused to let go of her arm. She waited, enjoying the small pleasure of his touch, but after a moment, asked again. "Why what, my lord?"

Ranulf didn't move, but in a low voice answered, "Pick one. Why did you return to Hunswick when you thought I was in danger? Why are you still here? Why did you stay with me last night? Why are you not frightened of my appearance when so many are?" Then his head swiveled around so his gaze could lock with hers. "But mostly I want to know why you kissed me."

Bronwyn's heart stumbled. They were the same questions she had been asking herself all afternoon and the answers she had come up with were not ones she intended to disclose to anyone.

Pride gripped her. If he had questions, so did she.

She slid her wrist out of his grasp, but refused to move away from his side as if she were running away. "So many questions, my lord. Their number rivals my own."

Ranulf blinked. Had he actually posed every one of his thoughts aloud? Damn. Confidence was not something he typically lacked, but he needed to know it wasn't pity that drove her to kiss him.

It hadn't felt like pity. He had experienced charity kisses before and he would rather be gutted with a blade than receive sympathetic affection. So much so, that a few years ago, he had stopped all carnal relations, refusing to suffer another compassionate word or touch. It wasn't worth it.

"Then answer just the last one. Why did you kiss me?" he asked in a low voice while leaning forward to study her reaction.

Her tongue nervously whipped across her bottom lip and hot memories of what it had been like to taste and explore its softness rippled through him, urging him to pull her into his arms and enjoy her lips once again. Only willpower and a lifetime of hiding his feelings kept him in control.

Unaware of how close she was to being ravaged, Bronwyn gathered her courage and decided to make Ranulf just as uncomfortable as she. Casting him a crooked smile, she said impishly, "No. I distinctly remember it was *you* who kissed *me*."

She sauntered over to his other side, keeping her back toward him, and waited for his clever retort. When she received none, she glanced back and realized her folly. She was on his left side. Ranulf had shifted to what looked to be an uncomfortable angle, but he would have to swing his legs practically over the armchair in order to see her. It was pride that was keeping him silent, not acquiescence. Victory would not be as sweet if not earned on equal terms.

Meandering back toward the chair to his right, she sank down, curling her feet up underneath her. Immediately, Ranulf shifted to a more comfortable position, wincing just slightly when he used his left arm to pull his leg up to rest his ankle on his knee.

Bronwyn bobbed her chin. "Maybe you should go back to bed and rest."

Ranulf grunted, hating that he appeared weak in front of her. A minute ago, she'd gone out of his vision, reminding him that he was only half a man.

"I *am* resting," he growled. "If I weren't, I would be out there—working."

"Working at what, my lord?" Bronwyn questioned, crossing her arms. "You may have lived in or near a great many grand homes and estates, but I doubt if you've ever been in charge of maintaining them."

"Maybe, but it didn't stop me from being pulled into at least a dozen discussions about when these people should hunt for quail, numbers of bonfires to be erected, menus for God knows how many feasts—"

"Twelve," Bronwyn interrupted with a playful grin. "One for each day of Twelfthtide. You know. That merry part of the year that follows Advent or did your studies only focus on the wearisome holiday customs?"

Ranulf ignored her tease, but returned her smirk with one of his own. He stretched out his legs in front of him, feeling strangely better than he had a minute ago. "Twelve feasts? More like fifty. I think the people here like to do nothing but celebrate."

"Happy people do. Have you never been content enough to just enjoy the season?"

Fact was, this odd little conversation was filling him with a deeper sense of peace than he could remember having since he was a child. Usually he ignored the proceedings involved with Twelfthtide, but not this year. "And then there was the question about you."

"*Me?*" Bronwyn squeaked in surprise.

"Aye, you seem to have my men in a stir about who should be assigned to Syndlear."

The mention of Syndlear startled Bronwyn. "Oh," she whispered. For a brief moment, she had felt like part of a couple that was at complete ease with the other, able to tease and banter without concern. But she *wasn't* part of a couple, and pretending she was or even that she could be was becoming very dangerous to her emotional state. It was much safer if Ranulf didn't know how much he affected her.

"I myself like . . ." She paused for a second straining to remember the young soldier's name that was at the gate. "Tory. He's . . . sweet. He could return to Syndlear with me tomorrow since you are on the mend."

Ranulf's body instantly stiffened. He had not intended for his comment to be interpreted in such a way. Just the opposite. Instead of being flattered, she produced a name and offered to leave. Well, *she* wasn't going to leave in the morning, but Tory sure as hell was.

"What if my wound gets worse?" Ranulf posed gruffly.

"It is fine."

"It may not be. Remember. I don't get fevers. I'm not like other men."

You sure aren't, Bronwyn murmured to herself. "All you need is rest," she stammered. "I'll . . . I'll have Constance look at it tomorrow."

Ranulf arched a brow. Bronwyn was nervous, proving he was not the only one sensing the sexual tension growing between them. Ranulf could not recall feeling this alive in his entire life. He was teetering on the dangerous edge between joy and agony, and more than anything, he needed another kiss. "Fine, angel. I'll go rest, but you are coming with me to check my wound."

Struggling to maintain the upper hand, Bronwyn stood up. "If you insist, then I will look at it now—

and here." She waved her finger for him to uncross his legs as she moved closer. "Lean back."

Ranulf watched her small fingers as they signaled for him to push aside the opening of his shirt. Imagining how they would feel against his naked flesh, he rose, undid his belt, and pulled the tunic over his head before tossing both items onto a nearby empty chair. He knew he was playing with fire, but he couldn't help it.

Bronwyn's eyes grew large. It was as if Ranulf knew her emotional state and was daring her to maintain any self-control.

She glanced around the room. A couple of servants were standing near the kitchen passageway, deep in discussion—probably about her and Ranulf. Rumors would soon be spread everywhere. Any other time or circumstance that knowledge alone would have been enough to make her walk away, but in three days she would be gone. Rumors be damned.

Leaning over the chair, Bronwyn pulled back the shirt opening. She reminded herself that she had seen him in less, but her heart had not been in jeopardy then. Trying her best to ignore his masculinity and keep as much distance as possible between them, she loosened the bandage so that she could see underneath without removing it altogether. Completely closed, the wound was healing even faster than she had predicted.

"You're fine," she said as she pulled back. "The powder stings horrendously, but it works. If you promise to minimize your activity over the next couple of days and not exert yourself, you can probably remove the bandage."

"Then remove it now," Ranulf ordered, his tone soft but serious.

Bronwyn ground her jaw, suspecting that his reasons for keeping her near were duplicitous. Her mind screamed to leave right now and head for Syndlear first thing in the morning. It was the sensible thing to do and she had always been sensible. Truth was, until Ranulf, nothing and no one had ever tempted her *not* to be. Still, he didn't need to know that.

Walking over to the hearth chair next to them, she pushed his discarded tunic aside, picked up his belt, and found the attached misericorde. The extremely sharp narrow dagger had been created to strike through the gaps between armor plates and therefore was perfect for what she intended. Pulling it out of its sheath, she spun the long, thin blade expertly in her hand, catching it in a dead stop. "Since I am removing the bandage, I might as well remove the stitches too," she purred mischievously.

Ranulf stared incredulously at the feminine vision before him casually wielding his knife in her palm. Either she was very skilled with the slender blade or she wanted to make him think that she was. Coupled with the devious twinkle in her eye, it didn't matter which was the truth. This was a bad idea. "Are you sure you know what you are doing with that thing?"

Bronwyn glanced at the dagger and then back at him, raising her eyebrows in an obvious mocked attempt at innocence. "Well, I could use *my* knife, but it is much bigger. I really think yours is better for the task."

Ranulf, unconvinced, tried to rise, but she pushed him back down, this time situating herself between his legs, a position both ominous and alluring. Then one stitch at a time, she manipulated the tip of the cutting edge, slicing the string and pulling it free.

Ranulf could ignore the painful tugging sensation, but every time one of her breasts accidentally brushed against him, he had to hold his breath and grip the arms of the chair. Suspecting she might believe him weak and possessing a low tolerance for pain, Ranulf searched for something to distract him from what she was doing. Only one topic came to mind. Their kiss.

"About this morning. Your memory is faulty."

Concentrating, Bronwyn was just about to sever the final stitch. "How so?" she murmured.

"I believe *you* kissed *me.*"

His nearness coupled with the unexpected reminder of their embrace caused her hand to quiver just as she sliced the last stitch, giving him a small scrape.

"Ow! You did that on purpose!"

Bronwyn jumped back. She was no longer nestled between his legs, but neither was she out of his reach. "I did no such thing. Besides, it is a small scratch, so stop disgracing yourself by acting so cowardly," she scolded, waving the sharp blade around as if it was another appendage.

"*Cowardly?*" Ranulf bellowed as he jerked the knife out of her hand. "You, angel, should be thanking me for being damn near to a *saint*! You have to be one of the most difficult women I have ever met."

Bronwyn's chin popped up angrily, her deep blue eyes flashing. "I'm not difficult. *You're* the one yelling." She turned, grabbed his tunic, and threw it at him. "I'm done. You can get dressed now."

Ranulf stifled an oath and tugged the black-and-gold garment over his head in frustration, refusing to wince as he twisted his injured shoulder to slip his arm through the opening. Nothing about the last few minutes had gone as planned. She was supposed to succumb to her physical need for him, not drive him mad to the point of losing control. He had known her for less than three days, and yet she was making him think and act in ways that were just not him.

"What did you say?" Bronwyn asked.

Ranulf scowled, hating to be caught mumbling. Something else he never did. "I said that I don't yell! I don't shout! Ever!"

"I find that hard to believe, my lord, for I have heard you do quite a lot of both since your arrival," Bronwyn said smugly, ignoring her inner voice to leave immediately. No longer could she pretend Ranulf was in need of assistance. He was virile, strong, and awakening an irresistible sense of awareness within her.

Ranulf opened his mouth to argue, when he realized she had done it again. She had changed the subject, putting him on the defensive. Plopping back down onto the chair he had been occupying, he casually crossed his ankle so that it rested on his knee. "The kiss, angel. You still haven't answered my question."

The gleam in his eye revealed that his confidence had returned and Bronwyn felt like stomping her foot. The man would not win this contest of wills, for that was exactly what it was. Her versus him. And she refused to be the one to cave in. So if he wanted to talk about their kiss, then they would. "But I did answer it, my lord. *You kissed me.*"

A disturbing knot grew inside him, wondering if she truly was offended, but then he spied the sparkle of raillery in her eyes. "Don't feel embarrassed, angel. I enjoyed it. Immensely," he added as he reached over to grab his mug of mead.

Mustering up the last bit of her self-respect, Bronwyn narrowed her gaze and smiled icily. "I may have been one of many women who felt a fleeting desire to kiss you, but you will never have to worry about me being one of them again." She rose and moved to do what she should have done much earlier—leave.

Many women? Try none, Ranulf thought. The honesty in the spark between them was rarely experienced by anyone and, for him, even rarer. So when she stepped around the chair to leave, he instinctively reached out and grabbed her by the waist, pulling her down onto his lap. Catching her chin between his thumb and forefinger, he turned her head so that he could read her eyes. And there, reflecting in the darkening cobalt depths, was the truth. She wanted him and her feelings were just as strange and startling to her as his were to him.

"I don't believe you, angel. I think you wanted to kiss me and desire to do so again, almost as much I want to taste you." Then his mouth came down on hers before she could even think of resisting.

Need and longing seeped through the featherlight kiss, penetrating every fiber of her body. Bronwyn could feel the urgency behind it, but also the tightly reined control as his lips tenderly, coaxingly persuaded her mouth to open. She succumbed to his will and that of her own and kissed him back hungrily, uncaring that she was admitting that he was right. She did want to kiss him and touch him in ways her mind had only fantasized about doing with a man. Her hands wound their way from his chest around his neck, pulling him closer to her. The world disappeared and all that remained was Ranulf and what he was making her feel. She was at last a woman, whole and desirable.

A quiver rippled through her body and Ranulf felt his self-control slip as he slanted his mouth over hers again and again, his tongue stroking, caressing every corner of her mouth. Her honest desire for him was ripping away all his carefully constructed defenses, creating an urge to satisfy swelling primal needs with more than just a kiss.

Other women had toyed with him enough to get him physically aroused, but this was much more. Bronwyn wasn't trying to excite him. It was the other way around, and he was succeeding. In Bronwyn's arms, he was a man, whole and strong and desirable. With her, he found real passion and its effect was intoxicating. Every nerve ending was alive with the sincerity of her response and he wanted more.

Immersing his left hand in her soft hair, his right traced the contours of her neck as his mouth continued to make slow love to her with his tongue. She was perfection. The softness of her skin, her smell, how she tasted, responded to his every caress. And the more he touched, his need to know every inch of her and feel her body next to his only grew.

Bronwyn heard a sound and realized it was coming from her. His lips had hypnotized her and the light touch of his fingertips was transporting her into a realm where all realities and concerns drifted away. She had entered into a place where torture and delight were indistinguishable, where her whole being strained toward the fulfillment of a desire she didn't understand. "More . . ." she heard herself beg just before his mouth again sought hers in another mind-numbing kiss.

Ranulf knew he was dangerously close to losing control, but her rapacious plea drove him to continue. Just one more touch, one more discovery, and then he would stop. Ever so slowly, his fingers trailed down the veins of her neck and then along the collar of her chemise, tracing their way to the upper part of her breast. Detecting the buds peaking up under her attire, his thumbs flicked lightly over the firm nipples.

When he felt her body respond to his touch, he circled the small mounds round and round, until she was quivering under the assault. Nothing could have been more arousing. His body demanded fulfillment, leaving him a choice: He could either stop, or pick her up and haul her upstairs.

As his lips released hers, Bronwyn closed her eyes and drew in a slow deep breath, marveling at the speed her heart was thumping. She could deny it, but she had wanted this to happen. Their first kiss had introduced her to the sensations of passion and desire, and she had longed to know more. Even now, she could still feel his hands as they cupped her breasts, kneading them until she was aching and hot for something she could not define. She would have yielded to his guidance, resigned her values, and permitted him every advantage under his touch. And all because she needed him for some inexplicable reason. Ranulf was who she had been looking for and never been able to find.

"Why?" she sighed in a raspy whisper, needing to hear that he felt something akin to her own shaken emotions. "Why did you kiss me?"

Ranulf froze. He didn't know how to respond. He couldn't say, "Because with you I am whole. With you I know who I am. With you, I become a man in every sense of the word. Because when I am with you, I am not afraid." Such honesty would scare even the strongest of wills and passions. So he opted for something far diminished from the full truth. "Because you are the most beautiful woman I have ever seen," he replied.

Bronwyn felt like she had been punched in the stomach.

Beauty. That was what drove him. And if that was what created Ranulf's desire, whatever passion that sparked between them would be instantly extinguished the moment he met the real Lillabet.

Bronwyn cast him a slight smile that did not reach her eyes and slipped off his lap. Ranulf watched as she retreated to the hearth, pretending to warm her hands by the fire. He knew instantly he had said the wrong thing.

It had been years since he had been with a woman and he couldn't remember ever truly trying to woo one. He had never wanted to before. Less than a minute ago, he had been given both opportunity and motive to convince her that his desire for her was real, and deep, and not just lust being satisfied. And he had failed miserably.

Ranulf rose out of his chair and glanced behind him. The room was empty but three women were whispering in the passageway, leading to the kitchens. All refused to look at him, trying to hide their expressions behind their hands. The back of the large hearth chair had hidden him and Bronwyn, but even a small child could have figured out what they were doing. He probably should be grateful as they most likely kept anyone else from entering the room, but right now he wanted complete privacy, not just a limited audience.

Ranulf signaled for them to leave and accompanied the gesture with a look that made it clear that no one else was to enter the Hall until he said so. Then he moved in behind Bronwyn and pushed her hair aside, giving him access to her neck. He bent his head and lightly kissed her nape. She stiffened. "Don't, angel," he whispered against her skin. "Don't pull away from me. Please. I want you and you want me, too."

Bronwyn wanted to resist, to walk away and protect her heart, but her body defied her will, succumbing to her more primal desires. What could it hurt? She knew the truth. This would be the last time. And it would have to survive a lifetime.

His lips created a line of searing kisses down her neck as his right hand stole around her waist, reacquainting itself with her body. Slowly it moved up to cup her breast and Bronwyn felt the last of her defenses crumble. Encouraging him, she leaned back and allowed his fingers to slip underneath her neckline, sending a shock wave through her entire body. At the same time, his left hand started its own descent. Lightly massaging her shoulders then biceps, his fingers moved lower until they grazed her forearm where she had slashed it earlier, sending sharp stabbing fire through the limb.

Bronwyn let go a sudden shriek and, with a jerk, pitched herself forward. The realization of what he had been doing, what she had been allowing, washed over her. She could feel Ranulf's eyes boring into her back as she covered her face with her hands to hide her tears, humiliated. Her sudden reaction had been instinctive, an attempt to stop the agony. Even now her arm throbbed angrily, but eventually that pain would diminish and disappear. The shame she would carry for life.

She had practically invited him to touch her and would have let him do much more if it hadn't been for her arm. She knew it and he knew it. What he didn't know was why she pulled away. No doubt he believed her to be a tease, or even worse, a child afraid of what was to come. And she was afraid, but not of what was about to happen, but of what never would. For she was not Lillabet and Ranulf was not her intended.

Ranulf stood immobile, unable to move toward her or step away, until he knew her frame of mind.

It wasn't hard to guess. She had been the one to realize what was happening and stopped him before he ruined her. Although he intended to marry her, this was not the way he wanted to get Bronwyn to the altar, through tricks and ploys. He raked his fingers through his short hair and berated himself for being too eager, too impulsive. What had he been thinking?

Despite Bronwyn's suggestion that she was like the other women he had bedded, she wasn't. And he didn't want her thinking that he regarded her as such. But how does one say, "When I hold you in my arms, I lose all reason?" He could have sworn she was in the same state.

Her response had been genuine, even welcoming. Yes, he had gone too far, but she didn't have to scream. She could have just pulled back or asked him to stop. Then again, maybe she had just remembered the farce she was playing, and what they were about to do was far beyond that of sisterly intervention. They needed to talk and she needed to confess to her ruse so he could make it clear that they were to be wed anyway. Soon.

"We need to talk."

Bronwyn pulled her arms around her chest and hugged herself, keeping her back toward him. "About what?"

"About us."

"What about us?"

"Look at me," he ordered and reached out to her shoulder, gently compelling her to obey. "You are not unintelligent. We cannot be in each other's company without—"

"It was just a kiss, my lord," Bronwyn finished, glad her voice sounded steady and not what she was truly feeling.

Ranulf's gaze narrowed and he could feel his composure disintegrate. She could belittle what had happened between them but it would do no good. He may not have had her, but he had seen and touched enough to know she had never been with another man. And she never would be. "It was far more than a kiss, and before we share too many more of those, we need to be married."

Bronwyn's jaw dropped. She hadn't considered

this as a possible outcome. But she should have. She gulped. "Because of a kiss?"

Ranulf's brows shot together. She seemed really incredulous. "Yes! I mean, no. I mean because of what's bound to happen next, and do not pretend you don't understand."

Bronwyn cursed her foolish, selfish desires. Of *course* he wanted to get married. He thought her to be Lillabet. Telling him that he was not obligated to her, but her sister, was out of the question. Her only option was to get him to understand that he wouldn't be marrying anyone. That he didn't need to. "I refuse to marry you out of obligation."

"And I wouldn't want you to!"

His emphatic response was not what she had expected. Hadn't he come north with plans to marry Lily, regardless of her feelings on the matter? "You wouldn't?"

"Hell no!" Ranulf bellowed, throwing his arms up in the air in obvious frustration.

Bronwyn swallowed, wishing she could be herself but knowing she couldn't. "Well . . . good, because I would never marry a man I didn't love."

"No one's asking you to!"

"*You* are! You and the king."

"Forget that," Ranulf countered. He stepped in close and seized her forearms in a grip that didn't evoke pain, but kept her from pulling away. "None of that matters. What is happening between you and me changes everything."

Bronwyn shook her head. "Not to me. It was just a kiss," she lied.

"I don't believe you," he rasped just before he crushed her to him with a savage intensity.

Her hands curled into fists and started to push against his chest, but they soon flattened and began to knead the muscles underneath. Encouraged, Ranulf thrust his tongue into her mouth, hungrily pressing his lips against hers. She instantly succumbed, and he soon lost himself in her softness. Her breathing became erratic, and once again he could feel the wave of need and desire overcome his reason. His grip increased, squeezing her arms pinned between them.

Bronwyn cried out, "I . . . can't!" The pain shooting through the injured flesh was intense and crippling. The moment she was released, she swung around to cradle her arm where he could not see. The burning sensation refused to fade away, and she struggled not to tear.

Ranulf was behind her, and after what seemed like an eternity, he broke the deafening silence. "Do you think I am a fool? Do you think I am unfamiliar with the games you play? I found out at a very young age that fate is pitiless and women like yourself are its ally."

Bronwyn opened her mouth to explain that her cry was not against him, that she had been in pain, but her voice broke. His words were cruel, meant to hurt, and their aim had been true. Ranulf was not the man she had believed him to be.

She spun back around, letting anger mask her pain. "*You* stopped *me*. *You* kissed *me*. It was you"— she swallowed—"who touched me."

"Well, put your fears aside, woman. *You* shall not have to endure *my* touch again," he sneered, the vehemence he suddenly felt for her unmistakable.

She watched as he did a slow, deliberate pivot

and walked away from her. Taking a deep breath, Bronwyn aimed her own stride toward the back staircase when the Hall's doors sprang wide open.

A shadowed figure with a purposeful stride entered, "Who the hell ordered the servants to keep everyone out? You know better than most, Ranulf, the dangers of a hungry mob."

Tyr halted his advancement just as the doors swung back closed. Something was going on, and it wasn't good. Bronwyn was obviously trying to slip out of the room and Ranulf was bent over one of the tables, leaning on his knuckles—something he only did when he was confounded or highly annoyed.

Tyr arched a brow severely and pointed his finger, waving it so that it bounced between them. "What's between you two?"

"Nothing," Ranulf growled.

Tyr shifted his jaw and slid his tongue across his teeth as he tried to decide if or how he should rebuff Ranulf's clearly false statement. He and Bronwyn looked as if they had done something awful, but it was hard to say what or who had been the culprit. Usually Tyr avoided Ranulf when he was in one of his rare emotional moods, but today was different. Today, his friend had displayed an assortment of feelings—frustration, confusion, compassion, guilt—none of which Tyr could remember Ranulf exhibiting in the past year, let alone all at one time, or twice in one day. Whatever was happening between his best friend and Bronwyn, Tyr intended to personally watch it unfold.

Stepping over a bench, he sat down and pointed

to the food that had been placed out on the tables, getting cold. "Where's the meat?"

"That woman refuses to serve it during Advent," Ranulf grumbled, wagging his thumb toward Bronwyn, but not actually looking at her.

That woman! Provoked, Bronwyn marched up to Tyr and hissed, "I already told his lordship that there were plenty of geese he could eat. He and his men just needed to hunt them. With so many unexpected extra mouths to feed, it would be beneficial to all if at least some of his soldiers contributed."

Tyr's eyes darted between the two hostile figures. "Well, then why don't we go hunting tomorrow?" he offered cheerfully, knowing that a sunny disposition right now would rankle his friend.

Bronwyn flashed Tyr a radiant smile. "What a sensible suggestion. After the past few days, it would be refreshing to spend some time with a charming gentleman and give me a chance to get away from certain . . . frustrations," she said as her gaze leisurely swept over Ranulf. "I can show you the choice spots."

Tyr let go a low chuckle. No wonder the women at court never interested Ranulf. None of them had the audaciousness needed to penetrate his thick shell. Tyr returned Bronwyn's smile and picked up a handful of almonds. "That would be great. It will also give you a chance to meet more of the men."

Ranulf didn't move, but his knuckles had turned white. "The last thing the men need is a woman around who enjoys toying with their emotions."

"I do not toy, my lord, but I suspect manners and general kindness may appear that way to someone who has the *emotional capacity of a stone.*" Her voice had risen at least an octave, giving away her confusion and hurt pride.

Oblivious, Ranulf slowly shifted his gaze to hers and grated back, "If I am a stone, madam, then perhaps it is because I look like one. I'm sorry that I don't have Tyr's smile or Tory's sweet nature. Men like me do not appeal to women like yourself. I would be a half-wit to think otherwise."

Bronwyn's back straightened. Her blood pounded and tears would be flowing any minute, but she refused to cry in his presence. Of all the men, she had thought Ranulf to be different. Oh, how wrong she had been. Someday she would be glad that fate had intervened and saved her from what would have been a grave mistake.

"There are worse things in life than having a few scars, something you should have discovered long ago, my lord. And until you started using them as an excuse, I *never* thought you to be a half-wit. But I am glad that you have clarified that point, for you're right. Such a man is unappealing." Feigning confidence and joyful expectation, she swiveled toward Tyr. "I will join you tomorrow morning in the bailey in front of the stables."

Both men stared, unable to stop themselves, as she sauntered out of the Hall and through the door that led up to her chambers.

Tyr watched the rhythm of Ranulf's pulse in the bulging veins along his neck. If Bronwyn were a man, she would right now be fighting for her life. There were probably only three people in the world who could provoke Ranulf and live to see another day. Him, Ranulf's commander and friend Garik, who had stayed behind in Normandy—and now that woman.

Asking Ranulf what the hell was going on and just what had possessed him to pick a fight with a woman he was obviously attracted to would be a waste of breath. His friend was too busy trying to convince himself that he despised her. It was an absurd goal. Until Ranulf realized that it wasn't anger he was feeling, the man would remain frustrated and become more and more unbearable.

Open confrontation would only cause Ranulf to leave, remain in denial, and keep hurting himself and the lady to whom he was losing his heart. Tyr had always abided by their implied rule of friendship—not to interfere—but that was before Bronwyn. She was visibly interested in Ranulf and truly hurt by his rejection. There was no one in the world Tyr was closer to, and watching Ranulf torture himself was insane.

Leaning forward, Tyr grabbed a mug of mulled wine and swallowed a large gulp. He gestured toward the door with the cup. "I say, she is sinfully attractive when she's angry. You may not claim to have a way with the ladies, but when you want to make one mad, you are indeed an expert."

Ranulf clenched his teeth and said nothing, but sent Tyr a flash of warning.

Tyr dismissed the look and pressed on, opting for a flank attack. "You know that dress she was wearing? She should wear that color more often, complements that odd color of blue in her eyes."

Ranulf sank onto the bench across the table from Tyr and raked his hands through his hair. "Take my advice and avoid looking too long at them. They can confound a man. Make him believe in lies."

"You might be right," Tyr agreed and moved to pour himself some more wine. "But when a man can't think straight, is it she who is telling the lies or is it he who is telling them to himself?"

"If you are trying to make a point, don't."

"No, no point," Tyr sighed and swirled his mug. "Just that she was looking pretty tonight. Did you not think so?"

"No."

"Well, I did. I especially liked the hair. Normally I do not like stuff being all free like that, gets in the way. I usually prefer a woman's hair to be pulled back and tidy, but hers . . . well, I just might change my mind."

Nothing from Ranulf. Not even a twitch. Damn. The man was stubborn.

Tyr swallowed the mug's contents for fortification. If he got out of this with his skin still intact, he would be lucky. He had maybe one more shot before Ranulf got up to leave, so it had to hit—and hard.

Tyr rocked the bench back and hummed, "Looked like silk, wonder if it feels like silk. I once had a woman with hair—"

"Damn you," Ranulf uttered through his teeth. "Be quiet or get out."

"What do you care? You may not like her, but I do. And not just in the face. I'm actually looking forward to tomorrow and spending time with the lady. And after her jumping onto the idea of coming hunting, I think she feels the same."

"She does not like you."

"I beg to disagree. She thinks I am charming. Said

so herself. But then it wasn't I who said she was trying to seduce every man around her."

Ranulf pounded his fists on the table, startling the servants who had recommenced prepping the trestles with food. But he didn't deny the accusation.

"My God! You really like her, don't you? I knew you were attracted to the woman, but you *really* like her. I should have known. From the moment you returned to camp that night, grumbling about how the women in this area were too damn pretty, I knew a female had finally burrowed underneath that hardened exterior. I just never dreamed you would also get to *her*."

"I hope I'm around when a woman finally lays claim to your sanity. With your impetuous personality, your actions will be far more out of character than mine."

Tyr clapped his mug on the table and threw his hands up in the air. "Not me. I swore an oath against women and commitments, and it is an oath I intend to keep. But you, my friend, are not me and do not have my reasons for rejecting happiness. Go to her, a woman like that would forgive a man, she might even find life in a stone. So much so, that she may even consider marrying him. Of course, he might have to grovel a little."

Ranulf pushed himself up, wishing Tyr was correct. Unfortunately, Bronwyn wasn't about to marry a man like him, not before and certainly not now. "I'm going to take a walk."

Bronwyn stepped into her room, leaned against the door, and squeezed her eyes closed. Why was

God taunting her? Never had her emotions been so shaken and taken to extremes in such a short period of time.

Ranulf infuriated her, but when she was in his arms, she felt like a woman, beautiful and alluring, something she hadn't thought possible. Something she had never truly felt within herself. And now that she had, she wanted to experience it again and again. But she had to stop wishing for a miracle.

Her sisters needed to be protected and so did Ranulf. He didn't know about Luc and his hired mercenaries. She could tell Ranulf about the baron and his ruthlessness, but that would only put him in a futile position. Either Ranulf would feel ethically forced to hand her over, belittling himself in front of his men, or his pride would make her stay and, as a result, lose everything. One just did not flagrantly disobey a king's decree.

However, if she and her sisters disappeared from Hunswick, so would the danger. With the three of them gone, Syndlear would revert to its vassal's owner—Ranulf—and there would be nothing Luc Craven could do about it. Leaving was her only choice.

Bronwyn pushed herself off the door and unlaced the snug bliaut. Pulling it off her head, she draped it over the chair and fingered the soft rich blue material. What a waste beautiful clothes were on her.

She walked over to the hearth and stoked the fire. Once the room warmed enough, she removed the rest of her undergarments, casting them alongside the jewel-colored gown. Tomorrow, during the hunt, she would slip away and head to Syndlear. From there, she and her sisters would journey north.

With a sigh, she pulled the coverlet back and

slipped into the bed, enjoying the feeling of the soft, worn linen sheets against her naked skin. She had only two more days of this personal, private luxury.

Ranulf sank farther down into the same chair he had been in when he'd nearly lost control with Bronwyn. The hour was late and the Hall was nearly empty. Only a few servants remained, cleaning up and taking down trestles from the evening meal. He had eaten the last bit of fish and bread, which were both good, but without butter, cheese, or meat, it felt more like a snack. And after two days of the sparse fare, more and more of his men were electing to sleep outside the castle walls—and fending for themselves when it came to dinner. The meat they cooked wouldn't be tasty, but it would be far more filling.

He almost wished he could be one of them. This afternoon had been a disaster. In the span of his and Bronwyn's relatively short interaction, he had felt hopeful, elated, guilty, incredibly jealous, envious, and deeply angry.

And worse, she knew why.

Her accusation had been uncomfortably accurate.

It had been a long time since he had mulled about his injury or what it had cost him. For years, his scars had impeded necessary relationships and negated the idea of finding voluntary ones, such as companionship. Passion, he quickly discovered, had to be reciprocated for it to be called such; otherwise it was just an animalistic lust to be satiated and forgotten. As he grew older, he learned that pleasure and desire were far from common and few couples truly shared either. That helped.

Then he had met Bronwyn, a wisp of an angel who had demonstrated more honest passion than he had received from anyone, let alone a female. And she had every right to hate him.

First, he had ordered her out of her home, then insulted her, and after she had saved his life, he had practically mauled her—twice—and then to make sure that it never happened again, he essentially accused her of being a harlot, and why? Because just the idea of Tyr and her spending a morning together hunting made him crazy with jealousy.

Even now she was probably berating herself for allowing the kiss and cursing him for initiating it. She certainly wouldn't ever allow herself to be put in the position to be touched by him again. She had probably thanked God a thousand times for making her come to her senses before things truly went too far. For he certainly hadn't intended to halt that last embrace. In truth, he had forgotten everything—that they were in a public hall, that servants were around, that she was innocent, even that he was the last man any woman—especially a lady—would want forced upon her. He had been consumed with desire. Desire to kiss and caress every inch of her, desire to make her come alive with passion, and to make her his in every way. And all that emotion had transformed into anger, then raging jealousy, and now remorse and regret.

He didn't know what to do with such strong feelings, and burying them as he had been doing all his life was impossible. They were too strong and had come to him too fast. As a result, he had prematurely ended any chance he might have had for happiness. And it wasn't until she left that he realized just how much he wanted to know her better and have her know him . . . and possibly like what she saw.

So he had left to think . . . and to take care of some things. He had first headed for the gatehouse to find young Tory, the man who had captured Bronwyn's attention long enough for her to determine his "sweet" nature. Tory wasn't there, but Norval was. The older soldier was married with several children, making him the perfect guard for Bronwyn. Ranulf gave him instructions to watch her—slyly—but no matter what, she was not to exit the gates of Hunswick.

He eventually found Tory at the stables. The young man had a sappy smile and facial features Ranulf knew the opposite sex found to be attractive. He was tempted to give the boy battlement duty for the winter, making him stay up nights and sleep days, but he ordered him to Syndlear instead.

Ranulf then escaped the castle and went for a walk until his shoulder began to truly ache. Upon his return, he had gone to his solar only to leave again immediately. Her fragrance was still in the air and laced his covers. Alone in his room was the last place he wanted to be. So, he had gone back to the Great Hall and had not left the hearth chair since.

"Would you like some more wine, my lord?"

Ranulf blinked and cocked his head to see who was speaking. The woman was small but she possessed the full figure a woman received after birthing multiple children. She had frizzy brown hair and freckles along her cheeks and nose that kept her looking younger than she probably was.

He shook his head and watched her take the

pitcher and his mug away. He wasn't used to having servants. His family had been far from poor, but for the past decade he had been at the disposal of Henry and in many ways a servant himself. Now that he was one of those rare men with limited power over others, he had a choice: Be like his father and abuse his station, or set expectations and reward those who met them.

The woman returned to clean the table with a damp rag and then moved to put another log on the fire. "There's no need," Ranulf said, halting her just as her fingers wrapped around the heavy piece of wood. She rose and wiped off her hands on the cloth tied around her waist. Just before she moved back out of sight, Ranulf coughed to regain her attention. "What's your name?"

Both her nut-colored brows sprang upward. "I . . . um . . . most around here call me Chrissie, my lord."

Ranulf shrugged with his chin and nodded. "Thank you, Chrissie. You and the others can retire. I will see to my needs for the rest of the night."

Chrissie stood still for a second with large questioning eyes, before scampering back into the passageway. Ranulf thought she had done as he had instructed, when he overheard two voices, one he recognized belonging to the nagging nursemaid, Constance.

"You wouldn't believe what just happened, Constance. It was just as Lady Bronwyn said, and to think I didn't believe her!"

"Why? What happened? What did the young lord say to you?" Constance half asked, half demanded.

"Well, earlier this evening, when I brought food up to her ladyship, I mentioned how much we miss his old lordship and how awful we thought it was that she was forced to stay behind and take care of the new lord when it was she who was the one feeling so poorly. Of course she told me that the young lord had *not* forced her to stay, to which I said, 'Then why is an old guard ordered to watch this Hall and your room?' She looked out the window at that very soldier and smiled! I'm telling you she smiled! She told me his name was Norvin or something and that he was a very nice man with *five* children and that he had been a farmer and wants to be one again when his family comes in the spring and that my James should go meet him and—"

"Chrissie, your mouth goes faster than a fox being chased. What does this have to do with what the—"

"I'm getting to that. So *then* milady told me that the young lord was just seeing to her safety. Of course, she even tried to convince me that we needed his lordship. She told me we should just be patient, and probably before the night was out the young lord would take the time to learn our names. Can you believe that! Of *course* I thought she was trying to be nice, because a man like his lordship isn't one to take time out to pay attention to those around him . . . but Lordy . . . *he just asked me my name!*"

"Did you tell him?"

"Of *course* I told him, and then he told me to retire. Wait until my James hears this. Me retire before the lord? Only Lady Br . . ."

Ranulf struggled to hear the rest of their conversation, but they must have stepped out of the pantry and back into the kitchens for the voices became too faint to hear. Listening in on another's conversation wasn't one of his typical pastimes. The few times he had accidentally been in a position to eavesdrop, he had found the topic uninteresting and moved out of earshot. Tonight, however, he had been riveted.

Bronwyn should hate him after what he had done. She should despise him, but then how could she have spoken so highly about him? And Norval? And how did she know about Norval *and* his family? She had obviously spent more time with his men than he had realized. But could she really have reacted so nonchalantly upon discovering his plans to keep her here? And what did Chrissie mean about Bronwyn feeling so poorly? Had she been crying?

Suddenly, Ranulf needed to see her, and tomorrow wasn't soon enough.

The winding back staircase led to a long narrow corridor. At its end was a portable pallet for a chamber servant to sleep on and be available. Unsurprisingly no one was there, and Ranulf doubted one slept there very often, if at all.

Three doors lined one side, but only the last had a faint glow of a light shining through the cracks. Ranulf knocked and waited. When no answer came, he nudged it and felt momentary elation when he discovered it was not barred. Swinging it open, he stepped inside and right into a bucket of water placed just to the left of the door. Grimacing, he cursed his missing eye and slid the pail over with his now wet foot to shut the door. Then he looked around, his eyes stopping on the bed. The curtains were gathered aside and he could see Bronwyn's sleeping form. She was on her side and the coverlet was pulled up over her shoulders, leaving only her face visible.

The sight was a salve to his soul.

The pressing need to speak with her and get answers had ebbed, but he was not prepared to leave, not yet. Deciding to get out of his wet stockings, he slipped off his shoes and leggings and then untied his belt. Three padded chairs similar to the ones in the Hall and in his solar were placed in a half circle around the hearth. The chairs had been meant to line the main dining table, but it seemed his predecessor had found better uses for them. Having spent too many uncomfortable nights on hard stools and benches, Ranulf agreed with the decision. Grabbing one, he twisted it around so that he could watch her sleep as she had him.

He was about to sit down when she spoke, causing him to freeze midair. "Be still and stop making noise, Ranulf, or I will just get even madder than I already am at you. And then you will see."

Ranulf took a step forward, searching for reasons to defend his decision to be in her room, when her voice trailed off with a sigh as she nestled farther down into the covers. The woman was asleep and had no idea he was there. Reassuring peace came over him. She thought about him in her sleep.

Ranulf had just settled down when Bronwyn stretched and flipped over on her back, causing the covers to slide off her shoulders and pool around her waist. The innocent action revealed a sight that took his breath away.

Honey-colored waves fell against softly rounded uptilted breasts. Smooth pale skin glowed in the moonlight. She seemed unreal, ethereal. A wild beauty and absolutely the most desirable, beautiful woman he had ever seen in his life.

He hadn't been prepared. So the moment air passed through his lungs, it was expelled violently with all the pent-up passion coursing through his loins. "Where the hell are your clothes?!"

Bronwyn arched her shoulders back and frowned at the abrupt shout. Irritation laced her furrowed brows and she squinted to discover who was snapping at her. Seeing Ranulf, her expression softened into a smile and she moved her arms over her head and stretched out of habit. Ranulf's eyes grew wider and his jaw dropped. Bronwyn became instantly awake as the cause of his reaction dawned on her.

Mortification filled her blue eyes as she reached out and snatched the coverlet, clutching it to her breasts. "What are you *doing*? Why are you in my room?"

Ranulf took several deep breaths and flexed his fists propped on his hips. It didn't matter that she was now covered. He couldn't think. "Why aren't you wearing your shift?" he finally managed to grit out.

Bronwyn sat up straighter, squaring her shoulders. "It's over there on my chest where it always is at night. I have never slept in clothes. They twist all around me and give me nightmares about someone tying me down. Now will you tell me *just why you are in my room*?"

The venom associated with her question was undeniable. She wasn't happy at all and he couldn't blame her. But he was not about to leave. "You've been sleeping in clothes for the past two nights!"

"Not in my room! And I wasn't *alone* just like I should be right now."

"Well, you aren't alone now and I am *not* going to

leave. We must talk." He marched over to the chest, seized the undergarment, and threw it at her. "Put it on."

Bronwyn took the wadded material and tossed it back as forcefully as she could. "No. I will sleep as I am. And you *are* going to leave. We can talk tomorrow."

"Tonight, angel."

Bronwyn issued him her iciest smile. "Tomorrow, your lordship."

Ranulf took several steps forward until he was less than a foot away from the bed. He leaned toward her and held out his fist with the shift twisted around it. "Listen, angel. You can either talk to me with something on or not, but unless you can physically throw me out of this room, we *are* going to talk. Tonight." He then let go and the linen material floated down onto her lap.

Bronwyn wrinkled her nose and pursed her lips in silent defiance. The man wasn't wearing too many clothes himself. Most were draped over the side of one of the chairs. When had he arrived? Just why was he there at all? To make her apologize or send her home? When she had spied Norval's presence standing guard, a small flicker of hope had sparked inside her. Ranulf wouldn't order someone to keep her from leaving if he wanted her gone. But maybe she had been wrong.

She grabbed the chemise and bit her tongue to keep from mouthing a retort as he nodded in approval and stepped away from the bed toward the hearth. Slipping out of the covers, she stood up and turned so that her back was to him and angrily pulled the fragile garment over her head. Now somewhat clothed and feeling less disadvantaged, she spun back around, prepared to do battle. But Ranulf was no longer in the mood for a fight. The blood had drained from his face and he was gripping the back of one of the chairs for support.

For an instant, Bronwyn was mystified at his sudden change, but then she recognized his horror and realized just what she had done. She had forgotten who she was, what she looked like, and now he knew the truth.

Woodenly, she moved toward the window and looked out, pulling her arms tightly around her, trying to fight the tears that were threatening to fall. After an interminable silence, she heard a log being tossed into the fire. The tension in her jaw increased as she braced herself to turn around and look at him. But he was not studying her. He was standing by the mantel staring at the orange and yellow flames with one arm just over his head propped against the stone wall. She wondered if his words about her supposed beauty were echoing in his ears as they still were in hers.

The pain in her forearm was throbbing from being held so tightly. Her legs started to wobble, warning her that the rigidity of her frame for the past several minutes could no longer be sustained. She walked to the chair she always sat in when her sisters were there and sat down, tucking her toes underneath her. She braced her injured arm on her leg and let the tears fall. This time, she did not try to stop them.

Ranulf pushed himself back to a standing position. Purposeless rage filled him for it was aimed at a cruel event that had happened long ago. He now understood Laon's baffling assessment of his eldest daughter. Her back mirrored that of his chest. Mottled flesh, disfigured from fire. He also understood why she had kept it concealed. Bronwyn had survived a horror only a few knew and could understand. But why didn't she realize that he was one of those few?

Ignoring the chairs, Ranulf settled down onto the worn rug and faced the fire, resting his forearms on his bent knees. "Why didn't you tell me?"

Bronwyn didn't answer. She didn't know how, so she stared, mesmerized by the muscles on his back. Even through the tunic, she could see his strength.

"I need to know, angel."

The guilt in his voice was palpable, forcing her to speak. "Because I saw how uncomfortable your own scars—especially the burns—made you." Her voice seemed so small and weak. She wasn't even sure it was hers.

"How." Again his prompt was less a question and more of a command.

"I truly remember nothing. I only know what I have been told."

"Tell me . . . please."

Bronwyn swallowed, not sure what drove her to answer—his needing to hear how it happened or her needing to tell the story. "When I was young— very young—there was a fire at Syndlear. No one knows why and I'm not sure it matters. My father was gone. We had a few posted guards and they alerted us to the danger. My mother was able to get my sisters safely out and then she came back for me. But by the time she pulled me out of the bed, the flames were at the door and the hall. She held me in one arm and wrapped us both in a wet blanket as best she could, leaving only her arms and hands and my back exposed. We nearly died, but Lord Anscombe brought us down to Hunswick, where we were cared for and, by some miracle, survived."

Ranulf closed his eyes. It explained so much. Why she didn't see his scars, why they mattered so little, how she and everyone else could be blind to them. Because she understood. She knew what they were . . . and what they weren't.

Bronwyn had called him a fool, but he was so much more.

"I'm sorry."

Bronwyn bristled. "Don't be." She didn't want his pity. "My mother was the most beautiful person I have ever known."

Ranulf studied her distress defined by taut lines in her neck and struggled to find a way of asking just how he could make amends. Her left arm was stretched out along her leg and she was holding it as if to keep it there . . . as if it were hurt. He moved over until he was kneeling in front of her and immediately she dropped her arm to her side and out of his sight. He knew then that something was definitely wrong.

"Let me see your arm."

Bronwyn shook her head. "It's nothing."

"Angel, I'll admit that most of the time you will be victorious when we fight, but tonight you aren't going to win any battles. Now, let me see your arm."

Bronwyn blinked, her large blue eyes growing even bigger. He spoke as if they had a future, as if he wanted there to be a future. That's why he had come to her room. Because of what had happened that afternoon. And it was happening again.

He was pale, tired, and in her bedroom, and they were both half dressed, and it felt . . . right. The situation should seem wrong and immoral, but despite their fiery tempers, she felt safe with him and didn't want him to leave. She also did not want him to berate her for not taking care of her arm, something he was sure to do when he saw the now very angry wound.

He put out his hand, palm up, and waited for her to comply. Squaring her shoulders, Bronwyn mustered what she hoped to be a cool demeanor and raised the linen sleeve to reveal her careless mistake. "It looks far worse than it feels and you really needn't worry about it. I'll have someone tend to it in the morning," she spurted out, the speed of her speech belying her outward behavior.

Ranulf supported her arm at the elbow and examined the gash, lightly probing the skin around the wound. "When did this happen?"

Bronwyn licked her lips. His voice was hard, lined with anger, but his touch was incredibly tender, gentle, and nurturing. "Earlier today. After I left your room this morning."

"How? Who did this to you?"

Bronwyn sensed his anger and it was rising. She reached out to stroke his cheek to calm him, but it didn't help. "It was my fault, Ranulf. I was clumsy and not looking. I knew there was exposed metal on the tub I was using so if you are searching for someone to blame, then you have only me. I would tell you if it were otherwise."

Ranulf released her arm and rose to his feet to head for the basin of water on the small table by the bed. He grabbed the drying cloth and forcefully dunked it into the cool water. Seeing her with an injury that was obviously causing her enormous pain was tearing him up inside. He would rather be stabbed a dozen times than to see her hurt.

"It was just an accident. There is no reason to be so angry," Bronwyn repeated.

"There are plenty of reasons for my anger, the least of which is you being in a tub known to be dangerous."

Bronwyn felt her own temper start to flare. "Well, then I am the one paying for my mistake. I have not complained. It is *you* who are making this more serious than it is."

Ranulf returned by her side and dropped back down to his knees. Retaking her arm, he lightly tapped the red skin. Each time she flinched despite her desperate attempts not to. "Where is that powder you used on me? You sent that woman to get it from your room, is it still here?"

At the idea of his using that stuff on her, Bronwyn yanked her arm out of his grasp. "That is completely unnecessary. The wound will heal on its own." Ranulf's ominous auburn gaze bore into her own. Few times in her life had she been around someone truly angry, and right now, his fury was aimed at her. Bronwyn shrank back. "You have no right to be cross with me."

"I have *every* right to be mad at you. Or are you going to deny that *this* was the reason you pulled away this afternoon? Not shame."

Bronwyn held his gaze. He was right, but he was also wrong. "And what was your excuse? Or are you going to deny walking away, whispering how you wished you could take it all back. That our kiss never happened."

Ranulf paused, hovering the cloth above her arm for a second before he let go and fell back against his heels. "I admit I was upset."

Bronwyn's brows rose. "No, my lord, you were livid. At me."

"Well, I'm not anymore."

Bronwyn wanted to laugh aloud. He was done being mad so she should be. He admitted his anger, apologized—not for insulting her—but for an injury he had nothing to do with, and now that he was ready to drop the argument, she was supposed to just happily do so as well. She shook her head and chuckled. "Truce?"

"Ask me after you give me the black powder."

Bronwyn recoiled. "No, Ranulf. That stuff is only to be used for emergencies and this small scratch is far from that."

"Look at it, angel. It is red and angry and you know that it is too late to be just cleaned and bound. By tomorrow night, that *scratch* will be much more. You have no choice, for I'm not giving you any. So where's the powder?"

Wanting it now just to be over with, Bronwyn used her chin to point toward the large, engraved chest in front of her bed. "You'll need to make a paste."

Ranulf opened the top and rummaged for a second, hampered by the dim light, finally pulling out a small bag and the wooden cup it was sitting in. She watched as he poured the contents into the mug.

Suddenly she was desperate for conversation to divert her mind off what was about to happen. "I guess this Twelfthtide, you have a lot to celebrate. You have much to thank God about."

Ranulf snorted. "I'm not thanking God. More like something else."

"But what about your title? These lands? Hunswick?"

"I didn't want them. They were forced on me."

"Forced? I understood that you and the king were friends. That he brought you back to his lands in Normandy and gave you the opportunity to gather wealth and men."

Ranulf finished mixing and went back to the chest. He pulled out a clean dry cloth and started ripping it into three narrow strips. "The reason the king asked me to serve as a commander in his army was to ease his conscience. As far as Twelfthtide," he said, pausing to point at his scar and missing eye, "I don't celebrate it. God abandoned me so I have abandoned him."

Bronwyn's jaw visibly dropped as Ranulf scooped up her elbow for the third time. "You lived! You still possess your sight, and your hearing, and your ability to move. You are still handsome . . . and yet you think God abandoned you? You are wrong, Ranulf. You are incredibly wrong. God saved you."

Ranulf was thrown by the vehemence of her accusation. He had always considered himself unlucky and never thought that his survival alone made him fortunate, and retaining the will to live, even more so. Rattled, he redirected the conversation. "And what about you? Why are you still at Hunswick? You are far past the typical marrying age of a noblewoman. Or are you letting your scars keep you from accepting?"

"No, my scars have nothing to do with my lack of

wedded state." He was close to the truth, dancing all around it, but he hadn't stumbled on it yet. But he would if he ever met her younger sisters. He, just like the rest, would gravitate toward them, forgetting he ever once had any interest in her. The only reason she was getting this rare bit of attention now was because Edythe and Lily were not around.

"What about your sisters? Do they have scars as well?"

Bronwyn shook her head and smiled genuinely. "No, but my parents lived in fear that it could happen again. My father had studied as a mason in his youth before helping King William fight the Anglo-Saxons. As a result, he spent his fortune creating back stairs to every floor in Syndlear. He ordered two buckets of water to be kept in every bedroom and even rebuilt portions of the keep walls to create fire holes for our safety. But we only ever used them for storage."

Ranulf returned to her side. "Buckets of water, huh? I guess that explains why I stepped in the one placed by the door."

Bronwyn smiled, imagining the event. "Habit. I don't know if I could sleep without knowing they were right there."

"Are your sisters like you?"

The question was innocent, but a reminder nonetheless. "No. I am the dull one. I have no color while my sisters are infused with it. Edythe is sensible, but possesses a fiery Scottish temper when riled. My other sister has both beauty and a sweet disposition. Life favors her, L . . . Bronwyn is just luckier than most," she finished, catching her near mistake just in time. She would have to be more careful.

"Well, they couldn't compare to you."

It sounded good and it was nice that he believed it, but it wasn't reality. "I doubt you would feel that way if you ever met my younger sister."

"You're wrong," Ranulf argued. Then he held her arm steady and smoothed the black paste on the injury.

Bronwyn could not help herself and cried out as the wicked concoction came into contact with her raw flesh. Immediately, Ranulf bound the arm and then masterfully picked her up and slid into her seat, cuddling her on his lap as her cries slowly receded. He wanted to do more. To kiss her and force her mind on to more pleasant things, but he refused to give in to what he knew was a personal desire rather than a mutual one. Tonight, he had been given a second chance, and this time, he was going to remain in control.

Bronwyn sniffled and glanced at her bound arm. "Another scar," she sighed.

He tucked back a long lock of her hair behind her shoulder. "You are so very beautiful. How you view and treat the world around you . . . that kind of beauty is more enticing than any I've ever known."

Bronwyn lay still against his chest. Of all the things she didn't want to hear, especially from him. "Please, don't ever say that to me again."

"Why? It's true. No other woman can compare to you and I will never be attracted to another."

Bronwyn pulled back and slipped off his lap, avoiding his grasp. She faked a laugh to mask her pain and said, "No one should ever say those words to someone else. You should know that better than anyone. Beauty is fleeting and there is *always* another whose physical appearance can capture even the most devoted of hearts."

Ranulf sat quietly, his expression grim. He wanted to refute her comment, for he had met many other supposedly gorgeous women, who fit every man's dream of a goddess. Every man but him.

Ranulf reached over and plucked his leggings and shoes off the chair next to him. He pulled them both on and then looped his belt around his waist. If he stayed, he would try to convince her of the sincerity behind his words. But before he bedded Bronwyn, she needed to end the lies between them.

Tomorrow they were going to talk. From now on, there would be no secrets, no deceit—only the truth.

Lillabet rocked back and forth in her room at Syndlear, clutching her mother's tapestry for comfort. Daylight would soon arrive. She hadn't been able to sleep, nor would she be able to until she made things right. Until today, she had no idea how much Bronwyn had been shielding her and Edythe about Luc Craven. Bronwyn had glossed over the encounters she had with the man. Lily had always understood that Luc was very unpleasant—too unpleasant to consider marrying, but until today, she had no idea just how horrific that possibility was.

When she had slipped past unseen by the guard posted to her as she did every day for her afternoon walks, Luc Craven had confronted her, demanding to see Bronwyn. Lily had tried to toy with him, as was her habit to control the situation with any man, but this time her tricks had not worked. And that was when she made her biggest mistake. She had let it slip that Bronwyn was not there. Instantly, the baron's mild demeanor changed and he had become enraged, declaring that there was no place Bronwyn could hide he would not find her.

For the first time in her life, Lillabet had felt and still continued to feel true fear. Luc had sworn Bronwyn would be his. *Never,* Lily vowed to herself once again. Never would she let her sister be a victim to such a man.

She had been purposefully naïve to the unpleasantness of the world for too long, with no inclination of changing. She hadn't realized that naïveté came with a price, and this time the cost of innocence was too high.

Tomorrow, whether Lord *Deadeye* liked it or not, she and Edythe were returning to Hunswick. It was her turn to protect her sisters and make the sacrifice. Tomorrow, she was finally going to grow up.

Chapter Five

Medieval holiday entertainment came in many forms—decorations, food, bonfires, acting, gambling, even the servers often came out in song. Greenery such as ivy, evergreens, and holly adorned homes and dinner tables, bringing a festive spirit and scent to the air. Families would extinguish all other flames when the bonfires were lit and join together, symbolizing unity of the village. Amusement would be found in a variety of ways from playing instruments like the harp or lute, games such as backgammon and early versions of chess and dice, or even a simple play given by the locals or visiting performers. These decorations and festive activities would last until the feasts on Twelfth Night, just before Epiphany.

Ranulf stirred in his bed and opened his eye, relieved to see daylight filling his solar. The sounds of several items falling off a cart, followed by an assortment of shouts and grunts, confirmed that the castle was awake and alive with activity. He must have finally fallen asleep just before dawn.

Groaning, Ranulf squeezed his eyelid back shut, feeling the weight of his fatigue more than usual. Sleep was not something he received overwhelming amounts of, but never had his mind been plagued with repeating thoughts and conversations . . . not to mention a physical need near painful. Supposedly the priest assigned to Hunswick wasn't going to arrive until tomorrow, which meant one more night of unrest, and of haunting memories of Bronwyn lying asleep on her back . . . naked.

The argument outside was escalating. Ranulf threw off the coverlet and moved toward the window, searching the bailey for the source of the commotion. As he suspected, a cart had toppled, but it looked like the situation was being rectified without interference. Ranulf was about to step away when he spied Bronwyn and Tyr standing just outside the stables, laughing. The sight rankled him enormously.

The woman showed no signs of sleeplessness, nothing to indicate that last night bothered her in the least. If anything, she looked refreshed, wearing a bright gold gown created more for court than a goose hunt. Tyr must have said something funny because Bronwyn threw her head back to laugh, freeing some of her tawny locks from its snood. Renewed pains of jealousy began to crack Ranulf's carefully controlled exterior. He knew it was ridiculous never to want another man to appreciate her beauty, to know her laughter, but until Bronwyn was his in every sense of the word, he would not be at ease.

Then Tyr reached up and brushed something off her cheek and Ranulf's self-discipline exploded into a rushing torrent of anger and possessiveness. His best friend! On his land, touching his woman!

Unthinking, Ranulf snatched his tunic and wrenched it over his head. After pulling on his leggings and shoes, he grabbed his belt and sword, fastening them as he exited the room. He ignored the servant, who had been patiently waiting just outside the door for instructions, and bounded down the stairs with only one thought—pummeling his soon-to-be ex-friend.

A warm wind hit his face as soon as he left the Tower Keep, and it was filled with humidity. A storm was brewing and behind it was the winter weather that should have arrived weeks ago. Marching toward the stables, he saw Tyr and Bronwyn still conversing. Upon seeing him, Tyr issued his typical lopsided grin of welcome. Bronwyn, however, showed little expression. She just stared questioningly at him with aggravating composure.

"Where's my horse?" he asked directly.

Tyr stepped inside to see that Pertinax was saddled. Bronwyn pointed to Ranulf's shoulder. "Are you sure coming is wise?"

Ranulf plucked her wrist out of the air, just below where he had bandaged it. "I know you shouldn't be."

Bronwyn arched her brows and gave her arm a firm tug to reclaim her limb. "I am only riding to show your men the most populated places along the lakeshore for geese. They will be doing the work. You, on the other hand, shouldn't be working a bow with that shoulder for at least another week."

"I came not to hunt," he growled. "I have seen little

of Hunswick beyond that of the Great Hall and my bedchambers and it is time I see the lands that were thrust upon me."

Tyr reemerged from the stables pulling the reins attached to three horses. He tossed Ranulf his and handed Bronwyn the straps to a brown mare. Taking them, she sauntered closer to Ranulf's side, her deep mist-colored eyes sparkling with defiance. "I don't know what has you so riled, but if you cannot at least pretend to be pleasant, then I suggest you stay rather than ruin the outing for everyone."

Before he could conjure a smart retort, Tyr joined them. "Doesn't her ladyship look beautiful this morning?"

Ranulf raked her up and down and scowled. "What she is, is too damn bright to go hunting."

With an intentional snub that said more than any words she could have mustered, Bronwyn turned from Ranulf and favored Tyr with a placating smile. "Thank you. It's not true, but I appreciate your attempt to make me feel otherwise."

Ranulf forced his jaw to unclench. Bronwyn's deflection was not an attempt at being demure; she truly did not see herself as the vision she was. And why should she? Even her father had not seen it, mostly because he saw himself in her, and he had a definite preference for dark-haired women. Unfortunately, Tyr did recognize the beauty before him.

Bronwyn was stunning, intentionally so, almost as if she were personally daring his men to avoid her allure. Her hair had returned to its netted coiffure. A gold band adorned with pearls came around her forehead, disappearing at the nape of her neck behind the matching snood. She wore only one piece of jewelry, a long gold necklace supporting a pearl cross with a sizable ruby in the middle. Her silk dress shimmered with a subtle woven pattern of flowers. Ranulf hadn't seen cloth that fine since he left the king's estates in Normandy.

The style of her bliaut was also different. While it did not reveal the amount of kirtle as her other outfits, the sleeves beckoned a man's imagination as they fitted down her shapely arms ending in a wide opening, lined with pearls. The neckline was round, not high nor deep, and was unadorned. The waist hugged her perfectly and the braided belt rested easily on her hips. Any man who had been unaware of her physical curves before was fully cognizant of them now.

The overall effect was mesmerizing, alluring, captivating. Not only to him, but to every man around her, driving Ranulf insane. "I doubt another woman in two hundred miles even knows of silk's existence and you're wearing it to go hunting," he grumbled as he moved his horse out into the bailey. He knew he was being unreasonable, but more and more he thought of Bronwyn as his and his alone. That no one else understood this only flamed his jealousy.

Bronwyn reared back, stung by his harshness. A clouded expression overcame her face as hurt transformed into anger. "The dress so happens not to be mine, but my sister's. *My* clothes went to Syndlear after *you* ordered us to leave Hunswick!"

Grabbing the horn of the saddle, she swung her leg over the brown mare's back, fighting the gold fabric, which refused to lie nicely behind her. Finally, after arranging the hem so that it draped in such a way it would neither tug when she rode nor bunch immodestly, she sat regally and stared down at him, as if she were sitting upon a throne. "And as far as the material being silk, it was the last thing given to us by my father. We received word only the day before your arrival that he had died on route back to England."

The mentioning of Laon's death hit Ranulf with unexpected force and he had no idea how to respond. Saying anything and not revealing that he had been with her father when he had passed would feel like a lie and they had enough of those between them. So he said no words of comfort, gave no apologies, offered nothing to show he cared. He knew that in doing so inflicted pain, but the truth would have hurt her more. Unable to continue seeing the growing sadness in her eyes and know that he was the cause, Ranulf silently mounted Pertinax and kicked his steed toward the gatehouse, leaving Tyr, Bronwyn, and the rest to follow.

A half hour later, Ranulf brooded in silence as the group moved beyond Hunswick and closer to the spot where he first spied her. Her sorrow had not left her eyes, but his men had been oblivious. Indulging them, Bronwyn had chatted congenially, answering questions lightly and enchantingly. His men were infatuated and their every sigh, every verbal fumble only confirmed their condition. Ranulf was just about to halt the ceaseless line of questions when Bronwyn did it for him.

Stopping at a small clearing nestled against the lake's shoreline, she called out to Tyr, "The geese typically gather just beyond the next bend. I need to check something and will join you in a moment."

Ranulf gave a quick tug on the reins, halting the

large destrier, and signaled Tyr to keep moving. Then he waited till the group passed before prodding Pertinax toward the very spot where he had first spied her. He remembered that day perfectly, including the man who had attacked her. The memory served as a sharp reminder that he had yet to find out just who her tormenter was and if she was still in danger.

Asking her would be fruitless. She first would have to own up to her identity, and she wasn't about to do that with the sparks of animosity flying between them. He needed to get his possessiveness under control and that wouldn't happen until he knew she was his. Not just in his own mind, but in everyone else's.

Bronwyn issued Ranulf a look of surprise as he slipped off his horse and tied it to the same bush she had used for her own mount. His comment about her choice of dress had hurt deeply.

She, too, had received material for a gown from her father. Hers was a shimmering dark silver, which accentuated her eyes, but it had been one of the few things she had packed and taken to Syndlear. Still, she had spent extra time that morning preparing her hair and had especially chosen Lily's yellow dress because she thought it might make her appear more like the women of court whom Ranulf had been with the past few years. It was a little snug and the color didn't suit her like it did her darkhaired sister, still Bronwyn thought she looked pretty.

But Ranulf had hated it. Everything in his demeanor and expression screamed for her to go back to her room and change. Pride had caused her to snap back, and as a result, a gulf of misunderstanding now lay between them. He had ignored her so she had done the same, keeping her conversations with his men or Tyr, whom she found affable and very interesting. And today, very informative.

She kept her back toward Ranulf and pulled at one of the leafless orange and yellow flowers covering a bush just to the side of her tree.

"What is that you are picking?"

"Witch hazel," Bronwyn answered as she spun the slender dark yellow stem in her hand. She inhaled its scent and sighed. "It grows in the winter when so few flowers do. That's why my mother loved it. It's bright and pretty and it smells sweet, like spring."

"So you planted it near her favorite tree."

Bronwyn turned just her head around. "How did you know this was her favorite tree?"

Ranulf shrugged. Bronwyn's wistful expression matched that of the tune she had been singing, the haunting sounds of remembrance. "I saw you here before."

"That's right. You were here that day."

Ranulf didn't answer. He didn't need to. Instead he waved his arm at the view. "I can see why you like this spot."

Bronwyn strolled closer to the water's edge. Boulders randomly lined the shoreline and extended into the water. As a child she used to jump from rock to rock. "This is where I come to think. After my mother passed, I would come here every day and just cry. His lordship—your cousin—knew but he never said anything, never stopped me. He knew that for some reason it gave me comfort. I am going to miss it."

Ranulf moved to stand by her left side, bringing

her back into his limited line of sight. "I'm not an ogre. You can continue coming here in the future."

Bronwyn nodded and gave him a quick placating smile. "So, tell me, just how long have you known the king . . . I mean personally?"

Ranulf pivoted and followed her with his vision as she went back to the prickly bush to pick more flowers. She was shutting him out and he didn't know just what it was she was protecting or why. But pressing would not gain her trust. "Not long and yet forever," he finally answered.

Bronwyn's mouth curved into an unconscious smile. "You know, that is exactly how I feel about you."

As soon as the words popped out, Bronwyn immediately bit her bottom lip. She shouldn't have said her thoughts aloud, but in a way she was glad she did. She wanted Ranulf to know after she left for Scotland that he hadn't been just anyone and that his company these past few days had been important to her.

"I've wondered what you were thinking about that day, before that man . . . disturbed you," Ranulf remarked, taking a risk, encouraged by her admission.

"It doesn't matter now," she answered with a semishrug. "But you should know that I will always be grateful for your interference that afternoon. I normally can handle men and have been protecting my younger sisters for years, but I'm afraid to think of what would have happened if you had not been there." She paused and took a deep breath, seeking the courage to continue. "I have never needed saving before. People always come to me for help. It is nice to know there is someone else who will take my place."

Her small speech rattled Ranulf, but it shouldn't have. After that first day, ordering her and her family off his property, of *course* she believed he wanted her gone. He hadn't talked of marriage and that was because she hadn't been truthful with him about who she was. And she wasn't ever going to admit to her identity while believing she was going to have to leave.

He gave in to the compulsion to pull her into his arms. "You're not leaving."

"I have to. My sisters . . ." Bronwyn argued, but she did not pull away.

"You said 'younger sister' the other night. I was told that Bronwyn was the eldest."

Bronwyn instantly stiffened and stepped out of the embrace.

Ranulf remained where he was. "Angel, whatever it is, you can tell me. You can trust me."

Her blue eyes studied the single auburn pool staring at her. In it was so much sincerity. She wanted to end the farce. Have him call her by her real name and not just "angel." To know if he would repeat his words with equal tenderness if he knew she was not his intended but the comparatively ugly older sister.

She was saved from deciding when the deafening unique sound of honking geese filled the air, making it impossible to continue their conversation. When the sounds started to die down, Tyr emerged into the clearing announcing that they had found the flock. With a frustrated grimace, Ranulf gestured that he and Bronwyn should mount and rejoin the group.

As soon as they arrived at the place where others were gathered, one of the village hunters proudly held up four monster birds. "Look, my lady, won't this be a great addition to the night's meal of pig and lamb?"

Tyr's hazel eyes grew large as he moved his horse closer. "Did you say pig and lamb?"

The hunter bobbed his head proudly. "Everyone at Hunswick is eating especially well this year since her ladyship"—he paused to nod at Bronwyn—"cleared all the storages of meat, giving us villagers and farmers a share. Won't find a man around who won't be willing to help out to replenish what we took for the feasts."

Ranulf nudged his horse forward until he was beside Bronwyn. Pivoting in the saddle, he arched the brow over his good eye and said, "Devout follower of Advent, eh?"

"Maybe I should have said recently devout," Bronwyn clarified.

A roar of laughter broke over the crowd. Tyr wiped away the tears forming in his eyes. "Oh, she got you, Ranulf. I *told* you not to evict a woman from her home. They have all kinds of ways of exacting revenge, and keeping a man from enjoying a good meal . . . well, that was brilliant and evil."

Bronwyn waited for Ranulf's rebuke, but instead, he joined his friend, and within minutes, the whole group was laughing, though only a handful truly understood why.

Three hours later, the geese had dispersed and the group, which was now almost to the other side of Bassellmere, was starting their ride back. Additional hunting would be needed to replenish the other meats, but they had more than enough to satisfy everyone's hunger that night as well as for the first few Twelfthtide celebrations.

Surprisingly, Bronwyn had enjoyed the outing immensely. Whatever tension that had been eating at Ranulf when he awoke that morning was now gone. Instead, she was able to witness how he was with his men, relaxed but with a cunning sense of humor. In return, they treated him with a respect and ease one only felt after years of companionship. And she had been welcomed into that small community through both teasing and the acceptance of her snappy returns. Best of all, Ranulf didn't seem to mind.

He rode beside her, most of the time, almost as if he were announcing to everyone that she was his future wife. That she belonged to him. She was living a fantasy but she couldn't bring herself to end it.

She had fallen in love. Deeply, irrevocably.

She had not intended to give her heart away, and never dreamed she could have done so in such a short period of time, but she had. She had started falling while arguing with him that first day on the battlements, but it wasn't until last night that he'd claimed her whole heart. There would never be another for her. She intended to soak in every minute, revel in every smile so she could relive this day over and over again in the future. Ranulf would learn the truth soon enough. Tomorrow she would ask to visit her sisters, knowing she would never see him again. And once safely in the confines of Syndlear, she would send word with the truth of her identity and why she had lied, hoping Ranulf would at least understand, even if he could not forgive her.

A shout from one of the men got her attention. They saw some deer, which tended to be quite elusive in the winter months. Ranulf waved them ahead, indicating that he and Bronwyn would follow but not to wait.

Bronwyn maneuvered her horse around a large thistle bush and pulled her mount to the right to wait for Ranulf. It was becoming increasingly more natural to adjust her position so that she remained on his right side and within his line of vision. "Tyr says that you are quite rich and that is why you can afford so many men."

Ranulf frowned. "Tyr speaks too much."

"But it's true, isn't it?"

"In a way," Ranulf hedged. Truth was, he was very wealthy compared to most commanders under Henry's rule. Everyone knew the king possessed a large fortune, and with his frugal inclinations, they did not rapidly diminish under his leadership. Consequently, Henry was able to be very liberal with his money when he chose, and as a result, he let a loyal few keep much of what they reaped in battle. And Ranulf had reaped much over the years.

"I guess it's nice to know that our new king is generous."

"If you say so. The last time I experienced his merciless generosity, he made me accept this title. Told me the responsibility of being a lord suited me. Me!" Ranulf scoffed.

"Doesn't it, though?" Bronwyn countered.

Ranulf twitched his mouth and glanced to his right. "To assume responsibility for men's lives during battle is one thing, but to assume it afterward means and affects much more, including their wives and children, making the burden far more difficult."

"I understand," Bronwyn murmured.

Ranulf glanced at her, surprised by the sincerity in her voice, but she probably did understand. For months, the lives dependent upon Hunswick had been thrust upon her, and just because she had risen to the responsibility didn't mean she had aspired to it, or even wanted it.

"I doubt many would, but you . . . you might. Still, I am fortunate. The lands are rich and many of the farms are unmanned, giving my men and their families a chance they never would have had."

Bronwyn expressed a gentle laugh that rippled through the air. "Those farms were last tilled by Saxons, and as far as the houses on them, only remnants remain. They will have to be rebuilt."

"My men won't mind, especially if it means they can settle down. Their wives are even more eager to do so."

"Wives?" Bronwyn repeated as she ducked almost successfully underneath a low-hanging branch. A stray twig caught her hair net.

"They're still in Normandy waiting with their husbands and families until spring to journey here. Once they do, we will rebuild houses and fortify Hunswick. Even Syndlear if needed."

Bronwyn pulled out the small branch but, in doing so, dislodged one of the pins securing the snood. She tried to reach back with one hand to find the errant pin stabbing her scalp, but couldn't while continually pushing aside the foliage. "I need to stop."

Ranulf spotted a small gap in the thicket located next to the water and, after she dismounted, guided both horses to the shore for a drink. The grass had turned winter yellow but it still remained soft and thick. The view of the lake from the secluded spot was calming and peaceful . . . at least to him. He turned to see just what was causing her to mutter irritably under her breath.

Bronwyn was standing there with two pins in her mouth, angrily searching for more. Clearly frustrated, she spit them out and began tugging at the netting, trying to free her mane from it altogether. "Do you miss your old life?" she asked. "I mean, Hunswick and the Hills must seem quite dull in comparison. We do not have the amusements you are used to."

"No, I will not miss court," Ranulf managed to get out. She was obviously trying to distract him, but that would be impossible until she stopped wrestling with her snood. With her hands behind her back, her gown was pulled tight across her chest, making each one of the perfect swells he had memorized the night before significantly more prominent.

"Then, what about Bristol? Do you miss your childhood home?"

Ranulf swallowed but it did not help as his mouth had gone dry. Between the dress and the slow release of her hair, it was near impossible to concentrate on her questions. "I miss no home, angel, for unlike you, I never had one."

His voice had become raspy as he remembered the feeling of her arms around him, his lips against hers. That was what home was about. Not a building, but a feeling of acceptance, comfort, safety . . . and desire.

Bronwyn bit her bottom lip and it was Ranulf's undoing. Watching her was becoming akin to torture. "Stop," he ordered and came up behind her. Her hair had become a tangled mass under her endeavors. Carefully, he found and pulled out the remaining pins, as well as a couple more thorny twigs, and removed the snood. Bronwyn sighed with heartfelt relief. Tilting her neck back, she shook her head and let the heavy locks fall. Unable to stop himself, Ranulf buried his fingers in the dark gold and whispered, "With you, I just might have found the home I never had."

Bronwyn was so surprised that for the space of maybe a heartbeat she didn't even move. Then slowly she turned around, and seeing the fear in his expression, as if he had revealed too much, she pushed all reason aside and followed an urge she didn't care if she regretted later. Cupping his cheek in one palm, she slid the other around his nape and curled her fingers into the short crisp hair at the back of his head. Then she closed her eyes and pulled him down so his mouth covered her own.

She parted her lips, and their tongues met, sending a tingling sensation throughout her body. She made a small hungry sound deep in her throat and he lifted her slightly, gathering her closer to his chest to increase the intensity of the kiss.

Ranulf's reaction to her heart-stopping gift was immediate and profound. He was hard and hot with wanting her and seconds away from being unable to stop himself from laying her down and making love to her in a way that would brand her forever to him. Breaking off the kiss, he lifted his head and sucked in air.

Immediately she rocked against him, going up on tiptoes to seek his mouth again. "Damn," he muttered and bent his head once more, this time kissing her harder, exploring her mouth with an expertise that made it clear there was no turning back.

Bronwyn met each thrust of his tongue with one of her own, unaware of what it was doing to him. All rational thought had left her. All she could feel were the hot little ripples of pleasure he was creating all over her body, awakening something deep inside that both frightened and excited her. Splayed over her back, his hands were big and strong. She sensed the tension in the arms around her and the rigidity of his shoulders and neck beneath her fingertips. Everything about him was bigger and excitingly harder.

Rocking her against him, Ranulf kissed her mouth, her cheek, her ear, reveling in the ever-quickening beat of her heart, short fast breaths, and trembling frame. His own body quaked, and burned, and throbbed. Marriage, truth, her father—all these things became secondary. Right now, Bronwyn was more than he ever imagined. More than he had ever wanted and the intense desire he had striven to repress now claimed his entire awareness. He needed to see and taste all of her. Consume her until she was one with his soul.

His hands parted the edges of her gown and slid underneath the shift, pushing it from her shoulders. Feeling the soft, delicate skin, he groaned and devoured her lips once more in a desperate claiming to which she submitted willingly, eagerly. His fingers continued their free exploration, slowly caressing the bare skin of her neck and shoulders, getting drunk on the warm silkiness of it. Inch by inch, the sleeves moved down her arms until both the gown and the chemise beneath hung at her waist.

Bronwyn quivered at the first callused touch of his hands as they moved up and cupped her breasts. Her nipple hardened in startled reaction and the hot sweet throbbing between her legs seemed to increase, times ten. She clung to him as his mouth continued its steady, head-spinning assault, kissing him back.

Teasingly, his fingers skimmed and circled her breasts, letting his thumbs periodically stroke and tease each hardened nub. It was torture. It was heaven. His light touch seared her skin and she thought she would never get enough. And still he circled round and round, until she was panting, aching hot for what Bronwyn knew not, but he did.

"Please," she half whispered, half pleaded against his lips. He answered her demand and closed both hands around her heated flesh, gently at first and then tighter. It wasn't enough. Her nipples were throbbing, tightening against his palm, straining for release. Still she wanted more.

Bronwyn reached out for Ranulf's tunic, but he caught her hand. His want was too great and the bare wisps of control he still had would soon be gone. He needed to bury himself deep within her, but he was determined to do so without scaring her. This would be her first and in many ways his as well. He was finally going to make love to a woman and be made love to in return. He was not going to allow either one of them to rush their inevitable union.

Ranulf caught her chin between his fingers and tipped up her face. He then kissed her. Hard. And when he felt her shudder against him, drawing her back under his spell, he began to unlace the back of her gown, not daring to raise his mouth from hers for fear that he might somehow lose her. Slowly, he pulled the strings until, several moments later, the golden material cascaded into a pool at her feet.

Her body pressed against him and his chest heaved with the effort it took to breathe. Ranulf felt the pent-up tension of passion grow as she ran her tongue across his lips. His legs began to tremble and he felt her own begin to quake. He needed to lay her down before they both fell.

Sweeping her up into his arms, he caressed her back, feeling the textured skin beneath his fingertips. All he could see and feel was stunning beauty. He laid her down on her discarded linen shift, wishing he had a bed, or was on the fur rug in front of his hearth as he had imagined multiple times the previous sleepless night. But he wasn't going to let this opportunity pass. His angel was his in mind and soul, and soon she would be in body.

Bronwyn watched as Ranulf stood back up again, naked beneath his gaze, and began to yank impatiently at his clothing, until they were all discarded and he stood nude before her. The hair on his chest was nearly black as the night, and the muscles of his torso formed a perfect V. Across his shoulder and upper chest, the mottled scars of burns long healed were far from unpleasant; rather they gave her a sense of protection. Here was a man who would fight and survive.

Her gaze trailed downward past his lean hips to his powerful legs and what was between them. Bronwyn had never seen a man like this before. She had heard much over the years and knew what to expect, but she doubted many men looked like Ranulf. He was hard and thick, almost begging to be touched.

Instinctively, she reached up, but her efforts were immediately stymied before they reached their goal.

"Do not . . . do that," he whispered hoarsely.

Bronwyn recoiled, regretting her impulsiveness. "I'm sorry."

Ranulf squeezed his good eye shut and shook his head, knowing she misunderstood. But he was scarcely breathing, barely restraining himself, and if she touched him, it would be over. "God, no, angel. Another day it will be my turn. This time, let it be all about you," he said with a quiet plea, lowering himself slowly on top of her, his gaze never leaving hers.

With the feel of her flesh against his overheated senses, he pulled her into one more mind-drugging kiss, fearing that she might suddenly realize just what was happening and ask to stop. But her welcoming response assured him that she wanted their union as much as he did. He splayed his fingers possessively over the soft skin of her belly, feeling the pounding of her heart. Bracing himself on his elbow, he cupped her face with his other hand and whispered, "You belong to me . . . do you understand?"

Bronwyn nodded, biting her bottom lip as a single tear fell down her cheek. His dark amber gaze glittered with renewed passion as he once again closed the distance between them.

She felt his hands touch her everywhere, caressing, learning every inch of her skin. Never had she dreamed hands so large and hardened with use could also feel so warm and gentle. His mouth closed over hers for a long, searing moment, and once again his fingers were on her swollen breasts, rubbing his calloused palms against the pebbled nipples. She shuddered in response. Splaying her own fingers over his back, she began to trace the tense muscles they found, drinking in his strength.

Then his lips were gone, returning to tantalize her as they moved down the length of her neck, pausing at her shoulder before moving lower. Then he stopped and hovered above her chest. Bronwyn's breath quickened and her breasts heaved in expectation. Desire washed over her and instinct forced her to arch her back until she made contact.

He took the hardened nipple into his mouth and flicked his tongue once across the tip. And then again, and again until she could take no more. "Ranulf," she whispered between heavy breaths and pressed his head to her bosom. At first, he refused to increase the pace, continuing to toy with the sensitive flesh, but at her protest, he began to suckle.

Bronwyn had never felt anything so wonderful. His mouth let go and he moaned uncontrollably as he moved to kiss the slope of her breasts. When he reached the other pink bud, she refused to wait and arched up into the heat of his mouth. He complied, branding her with his tongue as his other hand gently caught the other hard nipple between his fingers and squeezed carefully. She cried out, the sensation almost too much to bear.

Ranulf could feel her hands running through his hair pulling him closer, her abandoned response only adding to his own pleasure. His desire had become painful, and very soon he would no longer be able to deny himself release. He kissed the sweet, scented curve of her breast and trailed his fingertips down until they laced through the soft thatch of hair between her legs.

Bronwyn simultaneously tensed and gasped in astonishment. He closed his hand gently around her and whispered in her ear, "You are so beautiful, you take my breath away. Trust me, angel."

Bronwyn stared up at him with a mixture of confusion and vulnerability, but she didn't move, didn't even breathe until his lips touched hers. Then she sighed as he kissed her softly, reawakening the passion that had been building within her. Her last formed thought was this was not real, but it dissolved as her hips began to move against his massaging hand, her body now craving his touch. She would not stop him. This was her chance to discover what it was like to be consumed, savored, loved by a man. The memory would have to last her a lifetime.

Slowly Ranulf drew his fingers through the hot dew gathered between her legs, proof of her own need. He had been taught what excited a woman, but rarely practiced it, uncaring if his partner enjoyed the experience. Sex had been a physical release, nothing more. Until now. Of all things, he wanted her to know the intense pleasure that he could create. They both had been alone for too long. Never again. Every night could be like this.

Ranulf moistened his finger and then coaxed her small bud of desire into a tingling fullness. Her body began to vibrate with liquid fire and she opened her legs to him, rocking against his palm, unconsciously beckoning him for more. Slowly he parted her with one finger and slid into her, exploring her with deliberate possessiveness. Bronwyn moaned and lifted herself against his hand, pushing him deeper inside.

He introduced another finger and began to separate them, stretching her gently, widening the slick, hot channel. She trembled and began to writhe beneath him. His already painful arousal demanded release.

As slowly as he could manage, he settled himself between her silky thighs and probed gently, dampening himself in the moisture between her legs. Her body clenched in reaction. He kissed her and looked down. Her eyes were squeezed shut in anticipation. "Angel, look at me." When she finally did, he said in a hoarse whisper, "Don't be afraid of me. I could never hurt you."

His amber gaze had turned dark, unfathomable, with a fierce need for her to believe him. She had been terrified, but his sincere entreaty restored her calm and she began to relax. Every sensation he had introduced her to had captivated her, driving her to the brink of this. He seemed to know exactly how and where to touch her so that she only half understood what he was doing, but she did know that she didn't want him to stop. The tension suffusing her body was screaming for some kind of release, which Bronwyn knew only Ranulf could give. She just wished he wasn't so big.

Feeling her thighs ease, Ranulf opened her and began to make a place for himself in the very heart of her. He wanted to wait and go slowly, letting her drive the pace, but the throbbing had become unbearable. Every muscle had tightened almost to the point of pain. Never had he experienced this obliterating level of need.

He moved his hand on her thighs, urging them farther apart, pausing when he felt the shield of her virginity. Then he slid into her in one swift thrust that wrenched a cry of surprise from her throat.

She gripped his shoulders very tightly and he started to stroke away the pain, until her body was once again vibrating with liquid fire. Everything about their union was right. Bronwyn was meant for him and he had been meant for her and no other woman. He had finally found his home.

Instinctively, she lifted herself. Ranulf grasped her hips and guided her in the primal rhythm. He tried to slow the pace but control eventually escaped him. She was mindless with passion, writhing as their souls communicated. Every sense, every thought was caught in a whirlwind. The air around them turned into steam as he felt his release welling up from the base of his spine, rushing like an immense wave, until with a great shudder, he surged forward into her one last time. He heard Bronwyn call out his name as his whole body pulsated with erotic release. A triumphant groan of satisfaction escaped his lips before he sagged against her.

Bronwyn fought to catch her breath. Nothing— *nothing*—had prepared her for this. What they shared was a raw act of possession. In his arms, she had stopped thinking, only feeling. He was everything she had ever wanted in a man.

Drawing in deep breaths to abet his own recovery, he finally mustered the strength to roll over. Bronwyn threw a leg over his and cuddled next to his side, sighing as he stroked her hair. Complete and utter contentment. Why he was born and had been allowed to survive finally made sense. It was all to bring him to this place and this woman. A lifetime of her . . . of this . . . everything they both had endured had been more than worth it.

Bronwyn rose up on an elbow and smiled at him.

Feeling inspired and empowered to touch and do whatever she wanted, she began to trace the scar on his forehead, following it down over his eyelid and onto his cheek. "Does it ever open?" she asked about his missing eye.

Ranulf grinned back. No one had ever asked him before. And he suspected many had wanted to. "No. I can lift the lid, but to open on its own, the muscle needs the support of an eyeball."

"Hmm," she hummed, outlining his facial bone structure. "You never wear a patch."

"They hurt."

"So?"

Her answer startled him for he always thought it a good reason. If the retort had been from anyone else, he would have disregarded it, but coming from Bronwyn, he wondered if she wished he did wear the dreaded item. "Do you want me to start wearing one?"

Bronwyn rolled her eyes and playfully slapped his chest. "Don't be daft. You don't need to wear a patch for me or anyone at Hunswick. But I do think you should in certain company." She settled her chin on his shoulder, but kept her eyes locked on his. "Anyone can be shocked, but they shouldn't be judged for that first encounter when they are. You can't intentionally try to bate someone into a reaction and then be mad when they do."

Ranulf remembered her father saying something similar. "Enough talking," he said and pulled her up into a long, lingering kiss.

He loved her. He had from when he first saw her. Their coming together had been inevitable since that morning when he awoke and heard her speaking about him. He had hoped it would happen under the veil of honesty. But it didn't really matter. She was his now and there were other ways to get her to admit the truth before they married, which could now not be soon enough. It was going to be torture staying away from her bed until the priest arrived tomorrow.

All of a sudden, a much colder and stronger wind whipped around them, reminding them that a winter storm was coming. Ranulf felt Bronwyn's body shiver. "We need to dress and return."

Bronwyn sighed and moved to get up, but just before she rose, Ranulf drew her down into one final embrace. "In the spring, we are going to have to come here and try this again," he mumbled against her mouth.

Bronwyn pulled back, bit her bottom lip, and started to dress. As she laced the sides of the bliaut, something along the distant ridge caught her eye. The vegetation didn't grow thick around Syndlear, and any movement, especially if someone was wearing metal, could be seen on a bright day. Disguising her endeavors, she stole several more glances at the remote hills. She was sure the men she saw belonged to Luc, sent to watch Syndlear and to keep her from doing exactly what she planned . . . running away. Making their escape from her childhood home would no longer be easy.

Bronwyn considered telling Ranulf everything, but again as she played out the consequences in her mind, it was just not an option. Her blissful fantasy with Ranulf was over. With Luc spying on Syndlear, she and her sisters would have to depart from Hunswick, and the moment Ranulf saw them, she would have to tell him the truth and live with the consequences. But she had no choice. "Ranulf, I was wondering if my sisters and the servants who accompanied them can come down and have Christmas at Hunswick? Syndlear had not been prepared and—"

"And nothing," Ranulf answered, interrupting. "Of course they can come back." Her question was an answer to several prayers, including a new one for he, too, had seen movement in the hills while he had been dressing.

He needed to get back and speak with Tyr. Before the night was out, Ranulf intended to know just who had hired the mercenaries to watch him so closely. In his experience, lords and barons often liked to study their neighbors—especially new ones—and learn their weaknesses and strengths. It was usually accompanied with a brief show of power.

Vacating Syndlear was now a priority. Ranulf had only a few men, but they were some of his finest and could match a much larger unskilled army. But it would be easier if they were all together so he could react more effectively if needed.

Meanwhile, he needed to form a plan to compel Bronwyn into confessing her feelings and the truth. Given her request, he was fairly confident she was ready to divulge the latter, but he needed to be secure in her feelings for him as well, if not more.

It may have been a while since a woman had warmed his bed, but Ranulf was well enough versed in the act to know that what he and Bronwyn had shared was unique. And what made it so special was that it was not just a physical act, but an emotional, even spiritual one. Together they had given pieces of themselves and he needed her to admit she felt the same.

Luc pulled his horse behind a thicket of trees to avoid being spotted as the couple left to return to Hunswick. He had wanted Bronwyn for as long as he could remember. Everyone loved to point out the beauty of her sisters, but neither had ever held any interest for him. He had been the first to recognize Bronwyn's splendor, and had coveted his unique appreciation of his golden angel.

For years, his father had tried to entice him to marry other more powerful, wealthier women and he had refused. As a consequence, he had endured his father's brooding anger. But now that he was baron, he could do what he wanted. And he wanted Bronwyn.

When news came that the new Lord Anscombe had evicted Bronwyn and her sisters from Hunswick, Luc had been elated. He had immediately set out for Syndlear, eager to comfort his bride and try once again to convince her of the futility of refusing his hand. Then, he had learned from her little insipid sister that Bronwyn had been forced to stay behind at Hunswick.

Luc could only imagine Bronwyn's challenging response to such coercion and headed south to Hunswick. He had hoped to encounter her again on one of her solitary walks and finally play the part of hero.

But today she had not been alone.

Luc had been frozen, staring, unable to turn away as the couple entangled themselves in the act of making love. Slowly, a coldness crept over him and in its wake left an emotional void.

Deadeye Anscombe had taken what was his. And Bronwyn had gone willingly. In doing so, she had forsaken not only him but the future happiness of her sisters.

Soon. Very soon . . . all would pay.

Bronwyn passed through Hunswick's gates determined to enjoy her last night with Ranulf. Tomorrow would come soon enough and with it the end of her happiness. Until then, she was going to bask in the warmth and acceptance she had found in Ranulf's arms.

Just as she emerged into the courtyard, one of the younger farm boys ran up to her side. Tears streamed down his face as he murmured something about how no one was letting him be in the play the village was preparing. Bronwyn slipped off her horse and handed Ranulf her reins. When he popped a teasing brow, she asked, "I give you a choice, take care of the boy or my horse."

"Don't think such maneuvers will always work," Ranulf cackled and jumped off Pertinax's back, keeping her reins with him.

Bronwyn's laughter filled the air. "You chose wisely, my lord. Little Robert here can be quite a handful."

"Huh. Well, I'm going to send someone for your sisters and I'll see you at dinner." Ranulf gave her a wink.

"Soon I hope! I'm starving," she declared, beaming

him an enormous smile as she escorted the boy back across the courtyard.

Ranulf watched appreciatively as she disappeared around the corner toward the Great Hall, focusing her attention on the now very rapid discourse from the want-to-be mummer.

Turning to face the opposite direction, Ranulf guided both horses toward the stables. Halfway to his destination, he spied Tyr and he wasn't alone. Two women were next to him, and both were very beautiful. Bronwyn's sisters had obviously jumped to the same conclusion and decided to return to Hunswick despite his orders to stay away.

Edythe was exactly as Laon described, petite and full figured with vibrant dark red hair marking her maternal Scottish heritage. Her sister was tall, her frame similar to that of Bronwyn's—lithe and naturally graceful. Her striking raven-colored features would make most men cave to her every desire, and he could see, even at a distance, that she was well aware of the fact. The flirtatious interplay between her and Tyr made it obvious she was in many ways still a child and had yet to mature into her body. Experience, wisdom, control—these things she had yet to gain and never would until she was allowed to face and triumph hardships. Her family had not done Lillabet any favors protecting her like they had. Thank God he wasn't going to have to marry her.

But just as the thought disappeared, he snapped it back. Jealousy had awoken him to the truth about his feelings—even if only to himself. The disturbing emotion might be the quickest way to prove just how Bronwyn felt about him.

Resuming his march across the courtyard, Ranulf felt the piercing royal blue eyes of Bronwyn's middle sister. Edythe was as shrewd as she was beautiful and he suspected she was not one to be tangled with. Blank calculating stares like hers spoke as loudly as words. He knew. He had given them enough. Life had taught Edythe not to trust.

He wondered how his Bronwyn, whom he was sure had suffered and endured more than both sisters together, had maintained her goodness and optimism. She naturally sought balance and was even able to impart a little of her strength to him. No longer did Ranulf feel angry or bitter about the past. Instead, he wanted to take whatever he had learned to make his future, and that of these people, better.

Finally seeing him, Tyr waved him over with an uneven grin Ranulf knew not to trust. Tossing both reins to a stable boy, he sauntered over to the threesome. Edythe and Tyr faced him, but Lillabet had shifted so her back was to him, making her unaware of his presence.

Before Ranulf said a word, Tyr gave him a wink, hinting for him to play along. "Um, Lady Lillabet, would you please honor me by repeating your last remark," Tyr requested with hidden mirth.

Lily threw her hand up to her breast in mock protest, moving closer to Tyr's side. "Really?"

"Really," Tyr repeated. "I could use some amusement right now."

Ranulf spied the narrowing of Edythe's eyes and thought he saw her sneak out an arm and elbow Tyr in the side, but if she did, his friend showed no reaction.

"Amusing? Why it's not amusing at all," Lily gushed.

"I'm offering to sacrifice myself into marriage! Of course, I was surprised by the idea, but to save my sisters and keep them in their homes, I have decided to agree. I *will* marry you," she finished, placing a possessive hand on Tyr's forearm.

Tyr's already wide grin grew even bigger. "I appreciate the offer, and while you are indeed a pretty little girl, marriage and I are never to be."

"But the king . . . I thought you had to . . ." Lily sputtered.

"Now, my friend here, Lord Anscombe, I believe he is eager to have a bride," Tyr said, pointing to Ranulf, who wasn't sure if he was amused, insulted, or bored. "Here is your groom. Lord Anscombe of Bassellmere."

Lily whipped around. Her eyes were the color of gray mist and had turned saucer size. Her surprise was genuine, but her next move shocked even Ranulf. Straightening, she took a sizable gulp and announced, "As I was saying, my lord. I am ready and willing to marry you."

Ranulf stole a glance at Edythe, who was ignoring the unfolding situation. Her focus was on Tyr and had been since he had made his nonmarital declaration.

Taking a deep breath, Ranulf returned his gaze to Lily and reminded himself of the plan. Guilt panged him, but not for the lies he was about to tell the young woman, for he was positive Lily had put Bronwyn in the position of lying for her. And Lily's own feelings for him—or lack of them—were certainly not in jeopardy. So his plan held little risk and great reward.

He only regretted the brief distress he was about

to cause Bronwyn by accepting Lily's proposal. It would be worth it, though, when Bronwyn raced down to face him and demand that he retract his promise. After she admitted her feelings, he would then confess his.

This will work. It has to, he vowed to himself.

"Well?" Lily pressured, recapturing Ranulf's attention.

Tyr leaned back on the wooden frame supporting the structure behind him and crossed his arms. "I would also like to hear your answer to this one."

"One what?" Ranulf parroted back.

"I just asked how you intend to protect my sisters if I should marry you."

Ranulf stared at Lily, baffled. "What are you talking about?"

Tyr aimed his chin toward the hills. "She's talking about our overly attentive mercenaries. Seems their master wants Syndlear and intends to marry to get it."

A scowl came across Ranulf's face. He had seriously misjudged his watcher's intentions. Anger, hot and dark, raced over his nerve endings, along with the need to protect Bronwyn and those she loved.

"Once we are married, those angry little scowls won't be allowed," Lily pouted, feeling ignored. "I want a handsome husband . . . or at least as handsome as he could be."

Ranulf fought for patience. "You and I. We need to talk. Starting with just why you asked your sister to lie for you." He didn't *want* to talk to Lily, but he suspected she was the one person who knew everything that was going on and was naïve enough to tell him about it. And if his watcher wasn't after him, but one of Laon's daughters, he needed to know who, why, and just exactly what he wanted.

Edythe watched as the real Lord Anscombe guided her younger sister with a heavy hand to a quiet secluded corner of the bailey. She suspected she should join them, but she was tired of Lily getting away with her whims and it looked like her future husband wasn't as gullible as the rest of the men they had encountered over the years. Neither was his friend.

"I told her that it was a bad idea," Edythe mumbled under her breath.

"Must be nice to know everything."

Edythe sent Tyr a silencing sideways glance. "I'm practical."

"And openly opinionated," Tyr added matter-of-factly.

"*And* usually right," Edythe added, turning to face him squarely. She wished he wasn't so good-looking. Deep dimples, dark hazel eyes, and reddish-brown shoulder-length hair, the color she wished hers were instead of its intense auburn hue, all in a superior male body. Men that handsome weren't to be trusted. "You don't know my sisters like I do."

Tyr grinned down at her. Damn, he was tall. And he wasn't put off one wit by her aggressive demeanor. In fact, he was enjoying it. "Your elder," Tyr began, "is unaware of her underlying beauty, which is probably what makes her such a compassionate leader."

"Perhaps," Edythe tentatively agreed. "But if you truly knew Bronwyn and had not just observed her, you would know that it is her nature. I doubt any change to her appearance would make her any more or less of who she is."

"And you're envious of that."

Those words stung. Edythe had never cowered from the truth. Then again, it rarely was delivered so unsparingly. "Envious, no. I do not covet my sister's nature, nor do I desire to be exactly like her, but I sometimes wish I had more of her restraint." And before he could comment on her admission, she prompted with a slight dare to her voice, "If you know so much, then tell me of Lily or are you too swayed by her beauty?"

"Aye, she's beautiful, but also complicated and young. She is an . . . an opportunist, but not necessarily a selfish one."

"Ha. She can be. Lily's world revolves only around her."

Tyr chuckled and the sound sent ripples of awareness down her arms. "I'd rather talk about you, Lady Edythe."

"I'd rather not."

"Lady Edythe," Tyr repeated, drawing out her name. His forehead wrinkled. "No. Don't like it. A girl like you needs a nickname."

She hadn't been a "girl" for several years, and Edythe was irked that he saw her as such. "That's one thing I'll never want."

"That's a shame. Everyone should have a nickname."

"Really, then what's yours?"

Tyr licked his lips and in a low voice lied, "Bachelor."

"Fitting," Edythe retorted. "I doubt with your type

of self-serving charm, too many women vie to change that status."

Tyr clucked his tongue, completely unfazed by her ridiculous barb. "Ed, I think. Little and sweet . . . just like you."

"Thòin," Edythe hissed and moved to walk away, not dreaming for a second that he would know Gaelic and understand what she meant.

"Bauchle," Tyr chirped back in retaliation. Edythe spun around, her jaw open, but before she could retort, he added, this time with a Scottish brogue, "Ed, even if I didn't know my own language, certain words are known far and wide, and 'ass' is certainly one of them."

Straightening, she puffed out her chest and poked him in the ribs. "I may be many things, but untidy, fat, and your *wife* isn't one of them."

Tyr gulped. It had been a long time since he'd spoken his native tongue to a woman who knew Gaelic and he plucked the wrong insult from memory. He had just remembered it being about a woman and knew it wasn't flattering. "You're right. My apologies. But you, my pretty lady, are in desperate need of a nickname. How about one that is more fitting?"

"I don't want a nickname," she gritted out. *And certainly not one from you,* she hissed to herself. Why did he have to call her pretty? And why did she care?

"Well, *Ruadh,* you got one."

"Red? Lord, you are the most unimaginative—"

"Hmm, when you put it that away . . . Red . . . Ed. Quite memorable and easy to say. I like it!"

"You would. That nickname—if you can call it that—wouldn't suit a kitchen rat."

Tyr shook his head. "I disagree, and just remember that it was you and not I who compared yourself to such a repulsive creature. I would have said . . . a finch. Yes . . . small, loud, and with a sharp beak."

Edythe clenched her jaw and fought from stomping her foot. The man was impossible. To her every retort, he had a counter. "A beak you may want to avoid for I will use it."

His dimples turned into craters. "Aye, my lady, that you most certainly are not afraid of using. I think I actually see the small scars along your wrists and hands from where you missed your intended target and clipped yourself."

Edythe opened her mouth, ready to send out another assault, when the sparkle in his hazel eyes captured her attention. Tyr was not making fun of her. Rather, he was truly enjoying their conversation, and if she was being honest, so was she. Inclining her head in agreement, she curled her lips mischievously and said, "Inflictions all finches must learn to endure."

"Indeed they must," Tyr replied with a bow. "You, Lady Finch, are a genuine surprise. These past few days, your elder sister has been gracious, kind, and all things a lady should be when welcoming a guest, but it seems that only my friend Ranulf can turn her into a fiery tempest. And each time she does, it pulls him farther in. I see now why he is susceptible to such treatment."

Edythe briefly closed her eyes and gave a quick shake to her head. "You *enjoy* being insulted?"

"You have not insulted me, you couldn't. You don't know me well enough. Nor I you. We just merely sparred and I am finding that I like wit in a woman, a most uncommon trait where I have been. If I were not so decided in my ways, you, dear Finch, would be in trouble."

"Well, then I thank the Lord you are decided, for I am not easily swayed by a pretty face and you have a ways to go before you seem even moderately charming. And before you try to convince me otherwise, I must go see to Lily for she is looking overly animated and all too often the results of such excitement negatively affect me. Excuse me, sir."

Tyr bowed and stared as Edythe left his side and headed toward her younger sister. He had not lied. She was probably the most intriguing woman he had ever encountered. But it changed nothing. Marriage was not for him. Still, a pretty redhead with a cunning mind and a sharp tongue would be fun to pass the time with until he had to leave.

Bronwyn paced the floorboards in her room, chiding herself. If one kiss had not been enough, she should have realized that an afternoon in his arms would only create an insatiable yearning. The problem was she had fallen in love with him. With all her heart. And it just might be possible he felt the same about her.

Ranulf was the man she had been waiting for all her life, and now that she had found him, she wasn't sure she could give him up. The motivations behind her lies could all be explained, and if their positions were reversed, would she listen and forgive? Deep down, she knew she would.

He had asked her to trust him, and in that moment, she felt as if he had meant about anything and everything. If she truly loved him, then shouldn't she at least give him the chance?

Tonight, she would tell Ranulf the truth. Explain it all. Who she was, why she'd lied, Luc—everything. And somehow, Ranulf would come up with a plan to protect her and her sisters. And if he couldn't, then Edythe and Lily would have the option to travel north, but she would stay here—with him. With Hunswick and the people whom had known her all of her life.

Feeling the first true rays of hope in days, Bronwyn almost felt giddy, wishing dinner wasn't still several hours away. It did, however, give her enough time for a bath. Tonight, she would pay special attention to her hair. Entering the garderobe to see what other of Lily's frocks Constance had put in there, Bronwyn jumped when the door of her room sprang open and bounced against the stone wall. Something only one person would do.

Lily.

"Lillabet! What are you doing here? Ranulf—"

"Ranulf?" Lily asked as she cocked her head to her side and wrinkled her noise. "I had forgotten that was his name. Lord, what a mouthful."

"Cannot have gotten you here so quickly," Bronwyn finished, her mind racing with the ramifications of her sister's arrival.

Lily waved her hand and giggled. "No, silly, he's the one who sent us away, remember? But don't worry, I spoke to him. He isn't going to send us away again."

Bronwyn blinked several times. "No, of course he won't . . . but *what are you doing here?*"

Lily shook her head, and her whole face broke

out into a huge smile. "First, let me hear you say that I was right! I told you that you should be wearing bright colors and not those old drab ones." She gave Bronwyn a gentle push on the shoulder, compelling her to turn around. "Oh, I brought all your clothes back with me, but this dress is absolutely wonderful on you. I am so glad I left it behind. I would let you keep it except that the material came from Father, but you do look so pretty!"

Bronwyn stepped back with a frown, freeing herself from her sister's spinning grasp. "I'm not going to ask again," she warned.

Lily sauntered over to the bed and leaned against the edge. "I am here to save you and Edythe for a change."

Bronwyn took a deep breath and exhaled, not really in the mood to play games with Lily, yet knowing if she did so, it would be faster. "And just how are you going to do that?"

"Simple. We all three are getting married! And on Christmas. I am marrying his lordship, of course. Edythe is going to wed one of his best friends—who by the way is supposed to be quite wealthy—and lucky *you*, you get his lordship's commander! He tells me that Rolande is *especially* handsome."

Bronwyn grabbed the back of one of the chairs and took a deep breath. "I . . . don't understand. I mean I thought marriage was what you were trying to avoid."

"Well, it won't be a marriage in the real sense . . . for you and Edythe anyway, for the men you're going to marry won't actually be here."

"You mean marriage by proxy."

"Uh-huh. That was on purpose so you and Edythe can get an annulment later."

"But . . . but *marriage*? Why do any of us need to get married?"

"For more time, of course! I mean the best way to avoid marriage . . . *is to already be married*!" Lily gushed. "That will give his lordship time to meet with the new king and end that evil Baron Craven's aspirations," she ended with a scoff.

Bronwyn rubbed her temples. It still sounded as if Lillabet thought *she* was going to be the one to marry Ranulf. Bronwyn had to have misunderstood. "Lily, you are going too fast. I need you to start from the beginning and tell me exactly what Ranulf said."

Lily took a deep breath and exhaled. Then, much more seriously and slowly, she said, "I came back to undo what I did to you. I should never have made you pretend to be me. It's my burden to marry the new lord. So, I came back, saw him, told him who I was, and offered to marry him immediately . . . but only if he agreed to protect you and Edythe. Of course, he asked why you needed protecting, so I explained all about Baron Craven and that is when his lordship came up with this idea. After Twelfthtide is over, we are all going to London and meet with the king and get this whole mess straightened out. Then you and Edythe can get annulments and stay here at Hunswick. It's perfect!"

Bronwyn sank onto the hearth chair next to her. Her mind was spinning with questions, but she needed to ask the most obvious. "Are you *sure* Ranulf wanted you to marry him and not the commander?

I mean I thought you didn't want to marry his lordship and—"

"His commander? Are you worried? Don't be. I had his lordship describe them to me and they sound perfect. Edythe is going to marry his best friend, Garid . . . Garik—I can't remember, but they will live at Syndlear. He is supposedly a quiet man, who is not considered by most handsome, but neither is he hideous. But his lordship specifically said that *you* get to marry his commander Rolande and that way you can remain here at Hunswick!"

Hearing Lily keep referring to Ranulf as his lordship was driving Bronwyn insane. She stared at the floor, forcing herself to breathe. It was true. She should have realized it minutes ago when Lily mentioned that she had spoken with Ranulf. He had met Lily . . . he had *seen* her. Coupled with the fact that Bronwyn had lied to him, he obviously felt nothing but antipathy for her. "Um, how did . . . his lordship . . . take it when he found out I had been lying to him?"

Lily swished her hand. "Oh, that. I tried to apologize, but it seems he knew the whole time."

If Bronwyn thought she was in a state of shock before, she was truly in one now. Ranulf had been toying with her. She felt sick. How could she have been so stupid? He *knew* the first time he saw her she could not have been the famed Lily, his real bride. How many times did she need to learn the fickleness of a man's heart when in the presence of astounding beauty?

But nothing in her past had prepared her for this. This time she wasn't just to be rejected . . . but replaced.

"Are you sure you want to marry him, Lily? Marriage is a serious vow and you really don't know the man."

Lily rolled her eyes. "Who really knows anyone before they marry? And while his lordship may not be very handsome, he is exceptionally clever, don't you think? I mean, he did come up with the plan to save us all and let us stay."

"Yes, very clever," Bronwyn murmured. "But just what if things cannot be 'resolved' with the new king?"

Lily shrugged and twisted her hands chaotically. "Well, then you are protected through your marriage. His lordship assured me that his best friend would honor the agreement and his commander would have to if he ordered it. So do you?"

Bronwyn blinked, not understanding the question. "Do I what?"

"Do you accept?" Lily asked with exasperation. "His lordship said that the marriages would take place only if both you and Edythe agreed to the plan. Edythe said that she would do whatever you want, but you and I both know she would rather stay here than go to Scotland. Syndlear is her home. So please? I would miss you so much."

Bronwyn stared incredulously at her little sister. Lillabet actually seemed serious about marrying Ranulf regardless of Bronwyn's decision. "You really want this? If you marry him, then you understand that you cannot change your mind. Lord Anscombe is *here* and will undoubtedly claim his rights on your wedding night."

Lily sprang off the bed and kneeled down by Bronwyn's chair, nodding her head enthusiastically. "To be married to a wealthy nobleman who is close friends with the most powerful king in the world? Yes, I would. I mean I don't think he would be my pick if it weren't for the situation, but you have always told me that someday I would have to grow up and face life as it is and not how I want it to be. So here I am doing just that. His lordship is a good man—I mean you wouldn't have stayed to help him if he wasn't. So please say yes."

The reminder that it had been her choice to stay was a sharp prod to the gut. Bronwyn's pride finally bubbled to the surface, pushing all her other emotions—anger, shame, even jealousy—aside. Ranulf was shallow, but so was Lily. They were ideally suited for each other. "I happen to think this plan is perfect. It solves everything. My only reservation was your happiness, and if you truly want to do this, then Christmas weddings we shall have. I am actually looking forward to the day."

And she was, but not for the reasons Lily believed.

"Wonderful! Come and let's go tell his lordship. They will all be excited."

Bronwyn stood up and walked over to open the door. "No, you go down and tell everyone that I am relieved by the solution and couldn't be happier with the plan. I hope you and Edythe don't mind, but I think tonight I would like to eat alone. All the riding today tired me out more than I realized."

Lily widened her eyes and let go a small shrug of her shoulders as she moved toward the exit. She gave Bronwyn one last hug and kiss and then exclaimed, "Won't Father Morrell be surprised when he arrives tomorrow?"

Bronwyn nodded as a picture of the pudgy conservative priest's expression flashed through her mind. The man's already ruddy face exploded with color. There was a very good chance he wouldn't perform the ceremony on such short notice and it being proxy. And if he refused, Bronwyn wasn't sure how she would feel . . . relieved? Or hopeful?

Chapter Six

The Eve of the Nativity in medieval times primarily meant no more than the night before Christmas, the day observed as the birth of Christ. Modern-day religious traditions developed over the past few centuries. Some customs, such as decorating the Christmas tree, have related pagan roots, but primarily stem from mid-nineteenth-century influences. However, the Eastern Christian orthodoxy did practice a very strict fast day called Paramony through Christmas Eve, unlike the Western Church, which holds a Midnight Mass, typically performed much earlier in the evening.

The midnight hour passed, making it Christmas Eve and the beginning of possibly the worst day Ranulf could remember. The embers in the hearth were dying and he had no more logs for the fire. For hours, he had paced the planks of his solar unceasingly and every once in a while out of frustration and the need to do anything physical, he tossed a piece of wood violently into the flames. As a result, the room was hot, he ran out of logs, and his mind was no calmer for the effort. Over and over again, his thoughts repeated the folly of his decision and how he had been deceived.

Ranulf spun a small clay pot in his hand, the last happy duty he had attended to before Lily had relayed the bad news of Bronwyn's happy acceptance of his offer. The pot plus dozens more would be ready for St. Stephen's Day. His father had never observed the tradition of giving thanks to those who worked for him—especially monetarily—but Ranulf had the means and for the first time felt the compulsion. Tossing the pot onto the hearth chair across from him, Ranulf glanced at the tray of food to his side. The goose was the first meat that had been prepared and offered since his arrival and he had not even touched it. Everything about the meal reminded him of his perfect afternoon and how it had gone so wrong.

Sinking down in the chair, Ranulf intertwined his fingers over his stomach and stared at the ceiling. Nothing had gone according to plan and he could not fathom why. Making love to Bronwyn had been indescribable, emotionally wedding him to her for life. He had thought their coupling had meant as much to her. He had never intended for their first time to be in such rustic conditions—or to be so fast—but at the time, it had not mattered. Even now, when he conjured up the memory of her face and reaction to his touch, he knew—*knew*—she had connected with him, and not just physically, but emotionally. He certainly knew what it was like to be with a woman who felt nothing. So, why? Why was Bronwyn so eager to marry another man? And why was she so accepting of him with her sister?

When Lily had reemerged with the news of Bronwyn's full support to his plan, Ranulf had refused to believe it. Thinking just her pride had been pricked, he had been seconds away from marching up the Great Hall backstairs when Lily completed her accounting. Bronwyn had not just acquiesced to the idea, but had been eager to participate in it—all of it. Applauding his solution as perfect and looking forward to her union with his much younger, and much handsomer, commander. Ranulf made Lily repeat it twice, each time affirming that those were indeed Bronwyn's sentiments.

Ranulf pushed himself back to his feet and plodded to the window. With his hand on the frame, he locked his arm and leaned forward to look down at the courtyard. A few torches were lit, casting moving shadows in the breeze, indicative of his own mental state.

The idea of Bronwyn in his commander's arms was intolerable. Rolande, of all people! Why did he have to suggest *him*! But he knew the answer. Because Rolande would have been perfect for Lily.

The man was an incredible soldier and a damn good leader, but he was also exceedingly good-looking with jet-black hair, a tall muscular frame, and a suave personality that made Tyr's attempts to woo women look amateurish. Incredibly charming and very polished, Rolande knew just how to enchant a woman. His reputation was known to all, which was why Tyr had cornered Ranulf that evening about his ludicrous idea for a "solution." His friend had held nothing back, letting Ranulf know just what an idiot Tyr believed him to be.

Instinct and pride had caused Ranulf to blank his expression and hide his true feelings from his friend, but in truth, Ranulf had felt physically ill. Testing Bronwyn to prove her feelings for him had seemed like the perfect idea. But jealousy stemmed from deep emotion. Something Bronwyn obviously did not feel; otherwise she wouldn't have readily agreed to wed someone else. He had been a mere itch she had had for days, and once he had finally let her scratch it, she desired him no more.

And now he was pledged to Lillabet. Pretty girl, undeniably attractive—to all but him.

Almost every one of his men had stared at his supposed wife-to-be during the dinner service. And Ranulf couldn't blame them. If a man could dream up the most beautiful woman ever created, most would conjure Lily. And while Ranulf could acknowledge her beauty, the attraction and driving need to hold and caress her he had experienced with Bronwyn was not just lacking, it was nonexistent.

Understanding suddenly slammed into Ranulf. He lifted his hand from the window frame and slammed it back in place. How could he have been so blind? Lily possessed the type of beauty that captured young men's attentions and probably changed the mind of more than one suitor originally interested in Bronwyn. Could she believe his feelings for her to be so fickle? Didn't she know that she would always be the most beautiful woman he had ever seen, for she was the first to truly see him?

Damn woman just didn't trust him enough. Well, she better learn how. In the meantime, he wasn't going to let her punish them both with another sleepless night.

Bronwyn jumped at the abrupt and very loud pounding at her door. She pushed herself up to a sitting position on her bed and glanced out the window. It was pitch-black outside, hours before dawn. Only one person would be causing a commotion at such an hour and be able to get away with it. Ranulf. She rubbed her eyes and tried to ignore the deafening banging, hoping he would get the hint. He did not.

"Bronwyn, open this door or I swear on all the things you hold sacred, I will break it down."

Bronwyn slid her fingernails along her scalp and then through her hair. She wasn't ready to see him. What she needed was distance and had intended to minimize their meetings and, most of all, keep them public. Seeing him at night—especially alone— would be a form of torture and her heart was not prepared for the pain.

Unfortunately, her opinion did not matter.

Grabbing her shift, she threw it on, followed by her robe. Squaring her shoulders, she strolled over to the door and opened it. She leveled her slate blue eyes directly at his amber gaze. "What do you want?" she asked pointedly.

The moment the door slipped away beneath Ranulf's fist as she opened it, his heart had stopped. It had been racing with anticipation, but the second he saw her, he froze and stared, in shock. A pink crease line ran down her cheek. "You've been sleeping!" he bellowed, barging his way into the room. All this time, he had been frantic, concerned that Bronwyn was upset with him, worried about her feelings . . . and instead of weeping inconsolably, she had been blissfully unconscious.

Bronwyn flicked the door closed, turned to face her accuser, and admitted her guilt. "Maybe it's because I have had little sleep during the past few nights!"

Ranulf walked over and inspected the plate of food that had been sent up earlier that evening. It looked completely untouched, strange for someone who had declared herself to be starving when they returned. Maybe the afternoon's events hadn't left her quite as unaffected as she appeared. Pointing at the uneaten dish, he demanded, "Are you trying to starve yourself?"

"I wasn't hungry," Bronwyn ground out defiantly.

Cursing under his breath, Ranulf clutched the back of one chair and spun it around. "Sit down and eat."

Bronwyn stood firm, determined not to capitulate. Unfortunately, Ranulf was not in the mood to restrict their contest of wills to defiant stares and silence. In two steps, he was by her side, deflecting her attempts to push against his chest and keep him from advancing. He snatched her arm and Bronwyn yelped involuntarily. Growling, he moved his grip to her elbow and forcibly sat her in the chair. "Do not move." And then he pointed to the food. "Eat."

Bronwyn ignored the second order and watched him rummage through her things as he had before. When he pulled out another piece of linen and began ripping, she said, trying to discourage him, "My arm is fine. Just tender."

Seizing the basin of water, he walked back and

knelt down by her side, gesturing for her to out-stretch her arm. Exasperated, Bronwyn did as com-manded, knowing it would be easier than arguing. "You really are a beast."

A low hum of a chuckle rumbled through Ranulf's chest. "I've been called a beast before, but not be-cause I had bullied someone into letting me nurture them."

Bronwyn watched as he carefully pulled back her sleeve and unwrapped the binding. Relief flashed across his face. The wound had scabbed over and was just as she claimed, healing well. Bronwyn closed her eyes and took a deep breath. She could not do this. She could not let him continue to play with her feelings. Maybe he didn't know, maybe he didn't care. He had stolen her heart, and she needed to protect what little bit of her self-respect she had left.

"Thank you," she said in a soft voice. "I want you to know that I never meant to lie to you. I had to . . . for my sister."

"I know."

"Yes, you did," Bronwyn mumbled, reminded how enormous her folly had been. "How long did you know who I really was?"

Tossing the bloody binding aside, he tenderly bandaged her arm with the new cloth. "From the be-ginning."

From the beginning, she repeated to herself. He had been amusing himself. Rallying, she continued with more conviction, "Well, I'm glad we are both free now of our deception and can go forward as you have planned. I hope Lily told you how happy I was by the offer to marry your commander."

"She mentioned it," Ranulf grimaced.

"Who knows? Maybe Rolande and I will meet and decide to stay together, forgoing the annulment."

Ranulf rocked back on his feet, picked up the basin, and stood up, causing water to slosh on to the floor from the abrupt movement. She sounded so damn *happy*. He plopped the water bowl back on its table. And why shouldn't she be? "You will like my commander. He is as handsome as Lillabet is beautiful."

Pain flashed in Bronwyn's eyes, turning them dark, almost black. If Ranulf's aim had been to hurt, he had struck true, resulting in a desire to inflict similar anguish. "As long as he doesn't lie to me and make me out the fool, I will be content."

"I suspect he won't if you don't lie to him first."

Bronwyn pushed herself out of the chair as a frisson of anger shot up her spine. "Maybe I won't if he doesn't order me away from my home without the courage to look me in the eye when he does so."

"I never pretended to be someone else."

"In that you are correct, my lord. You made it very clear from the beginning that you were a hateful man," she seethed.

"Didn't seem to bother you when you used your female wiles to entice me to your bed," Ranulf hissed back.

Bronwyn marched over to the door and swung it wide open. "I wonder just how my sister will deal with your barbarism. She is sweet, beautiful, and innocent, but she also knows nothing about running a castle. So prepare yourself, my lord. In a few months you will have a rundown estate and no commander either, for after I use my *feminine wiles* on him, I doubt we will be staying here at Hunswick."

Ranulf stomped over and grabbed the handle from her hands. "Lily may be far less capable, but she has the only thing I ever demanded in a woman. She was honest."

The door slammed and the reverberating sound bounced back and forth down the hall. Edythe and Lily sat perfectly still and stared at each other, eyes wide open. For once, their thoughts were in accord.

When Ranulf had first arrived and started banging on Bronwyn's door, both had awakened wondering if they should do something. When the racket ceased, Lily scurried into Edythe's room. "What's going on?"

"I don't know," came Edythe's simple reply.

"Why is Ranulf so angry with Bronwyn?"

Again Edythe shrugged.

"Well, should we go and see if Bronwyn needs help?"

Edythe bit her bottom lip. The situation was foreign to her. She supposed they should go, but her gut was telling her to stay put. She was still debating the decision when voices rose again, and this time Bronwyn's was in the mix. And she *never* yelled.

The door slammed and heavy footsteps retreated. "I think . . . I think I was just insulted," Lily mumbled. "By both of them."

Seeing the stunned look in Lily's gray eyes, Edythe reached over to pacify her. "They also said some flattering things."

Lily slipped out of the embrace and shook her head. "Edythe, what have I done?"

"What do you mean?"

Lily bounded off the bed and passionately stabbed her finger toward the wall separating Edythe's and Bronwyn's room. "Them! Didn't you hear?"

Edythe nodded her head in relief. "I did. I just wasn't sure you had."

Slump-shouldered, Lily returned to the bed and collapsed on it. "Oh Lord, Edythe, I just announced to everyone that I was going to marry the man our sister loves."

"It's my guess that he loves her, too."

"I have to go and say something. Stop this. Take it back."

Edythe reached out and seized Lily's arm before she bounded off the bed again. "Do you think either of them is going to let you? Pride is dictating their actions right now. Neither is going to listen to anyone as angry as they are. They'll marry as planned just to spite the other."

"Then we better think of a way to stop them— and fast."

Edythe took a deep breath and held it for a second before letting it go. It was still early in the morning and it would be hours before the day began, but when it did, they had to have a plan. "You're right. But we're going to need help."

Edythe stretched her neck as far as it would go in an effort to see above those around her. Being short had its advantages, but in her opinion, it had far many more drawbacks.

Today had been a lesson in patience, and for once, Lily had not been the cause. The first test had been unexpected, though in hindsight Edythe should have predicted Bronwyn's resistance to participating in the Nativity ceremonies. Rarely was her sister stubborn against the wishes of her family and friends, but today mining the Cumbrian Hills for granite would have been easier. If it had not been for Father Morrell's timely arrival and subsequent pressure for *all* to be present at his sermon, Bronwyn would have remained in her room perfectly miserable, though claiming to be content.

Edythe's second, and if possible, even more infuriating trial had come in the form of a burly Highlander. Tyr had agreed with her goal of getting Bronwyn and Ranulf together, but not in his involvement. It was not until Edythe promised that the misery she'd rain down on him would be far greater than Ranulf's revenge that Tyr resigned himself to his fate.

Edythe stretched her neck again, searching the crowd. Finally, she saw Tyr winding through the families that were sitting around the semilarge bonfire situated in the bulging end of the courtyard. She widened her eyes and lifted her chin, clearly suggesting he hurry up. Tyr's response was to slide his tongue across his teeth and accentuate his swagger, slowing down his gait.

Huffing, Edythe edged away from Bronwyn's side and glanced at Ranulf. At least he was following the plan, although unwittingly. He had arrived and dutifully sat by Lillabet after she beckoned him to the spot next to her. He looked miserable and desperate. Almost as depressed as Bronwyn. This plan had to work.

Tyr sauntered up to the quiet group. "You look

beautiful tonight, Lady Bronwyn," he said in an excessively silky voice, all the while looking at Edythe.

Her bright blue eyes issued him a lancing stare at his ridiculously dramatic tone. Tyr shrugged back and squatted next to Bronwyn.

Lillabet saw the exchange and, fearing that Ranulf would catch on to Tyr's lack of sincerity, quickly diverted the conversation. "How is Christmas celebrated at court? Do they fast through the Eve of the Nativity, or are they persuaded, as Father Morrell is, to bring the event in with celebration . . . and food?" she asked and then daintily popped another piece of meat into her mouth.

"I suspect Father Morrell's preference for food and merriment is much related to the size of his girth," Edythe murmured through her pursed lips. Silence followed. Nothing was happening, and at this rate, nothing would and both of them would be married for several years before either admitted to themselves their true feelings, let alone to each other.

"Well, I love our traditions. Lord Anscombe—your cousin," Lily said, nudging Ranulf with her elbow, "created this one of starting the season outside, sitting around a bonfire with friends, family, and . . . loved ones." She leaned over and plopped a small chaste kiss on Ranulf's cheek.

Edythe saw the very slight, but definite recoil. *Excellent*, she thought. *Yes, Lily, keep reminding them both of how awful it will be . . .*

Tyr reached out to get a plate of food being distributed by a servant and handed it to Bronwyn, who gave him a thoughtful smile of thanks. Ranulf, who had been covertly watching the scene, let go a small grunt. Bronwyn picked up a piece of bread and started pulling it apart, but did not eat it.

A heavy stillness overcame the small group as Edythe and Lily searched for something to say or do to advance their cause. Meanwhile, Tyr, Ranulf, and Bronwyn waited for an opportunity to escape. Before either occurred, one of Ranulf's men, Tory, oblivious to the tension surrounding him, asked, "May I offer my congratulations, my lord? Not a woman in the world compares to your bride in beauty."

Lily typically basked in such praise, but tonight, all she could do was groan and give a dismissive wave at the good-looking soldier in hopes that he would leave before opening his mouth again. Meanwhile, Edythe crossed her arms to hide her hand pinching Tyr into action.

Just as covertly he snatched her fingers and squeezed them until he heard Edythe's sharp intake of breath. He did not need her encouragement. He could see the hurt echoing in Bronwyn's eyes and it angered him to see her in such pain, first by his friend and now by a soldier's careless remarks. Leaning over to Bronwyn, he whispered in her ear, "Tory's wrong, my lady. You are far prettier and far more attractive."

Edythe smiled. Tyr's tone was perfect. Sincere and just loud enough for everyone to hear. She lowered her eyes and covertly studied Ranulf. The man did not move. Nothing. Not even a quick look of disapproval. Edythe risked another poke at Tyr, this time removing her hand quickly before he could capture it in another viselike grip.

Tyr's reaction was immediate as she suddenly

found herself the object of a very angry and palpable stare. She swallowed and looked away, knowing she had just pushed the Highlander too far. *Well, if you don't try harder to make your friend jealous, a small poke in the side will seem trivial compared to what I will do to you, Tyr Dequhar,* she vowed, but only to herself.

Moments later, relief flooded her though when Tyr reached behind Bronwyn and awkwardly pulled her wrap around her. "You look troubled, my lady, for a woman about to get married. Don't be. Rolande is an exceptional man with a unique ability to make any woman feel very comfortable—and what I understand—very happy in his arms."

Edythe's head jerked up and she stared open-mouthed at Tyr. Was the man obtuse? How was openly telling her sister that her future husband had been with many women and made them all very deliriously happy going to help?

Tyr returned her stare with a smirk that said many things, including, *"What? Why are you looking at me like that? You wanted a reaction and I gave you one."*

Edythe squeezed her eyes shut but reopened them immediately upon Lily's gasp. Ranulf was standing, looking down. "Good night, Lady Lillabet. I will see you in the morning in the chapel." Then he issued a single pointed stare at Bronwyn—the first direct look he had given her all evening, and added, "And good night to you, *my lady.* May tomorrow bring you the future comfort and happiness you deserve."

Then he turned, and all the heads and eyes in the crowd followed Ranulf across the courtyard as he headed alone toward the Tower Keep. *My lady,* he had said. Those two words Ranulf had emphasized conveyed more than a thousand speeches. If there was any doubt Edythe had about his feelings that erased it. Ranulf had practically announced to all present that, despite everything, Bronwyn was not just a lady, but *his* lady. He also made it clear that it made no difference.

When he finally disappeared from view, Bronwyn in turn, rose and nodded to Father Morrell. "I . . . I'm sorry, Father. Your sermon was lovely as always, but I am fatigued from all the preparations." Then she flashed Tyr a brilliant smile that would have deceived anyone unless they saw the tears gathering in her eyes. "Tomorrow, then?" she asked.

Tyr nodded and Bronwyn pivoted, moving toward the Great Hall and her bedchambers above.

"Do something!" Edythe hissed.

Tyr rolled his eyes and murmured, "Haven't I done enough?" But seeing Edythe's imploring look, he jumped up and joined Bronwyn before she passed through the large two-door entrance.

"My lady," he began, reaching out and clutching her arm to stop her, "Ranulf knows not the mistake he is making."

Misunderstanding, Bronwyn shook her head in disagreement. "If that is true, then it is a mistake every man alive wants to make. My whole life, all prefer my sister Lily. And they should. She is sweet, good, and beautiful."

Tyr shrugged his chin and crossed his arms. "Aye, she is indeed handsome, but I have known Ranulf a long time. He won't be happy with her. Lily won't challenge him."

"Like Edythe challenges you?"

Tyr rolled his eyes, bobbing his head side to side,

not denying the accusation. "Aye, Finch is a far more palatable companion for life," he chuckled, not denying the accusation. "It is a good thing for us both that I have sworn never to marry or I just might be vulnerable to someone like her."

Bronwyn cocked her head to the right, but she did not pry. "You're a good man and loyal friend, Tyr. I am glad it is you I shall be standing next to in the morning."

Tyr swallowed, seeing the sadness in Bronwyn's eyes. Damn his friend for doing this. "Neither of you have to, you know. Get married. If you are doing this because of that baron Lily mentioned, I can assure you that Ranulf—even I—would protect you three."

"No," Bronwyn said quietly but with unwavering conviction. "That would mean fighting and death. I will not have that on my conscious when it can be easily avoided. I'll marry to ensure Edythe is safely protected and then I think I will leave. Edythe can stay at Syndlear. She loves it more than any of us."

"Leave?" Tyr choked in surprise. He wondered if Ranulf knew about this part of Bronwyn's plan.

She took a deep breath and looked around, hugging her arms. "My being here . . . would be too hard, you know, with memories of my father everywhere and . . . honestly I don't think marriage was ever my destiny, especially with someone I don't know. Even with a handsome charmer like Rolande," she inserted with a bit of joviality. Then more seriously, she continued, "I'm actually eager to leave. Starting a new life, with my mother's family that I have never had the opportunity to get to know . . . that has an appeal to me, now more than ever."

Tyr didn't say a word. She looked hopeful and he did not know how to tell her that it was all for naught. Ranulf would never allow Bronwyn to leave, despite his more recent actions and words. Her only hope was to disappear tonight and Tyr almost encouraged her to do so, for it was probably the only way to get Ranulf to admit to his feelings before he promised himself to a life of misery.

Edythe repressed the urge to run up and shake Bronwyn until she came to her senses. Anyone looking at either Ranulf or her sister could see the depth of their feelings. Unfortunately, they were equally stubborn, which spelled doom for them both.

"What are we going to do?" Lily asked as she stared at the huge flames of the bonfire. Her forlorn voice echoed Edythe's own concerns. "We can't force them to marry."

Edythe gave a quick shake of the head, agreeing with her younger sister. Coercion in any form was not the answer. Whenever she tried to pressure Bronwyn into or out of something—whether it was big or small—she had always failed. Not even their father or Lily had such power. "Both have too much pride. And tomorrow they will regret the power it has over them."

"If only we could *make* them marry each other. Leave them without any other choice."

Edythe blinked as Lily's passing comment began to take form. She glanced back and verified that Father Morrell was not in hearing distance. "Maybe, dear sister, we can." Then without warning, Edythe jumped up and ran toward Tyr, whose long stride was aimed purposefully at the Tower Keep. "Tyr, we need to talk."

He stopped in midstride and looked down at her petite form. "No, *we* don't need to talk, Finch. Ranulf and I do," he clarified and recommenced his march.

Edythe picked up her gown and ran to get in front of him. "Wait. Do you really think one more conversation is going to change anything?"

"No," Tyr growled. "But something needs to be done. Ranulf isn't acting rationally. I thought he would calm down from whatever made him mad and see reason by now, but I actually think he is going to marry your nit-wit of a sister and she is going to let him!"

"She only agreed because that's what she thought everyone wanted her to do!"

"Well, Lily picked a perfect time to start thinking of others."

"At least she is willing to do something drastic to save her sister from misery. Are you just as loyal?"

Tyr raked his fingers through his dark auburn hair, rubbing his scalp in frustration. "It's not a question of loyalty. I'm just at a loss as to how to stop a wedding two people are determined to have."

Edythe's lips curled into a very large and very mischievous smile. "Who said anything about *stopping* the wedding?"

Tyr paused, arched a brow in curiosity, and then lightly tapped the end of Edythe's nose with the tip of his finger. "Just what crazy plan do you have in mind this time, Finch? And it better not involve the silly notion of jealousy."

Edythe swatted his hand away, ruffled that he treated her like a child when it was the last thing she felt when around him. "Fine, I admit my first plan didn't work, just as you predicted. But this will. *If* you could use all that charm in a more productive manner and manage just one or two things."

Tyr listened as Edythe carefully detailed her idea. It was crazy and things would have to be timed perfectly, but he had to acknowledge that this one had the potential of actually being successful. Grinning, he nodded in agreement to his role in the latest plan. "You know, Finch, I actually think I like the way your mind works."

Oh, there would be a wedding, just as foretold. Only it would be unlike any ever heard of.

Chapter Seven

Saturday, December 25, 1154
Christmas, The Feast of the Nativity

Christmas is the annual celebration of the birth of Jesus Christ and typically involves a lengthy mass followed by a great feast. In the first millennium, pagan Yule celebrations still had enormous influence in Christian communities, and therefore, the holiday ranked low in importance and prominence compared to other feasts during this time of year, most notably Twelfth Night. It was not until the crowning of Charlemagne in 800, then Kind Edmund the Martyr in 855 and England's king William I in 1066, that December 25 became a more notable date for celebration in the Christian world.

"Edythe, no!" Bronwyn hissed through gritted teeth. It was humiliating enough participating in the wedding farce, and she was not about to add wearing a wimple on top of it. The severe white headdress was confining, uncomfortable, and—in her opinion—

ugly. Why both her sisters thought such a contraption should be worn during the ceremony was beyond her. The only saving grace of the day was that her father wasn't there to see it and be disappointed.

Gripping the white prison in her hand, Edythe shoved the garment toward Bronwyn. "I don't want to wear one either, but Lily does, and since she is the one who really *is* getting married today, we are going to oblige her. You are the only one not ready."

Bronwyn snatched the wadded mass from her sister's grasp, and Edythe gulped in relief. Bronwyn's touching the dreaded thing was the first step in convincing her to wear it. And she had to—all three of them did. Facial covering was crucial if this was to work.

"But why?" Bronwyn moaned, unbundling the now wrinkled clump. She started to re-form the distorted wire frame, her face full of aversion. "It's only Tyr and he has seen me in my net many times before."

Edythe grimaced and threw her hands up in the air, murmuring that she knew this was going to be the hard part. Lily sat down by Bronwyn and held her hand. "Please, do this for me."

"I already agreed to the dress."

Lily licked her lips. "I know it sounds ridiculous, but I will feel much more comfortable about my own vows if we are all dressed more traditionally. I need your support."

Bronwyn rolled her eyes. "Covering one's face is traditional? I have never heard such nonsense. Besides it sounds dangerous. Don't you want to be looking at your groom when he makes his vows?"

Lily shook her head and Bronwyn exhaled, believing she finally understood. "Then don't marry him. We can still leave—"

Lily closed her eyes and squeezed Bronwyn's fingers. "You misunderstand. I want to marry today. Very much. I will say my vows with no reservations. But I won't be able to—"

"Unless we agree to wear *these*." Bronwyn lifted hers up and tried one last time to change her sister's mind. "Mine is terribly wrinkled. Not at all appealing."

Lily kissed Bronwyn's cheek. "It will be fine. I'll see if the cook can lay something hot on it to remove some of the larger creases."

Edythe leaned against the window frame as the tension moved from one hurdle to another. Almost an hour ago just after dawn, Tyr had entered the chapel and he had yet to emerge, which could only mean one thing. He was having as much difficulty with Father Morrell as she was with Bronwyn. Then, as if he heard her thoughts, Tyr stepped out from the small enclosure and headed straight toward the Hall, most likely to find her. "I'll be right back. I'm just going to run down and check to make sure all is ready," Edythe gushed and then flew out of Bronwyn's bedchambers before her sisters could stop her.

Rushing down the back stairs, she slowed upon entering the large room just as Tyr came through the main entrance. She wiggled her finger for him to follow her outside and behind the small wooden building where the fur pelts from recent kills were hanging to dry. He stopped right beside her, not touching, but close enough to be unnerving.

Tyr reached down and flicked the stiff covering on the wimple. "Attractive," he teased.

She swatted his hand away. "Stop it. It's necessary."

His hazel eyes openly appraised her deep green gown and sparkled with approval, causing her racing heart to skip a beat. "No, I mean it. You, Finch, look incredible. Your sapphirine eyes could snatch a man's soul."

Edythe couldn't tell if Tyr was serious or not. His grin was enormous, making his dimples even more prominent and alluring. The man was devastatingly handsome and he knew it. *Flatter me all you want, Highlander, I'm immune to your charm,* she told herself, knowing deep down that it wasn't exactly true. "Never took you to be an admirer of wimples."

"I'm not. It should be a crime to hide your thick red mane," Tyr said seductively as he fingered the long white linen as if it were a lock of hair.

"Ha!" Edythe exclaimed with a snort. "You have no idea what my hair looks like as I have always worn it up and in braids."

Tyr leaned in close until his mouth brushed her ear. "Maybe you're right. Some redheads do tend to have hair that is unkempt and quite unpleasant. You may be providing a service of mercy by hiding it even now."

Edythe cocked a brow and smiled impishly. Time to fight back. She wasn't a practiced flirt—not like Lily—but she did know how. What was more, she knew exactly what would rattle Tyr. Walking her fingers up his chest, she whispered, "Aye, it is a kindness, for my hair is long, wild, and incredibly soft. But since I have chosen to marry another, you will live in want to discover if what I say is true."

"You marry another only because *I* refused to marry *you.*"

Edythe tilted her head back until they locked

gazes. "I would be insulted, but you refuse to marry anyone."

"You and every other woman are lucky that I know my limits."

"Aye," Edythe replied, mocking his burr. "Besides I understand the man I am to wed is far better than you."

Tyr took a step back, suddenly needing space. "You didn't choose him, I did. Ranulf asked me what I thought. So know this, Finch, your husband is the man *I* selected."

"Well, it won't matter unless you were able to convince Father Morrell about the ceremonies. You were in there a long time."

"Where's your faith? I was so good at convincing him of our plan, the man probably would profess it was his idea."

"*Our* plan?" Edythe repeated, unable to hide her mirth.

"You wouldn't begrudge me a little credit, especially as it would enable me to tease Ranulf with the fact for the rest of his life."

Edythe laughed aloud, wishing that she could keep from turning soft inside when Tyr smiled at her. "In that case, did Father Morrell agree to *all* of *our* plan?"

"Everything. I told him that due to the unusual circumstances and to keep the villagers focused on Christmas and not their lord and new lady, maybe it would be best to have the ceremonies without an audience and in the order you suggested."

"So all we have to do is keep everyone from meeting until it is too late."

Tyr nodded. "See if you can persuade Bronwyn

to wait in the inner close on the other side of the chapel. There, she won't see anyone coming in and out, and even more importantly, no one will see her."

"What about his lordship?"

Tyr licked his lips, unconcerned at the notion. "Ranulf will be easy. He already told me to come get him only when it was time. A most uneager groom."

"He said that?"

"No, but one of the servants told me that if any message was to arrive from Lady Bronwyn, he was to be notified immediately, even if that meant interrupting his own wedding ceremony."

Edythe frowned. "I overheard Bronwyn give similar instructions to Constance this morning."

"All we can do now is bring them to the altar."

"Afterward they are going to have to clean up their own messes."

Tyr laughed out loud and nodded his head. "Agreed," he said, intertwining her arm with his as he escorted her back around the shack and toward the chapel.

Neither had been aware they had been observed the entire time.

Ranulf told himself for the tenth time to look away, but he continued to stare at the couple conversing directly below. He could not see Bronwyn's face as she was wearing a wimple and the angle was almost vertical, but he could make out Tyr's demeanor.

At first, Ranulf thought they were discussing the upcoming nuptials, as Tyr was going to stand in for Rolande. He watched his friend's demeanor intently, waiting for a sign that Bronwyn had changed her mind, but the conversation looked far from controversial. It looked almost intimate with Tyr whispering in her ear and she remaining close.

Ranulf felt a wave of jealousy hit him, but before he could act on it, Tyr pulled back. His face had grown animated as if he was sincerely excited . . . and then he laughed. A real laugh, not the half chuckle his friend typically produced when amused, but the type that originated from within and was almost always shared.

Ranulf's apprehension about his decision suddenly vanished. After witnessing Bronwyn's lethargy last night, he had considered stopping the proceedings and ending the farce. At the very least, he had decided he wasn't going to marry Lily. But if Bronwyn could feel such ease and merriment at the prospect of his marrying her sister, then why shouldn't he? Lillabet was undeniably beautiful and most likely would be compliant and unchallenging as long as he adorned her with pretty dresses and mollified her with infrequent trips to court. She wouldn't provide him passion, but she would give him sons. It would be enough.

I'll marry her, angel, and find a way to forget you as you have forgotten me.

Ranulf stirred at the sound of someone knocking. He rose from the hearth chair and opened the door, surprised to see a small servant boy and not Tyr telling him it was time. His friend had no doubt already served as proxy and Bronwyn was now married. He scowled at the lad, who scampered away immediately, leaving Ranulf to descend the staircase and walk toward the chapel alone.

Aside from a few people who were shuffling around the stables, not a soul was in sight at the nether bailey. Perhaps they were all inside the chapel, waiting.

The morning sun burst into the dark room as he opened the doors. With the exception of Lillabet and the priest already at the altar, the place was empty. The door closed behind him. At the sound, he could see Lily's back stiffen. She didn't turn around and he was glad. He did not want to see her expectant shining face and be forced to smile in return.

Unhurried, he moved down the center aisle to her side, reminding himself that he was lucky. He had never thought to marry at all, let alone to someone all men desired. And he should desire Lily. She was beautiful. Her figure swathed in silver was similar to Bronwyn's, tall, lithe, and curvaceous in just the right ways, but without Bronwyn's spirit, she was just a pretty face.

Arriving at Lily's side, he looked down and saw the damp spot darkening the shimmering silk sleeve. Another drop fell onto the garment. Lily was crying. If she was this upset at the altar, what would she do in his bed? Suddenly, he didn't care. Relief flooded through him as if a great weight had suddenly been lifted.

Before Father Morrell could start his speech, Ranulf turned toward her, picked up her hand, and said, "Lily, I cannot do this. I don't want this, and by your tears, it is clear you do not want me either."

Hearing Ranulf's voice, Bronwyn froze, unable to

move or speak. She had felt dead inside standing at the altar. When Tyr had entered and made his way to her side, she couldn't even make herself look at him, and was wondering how she was going to be able to speak the vows that represented a life she desperately wanted—but with Ranulf.

Hearing his deep voice, Bronwyn twisted guardedly. Was Ranulf playing some kind of trick? Had he not married Lily earlier? She lifted her veil to see unhampered by the fine linen and verify it really was Ranulf standing beside her. His steady gaze instantly became remote, the amber color of his good eye turned dark and ominous. Everything about him— the granite hardness of his jaw, the severity of his demeanor—made it clear he was far from just unhappy. He was furious at the situation and the last thing in the world he wanted was to marry her. Whatever was going on, Ranulf was not party to it.

Ranulf was just as shocked as Bronwyn, but he had no trouble finding his voice. "Just what kind of game are you playing now?"

His booming attack was just the trigger Bronwyn needed to find her own ability to speak. "I am playing no game, my lord, and I am done trying to play yours," she declared through clenched teeth and then pivoted to leave.

She had not made it three steps when the chapel doors sprung open. Edythe and Lily ran in, dragging a very rattled Tory. Tyr followed and closed the door, with a pleased look.

Bronwyn stopped in her tracks and pointed, yelling at Ranulf, "See. There. It's a mistake. Tyr is here now and can . . ." Her voice dwindled off as she realized Tyr was shaking his head.

"Tory and I have done our proxy duty, Lady Bronwyn, and you can look, but I doubt you find another man available to marry you today."

Remembering the vacancy of the courtyard, Ranulf glared at his friend. Whatever was going on had been cleverly orchestrated. "Explain. Now," Ranulf ordered, his tone leaving no misinterpretation of his meaning or the severity of his request.

Completely unperturbed, Edythe stepped forward, her face filled with self-satisfaction. "I look forward to meeting Garik—my *husband*," she said with glee, making clear that her nuptials had already taken place.

She then glanced at Lily, who moved beside her. Lily issued a pleading look to Bronwyn and said, "If Rolande is anything like Tyr described, then he and I are much better suited. You know that I am not ready to run a keep, let alone a castle. The wife of a prominent and good-looking commander is much more to my liking." Bronwyn's blue eyes widened in surprise, but only for a moment before narrowing again as her thoughts raced dangerously. Her future, her *life*, had been decided by those she loved and trusted. "Is this done?" she demanded. "Is this a proposition or are you both married?"

Behind her came a short, voluble cough from an increasingly flustered Father Morrell. "May I ask if there has been a mistake? I understood that three marriage ceremonies were to take place. Each alone. I have done two . . . and I thought this was to be the third."

Edythe went to pacify the round priest, who looked extremely perplexed and suddenly dubious about the morning's curious events. "I assure you the right couples have been married. One more must be done, just give them a moment to get ready."

Ranulf could barely control his anger at the idea of being manipulated in such a way. He glared at Tyr and then Edythe, who was standing between him and the priest, her dark green silk dress making a swishing sound as she shifted her weight. He then shifted his gaze to Lily and then to Bronwyn, momentarily studying all three—and the color of their gowns.

He should have guessed the truth that morning. It had not been Bronwyn he had been observing but Edythe. At his angle, he had not been able to discern their height difference, but the green silk had been notable and Bronwyn was wearing light silver. All the turbulent emotions of this morning swirled back to the surface. Feelings of betrayal, doubt, and shock that he could be so wrong dissipated as the truth of the situation overcame him. Bronwyn *had* been upset last night, and the aspect of marrying Rolande was causing her to cry even as she was about to announce her vows.

Bronwyn no longer felt sad. The tears that had plagued her since discovering Ranulf's preference for her younger sister vanished, leaving only fury in its place. She glared first at Edythe and then Lily. "I hope you can both find happiness with your decision, but I refuse to let you make mine," she ground out and then lifted her gown to hasten out of the chapel.

As she passed Lily, her sister's hand seized Bronwyn's injured arm, causing her to flinch, giving Lily just enough time to leap in front of her. "Bronwyn! You can't leave. You *have* to marry Lord Anscombe. You have no choice."

Anger rippled along Bronwyn's spine. How could her sister not understand? Ranulf had chosen Lily, and just because she had disregarded his choice did not change the situation. "You're wrong. I still have a choice."

Panic overtook Lily's face. "But you have to! If you don't, you will have to marry Baron Craven and give Syndlear over to him."

Bronwyn glanced back at Ranulf. His eyes blazed, and his large neck was the color of crimson. Her misty blue eyes, now the hue of a dark storm, returned to Lily. "Never. Never will I marry such a man. You forget. I have another option." Then, after maneuvering around her sister, Bronwyn once again headed outside.

The door from her exit slowly swung back shut on the quiet crowd. Lily and Edythe stood openmouthed, unknowing of what to do or say. The plan that had worked nearly flawlessly fell apart at the most critical part. Tyr, who had felt the icy glare of Ranulf's barely controlled temper, had opted to remain silent rather than give him more reasons to sever their friendship. But his honor was now at stake. He couldn't live with himself if something happened to Bronwyn in her rash decision to flee north to the Highlands in the middle of winter.

Speaking slowly and deliberately, trying to hold his own growing temper in check, Tyr asked, "Are you really going to let her leave Hunswick?"

Lily gasped and sank onto one of the empty benches behind her. "That's what she meant?" she murmured.

Tyr nodded, but his gaze never left Ranulf's, unable to fathom how his friend could remain stoic and motionless when Bronwyn was walking out of his life forever. "Aye, Lady Bronwyn told me yesterday that if she didn't marry she would leave for Scotland. I never dreamed that you would let her, Ranulf. Travel to the northern lands in winter? Are you really going to let her do that?"

Ranulf scowled at his friend for almost half a minute before answering. "No, I am not." Without saying another word, he strode out of the chapel and across the bailey toward the Great Hall.

Six days ago his life had been relatively calm and predictable. He had been far from happy with his fate, but he could have managed it. Upon seeing Bronwyn, however, his emotional state had been turned every which way and his mental stability along with it. Truths were lies and lies were truths. Then he had compounded the situation with even more lies, and as a result, he had nearly hurt Bronwyn and himself irrevocably.

In his experience, women were not forthright creatures and had to be tricked into honesty, especially when it came to their feelings. His plan to make Bronwyn jealous had been innocent, but he had not accounted for her strong sense of pride, and he should have, considering his own stubborn streak. Seeing and hearing her outrage at the situation, Ranulf had decided to give her the space and time needed to calm down before talking with her. Then, he would explain his intentions and convince her to marry him. But with Tyr's revelation, it became clear that option was not available. There was no time to convince Bronwyn of anything.

She was going to marry him now and calm down later. The woman was going to be furious with him, but that he could handle. In time, he would remind them both of just how good things could be between them.

Ranulf slammed open the Great Hall doors just in time to see Bronwyn fight her way through the crowded trestles on her way to the back stairs. Almost all of Hunswick was inside, waiting for them to begin the celebration. Claps started from somewhere and the crowd was all on their feet. Ranulf ignored them and deftly snaked his way around the people, capturing Bronwyn just before she reached the door to the back staircase. She tried to kick his shins in an effort to get away. "Leave me be, Ranulf," she ordered.

"Not now or ever," he issued back and threw her over his shoulder, careful not to reinjure her arm. Spinning around, he marched back outside and toward the chapel, unheeding of the pounding he was taking on his back from her fists or the open gapes from onlookers. Within minutes of his departure, he was back inside the chapel, depositing her in front of a very flustered priest. He grasped her shoulders firmly in his hands and said, "You can begin, Father. We are now ready."

Bronwyn twisted vigorously, trying to wrench free. "Damn you to hell," she hissed.

With each struggle, the wires of her wimple poked his chest, causing him a surprising amount of pain. He was about to yank the horrid thing off when she came to an abrupt halt at Father Morrell's rebuke. "I am shocked, my lady. You have always been a girl of common sense. To use such language, on Christmas, and in the chapel!"

Bronwyn bit down hard on her bottom lip, her

fury inflamed further. She forced herself to stand still and succumb to the proceedings. Ranulf may be keeping her here now, but that didn't mean she couldn't escape before night fell.

"And you, Lord Anscombe," Father Morrell huffed, "this is most irregular. How am I to know this lady comes willingly to this marriage carried upon your shoulder?"

"Father, you have one duty in front of you at this moment, and that is to wed me to this woman. The salvation of our souls can wait until tomorrow." The menacing tone in Ranulf's voice left no room for argument. Bronwyn wasn't sure what Ranulf would have done if the priest had been made of sterner stuff, but she doubted the outcome would have been any different.

Her mind was still trying to catch up to events when her body was suddenly engulfed by Tyr in a big bear hug. She must have said the right things at the right times for everyone around her was calling her Lady Anscombe. Lily and Edythe were embracing her, telling her that she and Ranulf might be angry now, but both would thank them later. That all their interference was a type of present to her. It was their turn to help her as she had been doing for them all these years.

Bronwyn wanted to scream and say that this was not what she wanted. She didn't want a man by default, and she most especially didn't want to be forever attached with one who preferred her sister. But nothing came out. It was just as well. Let them think she was happy. Tomorrow they would learn the truth.

The priest announced it was time to gather in the

Great Hall and begin the hand-washing ceremony. Ranulf nodded in agreement and escorted Bronwyn out of the chapel and across the yard. Once again, they entered the Great Hall. This time the crowd waited until they saw Edythe's and Lily's beaming looks of encouragement before rising in congratulations. Only after Ranulf and Bronwyn took their seats at the head table did the roar calm so that words could be exchanged.

Ranulf leaned in to whisper something in her ear, but the sharp bend of the wimple interceded. He nudged the tip aside and said softly, "Know this, I won't let you leave."

"Oh, my lord," Bronwyn hissed back as she continued to fake a smile to those around her, "if I want to leave . . . I will."

"And then I will follow you and be most unhappy at the effort."

Bronwyn dropped her sham expression of bliss to glare at him directly. "I wonder if you would truly care or even notice."

"You are mine, Bronwyn. Now and forever. And I *would* notice."

"Why should I care?"

"Because you would be destroying everyone's Christmas. For if you try to depart from Hunswick without my approval, I will find you and use every able man to do so."

Bronwyn openly gaped at him, realizing he was completely serious.

Father Morrell, in hearing distance of the conversation, made another one of his blaring coughs. He then gave them both a slicing look she hadn't thought possible out of the cherublike face and held up a bowl of spiced and scented water. "It is a time for quiet. A day for being with loved ones, and *sharing love together* . . ." The man had started his sermon, making further conversation just like everything else around her . . . impossible.

Chapter Eight

Saint Stephen was the first Christian to be martyred for his faith by being stoned to death shortly after Christ's crucifixion, furnishing him the highest of the three classes of martyrdom—by will, love, and blood. Though not definitive, some theologians date the holiday back to the Early Middle Ages (400 A.D.), originating with the nobles of England, who celebrated the day with food, fun, and gift giving of practical items such as cloth, tools, feed, grain, and often money to those who supported their rule. In medieval times, monetary gifts would be distributed to families in hollow clay pots called "piggies" with slits in the top, which would be broken to retrieve the money. Many records have this tradition as obligatory and not optional, and by 1871, the gifts were supplied via boxes, causing December 26 to be known as "Boxing Day."

Tyr swiveled his head, which was relaxing on the back of the comfortable chair, to see who was entering the Great Hall at the very late hour. Midnight had passed some time ago and besides a few snoring men passed out from too much food and drink, he and Ranulf were the only two left awake. The wind howled and slammed the door shut, but no one awoke. The sizable fire flickered, but it remained lit and more than able to keep the spacious room warm for a couple more hours.

It had taken time, and much ale, to get Ranulf to forgive the intrusive tactics to get him to the altar, but he finally had. The relief Tyr felt had been enormous. He could have borne not having Ranulf as a friend—he had endured the loss of much worse in his life—but he would not have liked it.

Ranulf sighed as he approached and sank down into the seat next to Tyr. He outstretched his long legs and balanced the heel of one foot on the toes of his other, staring at them. The man was tormenting himself and had been for hours.

Tyr slouched farther down into the chair, intertwined his fingers over his satiated abdomen, and closed his eyes. "I hope you don't need any more walks to gather your courage. Yesterday is over, my friend, and your wedding night will soon be as well if you don't hurry up and join your wife. Has it been so long you have forgotten how? Need any tips?"

"Not from you," Ranulf grunted, his tone laced with anger.

Tyr's hazel eyes popped open and glanced at Ranulf. "My God, you still sound jealous, and after all I did to ensure she became *your* wife!"

"Just you wait," Ranulf mumbled, wishing he could

somehow physically force Tyr to be silent. "Someday you will find someone, and with your impetuous personality, you will act far more out of character than I."

Tyr shook his head and closed his eyes again. "Not me. I swore an oath."

"An oath you made when you were barely a man," Ranulf mumbled, unable to expound further as he knew nothing about the reasons behind the ardent vow.

"Still, it is one I intend to keep. But," Tyr added in a mocking tone, "if there was ever any example of marital bliss that might get me to change my mind, it would be you and your devoted wife. I have never seen a couple more happy or excited to be married than you two."

"Someone should muzzle your tongue."

"Not until you leave. I need it to annoy you into getting up and going to your wife. Consider it another wedding gift."

Realizing his friend was serious and still drunk enough to disregard the possible consequences, Ranulf rose to leave.

"You can thank me tomorrow," Tyr muttered.

Bronwyn locked her arms around her knees and rocked back and forth on the rug in front of the fireplace. Her wedding day had ended alone and it seemed her wedding night was going to conclude the same way. And she was not sure how she felt about it.

When Ranulf had ordered her guard to escort her from the feast while it was still lively, she had thought he would soon follow to discuss the situation they were in and determine a course of action, but he never arrived. So she had tried to leave and had been stopped by Norval, who supposedly stayed to ensure her protection. Ha! Ranulf wanted to keep her trapped so that she wouldn't—or *couldn't*—leave. Why would he force her into a marriage he clearly did not want? Why had she not left the very hour she learned of his decision to marry Lily?

Bronwyn had been asking those questions and others repeatedly for hours. She was exhausted but unable to sleep. So she sat in silence and listened, wondering if Ranulf would ever return. When finally she heard the heedless bang of the Tower Keep's courtyard door, her heart lurched and the frustration that had been mounting rapidly changed to overwhelming sadness. She did not want to be married to Ranulf. Not like this. By the time the footsteps reached the solar door, a new set of tears were rolling down her cheeks.

Ranulf entered his chambers and his gaze immediately darted toward the bed, seeking Bronwyn's sleeping form. He had hoped if he waited long enough, she would be asleep so that he could crawl in next to her and pull her close. Then if things went ideally, Bronwyn would awaken in his arms, and before she realized what was happening, he could remind her of how much she enjoyed his touch and the pleasures it could bring.

But she was awake. And crying. And far from desiring his ideal plan.

Taking a deep breath, he sauntered up to the chair behind her and sat down. Her back was toward him, as she was hunched over her knees. Her long hair was still covered by the painful headdress and he longed to see it down. "Take that thing off and never don one again," he barked, not intending for his first words to be so harsh or critical.

Bronwyn blinked. She had forgotten she was still wearing the dreaded thing. After entering the solar and realizing the truth of her situation, everything else disappeared, including her own discomfort. Still, of all the things for him to say, his dislike for part of her outfit was not what she had expected. Then again, the unrelated topic helped to compose her own emotional state.

Slowly she rose to her feet and unpinned the white linen strapped around her chin so she could pull the wire contraption completely off her head. After shaking her hair free, Bronwyn tossed the miniature prison into the fire. Then without a word, she walked over to the peg where his pointed Phrygian cap hung next to the mantel. Only once had she actually seen Ranulf holding the odd-shaped item, and it had been at a distance and from the back. Even in his hand the large coxcomb peak had looked wrong. If she were ever to see Ranulf wearing it, she imagined he would be something between appalling and repulsive.

Yanking the cap off the stake, she tossed it, too, into the fire. "I hate that cap more than you dislike my wimple, my lord."

"No caps for me or for everyone at Hunswick?"

Bronwyn shrugged. She thought they looked ridiculous on all men, but to ban them in the middle of winter was absurd. "Just you," she muttered.

Ranulf leaned over and rested his elbows on his knees. He wanted to ask why just him, but he suspected he knew and he wasn't in the mood to hear the denigration aloud—or from her. Especially tonight. He stared at his thumbs and debated if he should ask the other question on his mind. "Do you need more time?" he finally asked.

Bronwyn blinked. *Time?* she wanted to scream. *All I've had was time.* "For what?" she snapped.

Ranulf gulped. "I don't know. I just . . . well, I mean I took a walk after you came here . . . to think. I thought you would want some time to do so as well, alone with no festivities to interrupt your thoughts. But if you need more time, I can leave."

Bronwyn forced her gaping mouth, which had slowly opened during his speech, to close. This whole time she had not been thinking anything. She had been feeling, and most of it was anger— all directed toward him. Suddenly at a loss for words, she crossed in front of the hearth toward the empty chair on his right and sat down. "I don't need more time to think," she asserted just strong enough to be believed.

Ranulf continued to stare at his thumbs, but he could see her sitting straight backed in the chair with her elbows resting on the wooden arms in his peripheral vision. The chair on his left had been closer to her, but she had moved to his right so that she would remain in his line of sight. The gesture had been unconscious, but at a deeper level, it had also been intentional. Not a soul in his life—even his friends Garik and Tyr, who had known him for years—was ever so deliberately considerate. Rather, he was always the one to make adjustments or move to where he could best see. Sometimes he felt like he was chasing events rather than participating in them. But not with Bronwyn. And in this one small act she reminded him of a fact he had almost forgotten. She was his soul mate.

Somehow, he needed her to understand how important she was without making her retract even farther away from him. "I want you to know that this marriage, despite how it came about, is an acceptable one to me. With you, I am . . . comfortable, something I don't feel around most people. Especially women," he clarified. "We are also . . . physically compatible and the people of Hunswick love you and see you already as their Lady. It is appropriate that you remain so."

Bronwyn was now even more at a loss for words. *Appropriate, comfortable, compatible* . . . not the words a woman wanted to hear on her wedding night. Passion, love, desire, these were the things she felt for him. It was one thing to be alone, but to be alone with someone you cared about was a torture Bronwyn wasn't sure she could endure for long. After their afternoon together, she needed to be touched by him, held by him, not just serve as sporadic company. "Would you expect this to be a . . . a real marriage?"

"As a lord, I need sons."

His answer sent a shiver down her spine. She was not sure if she was relieved or bothered by the indifferent reason. "I'm not sure that I can . . . be with you."

Ranulf's breathing deepened to an audible level. "I said I would give you more time."

"I don't need time," Bronwyn insisted with a wave of her hand and stood up to pace. "I need to know . . ."

She paused and looked at him, pleading for him to understand what she could not ask.

In one smooth movement, Ranulf rose and grasped her upper arms. "What, Bronwyn? What do you need to know?"

Bronwyn. He had spoken her name. Not an endearment. No "angel," no "my lady." She closed her eyes. "Nothing," she whispered.

Ranulf caught her chin between his thumb and forefinger and turned her head so that she was forced to meet his gaze. "Tell me."

Once again he was seducing her, and her body was coming alive in his arms. She wrenched free. "How can I lie with you when you wanted my *sister*?"

Ranulf caught Bronwyn's face between his hands and kissed her almost savagely, invading her mouth with a soft intimate aggression that seared her senses. She heard him make a soft, hoarse sound and felt his pelvis smash up against the junction of her legs. His hardness, evidence of his desire, was nestled so intimately against her that it rattled her nerves all the way down to her toes.

Deep inside her something responded to the obvious masculine need in him. A soft whimper came from deep in her throat and her fingers clenched around his shoulders. Gradually, the kiss softened until it was so tender, so full of feeling, she felt like she was choking.

He released her lips but he did not pull back. Instead, he traced the lines of her jaw with his fingers. "Does that answer your question? For let me tell you now, I never have and never will desire another."

His voice was deep, husky, caressing. The sensual sound nearly pushed reason aside. She had been so hurt. Bronwyn was not sure she could survive another disappointment. It would be better to run and live with the memories than stay and face that pain ever again.

Ranulf cradled her face in his hands and studied her eyes, consuming them as if he could discern the essence of her spirit. "I meant what I said, Bronwyn. I will never let you leave me. Never. So end your plans of Scotland and disappearing in the middle of the night, for I will hunt you down and claim what is mine. And you are mine. *And I never let go of what belongs to me.*"

His possessive speech riled her enormously. She wanted to retort that she belonged to no one, but it wasn't true. She couldn't retreat now even if a part of her still wanted to do so. She belonged to him, and his kiss proved that no matter what had happened or would happen, she would desire him and need him in ways that made leaving impossible.

Urging Bronwyn to her tiptoes, Ranulf pulled her close once again for another kiss, this time long and soft and deep, capturing her tongue and drawing it into his own mouth. "Promise me, angel. Promise me that you won't leave," he demanded huskily between breaths.

Ranulf wasn't spouting out words of love, but it did not matter. She was bound to him by law and by spirit. "I promise," she murmured.

A deep groan of satisfaction escaped his throat and his hand delved into her hair as he kissed her again and again, each time demanding more of her. Then his mouth was gone and she could once again breathe. He kept her close and buried his face in her wild mane.

After a few seconds, Bronwyn realized he was shaking. "What's wrong?"

Ranulf let go a brief snort, clearly disgusted with his own lack of restraint. "I cannot even kiss you without being in danger of losing control. And I cannot lose what little I still possess, not when I am so close. Damn, Tyr was right."

Bronwyn pulled out of his embrace so she could look at him. The amount of emotional intensity staring back at her made her heart race. "I don't understand."

With the backs of his knuckles, he caressed her cheek. "You are married to a most ignorant man when it comes to your sex. I have never courted a woman, sought after one, or cared about whether or not she received satisfaction in my arms. With you, though . . . I want so badly to give you pleasure, teach you and delight you in ways to make you happy—more than happy—and I am afraid I am going to fail."

Bronwyn's heart swelled, nearly choking her. Ranulf claimed no love for her—nothing of the intense feelings that she had for him—but he did want to please her and care for her. It was enough. It was time to let go of how and why they came to be married and to just love him.

Taking another step back, she slowly began to undo the ties of her bliaut. Her fingers shook with nervousness. Undressing in front of a man was not something Bronwyn had ever done before, and last time, Ranulf had removed her gown in a whirlwind of passion that had completely overtaken her senses. Tonight's coupling would be deliberate.

The silver shimmering mass fell to her feet.

Seeing his shocked reaction, she gained more confidence, and leisurely, she slipped her hose off each leg. "You won't fail, Ranulf. You have never failed at anything before." Then standing before him wearing nothing but a diaphanous undergarment, she leaned toward him and said softly, just above a whisper, "I trust you. I always have."

Ranulf felt her hands upon his chest and stared down at her, unbelieving fortune could have changed to his favor. This morning, he had been doomed for a dismal eternity, but instead, standing before him was a woman giving him everything he had dreamed of but never thought he would possess.

He laid his forehead against hers, breathing in her scent while collecting his thoughts. Ranulf craved to pick her up and carry her to his bed without further prelude, remembering how she felt, all soft and willing pressed up against him. His body quickened at the thought, and he silently cursed his own weakness. This time he refused to rush. Tonight was about her.

Bronwyn arched her head back and softened her mouth into the barest of smiles. She couldn't believe it, but she was nervous. Last time, passion had dictated everything, not allowing enough time or the ability to think about what she was doing. But now, Ranulf was restraining himself for her sake. She was appreciative, but what she really wanted was for him to make unrestrained love to her and show her once again what it felt like to be beautiful and desired.

Pulling back the opening of his shirt, he felt her lips kiss the warm skin of his chest as she inhaled his musky scent. "Angel," he groaned in a deep guttural voice as her mouth seared his skin. She lifted her head and he stared down at her. Bronwyn flicked her tongue over her lips and every muscle in his body seized. He turned her around in his embrace and she leaned back against him. How was he going to keep things slow? His blood was roaring in his ears as it raced like liquid fire through his veins. He closed his arms around her and began to loosen the ties of her chemise.

As the garment fell to the floor, he leaned over until his mouth touched the smooth white skin of her throat. A soft sigh escaped her lips, causing his loins to throb with increased need. Keeping her facing away from him, he quickly disrobed before scooping her into his heavily muscled arms. In three long steps, he reached the side of the bed and tenderly placed her among the pillows.

Shy of her own nakedness, Bronwyn reached out to him and tried to sit up, but Ranulf placed his hand against her shoulder, compelling her to lie back. The firelight flickered over her body and his heated gaze swept over her, taking her in from head to toe. She was beautiful. Perfect. His.

His jaw tightened and he closed his eye. How could he have ever believed that he could spend even one minute in the arms of another woman after being with Bronwyn?

Unable to wait any longer, he lowered himself until he covered her body with his own. His mouth swirled around her ear as his hand molded to her side, tracing a path to her breasts, making her bend to him. A low rumble of satisfaction escaped from deep within Bronwyn. She raised her head and pulled his lips down to hers, opening to him, tasting him hungrily as his thumbs cruised gently over her nipples, relishing her response.

Eagerly she pressed her body against his, and he felt himself grow harder. "We need to slow down," he said in a thick voice, feeling the throbbing mass of his erection nestled against her thigh, begging for release.

"I don't want to," Bronwyn replied, her fingers running up and down his spine. Lacing them through his short hair, she met his driving tongue, thrust for thrust, taking and giving back in turn.

He had wanted to touch her, kiss her, take the time to explore her entire body in every way he could before their lovemaking became heated, fueled by need. He wanted to connect with her body and soul.

Bronwyn closed her eyes and wished Ranulf would break free and take her like he had before. He tongued a path between her breasts and gingerly outlined them, bringing the pink tip to a crested peak. She quivered and arched closer to his lips until she felt his mouth take her nipple in. She moaned.

His slow gentle approach was driving her wild, creating a torrent of desire that was taking over her body. She wanted nothing more than to feel him on top of her, inside her, exciting her to new limits. She writhed under his touch, begging him to take her into his mouth once again. When he didn't, she slid her palm down his chest, across his belly, and lower.

The moment she touched his flesh, he shivered violently and jerked back. "I can't—" he began, but his body refused to listen and pushed forward into her palm.

Bronwyn had never considered the idea she had the ability to arouse his desire. At least not like this. It was empowering. But just as she was starting to experiment, cradling him in her palm and stroking him gently, he pulled her hand away. Bronwyn was about to argue, but when the heat of his fingers pressed against her intimately, all ability to think stopped.

As his hand closed gently around her, a deep tremor shook her and Bronwyn heard herself cry out. Slowly he stroked her, parting her with his fingers, opening her as he eased one in and out of her snug passage. The pace he had set was torment. She needed more of him inside her and started lifting up her hips until they pressed against his hand, demanding release.

"Ranulf," she breathed, going half crazy with need. Unmoved by her pleas, he continued to stroke back and forth, slowly drawing forth the wet heat, stroking the flames until she was writhing uncontrollably with desire.

Ranulf waited until he could hold on no longer, and with a low groan, he eased himself slowly and deeply inside her. She closed around him, hot and wet and so tight that it almost undid him. Then he began to move within her, slow and careful and very, very thorough.

Bronwyn called out his name, begging him with her voice and body to quicken his pace. And as her hips began to thrust, he obliged, bringing them into a passionate rhythm until their breaths turned into short gasps. His back was slick with sweat and his muscles trembled beneath his skin. He needed this.

He needed to feel alive again, to block out past fears that she had abandoned him.

He increased the pace until she clenched around him and any semblance of control he may have had was obliterated. Once, twice more he thrust deep inside her then she cried out in elation. Barely a moment later, her own name was uttered from his lips in an ecstatic gasp, and he collapsed in blackness. Nothing else existed. Only the feeling of being surrounded by heaven.

Bronwyn felt him shudder inside her and then the slump of his body falling heavily atop her, his breathing still affected by the exertion. She smiled and closed her eyes. The crazed passion of before had not been present, but even so, she felt replete, with the throb of his last thrusts still echoing within her. Once again, he had moved her in ways she would not have believed possible before meeting him. Tonight had not been about a rush to quench a thirst. Ranulf had desired above all else to give, and as a result, he had made her feel special.

"Thank you," she murmured against his skin, placing light kisses across his shoulders.

Ranulf flipped over to his side so that he lay next to her, enabling him to run his fingers up and down the soft skin of her arm and hip. "Imagine, angel, a lifetime of this . . . of you and me."

Bronwyn nestled her backside closer to him and nodded. She wanted that lifetime. She would never leave him, and even better, he would never let her go.

Light from the morning sun poured through the window, revealing the long-healed burns covering Bronwyn's upper back. Ranulf studied them thoughtfully, caressing the uneven skin with his fingertips, glad she could not remember the excruciating pain the fire must have caused. Slowly his thumb traced them down her spine. They were more widespread than his own, but her skin could not have been exposed to the fire for long for she had maintained the use of her muscles. Yet, the very scale of her injuries . . . it was a wonder she had not died. Any worse, and she would have.

Bronwyn stirred.

"Sorry I awoke you."

"Don't be," she purred, stretching her toes.

"Nothing," he vowed, "nothing like this will ever happen to you again."

Bronwyn froze as she realized what Ranulf meant. "It's strange, I can't remember the fire, or the pain. I can remember being trapped in bed next to my mother for long periods. My father remembered it all, and practically rebuilt Syndlear as a result. He never wanted his family going to sleep and being trapped in flames again."

"I can't blame him. I would do the same," he replied huskily, still outlining the contours of her back.

"Really?" she asked, flipping over. "Spend your fortune on expanding a keep that provides no additional room, no added protection, nothing but tiny escape holes in the wall that couldn't barely fit one adult, let alone a family?"

"Does fire scare you?"

"No," Bronwyn murmured, shaking her head. "Accidents do." She pointed to the dark red scab on his shoulder. "You were lucky. My mother died right after the North Tower was completed while she was helping arrange furniture on one of the floors. I am sure my father also met with a similar misfortune. I just cannot believe disease took him. No, something unexpected, something awful happened. So, no, not fire . . . accidents are what I fear. They have taken away those who I loved." With a sigh, she turned back over on her side. "And among those who I love are my sisters. I need to know they are not destined for misery because of me."

Ranulf sat up and raked his hand through his hair. He swung his legs over the side of the bed, knowing what she was about to ask. "They married good men. Besides Tyr, I trust no one more than Garik. And Rolande . . . well, he will be willing to settle down as soon as he sees Lily. He has not spoken of it, but I know he has been wanting to cast off his reckless ways."

Bronwyn bit her bottom lip. "I already knew the men whom my sisters married were good; they had to be if you respected them. But none of us were raised like other noblewomen, to be compliant and quiet. Edythe, especially. She considers herself realistic and tends to prepare for the worst, often coming across as mocking. I have seen her cutting wit injure the pride of many a man."

Ranulf gave a short grunt and twisted around so he could look Bronwyn in the eye. "It doesn't take long to understand Edythe, and trust me, Garik is just right for her. The man is intelligent and engages those around him. Edythe will be surprised to find herself liking him, but she will."

"But why not Tyr?" Bronwyn posed, rising to a sitting position. "He is quick and observant, and what's more, he will test Edythe's convictions and I think she would do the same for him."

"Ha! You mean that they actually search for ways to stump the other. Just listening to them is amusing and *seeing* them fight, with their height difference, is beyond entertaining and something I will be harassing Tyr about endlessly in the future. And," he interjected, seeing Bronwyn's mouth open with another question, "of everyone I know, Tyr is the most sincere about his declarations against marriage."

"You can't be serious. He's so . . . perfect," she murmured, her eyes wide in astonishment. "I find it hard to believe that *no one* has ever caught his eye."

Ranulf fought to suppress the twinge of jealousy darting through him, reminding himself that Bronwyn belonged to him completely, and that he—without any doubt—belonged to her. "I've never known him to take serious notice of anyone. Although your sister has come as close as any, I hope she understands that his vow is quite resolute. Don't fear. Garik's mind is just as fast and sharp. And he's shorter."

"Well, that is a plus," Bronwyn sighed. "But what about Rolande? Rumors don't portray him as a man desiring marriage."

In one swift motion, Ranulf bounded from where he sat and straddled her hips with greater agility than Bronwyn would have imagined given his size. His hands nudged her back down onto the bed and he began to reexplore her silken flesh. "He's my commander and nothing like me. Funny, outgoing, and quick to smile. Like Lily, his greatest asset can also be his undoing—he searches for the good in people and situations."

Bronwyn bit the inside of her cheek, trying not to let Ranulf see how his touch was getting to her. "Sounds like a bad commander. Don't you want somebody fierce?"

Ranulf paused. "Fierce? No. I want somebody competent."

"Doesn't all that compassion get in the way during battle?"

"I never said Rolande was compassionate, at least not on the field," he murmured, leaning over her and nuzzling her ear. "But he is quite the focus of the ladies, although I think Lily just might capture his attention. Especially, since—and don't take offense— these hills are not swarming with competition."

Bronwyn made an effort to shrug her shoulders and push him back. He only shifted his efforts downward. "Wouldn't matter if they were," she gasped. "If Lily wanted him, she would get him. She's . . . lucky that way."

Ranulf's mouth roamed to the valley between her breasts, chuckling as her body arched in response. "Mmm . . . maybe it just appears that she is lucky. She's always had you"—he paused to give her a quick nip—"and Edythe giving her whatever she wanted."

"Ahh . . ." Bronwyn moaned, straining to put her thoughts together. "I . . . I will admit that much of what you say is true, but after you have been around her awhile, you'll understand that it is not me . . . Lily really is lucky," she managed to get out. His tongue was velvet torture and the conversation about the future of her sister's well-being was no longer important.

"Maybe, but luck often runs out. I just hope she

can handle it the day hers does." Groaning, Ranulf took one nipple into his mouth and sucked, sending a shudder of excitement through them both.

Bronwyn felt herself liquefying and her hands started circling his broad back of their own accord. No longer able to speak or think, she crushed her lower body against him, rhythmically flexing and arching her hips.

Stimulated by her response, Ranulf's tongue delved lower, across the curve of her belly. His hands slowly caressed the insides of her thighs, stroking, teasing until she was trembling violently. Sinking down on his knees, he placed himself between her legs, ignoring his own sexual tension seizing his insides.

Hot, burning breath fanned the juncture of her legs as Ranulf kissed the inside of her thigh and then again, higher. At the unfamiliar caress, she gasped and tried to move, but Ranulf held her hips in position, allowing him to give her the most intimate of all kisses.

She couldn't move or think as he continued to taste until she was writhing, reaching for him, begging for what only he could give. And then he was there, at the core of her body, driving deep, seeking release and reassurance that she wanted him as much as he wanted her. Her own body clenched around him with every stroke, craving the hot, thick feel of him inside her.

Ranulf cried out at the intimate connection and instinctively pulled back and thrust again, sinking even deeper into the snug, tight channel of her body. Her nails dug into his back as he pressed his face into the curve of her neck, inhaling her sweet rose and womanly scent. Unable to slow or control the rhythm of their lovemaking, he plunged harder and faster. She in return wrapped her legs around him, spreading herself as wide as she could to bring him in farther.

Then he could feel her body seize and go into hard tight convulsions that carried her right over the edge as she cried out his name in surrender. Unfathomable feelings of possession slammed into him and he plunged one last time. Life stopped and eternity began. Never would he get enough of her.

Ranulf had no notion of how long he lay weak and satiated, unable to move or feel anything but her soft kisses on his hair. He held her tightly to him as he regained control of his limbs, and slowly rose to his elbows, taking great pleasure in the dazed and replete blue eyes staring back at him.

"Are you going to answer that, or should I?" Bronwyn asked, squelching a giggle, letting her hand slide downward over his body until her fingers curled gently around him.

Ranulf's body instantly responded. "Answer what?" he grumbled, as the sound of knocking penetrated his senses. When it did not stop, he roared at the intruder, "Go away!"

"I will not!" came Edythe's very short and surly reply. "The sun rose hours ago and we have been waiting patiently for Bronwyn's help with the evening's events."

Ranulf moaned. He couldn't believe Bronwyn's wantonness, teasing him when she knew her sister was on the other side of the door. Stilling her torturous fingers in a firm grip, he gritted out, "We're still deliberating your fate since you were so kind as to determine ours. So leave us alone."

Edythe let go a single, but audible "hrmph" in disgust and retreated. Bronwyn arched a playful brow and said, "Shouldn't we get up?"

With unexpected strength, he grabbed her waist and rolled over at the same time, positioning her so that she was astride him. "I don't think so."

Bronwyn licked her lips. "It is Saint Stephen's Day. The people will be waiting."

"For their pots full of money."

"So you know the custom," she purred, letting her fingers play with the hairs on his chest.

"Of course," he groaned. "I ordered the clay pots as soon as we got back after we went hunting. I'll pass them out tonight."

"Did you know that you, too, get a present?" Bronwyn asked as she leaned down to kiss his navel, smiling with delight as his stomach contracted.

Ranulf grinned back. "Really? And just what is in my clay pot?"

"Your present doesn't come in a pot," she purred, smiling as her hand slowly moved lower, making a trail for her mouth and tongue to follow. "And even more lucky, you don't have to wait until tonight either."

Chapter Nine

Saint John the Evangelist was a beloved disciple and his day is celebrated during Christmas to represent his closeness to the Lord. Although he was saved miraculously just before he was sentenced to die, his willingness to suffer death for the cause of Christ allows him the description of martyr—through will though not deed. In medieval times when celebrating Saint John's Day, it was customary to collect the herb Saint John's wort and hang it over doors and windows to keep evil spirits away. Another focal point of the celebration was the building of great communal bonfires, burning from dusk until well after midnight, to serve as a symbol of Christ himself—the burning and shining light. Feasts were enjoyed and songs were sung.

Ranulf swallowed. Bronwyn was stretching in her sleep, her hand touching him innocently in ways that created an instant lesson in self-control. He curled his arm around her middle and pressed his lips against her forehead, causing her to remove her hand, roll to her side, and snuggle closer to him. The kiss had been a natural solution to her unconscious embrace, one he had performed without forethought, as if he had done it a hundred times over several years.

One of her legs was lying haphazardly over his thigh, her foot nestled below his calf. Her hand now rested on his chest, tickling him whenever the tips of her fingers moved. Her nose was buried against his neck, and her hair, free from its braid, lay sprawled over her back and shoulders so that he inhaled whiffs of rose and witch hazel each time she moved. Ranulf was not sure if having Bronwyn in his bed provided more rest or less.

Yet whenever she rolled to the edge of the bed, the sudden feeling of loss grabbed him, arresting him from his sleep. He had not realized how unbalanced his life had been, but he had finally found true happiness. And if he ever lost Bronwyn, he would no longer be able to survive the loneliness he had previously endured.

He loved her. Fully and completely. She had, in just a few days, become his everything.

Before her, the concept of love had seemed vague, and when described, it sounded like a child's whimsy and not to be believed. Too many times he had witnessed a man or a woman swearing their love and then soon after moving their affections to someone else. So he had concluded long ago that love and lust were synonymous, a potentially powerful craving that, when satiated, disappeared. But lust did not explain what he felt for Bronwyn. He had been falling for her since the first night she had poured out her heart thinking him asleep. He had learned everything he needed to know then. She had captured his soul thoroughly.

Finding happiness scared Ranulf, but knowing that he possessed the power to ruin it terrified him. For Bronwyn believed all their dishonesty was behind them. And while he had been careful not to lie to her, Ranulf had kept one vital truth to himself. A secret he intended to keep. At least for now. Bronwyn had feelings for him, deep ones, passionate ones, but they were not necessarily the emotions that bound one to another. Even if he held her tight, Bronwyn would slip through his grasp if she knew the truth. He needed to secure her heart before she ever learned the events of that awful day.

Ranulf needed Bronwyn to fall in love with him.

The realization frightened him since he hadn't the slightest idea about how to woo a woman and make her fall in love. Rolande had often touted the expediency of a good love poem, but Ranulf could hardly string together more than a few sentences. Love songs were out of the question. He had never been inclined to making music, whether it was playing an instrument or singing. That left gifts.

The castle was fairly plain and undecorated. He could start there. She had one silk gown; he could procure more. And jewelry. Bronwyn wore very little. Did she not like jewels or was she never given them? Well, he knew she enjoyed horses. He would give her a stable of them to ride. Anything she desired she would get.

* * *

Bronwyn finished lacing up the ties of one of her newest, and therefore nicest, bliauts. Never before had she cared about how she looked and she found it secretly amusing that her concern began only after she already had her man.

She glanced out the window to the courtyard below. Ranulf was talking with Tyr and the steward about where to build the night's bonfires. Her husband appeared relaxed, almost a different man from the one who had defied her while overlooking the North Tower battlements. Bronwyn wondered if she had also outwardly changed. She certainly felt different. As if she had finally found what she had been searching for . . . and she hadn't even known she was looking.

A light tap on the door interrupted her musings just before Lily burst in the room and launched herself onto the rumpled bed. Seeing Bronwyn's raised brows of disapproval, she sniffed and said, "I saw your husband downstairs so I knew I could come in." Then her gray eyes welled up with tears until they began to spill and run down her cheeks.

"Good Lord, what is wrong?" Bronwyn asked, suddenly concerned.

"I was just trying to talk to that monstrous Highlander when he told me that he wasn't at all affected by my flirtations and to practice them on someone else." She wiped the tears away with the back of her hand. "Can you believe he said that? Like I would flirt with him."

Bronwyn gave Lily a reassuring smile and sat down beside her. "I would be careful when it comes to Tyr. If he hasn't noticed you yet, he probably never will and you would only look foolish if you kept trying."

Lily opened her mouth to argue but was prevented by another knock on the door. Once again, it opened without leave. This time by Constance, who entered in a huff, wagging her finger. "If you don't come down and deal with the kitchen servants, the festivities planned for the night are doomed." Disregarding Lily and the possibility that she and Bronwyn might have been talking about something important, the old nursemaid dropped down into one of the chairs. "And don't tell me to see the steward, for he's a good part of the problem. The man has been with his lordship all morning, and as a result, no one is doing their work."

Bronwyn licked her lips and attempted to wrap the snood around her wet hair. "What happened, Constance? They kick you out of the kitchens?" The old nursemaid gave her a withering side glance and Bronwyn knew she had guessed correctly.

"No," Constance lied. "I wouldn't go near the place with the cooks demanding help to prepare tonight's feast. The baker is barking at everyone, insisting on having his own help, and those trying to clean from yesterday's festivities are getting frustrated with the ones who are already trying to decorate the windows and doors for tonight."

Bronwyn sighed and tugged at the net, pulling it free from her damp mane. She tossed it onto the bed, deciding to leave her hair down. Her short treasured respite was over. "Lily, we'll have to talk later," she said wearily and left.

* * *

The dark gold of Bronwyn's hair gleaming in the morning sun caught Ranulf's attention the moment she exited the Tower Keep. People immediately starting flocking to her, accosting her with questions. Just watching the mayhem made him tired. He had seen Edythe manage a few issues, Lily received none and therefore dealt with nothing, and his steward had been occupied with him all day. Everyone had been waiting for Bronwyn. Unfortunately, his wife's management style, while obviously beloved by all, was clearly hectic and exhausting for her.

Stopping in midconversation, Ranulf marched over and swung her into his arms. He announced to everyone within hearing that all questions were to come to him and the steward for the rest of the day and then proceeded toward the Tower Keep. The rigidity of Bronwyn's frame and her sullen expression made it clear she was far from pleased, but Ranulf didn't care. He was enjoying the fact that he could pick her up and carry her in front of everyone instead of sneaking around their home.

Their home. He had never put much value into the idea of a home and realized the reason why was because he never really had one. Ranulf grinned to himself. Here he was, far from battle, in the cold, taking care of what some would call mundane responsibilities, carrying a furious wife in his arms, and he had never been happier or more at peace. What was more, he had the rest of his life to get used to it.

During the whole trip back, Bronwyn's frustration mounted. One day of marriage and the man was coddling her, taking over her responsibilities, sending her to her room. What was she going to do with her time sitting in the solar day after day? Couldn't Ranulf see from the deluge of questions he had rudely pulled her away from that he could use her help and experience in running Hunswick?

He kicked open the door, and spying Constance and Lily sitting by the hearth chatting, he snarled at them, "You, nursemaid, go find the steward and make yourself useful. And you," he directed to Lily, "may be my wife's sister, but these are *my* bedchambers and the days of you coming in idling in her room are over."

Both women's eyes popped open wide as they jumped to their feet. Seconds later, Bronwyn heard the scuttle of footsteps racing out the door. "And Lily better not come back with Edythe," Ranulf growled loud enough for everyone to hear as he finally placed Bronwyn on her feet.

"I don't think that will be a problem. No one is going to venture anywhere near this keep after that display of temper," Bronwyn vented through gritted teeth.

Ranulf ignored her hostile stance and bent down to give her a quick soft kiss on the lips. "Good," he murmured, massaging her palm with his thumb. "I understand how everyone around here loves you and desires to get a piece of your time, but after all that has happened, I wanted to give you one day to just rest and relax. Two things I am fairly certain you haven't been able to do in a long while."

Bronwyn held her breath. Was he really just giving her some much-needed reprieve? "But what about all the problems Constance mentioned?"

"All problems may seem urgent, but you and I know they aren't. I can handle what needs to be done."

"But how? You've never run a tower, let alone a castle."

"I'm a very smart man," he answered, nudging her toward the chair to sit down. "You, love, are no longer alone. You have me. You also have a capable steward who, though old, can help with decisions. And though you think I know nothing about Twelfth-tide, I am fully aware that this is Saint John's Day, the day of bonfires, sacraments, and blessings. You are my blessing as well as everyone else's around Hunswick, and in deference to all that you give, today is your day off."

Tears formed in her eyes. Ranulf brushed them away with his thumb. "Is it really so hard to lean on me? To let someone help you?" She shook her head. "Good. Now sit and relax and I will have food brought to you shortly."

Bronwyn watched as Ranulf moved the other chair in front of her and then propped her feet on its cushions. He was so much more than her husband and lover. He was her friend. He had not wanted to usurp her contribution or belittle it. Instead, Ranulf had done what no one had—he had recognized it. The enormity and pressure of what she did, and for one day, he wanted to relieve her of that burden.

"I love you, Ranulf," she whispered.

Ranulf was just reaching for the leather strap to open the door when he heard the precious words softly voiced. He was sure that his heart had stopped, his breathing remained half in half out, his eyes refused to blink, almost waiting for her to take it back, to add a caveat, to give some reason, but none came. He glanced back, nervous, the urge to deny her claim welling within him. He had not realized how vulnerable those words . . . from her . . . made him. They could undo his soul if not true. But she only stared back at him with misty sea-colored eyes, large and luminescent and undeniably full of love . . . for him.

As if God had breathed life back into him, Ranulf was back at her side, pulling her to her feet and into a deep embrace. "I am the happiest man alive and vow to make you even happier," he stated haltingly between kisses across her brow, cheeks, and lips.

Problems be damned. There was no way he could leave, not now. Desire roared in him, not just for her body, but for all the things she had given him— happiness, peace, and above all, love. Lifting her once again, he brought her to the bed and together their bodies and souls became one.

An hour later, Ranulf left her side and dressed. He went to the door and took one last peek at her supple slumbering form. He had to tell her the truth. She loved him, trusted him, and it was time to trust her. On Epiphany, he decided, after Twelfthtide.

They would have until then to enjoy their new-found happiness.

Bronwyn poked her head into Ranulf's day room. Tyr and Tory were there talking to him but they stopped when they saw her and waved for her to enter. She had left the keep earlier to ensure Lily and Edythe were not emotionally shattered from

Ranulf's earlier decree. Surprisingly, neither was upset by his mannerism and both were actually meekish about their own behavior.

Tyr and Tory quickly left, leaving her alone with Ranulf. He reached out and pulled her into his arms, wearing an enormous grin. "Just why are you so amused?" she inquired.

"Because I finally understand why you married me. I could never figure it out before. We hadn't known each other very long, and there were many reasons why you should not have, but now I understand."

Hearing his teasing tone, Bronwyn cocked a brow and mischievously replied, "You forced me to. That's why."

"I did not."

"Yes . . . you did. I left and you came and carried me back to the altar."

A wry glint appeared in his eye. "But you could have still refused. Be honest. If anyone else, besides me, had dragged you back . . . would you now be married?"

"I . . ." Bronwyn stammered. "How should I know?"

Her empty response didn't bother Ranulf for he had complete confidence in the real answer. "Well, I know. You wouldn't have married him."

"Maybe I would have," she said, challenging his supposition. "Remember I could have asked for an annulment."

Ranulf held her just a little tighter. "But you knew with me that wouldn't be an option."

Bronwyn could sense the tension rising in Ranulf and recognized its cause. Though he had yet to make the same claim, he needed her to convince him once again of the depth of her feelings. *Soon,* she told herself, *he will be able to say it back.* "I love you," she whispered and brushed his lips with her own, letting him feel the endless need and love inside her. "And I meant every word I said. I had found the man I had always wanted and married him."

"And you are mine, Bronwyn. Forever. You have been since the moment I first saw you."

Bronwyn arched her back and poked his chest. "I wasn't your first choice, but I am happy that I'm your last," she teased.

Ranulf crinkled his brow. "What do you mean?"

"Only that Lily was your first choice."

Ranulf let go. "She wasn't my *choice,*" he stressed. "That should have been clear at the altar when I told her—*you*—that I didn't want to marry her. I never wanted to. I can't even imagine kissing Lily."

Bronwyn stepped back, feeling confusion and the first sparks of anger. "Then why did you agree to marry her?"

"I have a better question, why did *you* agree to marry someone else?" he asked, raising his voice in response to her iciness.

"Why shouldn't I have? *You* were the one who chose the man for me!"

"Well, I never thought you would agree!" Ranulf bellowed, remembering his shock at learning of her quick acquiescence to the idea of becoming another man's wife. "Do you know the hell I went through knowing you had no problems marrying another man over me? After the afternoon we shared?"

Bronwyn threw up her hands. "I didn't *choose* Garik over you. You *rejected* me and for my sister, of all people. If I chose anything, it was time. Time to make sure Lily would be happy and to ensure Edythe really wished to stay. I had plans to leave."

"And do what? Go north and find someone else?" Ranulf half snarled, realizing how close she had come to ruining their future.

"Someone *else*?" Bronwyn parroted back. She grabbed his forearm. "Look at me, Ranulf. Until you, no one ever wanted me. And I find it a little ridiculous that you could protest about my finding someone else when it was *you* who chose Lily within minutes of meeting her!"

"Damn it, I did *not* choose her! I would have never married her. Pride got me to the altar, but I was stopping the farce before it went further. Hell, until you, I never thought I would ever want to marry. You have to know after the past few days that you are everything I will ever want and far more than I dared hope to ever find. It terrified me to think that you might not feel the same. So when your sister came up and offered herself to save you . . ."

"Wait a minute!" Bronwyn shouted as clarity started to shine on the events leading to their marriage. "You were *testing* me?" Then in a much lower, quieter, and colder voice, she said, "Damn stupid test, Ranulf."

"No more stupid than using your sister to *test* me."

"I did not use my sister," Bronwyn protested, her dark blue eyes ablaze with smoldering ire. "I never *sent* her to you."

"Because you didn't need to. But instead of asking Lily about anything, you just accepted her decree, never once considering how your quick *enthusiastic* answer would sound to me."

"And just what would you have done if you were me, Ranulf?" Bronwyn challenged, moving toward the door. "Groveled and begged when you learned you were played the fool or would you have somehow scraped the remaining morsels of your pride and accepted the offer?"

"Just where do you think you are going?"

Bronwyn yanked the door open and pivoted to look at him in the eye one last time before leaving. "Out to solve a problem. I love you, Ranulf, but that was one cruel idea and it nearly cost us each other. I need to do something productive to calm down. I'll see you at dinner."

Ranulf stood in front of one of the Great Hall windows and watched Bronwyn cross the nether bailey and hand some bundles of Saint John's wort to several of the villagers. Despite his gift of letting her rest, she had been there all afternoon, helping. He was still tense about their fight, but not fearful. Neither of them exchanged threats, just heated words and emotions and, most importantly, a promise to speak later. In an odd way it spoke well of their future together, their ability to fight without tearing the other down. And he had learned an important lesson he hoped he could remember in the future—when Bronwyn was angry, she wanted to be alone.

Consequently, he had spent most of the afternoon working from his day room, keeping his mind occupied. In between answering random questions about the night's festivities, he had met with the steward about finding a mason and rebuilding the North Tower in the spring. Afterward, he had met with the stable master to discuss what would be needed to shelter the horses that would arrive in the spring with his men. Next, he dared to enter the kitchens and ensure the evening meal would be on time. He had decided very quickly that Bronwyn would be best suited for such discussions in the future. Since then he had been in the Great Hall strategizing with Tyr about the movement in the hills. The numbers of men roaming the woods had rapidly diminished in the past two days, and without knowing why, Ranulf was on his guard.

The heavy doors to the Hall swung open and a gush of cold wind caught his tunic, whipping it across his legs. It had been happening all day as the servants went about decorating everything in sight. A deep short cough alerted him that this time it was something different and he turned around. There was no one there. Frowning, Ranulf twisted a little farther until he saw Tory, who—though unintentional— made a habit of standing on his left and just outside his line of vision. The young man's face was not a happy one.

"We have a visitor," Tory announced, his voice as grim as his expression.

Tyr, who had been standing across the room by the trestles sampling food as it was brought in, came forward. "Just who is this visitor?" Hearing his normal jovial tone turn serious, the handful of other soldiers in the room rose and joined him.

"Baron Craven. He wishes to pay his respects," Tory answered, keeping his gaze on Ranulf. By now, Lily's tale of the baron and his plan was well known among his men. Tory, along with everyone else, had no idea how his lord was going to respond.

They had fought for Ranulf many times, but no one, not even Tyr, had ever seen *Deadeye Gunnar* faced with this type of situation.

"Welcome the baron in, Tory, and escort him here."

Tory blinked in surprise, but nodded and left. Tyr grimaced and his face took on the hard, angular look of a warrior preparing for battle. "Ranulf, I should be dressed better for such a meeting, don't you agree?"

Ranulf nodded, glad his friend had elected to hang around Hunswick until after the holidays. Ranulf only wished that he, too, could leave and get his sword. The chances of him needing one were small, but often its physical presence could stop a fight.

The doors swung open again as Tyr left. Before they closed, an unusually tall man with wavy blond shoulder-length hair entered the room. His piercing light blue eyes scanned the spacious area, pointedly looking at the servants, who had recommended hanging the herb bundles. Finally, they landed on Ranulf. The baron's face cringed just barely as he saw the loose flesh of Ranulf's left eyelid and realized that he was not winking at him.

Ranulf should have expected the reaction. He had been getting it since the day he awoke after his accident, but in the past few days, it had been vacant from his life. His interactions with those at Hunswick had been as if he were any other man or lord. Consequently, he had forgotten his outward appearance and people's typical response upon seeing him. Usually, though, people looked away, but not Baron Craven. His eerie blue eyes continued to assess Ranulf so he did the same.

Overall, Luc Craven looked no different close up than he did from afar. Ranulf had spent enough time in court to know that outwardly the man before him would appeal to women, but that day in the woods Bronwyn had not desired the baron's touch, she had been repelled by it.

Again, the door opened. It was Tyr, brandishing not one sword, but two, in case Ranulf desired one after all. Ranulf sauntered to the head table and stood in front of the main chair without sitting down. "I must say I am surprised to have a visitor so late in the day. As you can see, we are trying to finish preparing for tonight's feast."

Luc stopped midway and gave a respectable, if not sincere, nod. "I apologize for not coming over sooner to welcome you to the Hills, but similar responsibilities prevented me."

The doors again swung open and closed as people continued to work. Ranulf ignored them, keeping his attention only on the baron. "I completely understand, but as Twelfthtide season has begun, I wonder how it is that you were able to break free tonight."

Luc pointedly eyed the servants hanging herbs. "I confess that I do not allow the practice of all the Twelfthtide customs. I find them a nuisance and a drain on my finances, not to mention the king's."

"I guess I am fortunate to know the king."

Luc inclined his head in acknowledgment. "I had heard you had worked for him for a number of years. An advantage that might make some of your titled neighbors a bit uncomfortable."

The corners of Ranulf's mouth lifted, but didn't

quite form a smile. "Perhaps nervous enough to have men—hired men—to watch my home and lands."

One of Luc's brows quivered, the only indication that he felt the effect of Ranulf's barb. "Then I suggest you be careful until you have made local friends," Luc said smoothly, determined not to show his frustration. "I came for two reasons. First, to pay my respects to you, of course. Your predecessor was quite loved. I expect it has been hard to step into the position when it was meant for your brother."

Ranulf raised an eyebrow. Another gibe. The man felt confident enough to issue hidden insults, but he stood in the middle of the Hall between tables, not exactly a civilized speaking distance. More like a cowardly one. Ranulf decided to test the baron and advanced a few steps. Immediately, Luc shifted to his left, casually walking toward the windows and keeping his distance. Though surreptitiously done, it was enough to prove Ranulf's guess had been accurate.

Ranulf returned to his chair and sat down with a pompous flair so out of character it caused several in the room to slacken. "My assumption of the title was unexpected, but not difficult," he said with a condescending shrug of his shoulders. "From what I understand, you are my nearest neighbor and not far away."

"Just less than a day's ride. My lands are equidistant to Syndlear, but on the other side of Torrens. Or did you not know that the mountain was named after Lady Bronwyn's beloved childhood pet?" Luc asked, smiling wickedly, believing his knowledge of Bronwyn greater.

Unaffected, Ranulf returned the dishonest smile. "Soon I should come pay you a visit, if welcomed."

"And that is the topic of my second reason for coming here. I would like a moment to meet with Lady Bronwyn and her sisters. I understand that they have recently left their home to spend Twelfth-tide in your company."

Ranulf's amber gaze suddenly went dark, and danger radiated from them. "If you wish to speak to my wife, I first must ask why."

"Wife?" Luc repeated, making no pretense at hiding his shock. "Lady Bronwyn is your . . . *wife?*"

Ranulf rose and was about to end this charade when the woman in question entered the room through the kitchen passageway.

Bronwyn had been talking with the cook when she had heard the last bellowed question, as had anyone else near the Hall. Immediately recognizing Luc's voice, she darted to the Hall, slowing only just before entering. Her eyes latched on to Ranulf for a brief second before pivoting to see sky blue orbs boring into her. "Baron Craven, I see you have met my husband."

Luc sauntered over to where she stood and grandly picked up her hand. Holding it for an extended period of time, he bent over and kissed it, his eyes blazing. "I see you forgot the promise made to me, a promise made by the king."

A low menacing growl came from Ranulf, and Tyr readied both swords, prepared to toss one to his friend with just a single look. "Let go of my wife's hands." The command held no compromise, only pain if not obeyed.

Luc squeezed the fingers and let them go. "I had

the understanding these fingers were meant for me. What would you do if someone stole your long-fought-for and finally earned bride?" he taunted aloud, keeping his attention solely on his lost prize.

Bronwyn's blue eyes darkened into angry thunderclouds. "A bride promised by someone now dead, not King Henry."

"Bronwyn . . ." Luc said, stepping in closer.

She took a step back. "As you pointed out at our last meeting, we are no longer children. You may refer to me as Lady Anscombe." Then with an abrupt turn, Bronwyn went and joined Ranulf, clasping his hand to hers, not for comfort but to keep him at her side. If Luc continued, things were about to become bloody. He did not seem to care that he was alone and making enemies.

Luc fought back a tremble of anger. He refused to show weakness. He was a noble and Ranulf could not kill him without cause, for doing so would come with consequences. "Then I demand to see her sisters!"

Ranulf felt Bronwyn's grip increase, warning him to stay still. She was probably right. However, it did not change his desire to get her out of there before things escalated. "As my wife's sisters were married on the same day, I have no doubt their husbands will also demand to know why."

Enraged to discover the leverage he held was nonexistent, Luc's eyes stabbed Bronwyn. "I should have been the one," he sputtered, advancing toward her, unheeding of the danger he was in. "You were for me. I refused all others, endured my father's anger all to have *you* . . . and you betrayed me to marry a cripple. How could you? He doesn't love you, not like me."

Bronwyn reached inside her bliaut and slid her palm around the leather girth hidden within. "It doesn't matter if he loves me, Luc, I love him."

"After what he did to you? How can you when—"

"You've said enough, baron," Ranulf interjected, his skin pale with wrath. Stepping forward in front of Bronwyn, he signaled his soldiers, who had been quietly entering the Hall, to encircle Luc. "I think it best that you leave now."

Luc gritted his teeth and remained silent, recognizing the look in Ranulf's eye. They were merciless, and another word would undoubtedly mean his death. But it did not matter. Hunswick was not his battleground. Here was the one place Ranulf was strong. Everywhere else it was the reverse. And Luc had seen what he needed to defeat Ranulf and take back what should have been his. His final probing question had not angered Bronwyn, but perplexed her. Luc took a chance and glanced at her one more time, relishing her still crinkled brow.

She did not know.

Luc artfully nodded once more, pivoted, and left the Hall, vowing to himself that he would have his revenge.

The moment Baron Craven was out of sight, Ranulf waved for his men to escort him completely off his property. Without even asking, Tyr tossed him one of the swords and grunted, "I'll see that it is done."

With that, Tyr was gone, leaving only a few servants, who had been praying that they would be able to escape before the fighting commenced. So when

Ranulf let go a clipped, "Leave now," all dropped what they were doing and hastened out of the room, suddenly eager to find their friends and loved ones to tell the tale. Finally alone, Ranulf spun Bronwyn around, closed his hand around the back of her head, and brought his mouth down to hers. He parted her lips with his tongue, desperately claiming her once again, needing to know that she was still his and only his.

Bronwyn moaned softly and tightened her grip on his shoulder, trembling at the intensity. To his every demand, she surrendered. When he finally ended the kiss, it was a long while before she opened her eyes. Staring back was anguish and love.

Without a word, he scooped her up into his arms and carried her to the hearth chairs, settling her on his lap. Ranulf cupped her cheek and she held her breath, his touch so tender. Then he kissed her once more, lightly, persuasively, pulling her closer to him.

Bronwyn leaned in to deepen the kiss when he broke free and sat her back up. "Hold on," he groaned and reached inside her bliaut to find the painful object stabbing his leg. He pulled out a small, but sharp dagger, which she had been clutching earlier. "Was tonight special or do you carry that thing with you all the time?"

"Not *all* the time," she answered defensively, her tone indicating that more often than not it was with her.

He eyed her and then put down the sharp blade on the table next to them. "Do you know how to use it? Or do you just feel safer with a weapon?" he asked carefully.

Bronwyn leaned in close again and let her lips

tease the place directly behind his right ear. "Someday I will give you a demonstration of my skills. But not now."

Ranulf swallowed, knowing what would happen if he allowed her to continue, and nudged her head down so that it rested on his chest. He was far from the mood to start a fight, but daggers were dangerous, and if not handled properly, they could give the attacker more of an edge than the owner.

Sighing, Bronwyn nestled closer. "Today has been a long day."

"I'm sorry about this morning."

"What did Luc mean, Ranulf? What does he think you did to me that would make me hate you or at the very least not want to be married to you?"

Instantly, the tension draining him returned. Bronwyn had not missed the baron's parting question or its meaning. He stared at the fire and slowly stroked her spine, wondering how to begin. Unable to find the words, he said, "There is something that you should know about my past. I had planned— and still plan—to tell you after Epiphany. It is not pleasant, but I also promise you that it will not change anything between us. I need you to trust me. Can you do that? Trust me enough to wait and believe that nothing you will ever learn of me or I of you will diminish what we feel for each other?"

Dark heavy lashes shadowed her cheeks. So Luc had been right. There was something she should know about Ranulf. But Luc had also been wrong. Ranulf was not hiding it from her and never had intended to keep it a secret. He wanted time and she could understand why. She felt as if she had known Ranulf a lifetime, but in reality, their time together had been very brief and mostly tumultuous. After weathering these past few days of doubt and distrust, she knew nothing he could reveal would change how she felt about him. But Ranulf had not had the years of familial love and acceptance she had received. He was still new to what they shared, and if he needed more time to believe it could not be broken, she would give it to him.

"Until after Epiphany," she whispered. "And whatever it is, I shall not leave, Ranulf. This is where I belong, with you, in your arms."

Her gaze locked with his, and Ranulf felt an overwhelming warmth invade his heart as it began to beat again. The fear inside him began to recede. He was going to survive, after all. "I'll never let you go, angel," he said, his eyes turning to molten gold.

"You better not," she whispered just before his lips once again consumed hers.

Chapter Ten

Childermas, the Old English name for Children's Mass, originated sometime in the fourth or fifth century and is recounted every year in the haunting melody and words of the "Coventry Carol." Though celebrated on different days depending upon religion and nation, it is always associated with the Nativity, commemorating the children two years old and younger massacred by Herod after his failed attempt to eliminate the child Jesus. The Christian Church honors these children as martyrs for they are the first killed by deed, if not by will, dying not only for Christ, but in his stead. The day's customs focus on children, who get to decide the foods and entertainment, but Childermas is also notably known as the unluckiest day of the year because of the horror attached to it. Consequently, in medieval times, work was avoided wherever possible and marrying on this day was heavily discouraged.

Bronwyn pushed the heavy brush aside and looked into the rocky clearing where she expected to find an injured boy. But it was no child standing in the center. Luc Craven had tricked her into leaving Hunswick, and going beyond Ranulf's immediate reach.

Last night, Tyr had come back declaring the baron had returned to his lands, and he might have, but Luc knew Torrens almost as well as she. He could have easily snuck back and evaded the few guards Ranulf had placed in the woods. Seeing the golden stubble sparkling on his sculpted cheeks and dark circles enhancing the dangerous glitter of his ice blue eyes, Bronwyn knew that was exactly what he had done.

She should have expected Luc would try such a move, especially after his humiliating departure last night. But never did she suspect a ruse when one of the village children told her that a boy had fallen off the jumping rocks and needed help. Ranulf had already left to fetch the youngest child for the feast that night. She had expected him back soon, but unwilling to wait while a boy was in pain, she had left, asking one of Ranulf's soldiers to be her escort.

"Gowan," Bronwyn said sharply, gaining the young soldier's attention as he waited for her to proceed. "I need you to return to Hunswick and find Ranulf. Tell him why I left and that I will be right here waiting for him."

Gowan flexed his grip on his sword. She thought he was going to argue with her, but he finally gave her a curt nod and returned toward the castle. Fortunately, he could not see through the brush; otherwise he would have recognized Luc and she would have never persuaded him to leave. As soon as the young soldier vanished, she gripped the small dagger hidden in the pocket of her bliaut and stepped through the brush, knowing that if she returned as well, Luc would follow.

Once inside the clearing, Luc advanced until he was standing just out of arms' reach in front of her. She flashed him a look of disdain and held her ground. "You should leave now, Luc, while you can. Ranulf won't be so understanding."

A shadow of triumph swept across Luc's face. "Worried for me?" he asked, his voice full of contempt. "How touching and very unnecessary. I know these woods nearly as well as you do, angel. Your new lord could only find me if I wished him to."

Bronwyn looked at him with mute defiance, hating to hear the truth. The landscapes of Cumbria were varied. On many the grass grew wild, unencumbered with trees. But around Bassellmere, the woods were thick, creating many places to hide, and Luc knew them all. In a year, maybe two, Ranulf would as well, but at this moment, if Luc decided to disappear, he could confidently do so.

"Angel—" Luc began, inching forward.

Bronwyn stepped back to maintain the space between them. "Don't call me that."

"Why? Is that what he calls you?" His cold eyes sniped at her. "It's a wonder you can even stand his touch, but I can fix that."

Luc's sudden change in attitude toward her put Bronwyn even more on guard. Last night, he had been incensed upon learning she was married and that she loved her husband. So what game was he playing now? He wasn't here to spirit her away, but something else. What was he trying to achieve? "You spent a lot of effort getting me here. Why?"

He shrugged, not offended by her question or her desire to keep her distance. "It was actually very little effort. No more than, say, the amount as you spent in sending the boy soldier to play fetch, leaving us alone . . . so you could learn the truth about your beloved *husband*."

"I'm not afraid of you anymore, Luc. Hurting me will be regarded as an act of war—a war you would lose and I think you know it. You value your life far too much to risk it on me."

"How little you know me, angel." The flames smoldering in Luc's eyes suddenly dimmed, leaving them ice cold and emotionless. "I *loved* you."

The hot breath she was holding burned in her throat. "That's not love, Luc. Your desire for power dominates anything you could feel for me. You never wanted me. You covet Syndlear and are angry it is forever out of your grasp."

Luc scoffed and began to pace. "I don't deny I wanted Syndlear. With it came everything I ever deserved, most of all *you*," he asserted, pausing to look her in the eye. He took a step in her direction. "And do not deceive yourself into believing the new Lord Anscombe is any different. You think I'm cruel and unkind, but I have never harmed anyone you loved. *I'm* not the one who killed your father."

Bronwyn felt the air leave her lungs as a bitter cold feeling of anguish gripped her soul. She examined Luc's face, seeking evidence of lies or exaggerations, but found none. He was telling the truth.

"Your lover didn't mention that, did he?" Luc continued. "Did he tell you that he *knew* your father?

That they traveled on the same ship? And that just before they reached England, it was your *husband* who pushed over several crates, crushing the one man who forced him into his duty? Didn't you ever wonder why the king ordered the new lord to marry Lillabet and not you? Penance, angel. Lily brings her husband beauty, but you . . . you come with land. But he defied our new king, didn't he? And you accuse me of desiring power."

"I don't believe you," Bronwyn choked, barely able to speak.

"Yes, you do," Luc countered, his voice laced with dark warning. He moved forward and grasped her upper arms. "That cripple took you from me. He tricked you, lied to you, but it is not too late. Come with me and I will see you get an annulment. We can still be together."

Bronwyn wrenched free and flung out her hands to keep him from coming close. Anger surged through her, temporarily driving out the sorrow. "If what you say is true . . . I don't know what I'll do, but I'll never be with you. I don't love you, Luc. I never will. And how my father died changes nothing."

Luc's eyes dimmed and she saw the fury boiling inside him. He finally understood that she would never be his; he had been clinging to a fantasy that would never come true. And with it, her belief that he wouldn't hurt her disappeared.

Bronwyn reached in her bliaut for her dagger and wrapped her palm around its girth, preparing to take aim. But then he pivoted and grabbed the mane of his horse to mount. His white-knuckled grip on the reins revealed his raging fury. "Take great care, Lady

Anscombe, for if I can't have you, I will no longer concern myself over your welfare."

Then he was gone.

The moment of imminent confrontation passed. Swallowing a sob that rose in her throat, she felt her legs give beneath her. Grief and despair tore at her as the enormity of Luc's revelation washed over her. Finally, tears broke free, as she allowed herself to feel the agony of her father's loss. When strong arms encircled her, lifting her off the ground, she did not stop them. She continued to weep until she had no more tears to shed.

Ranulf's blood raced and the tight knot in his stomach doubled. His heart pounded with every sob that overtook her limp body. He clenched Bronwyn to him tightly, wishing his sheer presence could diminish her pain, but with her continued silence, he feared that it was just the opposite.

When Gowan had found him and repeated Bronwyn's message, a cold fear like he had never known ripped through him as he realized what happened and that Luc was alone with his wife. As Ranulf tore off to find Bronwyn, Tyr had ordered the young soldier to remain behind, probably to save his life for leaving her ladyship. But Ranulf had been too busy blaming himself for not anticipating Luc's plan.

Bronwyn let go a soft whimper and he tightened his grip. She didn't resist, but she had not wrapped her arms around him. Instead, she huddled within herself, withdrawing from him. It was tearing him apart.

He should have told Bronwyn the truth last night.

He should have told her right after they met. But he had been afraid of losing her. And now he would.

Arriving back at Hunswick, Ranulf drove Pertinax through the gatehouse. He threw the reins at one of the stable boys and then swung down. He was about to slide Bronwyn off the horse and into his arms, when she slipped to the ground to stand beside him. He put his arm around her, tucking her protectively against his side, and guided her across the courtyard to keep onlookers from realizing something was wrong.

Just before he reached the Tower Keep, Father Morrell appeared before him. "My lord, I need to ask you about the Feast of Innocents and when you intend to bless the children."

"Do it yourself," Ranulf gritted out and stepped around him, keeping Bronwyn next to him. "Her ladyship is ill. Neither of us will be attending."

The priest tried to argue, but Ranulf left him stammering as he directed Bronwyn into the Tower Keep and up the stairs to his solar. He kicked open the door, and after settling her in the hearth chair, he went to throw another log into the fire.

Bronwyn pulled her knees up close and watched him from beneath lowered lashes as he moved to bolt the door. Was he caging his rage? Or had she imagined the slight tremor when he left her side? As soon as Ranulf turned around, she had her answer. He was furious. But at who?

She rotated her gaze to rest on the fire and rested her cheek against her knee. Ranulf moved behind her and she felt his knuckles graze her back as he clutched the frame of the chair. "Did he . . . hurt you? Touch you?"

His tone reflected what she had seen, fear and

potential uncontrollable rage. "No," she whispered, her voice raspy. She licked her lips. "He just wanted to talk. To tell me about what happened to my father."

Ranulf did not say a word, but she could feel his knuckles grow sharper as his grip grew tighter.

"Did you . . ." Bronwyn started, pausing in mid-thought. She had thought about directly asking if he had killed her father, but the question sounded too much like she believed he murdered him. "Was it you that caused the accident?" she finally asked.

"Aye."

Bronwyn waited, but Ranulf said nothing more. No explanation, no justification, no reasons. She had expected more, wanted more, needed something to prove that what Luc had told her was made up of partial truths, and mostly lies. But if Luc had been right about her father . . . then what of his other claim? Bronwyn pulled her knees tighter toward her chest. "Then you married me for Syndlear," she murmured, not realizing her random thoughts had been spoken aloud.

Ranulf abruptly released the back of her chair and in two steps was in front of her. Her statement had cut him deeper than any wound ever could. The first accusation he had expected, but the second? "What do you want me to say? No, I didn't marry you for Syndlear. Yes, I was there when your father died. He was a . . . good man. And his death was a great loss to me. If you are going to believe anything, believe that," he growled. "Or do you need to go run out and find your baron to confirm it?"

She shook her head and brushed away newly formed tears. "Please tell me what happened. How you met, where my father died, about Syndlear . . . I need to know. I need to know all of it."

Regret for his harsh words assailed Ranulf. He sank into the hearth chair beside her and faced her, his elbows on his knees. Her forehead was resting on her thigh, and more than anything, he wanted to gather her in his arms and hold her close, letting her use him as support, but he remained seated, and answered her question.

He told her everything—how he had met Laon, what happened, and the promise her father had made him make. Bronwyn never interrupted or stopped him and he found himself telling her more than he'd ever intended. How her father was one of the few to challenge his beliefs, his way of thinking. How Laon forced him to see a world that could benefit not just from his sword and bow, but from his experiences. That her father loved his daughters immensely. That he was a great man, who had a singular ability to persuade people to his position on things, even the new king and queen—something few could do. Throughout it all, she remained silent. Not moving or saying anything to give him an indication of whether he should say more or less. Finally, he could add nothing further.

Slipping down to his knees, Ranulf gathered her hands in his and tucked back a lock of her hair almost as if he was afraid to touch her. "Would you like to be alone?"

Bronwyn digested the question. Emotionally, she didn't want him to go, but if he stayed, she would crumple and cave in to the desire to be held in his arms. And she wasn't ready mentally to accept comfort from the very man responsible for her grief. Unable to put voice to her warring desires, she nodded.

Rising, Ranulf walked over to the chest by the window and pulled something out. She couldn't discern what it was and wasn't going to risk looking at him to find out. "I'll have some food delivered to you. Try and eat." She felt his lips against her hair. "I'm so sorry, Bronwyn," he whispered and then left.

Suddenly, she felt more bereft and desolate than ever before. Tears once again scalded her eyes, flooding them until she could not see. Unable to sit up any longer, she stumbled to the bed and let go all that she felt. For hours, she lay there weeping, overwhelmed with loneliness and the emptiness surrounding her. And when she could cry no more, she sat up, wishing Ranulf would return, for at last she understood much of her despair was because he was not there. Hearing about her father's death, she had initially felt as if the years ahead were suddenly vacant, with no one to share her happiness or her pain, no one to care whether she lived or died. But she did have someone. Ranulf.

Getting up, Bronwyn splashed water on her face and noticed that a tray of food was perched on one of the small hearth tables. She had been so deep in her sorrow she had not even known when it had been delivered. Walking over, she pulled apart a piece of bread and went to go stand by the window. It was dark but she could see people scurrying around the courtyard. The feast was still going on in the Great Hall, but she did not feel like leaving the room and participating.

After tossing another log on the fire, she resettled herself in the chair and nibbled on the meat, thinking over what Ranulf had told her. Yes, he had caused the accident, but it had been far from intentional. Still, she had other questions, starting with why had Ranulf believed it necessary to keep this from her. Didn't he trust her? When he returned, Bronwyn intended to ask.

After a while, her back began to hurt and her tailbone could stand to sit no longer. She crawled back into bed, wishing for Ranulf to return. Had he thought she wanted to be alone all night? For she hadn't. She had only wanted time to think, to digest . . . and mostly just to grieve. She'd never really had the chance before.

Unable to keep her eyes open any longer, she fell asleep, vowing that when she awoke, she would seek him out. Tell him that she was glad to know the truth. That it gave her peace to know he had met her father and that he was in heaven smiling because they were together. Tomorrow, she would tell Ranulf that he was right.

Nothing she would ever learn could diminish what she felt for him.

Ranulf knelt down and studied the shaded wooded path for a minute. Most of the time, Luc's trail could be easily discerned, indicating he either did not care if he was followed or just inept, but the sun was setting and it was getting harder to follow. When Ranulf started, he had not intended on tracking the baron for this long, but he had desperately needed something to do and be by himself.

When he had left, he had told Tyr that he would be back shortly, never realizing where his trek would

take him. His initial goal had been to stay away as
Bronwyn requested, but when he arrived to where
he had found her huddled, shaking and alone, the
simmering fury within him raged anew. Clues to
where the baron had gone beckoned him and so he
started to follow them.

It was not until Syndlear loomed in front of him
that he realized how far he had gone. The afternoon
sun beamed down on the vacated building. He went
in and looked around to see if any of the baron's
mercenaries had made themselves a temporary
home, but it looked unused. The empty stone structure was well fortified and, though not especially
spacious, in good shape. Situated at the top of Torrens, its view spanned far into the valleys on either
side of the mountain, making it an ideal outlook for
either the baron's land or his own.

He considered returning to Hunswick, but opted
to continue following the trail. Luc was traveling
alone and his route showed no indications he intended to stay on Hunswick lands. The baron was on
his way home, and its location and level of protection had become of great interest to Ranulf. Luc was
not an adversary—but an enemy. Soon, they would
meet again and one of them would die.

Carefully, Ranulf followed the path down the moun-
tainside. The wooded landscape had changed to a
rockier and steep terrain, with sparse vegetation to
hide his movements. He had been forced to stop for
fear of being seen, but soon resumed after night arrived, cloaking his movements. Quickly Ranulf realized
that the baron did not expect his or anyone's arrival
for he had to avoid only a few sentries, who were more
interested in sleeping than manning their posts.

Ranulf continued down the mountain, crossing one river, before he got to the valley below . . . and within eyesight of Baron Craven's home. The motte and bailey castle in sheer size could almost rival that of Hunswick. But it had one significant weakness many of the Saxon castles littering the English countryside still possessed. It was made of wood. Only a single plinth of a future curtain tower was being rebuilt of the local rock. It was no wonder the baron coveted Syndlear. He meant to dismantle it and use the already mined and shaped stones.

Ranulf took his time surveying the land and those who protected it. Five to six dozen hired men had meandered around before falling asleep, leaving only a couple actually awake enough to be considered on watch. If Ranulf and his men ever went into battle with the baron's purchased army, Ranulf knew he would prevail despite the gross difference in numbers. Still, there would be losses.

In the distance, the air growled and Ranulf could smell the rain. It was still far away, but the moonlight, which had been guiding him, had dimmed considerably by the clouds rolling in. He had seen enough. It was time to retreat and make his way back home.

He prayed that Bronwyn was now ready to see him, but even if she wasn't, she would just have to accept his presence. They were married and he was not about to lose her. It may take time for her to forgive him, but she would. Of that he was certain. She loved him, and more importantly, she knew that he loved her.

Just as the thought flashed in his mind, Ranulf realized she might not know. He had never actually told her. He had meant to, but somehow never did.

He needed to get back.

Chapter Eleven

Throughout history, there are accountings of a Christmas truce, where weapons were laid down, creating a period of peace. In recent years, the cease-fire would be on Christmas Eve, but in medieval times, the chivalric code called for a battle truce through the whole of Twelfthtide. The most well-known Christmas truce occurred in 1914 during the Great War between the French and Germans, later becoming a focus of plays, songs, books, and movies. In the Middle Ages, however, the more famed truces are those that failed. One of the bloodiest battles of the Wars of the Roses took place during the holiday season, when York forces attempted to attack unprepared Lancasters. Even court was not immune to the potential fickleness of the truce. Both Henry IV and his sons were very nearly murdered during Christmastide in 1399. Four years later, the holiday season again provided the cloak needed for a second—and

*again failed—assassination attempt. Queen Elizabeth I
had her own Christmas nightmares, both plotted and
executed. Even King Henry II of this story felt the
sharp spear of the truce's failure when his one-time
companion Thomas à Becket was murdered after an
inflammatory Christmas sermon.*

Bronwyn stretched. She had not slept well at all.
In the middle of the night, she had been awakened
by thunder and went to search for Ranulf, only to
be told that he was occupied. The storm had not
brought any rain, but it was indicative of upcoming
weather. Winter had finally reached Cumbria.

Curses followed by several shouts from outside
caught her attention. Rising, she flexed once again
to loosen muscles stiffened from sleeping in the
hearth chair and moved to peer out the window. Instantly her warm breath fogged the glass. It was cold
outside and the wind was rattling the panes. Thankfully, no feast or outside activities had been planned.
However, it was customary for those living close to or
within the castle to gather in the Great Hall throughout Twelfthtide to enjoy each other's company.

Bronwyn glanced back at the empty bed. Ranulf
had obviously decided to sleep elsewhere and was
waiting for her to leave before he came to the room
to freshen himself. Next time she would be much
more specific to the amount of time she needed
when asking to be alone. She had been allowed to
think, but none of her conclusions had ended her
turmoil. She needed to speak with Ranulf.

Another wail erupted and this time Bronwyn
looked straight down to see a small crowd just outside of the chapel. Father Morrell would explode.

After being forced to conduct three weddings on Christmas, endure Luc's invasion during the Feast for Saint John, and accept her and Ranulf's absence on the night of the Holy Innocents, the devout priest was probably on the verge of either a stroke or a mental collapse.

The group had moved into the shadows, most likely to protect themselves against the wind. She could make out Constance's hostile stance and a couple of guards, but the majority of the figures was facing the other way. She was about to go down and remind them about their dangerous location for such a boisterous activity when one of the shadows moved. The round, short silhouette could only belong to Father Morrell. Seconds later, Tyr stepped back into view along with both her sisters.

All looked to be angry or frustrated, including the priest, who was more than animated. She could not remember seeing any person of the cloth so visibly agitated. Her eyes darted elsewhere, looking for Ranulf, but he was nowhere in sight. Her desire to find him had to wait. Whatever was going on, a calmer head was needed.

Moving quickly, she donned her hose, woolen chainse, and heaviest bliaut, and at the last moment, grabbed a blanket to wrap around her shoulders. She then dashed down the stairwell and hastened toward the small party. Everyone quieted on her arrival, but the frustration in the air was palpable. As she was trying to decide who to calm first—Father Morrell or her sisters—her decision was made for her.

"Women," Tyr grumbled, gesturing toward her sisters.

"What about them?"

"I'm just glad I'm not one, that's all."

Bronwyn quirked her eyebrow at the idea and asked, "Where's Ranulf?"

Tyr pressed his lips together and frowned. "He's out and will be back shortly. If you need something, I'll take care of it."

Bronwyn gave a quick shake of her head and dropped the bulky wrap. The wind was biting, but when blocked, the heavy bliaut and thick chainse were more than enough to keep her warm. "I do not need anything. I was just wondering what was upsetting everyone."

"Nothing important," Tyr groaned, rubbing the dark circles around his eyes.

"Maybe not important to you—" started Father Morrell.

"See?!" Lily shouted, staring at Bronwyn as if she suddenly understood everything and was on her younger sister's side.

"I've had enough," Tyr bellowed back and started heading toward the stables. Bronwyn ran to catch up with him. "Don't start. I am not about to send anyone after a missing tapestry just to pacify two women and a priest."

Understanding dawned on Bronwyn. The only weaving she knew that could cause such commotion *and* have the support of Father Morrell was the one her mother had created of her daughters. "You are right," Bronwyn said matter-of-factly.

"Then maybe you can tell that to your sisters and make them see reason," he grunted, slightly calmer after hearing the three magic words. "I'm just glad

I don't have to deal with such nonsense for the rest of my life. When Ranulf comes back, I'm gone."

Bronwyn stopped and let Tyr continue toward the stables without her, suspecting there was much more to his frustration than even he realized. Turning around, she went back to confront her sisters, but they were gone.

She found them in her old bedchamber, slumped in hearth chairs wearing grumpy expressions. Both were arguing simultaneously, their anger and hurt unmistakable. When they saw her, their voices rose, chattering about Father Morrell and Tyr and how both men were incredibly unfair.

A half hour later, Bronwyn thought she understood the situation and why everyone was so on edge. She was not the only one who had little sleep the night before and all were emotionally drained. Normally, she could dispel her sisters' frustrations before they rose to such levels, but she had not been around.

On Christmas, Lily realized that she had forgotten her mother's tapestry in her rush to leave Syndlear and then had misled Father Morrell about having it. She had asked Tyr to recover the item and he had readily agreed, but it seemed he had not been specific as to when he intended to do so. Then last night, when Father Morrell came to retrieve the weaving to hang it behind him during his sermon about the Holy Innocents, Edythe let it be known Lily had left it at Syndlear. The priest had held his peace until this morning, but at the break of dawn he confronted Lily about her misdeeds. Lily in turn blamed Tyr, and soon after, insults were being slung about with no one, including the priest, being immune.

Bronwyn listened quietly. Then just as she believed both her sisters had completely discharged all their frustrations, Edythe exclaimed, "And just where were you last night? Everyone was very confused when Father Morrell gave the blessing . . . *alone.*"

Bronwyn hated dishonesty, even though burdening her sisters with the truth of their father's death was not something she wanted to do. At least not now. Not during Twelfthtide. Suddenly the dilemma Ranulf had been in became clear. But she knew based on experience that keeping such secrets brought only additional pain.

Taking a deep breath, Bronwyn told her sisters what she had learned the previous day. Both listened in shock to the news of their father. Lily ran to her room, but Edythe remained stoic. Bronwyn knew she would grieve later, in her own way.

"What are you going to do?" Edythe asked.

"I am going to ride up to Syndlear and get that tapestry," Bronwyn replied, rising to her feet. "While I am gone, Lily is going to muster up the courage to apologize to Father Morrell and you are going to pay a visit to Tyr and do the same."

Edythe's cheeks warmed and for a moment Bronwyn thought she was going to argue, but Edythe instead gave a quick bob of her head. Bronwyn almost felt sorry for her. Lily was going to have to do a month's worth of penances, but she suspected Edythe would suffer a far worse punishment in facing Tyr.

Bronwyn went to leave when Edythe reached out

and held her sleeve. "What should we tell Ranulf when he asks where you are?"

"Tell him I'll be back this afternoon and we will talk then."

Bronwyn had never seen Syndlear so deserted. Even during Twelfthtide, families usually took turns keeping the place running while most came down to Hunswick for the celebrations. This year, however, Ranulf had ordered everyone down to the castle for the winter, in order to keep from splitting his few forces between the two dwellings.

Logically, the decision made sense, but it was hard to imagine a battle of any significance taking place in Cumbria. Beyond small skirmishes between families, strife had been absent and Luc would not dare attack unprovoked. Based on what Ranulf told her, the new king would be quick to retaliate against such unsanctioned aggression.

She rewrapped the thick blanket around her and ventured inside. Despite the sun being high in the sky, its interior was dark and cold from the hearths not being lit. The lack of odor told her the place had been left clean. Even the rushes had been removed to help diminish the number of critters visiting while all were gone. Bronwyn glanced around to see if anything had been taken by vandals, but all looked to be as it should. Edythe would have been able to tell in an instant if anything was gone, for she loved this keep as much as Bronwyn loved Hunswick. For her, Syndlear held very little value. It was the people it housed that had any meaning. The building itself held too many dark memories, ones that she never could quite visualize, but hovered nonetheless just out of reach.

She moved up the staircase quickly to the third floor, eager to get the tapestry and leave. The overly large room had once belonged to their mother and had been converted to Lily's chambers when she became of age. On the bed was the forgotten weaving, folded and ready to be packed. Bronwyn went to retrieve the item when behind her the door slammed shut. A scuffle of something being wedged in the frame immediately followed. "Is someone there?"

"Only me," came a snide reply. "Your intended husband."

"Luc? What are you doing?" Bronwyn asked as she advanced to the door and tried to open it. It did not budge. "Let me out!"

"Begging for me to help you now? That's a change." A cold chuckle chilled her blood. "I thought you would never want me under any circumstances. Funny how you seem to run to the nearest man whenever you feel in trouble. What will you promise me? Your body?" Luc inquired, sneering.

"Luc, let me out now. If Ranulf finds out what you have done—"

"Your precious lord is right now caught in a trap I set for him."

Bronwyn held her breath. "I don't believe you."

"You should," Luc replied, the promise in his tone unmistakable.

"You wouldn't dare hurt him," Bronwyn whispered, trying to convince herself as much as Luc.

"Harm one of the new king's beloved noblemen? Not directly, but if your lover cares for you like he claims, then he will wish I did."

"You are just begging for an early death, Luc."

"Correction, *angel*," he countered. "Death is what *you* asked for by marrying him and not me. Do you not remember what I said about no longer caring for your welfare?"

The contempt he held for her was enormous. She had been naïve to believe that his plans of revenge ended with his revelation about her father. He still wanted to hurt her. His question proved that.

"Do you?!" Luc roared when she didn't answer.

"I remember," Bronwyn finally murmured, wishing there was some other way out of the room. There were secret passageways added to the solar and the rooms she and her sisters used as small children, but none had been constructed here. Only the storage spaces her father had built into every room above the first floor.

"Maybe I should have said that if I couldn't have you, no one could. If I had, would it have made a difference?"

She had been unprepared for the threat. *Agree to come with him and live, or stay and die.* Until now, she had assumed Luc intended only to frighten her by leaving her locked in the room alone until someone came to get her, which was probably tomorrow at the earliest. But Luc's plans did not have her living that long. "No, it would not have made a difference," she stated truthfully.

His cackle caused her to tremble. "That's what I love about you, angel. You have more courage than anyone—man or woman—I have ever met. I will miss that in Lillabet when I make her my wife."

Bronwyn slammed her fist against the door in protest. "She's already married!"

"I don't believe you. The woman I saw had not been touched by a man, and when I go to the king and tell him of her trickery to prevent me from what was mine . . . then an annulment is sure to follow."

"Don't do this, Luc. Please . . ."

"Too late, angel. Just know in the end I will have everything that was supposed to be mine, despite your efforts."

Fear twisted her gut as she heard his footsteps retreat. She raced to the outside wall and used the arrow slits to stare below. After several minutes, he appeared, mounted his horse, and rode off in the direction of his own lands.

It doesn't make sense, she thought to herself. Maybe she had been wrong about the level of revenge he sought. Then it occurred to her who was the real target. Ranulf. She started to pace back and forth. Of all the people she had ever met, Ranulf was the most capable. Luc might be setting a trap, but Ranulf was no ordinary prey. He would rescue her. Her job was to stay alive until that time.

She was hungry and thirsty. Walking over to the small table beside the bed, she picked up the pitcher next to the empty basin and sighed with relief. There was water. After drinking enough to satiate her thirst, she decided to save the rest and went to sit down on the bed. Worry was not her typical approach to handling problems, but as she was powerless to do anything else, her mind began to replay all that Luc had said, especially the comments regarding Lily. She had to get out.

Standing, Bronwyn returned to the door, hoping that if she hit it enough times, whatever was wedged on the other side would give free. On the fifth body assault with no indication that it was working at all, Bronwyn took a deep frustrated breath.

Smoke.

Icy fear twisted around her heart. She had not made a mistake. Luc did not desire to starve her out or have her rescued too late to help Ranulf. He had planned to do just what he intimated—he wanted her dead.

Bronwyn could smell the smoke stronger now and was transported back in time. Crumpling to the floor, she rocked back and forth just as she had as a little girl, waiting for her mother to save her. But no one would this time. No one would even try. Her father had sworn this would never happen again, he would make sure they were safe, he promised to protect his family and . . . suddenly Bronwyn remembered that he had.

Jumping to her feet, she ran to the little stone cubby that held all their childhood keepsakes and started pulling everything out. Old dolls, worn blankets, favorite whittled items, one by one, she tossed them into the room. Fire had not reached the door, but heat emanated from the floor below, indicating that flames were eating through on the other side.

Soon the small area was clear. Bronwyn grabbed the tapestry and threw it in followed by a couple of woolen blankets. Then, she started to wedge herself in. The cracking snaps of the floor giving away echoed in the stone death chamber just as she was able to get inside. Her fingers curled around the leather strap her father told her never to pull unless there was a fire. She gave it a yank. Nothing happened. She yanked it again, harder, and a large stone fell into place.

She was now safe from the fire, but she was also trapped with no way to get out.

Ranulf dismounted, glad to make it back to Hunswick before the dinner hour. He tossed the reins to the eager stable boy and headed out across the courtyard toward the Keep. He had not even made it halfway to his destination when Tyr intercepted him, scowling. Ranulf recognized the pained expression. His friend had a headache, most likely caused by Ranulf dumping everything on him, including his new family.

Opting not to ask the question that might initiate an hour-long conversation regarding the agonies of responsibility, Ranulf continued toward his destination. "I'm going to see Bronwyn."

Tyr stopped short and crossed his arms. "Not there you aren't. She went to visit her sisters this morning, who are quite wisely staying out of my way and Father Morrell's sight. Your wife's still with them."

"Thanks," Ranulf mumbled and changed direction only to be stopped by his friend again.

Seeing Ranulf's icy glare, Tyr shrugged unperturbed, and explained, "No woman—even one that loves you—is going to want to be in the same room with your stench. So if you are hoping to charm your lovely wife back into your arms, I suggest you take a bath first."

Ranulf inventoried his muddied state and realized his friend was correct. Clapping Tyr on the shoulder, Ranulf gave him a parting wink and ventured into the kitchens. Two days ago, he had vowed never to enter that domain again, and yet here he was. Not many occupied the room, but the ones who were there were buzzing with activity. Seeing him, Constance gave a little yelp and nearly toppled the beans she was preparing. She quickly recovered and sent him a scathing look before resuming her task. Well, the old woman was consistent with her loyalty to Bronwyn.

"I need a hot bath to be delivered to my bed-chambers, and you," he said, looking at Constance, "go find Bronwyn and have her meet me in the Great Hall." Leaving, he heard her mutter that she would go, but only when she was ready and not a minute before.

An hour later, Ranulf finished cinching the belt to his tunic and repeated the speech he had been giving himself. His plan was simple. First, he would hold Bronwyn and kiss her until she admitted that she loved him. Then, he would explain his own fears and she would forgive him. But most of all before the night was over, he would tell Bronwyn just how much she meant to him. By tomorrow morning, she would never again doubt his feelings.

Ranulf was just stabbing his dagger into its sheath attached to his belt when a solid single knock came from his day room. Ranulf gave a grunt to wait, but the door squeaked open regardless. Thinking only Bronwyn would be so bold, he stepped out of the garderobe with anticipation. Disappointment and then concern filled him as Tyr stood in silence with a very tense look on his face.

"What?" Ranulf asked without preamble. Whatever was bothering Tyr was not good and Ranulf had never been the type to guess.

A muscle flickered in Tyr's already clenched jaw. "One of the villagers just ran with news that they could see flames. Syndlear is on fire."

A brittle silence filled the room. Finally Ranulf raked both hands through his hair. He should have known Luc might try something. He should have waited for him to slip back onto his lands and confront him. "Damn, if Bronwyn wasn't mad at me before . . . how can I explain this? My shortsightedness has cost my wife her home."

"Thank God you had everyone come down to Hunswick."

Ranulf dived back into his garderobe and came out holding a hauberk and doublet. "Gather the men and have them all meet me in the Hall."

Within a half hour, Ranulf met with his men and began devising a strategy to draw out their attacker. Though there was no proof, Ranulf had little doubt it was Baron Craven. An accidental campfire would have caught the woods on fire and been less localized. Besides, the weather had been too damp in recent days to blame dry kindling and there had been no lightning storms in the past twelve hours. No, someone definitely had started the fire and the list of people who would gain by such an action had only one name.

"How many do you want to send north?" Tyr posed.

Ranulf twitched his mouth, thinking. "No more than a half-dozen. He wants us to be vulnerable here where it counts."

Tyr nodded. "I'll ride with Tory and four men of your choosing, leaving the rest to stay here. But I need to leave quickly before Edythe finds out. She loves that place and somehow the fire will be my fault. That I should have known it would be started and was unwilling to stop it."

"That doesn't make sense."

Tyr shrugged. "Oftentimes, neither does Edythe." He pivoted and was about to make his escape when a redheaded blur caught his peripheral vision, causing him to do a double take.

"Don't you dare go anywhere," Edythe ordered. Lily was right behind her.

Ranulf arched his head to see behind them, waiting for his wife to emerge. Meanwhile, Tyr's posture became hostile. "Didn't your apology provide you enough embarrassment for today?"

Edythe narrowed her green eyes. "Have no fear, Highlander, for I . . ." She paused and noticed his attire. "What is going on? Why are you dressed so?"

Tyr placed his hands on her shoulders and took a deep breath.

"Let me go," Edythe wriggled unsuccessfully.

"No. I don't want you to hit me when you hear the news." Tyr swallowed and prayed for strength. "There is no easy way to say it, but Syndlear—your home—is on fire."

A quiet filled the room. "Bad?"

Tyr nodded. "We can see the flames so I am afraid so, Finch." He had readied himself for pummeling fists, shouts of denial, and angry accusations. He had not been prepared for Edythe to fall against him, sobbing. "Sorry, love. I know how much your home meant to you. But I promise you, Ranulf and I will find the one who started it."

"It's Luc," she muttered against his tunic.

"If it is, then this time, the baron will pay with his life."

Ranulf, still not seeing Bronwyn, stepped around the embracing couple blocking the entrance, only to run into Lillabet. "You think Baron Craven started this?" she demanded, her voice high-pitched with an element of frenzy. "Then what are you doing here? You have to get there! You have to save her!"

Hearing her panic, Ranulf reached out and grabbed Lily's upper arms. "Save who?"

"Bronwyn," she wailed. "She rode up there this morning and she could still be there—"

Ranulf heard nothing more.

Chapter Twelve

The Feast of the Holy Family celebrates the family unit and the Holy Family: Jesus, Mary, and Joseph. During this time, celebration practices are simple, including prayer and a sermon that focuses on the remembrance of the family unit. This is followed by another feast in which everyone reflects on the value of family and elevates the concept in their culture, neighborhood, and community. These practices have been around for centuries, but it was not until the mid-1600s that the Feast of the Holy Family became a formal event. Even then, it was not recognized by the Church until 1921. Forty-eight years later in 1969, the Pope moved the Feast from the first Sunday after Epiphany to what is now often known as the "First Sunday after Christmas," making it one of today's Twelfthtide celebrations. The exception is if Christmas or Saint Stephen's Day falls upon a Sunday (as it did in 1154), then the holiday is held on December 30.

"Face me!" Ranulf cried out, daring Luc to leave his castle walls and meet him in one-on-one battle.

On the way to Syndlear, Ranulf's fear had grown to immeasurable limits, and by the time he had arrived, his blood had been pounding so hard in his veins, he could hear his own pulse. Then, in an instant the world had gone silent and remained that way. For the flames that had consumed Syndlear were gone. They had nothing left to eat. Only smoldering embers and scorched stone walls remained. No one could have survived.

Someone found Bronwyn's horse running loose nearby and brought it to him. Its charred reins and singed mane were proof the animal had been tied up close to the burning keep when it had struggled to gain its freedom and safety. There could be only one explanation as to why the horse had been left to defend itself; Bronwyn had still been inside.

Unable to look away, Ranulf had stared at Bronwyn's grave marker and let the rage and anger fill him until only loss and loneliness remained, devouring what was left of his soul. Speculations about the fire's cause started circulating around him, but not one idea was plausible. Vegetation was scarce next to the keep and the trees nearby were untouched. Lightning strikes required clouds that had dispersed long before, and unattended hearths would have died out or resulted in a fire days ago soon after everyone left. No, Syndlear had been destroyed intentionally. Bronwyn was dead and Baron Craven had just forfeited his life.

Ranulf could not prove his deduction, but it was not needed. He knew the truth, and it left only one choice—war. Peace be damned. The saints of Twelfthtide, the Church, his men, even King Henry—all of them . . . they would either understand his immediate need for blood or they wouldn't. Either way Ranulf did not care.

With only a handful of men, it should have taken virtually no time to prep for battle, but every minute had felt like an eternity. After assuaging Tyr's concerns by leaving just enough soldiers at Hunswick to protect Edythe and Lillabet, Ranulf had led his remaining men back across Torrens and toward the mercenary army. This time, however, the baron's soldiers were not relaxed. They had been waiting and were prepared for Ranulf's arrival, confirming Luc's guilt.

The size of the baron's hired army was far from insignificant, but even if it had been doubled, it would have changed nothing. Ranulf would have still led his nearly two dozen men through the deadly crowd, maneuvering toward the vulnerable timber castle.

"Face me or everyone here will know you are not a man but a coward," Ranulf taunted again. A minute later, he had his reward.

Luc appeared just above the wooden palisade, looking smug, overly confident, and easily within reach of Ranulf's arrow. "I heard about the fire. One of my men said that your wife was rumored to be inside Syndlear at the time. I guess it always was her destiny to be killed by flames."

Ranulf tightened his grip on the reins. "You killed her," he accused, his voice low but penetrating.

"Something you cannot prove. And now you are left with a choice. Come after me, the king will take your home, your men, perhaps even your life. Leave and you lose your honor."

"I will have you at the tip of my sword, baron."

"You're welcome to try," Luc said haughtily with a wave of his hand, indicating the small but hostile army who had encircled Ranulf and his men. "But it won't change the fact that Bronwyn will never again be yours."

The reality of the baron's hateful words slammed into Ranulf and he let loose a battle cry that could be heard throughout the valley.

Bronwyn stirred back into consciousness. Her stiffened muscles and joints burned, demanding to be moved. The fire must have died hours ago. The intense heat from the walls was gone and all the warmth had left the stones. Using the small breathing air holes as a window to the outside, Bronwyn surveyed the scene below. It was hard to make out, but based on the amount of moonlight, the sun had sunk behind the horizon several hours ago. Soon rescuers would arrive.

She squeezed her eyes shut and tried to remain patient by recalling what she could before blacking out. After the stone door had locked her inside, the smoke had slowly seeped in, consuming all breathable air. She had pressed her lips to the small holes in a desperate effort to inhale anything that didn't taste and smell like ash. That was the last thing she could remember.

Again Bronwyn tried to stretch. This time a little more successfully in her upper body, but crouched inside, she could not straighten her legs. Until she was freed from the small storage unit, they would be screaming for relief. Still, she was alive. Despite everything she had ever thought about her father's narrow-minded commitment to build the fire holes, they had worked. They had kept her safe. Hopefully, they wouldn't also cause her death.

She counted everything she could see, hummed every song she knew, but the silence remained. Where was everyone? Hadn't the flames been visible? Maybe help had come and gone while she had been unconscious, never realizing she was inside the wall, alive.

Panic began to flood Bronwyn and the need to escape became her sole focus. Skimming the surface with her fingertips, she found the edge of the large stone blocking her way out and pushed. The effort resulted in absolutely no change. Bracing herself as best she could in the confined space, she shoved against the barrier. Again, nothing. The stone door had been designed to be removed from the outside by adults, not from the interior.

Stifling a ripple of fear, Bronwyn took several deep breaths and told herself that Ranulf would not let her die. He would somehow know she had survived and come to find her. She just hoped he did it before she starved.

After wiggling back around, the faint red break of dawn could be seen glowing through the air holes. Night was ending. Moving closer to study the landscape, Bronwyn realized her view was not of Hunswick, but the other side of Torrens—toward the Craven castle. Furthermore, it was not dawn lighting up the dark sky, it was torches.

In the distance, shadows moved and every once

in a while a faint scream echoed across the valley. Bronwyn had no idea how long she stared out the holes, snatching morsels of activity, when suddenly the night sky lit up and the battle scene was no longer a struggle to see. Luc's castle was on fire. There was only one rational explanation for the razing of the noble's home—Ranulf had declared war. For him to make such a move meant he had already come to Syndlear and believed her to be dead. And without food or water, she would be very soon.

Tears flooded her eyes and the sick tune of Luc's departing comments sang in her memory. *Know in the end I will have everything that was supposed to be mine.* Damn. She had been right. Luc *had* created a trap for Ranulf. Not the one she had anticipated, but one far more devious and destructive.

Ranulf had everything Luc ever desired—her, Syndlear, higher rank and power, even the king's respect. But Ranulf's unprovoked, unsubstantiated attack, killing dozens of men, could be the one thing to change that. Bronwyn could hear Luc oozing charm as he described her husband to the king, spinning stories of Ranulf's lust for power, acting above the law—the one thing King Henry was rumored never to tolerate. Then add tales of her being promised to Luc and Ranulf's defiance . . . it was very possible that Ranulf would lose everything, all the while believing she hated him for the accident that took away her father.

Bronwyn cried out at the injustice. It couldn't be too late for them. She would yell and scream until someone came and found her. She had to tell Ranulf she loved him, and no matter what the king said or did, she would always be with him.

She would stay alive. She had to.

Ranulf studied the destruction surrounding him. The battle had ended several hours ago, but the war had just begun. All that remained of the baron's castle was smoldering ashes. The men who had fought for Luc had either fled or died. The fighting had been brutal and Ranulf knew he was lucky to have only lost only two men against the greater numbers, but their deaths would haunt him for a long time. Especially because the reason they were there, the reason they had fought, the very man that Ranulf had craved to face most—had not yet been found. The baron had disappeared just at the onset of battle.

A bloodied figure moved and Ranulf knelt down by the mercenary's side. The man gasped and it was clear he was in enormous pain and would soon be dead. Ranulf didn't care. Any of his remaining capacity for empathy had died with Bronwyn.

Grasping the man's shoulders, Ranulf gave him a choice. "Tell me where the baron is and I will bring you water."

Despite the pain wracking the mercenary's body, distaste overtook his expression. "I hate people like you and the baron, always thinking you are better than everyone else, entitled to more," he hissed. "Keep your water and your so-called kindness and may both your souls be damned to hell."

"Where is he?" Ranulf pressed, promised cruelty laced in each word.

The dying soldier coughed violently before finally answering truthfully, knowing it would be the most vindictive of all last actions. "Gone to see the new king. You may be the better leader, better soldier, better at everything . . . but the man still won. You could kill him, but he would still win."

Ranulf released the now limp frame and stood up, hating the fact that the dead man was right. Ranulf had gone to war without permission, and the instant Henry learned of the unapproved, unilateral decision, there would be repercussions. Being the king's friend would not help Ranulf's cause. If anything, it would hurt him. Henry had just assumed his throne and paramount to all was establishing authority and gaining the respect of his nobles, something that could not be earned by ignoring Ranulf's most recent decisions. Instead, Henry would be forced to make Ranulf an example by stripping him of his title and wealth—a humiliation unlike any he had ever endured, and yet he didn't care.

He didn't care about anything.

Tyr kicked aside an empty helmet and sheathed his sword. "That one say anything?" he asked, pointing at the lifeless man beside Ranulf.

"Nothing I didn't already know."

"Then the baron's gone to London then. We pursue?"

Ranulf shook his head. "We do not. Get the men and our dead. They are not to be buried here."

Tyr nodded, but before he went to see to Ranulf's bidding, he said, "You know what will happen then when the duke hears of . . ."

"Henry can have Hunswick and the title."

"All may not be lost. State your case. Henry's fair."

Ranulf shook his head. "The king wants to focus on conquering Ireland for his brother. He's not going to be pleased that I am causing problems in the north."

"But what if he offers the baron Syndlear as a stern warning to you? Or worse, decides to raze Hunswick? Henry's done it before, and if you don't tell him the truth about what happened, he might do it again."

Ranulf glanced at the dead bodies littering the valley and riverbed. His reaction had been justified but all the killing had not helped. The pain still remained and it always would. Bronwyn showed him what it was like to be complete and happy. Without her, a sickening hollowness consumed him. And nothing, no action, no inaction even if justified, would change that. He could search for Craven, find him, and even kill him, but it would change nothing.

"If that's Henry's decision, then so be it. After I see to the safety of my wife's sisters, I never want to see either Syndlear or Hunswick again."

Chapter Thirteen

First Footing is one of the primary celebrations of Hogmanay, a Scottish holiday that for many centuries was treasured over that of Christmas. The first person to cross the threshold of a home after midnight on New Year's Eve determines the homeowner's fortune—whether good or bad—for the coming year. Derived from pagan rituals and Viking invasions, the ideal visitor was a tall man of dark complexion, resembling as little as possible of the fair-haired invaders from the north. In medieval times, the first visitor would bear gifts, such as coin, bread, salt, coal, or drink, in exchange for food or wine. The tradition still continues in the United Kingdom today and is celebrated vigorously in Scotland, causing January 2 to be an official Scottish holiday, allowing for the recovery of enthusiastic merrymakers.

Lily strolled into the Great Hall careful not to make too much sound. The room was clean, just as most of Hunswick. She and Edythe had straightened their rooms that morning supposedly in preparation for First Footing, but in truth it was to keep busy. Everyone was searching for anything to occupy their minds from what they had lost. Her beloved sister through death and now their lord through paralyzing grief.

Lily stared at the large dark extended form staring into the hearth. Ranulf had spoken little since his return, eaten less, and moved not an inch from the Great Hall chair. Taking a deep breath, she ventured toward him, readying herself for his sour disposition.

"I told everyone to leave me alone," he mumbled, but the uncompromising stance behind the request was clear.

Lily picked up the mug beside him on the table and quickly put it back down upon smelling the odor of its sour contents. When news came that her sister's body could not be found among the ashes for burial, Ranulf had ordered everyone—including Tyr—to leave him be. The food and drink beside him had been sitting there for nearly a day and the ale had been from a cask opened almost four days ago for the Saint John's feast. Most of the villagers thought their lord was in the Hall getting drunk, but the smell alone proved he had not taken even a sip. Lily was not surprised. The desire to eat or drink had left her as well.

"My lord? I just wanted to say good-bye. I am leaving for Scotland after the First Footing."

Ranulf did not move. Lily didn't think he had

heard her even though she was standing right beside him. Then unexpectedly, he turned his head. "Tonight?" he asked.

She bowed her head, suddenly feeling as if she was abandoning him. "In the morning, with Jeb and Aimon. So far, the weather has been mild, but even if winter hits, they are from my mother's clan and know people we can stay with during the journey."

Ranulf resumed his firelight stare. "You don't have to go. Bronwyn wouldn't want you to leave."

"My heart will stay here, but I cannot. There are too many memories."

"You cannot flee them, Lillabet. They will follow you and haunt you wherever you are. Trust me."

Lily wringed her hands and shook her head as another wave of guilt washed over her. "If I stay, I will only remind others of what I did. I am the one that forgot the tapestry. I am the one that made the protest about it not being here."

"You didn't kill her."

"No, and neither did you. Baron Craven did."

Ranulf remained still, but Lily could see a rigidity overtake his frame. He was shutting her out. "Tory and Norval will escort you as well." Then as if he could tell she was going to argue, he added, "I made a promise to keep you and Edythe safe."

Lily nodded in resignation. Then, realizing she was standing on his left just where Bronwyn had said not to, she moved to his right side. "Thank you. I am sure Jeb and Aimon will appreciate the support, but Edythe is not going. She has it in her mind that Bronwyn would want her to stay and help you with Hunswick and there is no convincing her otherwise.

But she has Tyr, and I have seen the way he looks at her. He will keep her safe."

"He won't marry her."

"Not while she's married, no, but later," Lily insisted. "Like me, she intends to get an annulment. Then, she—"

"Wouldn't matter. Tyr won't wed, not now, not ever."

Lily crossed her arms and furrowed her brow. "I think you're wrong. You think I am young and naïve, but I know love. It was I who realized Bronwyn was in love with you. I saw how happy you made her and now I see it in Edythe's eyes. Don't prevent Tyr from being content because of what happened to you."

The accusation riled Ranulf into a reaction. He sat up and jerked his head around to give her a pointed stare. "You think I would do that?"

"I think you miss Bronwyn in a way I only wish I could someday understand. I think you were lucky, *supremely* lucky to have been loved by her, and she was just as fortunate to have been loved by you. But just because your time was cut short does not mean others are not meant for joy."

Ranulf rolled his eyes and then relaxed against the chair, massaging his temples. "Tyr has demons, Lillabet. Ones that would terrify Edythe. He won't marry her because of *them*, not me. He and I were never destined to be happy. He accepted that truth long ago. I am only now realizing he was right."

Lily took a step back. The fierceness of his declaration rattled her. "I'm sorry. I didn't mean to accuse you . . . I'm really sorry, Ranulf. I'm just lost without her. Bronwyn meant the world to me. She was beautiful and kind and everything to everyone. But with you, she was finally happy." Lily moved back to his side and knelt down beside him. "If you remember anything, remember that. You made her happy and she loved you."

Ranulf swallowed. "But did she know that I loved her?" he whispered, desperately seeking an answer.

He leaned over and rested his elbows on his knees and studied the floor. A tear splashed on the wooden boards below. If Lily thought his coldness unnerved her, Ranulf upset was significantly more disturbing. "Of course she did. How can you think otherwise?"

"I never told her, Lillabet. God, I never told her what I felt. She said the words, but I never did."

Lily squeezed his forearm. "But she knew. Bronwyn *knew*, Ranulf. She absolutely knew your feelings. She couldn't have loved you so deeply if she didn't. I promise you, she didn't need you to say your feelings to believe in them."

The squeak of the door behind her caught her attention and Lily stood back up as the steward approached and whispered into her ear. "We need to bring in the juniper for tonight. Do you think his lordship will mind if Tory did the First Footing? He has dark hair and it would be an honor for him to be selected."

Ranulf gripped the arms of the chair and pushed himself up. He faced the startled steward. "Choose whomever you want. Makes no difference to me."

Ranulf then moved to leave the Hall. Lily reached out to stop him, but he avoided her grasp. He knew what he had to do. He had to say the words he should have uttered when it would have mattered.

* * *

Syndlear was exactly as Ranulf remembered, a charred ruin. From a distance, the damage was hard to discern with the stone walls still standing, but inside it was hollow with only a useless stairwell remaining. The floors had been burnt out, causing their contents to crash below and burn to unrecognizable ashes. Only scorched beams and a few fragments of furniture were identifiable.

Ranulf jerked at the rafters, searching for anything of Bronwyn, but again, nothing but her disappearance proved she had been inside. Exhausted, Ranulf fell to his knees and, with tears streaking down his face, looked up at the visible sky. "Why not me? She had done nothing!" he half sobbed, half shouted. "Her people need her . . . I need her. Why didn't you take me?"

Bronwyn stirred to the desperate sound of Ranulf crying. Physically and emotionally drained from the lack of movement, food, and water, she was dreaming, hearing the one voice she desired above all others. This time it seemed real. But even if it was, it wouldn't matter.

Earlier that day or maybe it had been the previous one—she couldn't keep track—people had come, but not a one heard her cries for help. They had been talking too much among themselves to perceive her strained voice weakened by her earlier attempts when no one was close enough to hear. Then they had left, never knowing she was still alive, waiting for rescue. At that moment, she gave up and waited for eternal sleep to take her.

Another angry wail came from below. It was Ranulf! He had come, not to find her, but it didn't matter. He was there. As loud as she could manage, Bronwyn cried out, "Help! Please help me!"

Ranulf was moving to exit the keep when he froze. Bronwyn's voice had come and disappeared. The raspy sound was strained, barely distinguishable, but it definitely belonged to her. Was he going mad? Did he need her so badly that he was imagining her near him?

Then he heard it again. *Please help me.*

His heart rate doubled as blood and hope surged in his veins. "Bronwyn! Is that you?"

Silence surrounded him and he felt the tentacles of despair that had been plaguing him reach out once again. She had been a dream. A dream he could still hear. "Ranulf, don't leave me."

"I'll never leave you. I am yours forever. Even in the next life. I love you. Wait for me," he whispered and brushed away the tears that now flowed down his cheeks. He couldn't stop them.

"I love you, too." The sweet sound of her voice was fading. His angel was leaving him and going back to heaven. "Find me. I'm in the wall."

For a few seconds, Ranulf was too stunned to do anything more than just hold his breath. *I'm in the wall?* His gaze flew to the thick stone and studied them. He saw them then. The holes Bronwyn had told him her father had added after the first fire. The small outlets were visible and followed a logical pattern, except on the third floor. There, instead of an opening was a large stone resting on a stone ledge, secured from falling over by a small lip perfectly carved to keep it in place and prevent fire from getting inside. Her father either had been a genius mason or he had hired one.

"Bronwyn!" Ranulf shouted, this time with confidence that he was not talking to a ghost, but his still alive wife. "The floors are gone, so I'm going to need to find something to wedge between the stairs and the lip to reach you. Hold on just a little longer, love."

Bronwyn closed her eyes and released a deep breath. Ranulf was there. He had heard her. He knew where she was. She had hung on to life long enough to feel his arms hold her one more time.

What seemed like an eternity later, the stone door at last rolled away, crashing to the dirt floor below. Large hands reached in and gently pulled her free from the small enclosure. At the last moment, Bronwyn reached back into the hole and snatched the reason for her even being at Syndlear—the tapestry.

Finally released from what she had begun to think of as her tomb, Bronwyn held on tight to Ranulf as he carried her across the narrow plank to the staircase. Daylight was disappearing and the dusk of the room made the rescue even more dangerous. One false move and they would both fall to their death. The tension in his frame lessened once they were at the staircase and descending the winding steps.

"Can you walk?" Ranulf's first question was simple, very pragmatic, and on the surface, far from romantic. But Bronwyn could hear in those three small words that he had lived in the same hell she had been in the past few days.

"I don't think so. I can't really feel my legs anymore."

Ranulf nodded, glad to have a reason to keep her in his arms. He wasn't ready to let her go and was not sure when, or if, he ever would. He stepped over the burnt remains and moved outside, heading to a small nearby clearing protected by trees. Sitting her down, he laid her back against one large trunk and went to his horse, pulling out a leather bag. He handed it to her.

Bronwyn squeezed the contents into her mouth, relieved to taste water and not ale or mead. As she swallowed, she could feel the cool contents slide down her throat and into her stomach. It was then she knew that she really was going to live.

"Here," Ranulf whispered. "It's only bread, but you'll want to eat it slowly."

Bronwyn popped a piece into her mouth and just let it sit there for a moment, savoring its wonderful flavor. Never again would she take eating or food for granted. She watched Ranulf gather and pile twigs to make a fire. After being cold for so long, she instinctively tried to move closer to the heat, but her deadened limbs refused to cooperate.

Seeing her frustration, Ranulf moved to her side and began to massage her limbs. The pain created by the pooled blood circulating once again through her veins was enormous. "Where did you find the wood for the planks? I thought everything had burned," she said in a broken whisper, hoping the sound of Ranulf's voice would help focus her attention away from his painful ministrations.

"Outside there was a broken old cart. I tore it apart to use the boards," Ranulf answered in a low, husky tone that seemed to come from a long way off.

He kept his sight on her legs as he softly kneaded them. He knew that Bronwyn had hoped he would expound. She needed him to talk, but he didn't trust his voice. It was everything he could do not to break down. His whole adult life he had strived to isolate and control his emotions, for he had seen the weakness and vulnerability they created in their wake. And now when he needed to shed his emotions the most, the ability had forsaken him.

A soft sob escaped Bronwyn and Ranulf glanced up. New tears had formed from the necessary pain he was causing her. It tore him apart. Moving up to her side, he pulled her onto his lap, framed her face in his hands, and with his thumbs, wiped the wet streaks, smearing the soot that clung to her cheeks. Then slowly, he lowered his mouth and brushed his lips lightly across hers, kissing her tenderly, lingeringly, and with a possessiveness that hinted of enormous restraint. She began to respond as she did every other time they kissed. But before she could persuade him to deepen the embrace, he released her lips and drew her into his arms, holding her as he dropped soft kisses onto her forehead.

"I'm so sorry," Ranulf whispered, his voice full of remorse and self-loathing for what he still needed to do. "But I must continue. I promise the pain will pass."

Bronwyn lifted her head from his chest and shifted off his lap so that he could once again massage her legs. "Then I'll be able to walk again?" she asked, staring at her two immobile limbs. "They look so . . . pale."

Ranulf paused and pushed another piece of bread into her palm, motioning for her to sit back and eat it. Then his fingers resumed their unpleasant task of kneading the sensitive flesh. "The firelight doesn't make it easy to see, but I can already tell that the circulation is returning. The skin is much warmer to the touch and the unnatural color is gradually lessening. You're going to be fine."

With the last few words, his speech had become halted, and his hands started shaking, forcing him to stop. He had not been lying—although he would have. She was going to recover completely. He had been given a second chance.

"I love you, Bronwyn. I always have," he whispered, unmoving, still staring at her legs. "From the first moment I saw you, you lit up my soul. Such happiness doesn't come to men like me. I thought if I said it aloud, then it would all disappear, I would lose control . . . and you." He paused and tilted his head to look at her directly. "I won't ever make that mistake again," Ranulf vowed. For the rest of their lives, she would know just how much she meant to him.

Bronwyn gently leaned forward and peered into his face before reaching out to stroke his cheek. "I was so afraid, Ranulf. Not of dying, but of not seeing you one last time. I should have told you that I understood why you didn't tell me about my father. That I do trust you and never stopped loving you."

Ranulf clasped his hand around her neck and drew her lips to his. This time the kiss was sensuous and filled with renewed promise. She was the fire in his blood and as necessary to life. He probed the warmth of her mouth as his hands tenderly caressed her spine. Responsive to his touch, Bronwyn moved in closer, shivering with need. His body ached for more, but he feared crushing her frail frame. Still he could not muster the will to break the embrace and gave in to the desire for one more sweet kiss.

When he finally lifted his head, Bronwyn lay in his

arms, reveling in their strength, feeling like she was floating on a blissful cloud. She trusted this man above all others. He'd been hardened by years of being alone, but from him, she received a tenderness unlike any other. He comforted her with a masculine calm. His presence brought her a kind of security. She lifted her gaze and traced the silver scar on his cheek. "I knew you loved me," she said softly. "I have known for some time."

"Lily said you did."

At the mention of her sister, Bronwyn pushed against his chest to sit up. Her legs cramped at the effort, but no longer did they scream in agony. "We have to go! Ranulf, we have to leave right now. We have to get back to Hunswick. Luc is after my sisters and I—"

Ranulf placed a finger over her lips. "They are safe, love. Tyr hasn't left Edythe's side and I have ordered two men as guards to Lily, even though she doesn't know it. Baron Craven cannot get to them."

Pulling his hand down, Bronwyn sought additional reassurance. "But you, are you safe? I saw the battle, and the king—"

This time, Ranulf used a soft lingering kiss to silence her concerns. "As long as you are mine, nothing else matters."

Bronwyn chuckled. "Nothing? What about Hunswick? My sisters?"

"The people of Hunswick will recover the instant they see you and both your sisters are stronger than I would have thought. Even when I left, they were preparing for Hogmanay because they knew you would have wanted it."

"Tonight is First Footing?" Bronwyn squealed, her

eyes dancing with happiness. "If we leave now, do you think we could arrive in time?"

Ranulf furrowed his brows. The ride was long and she had only just started to recover. "It might be too painful."

"Ranulf, First Footing is my *favorite* holiday. My sisters and I have always welcomed the first visitor and this year will be no different. I want to be there."

Seeing the longing in her eyes, Ranulf could deny her nothing. But this year, it would be different. She would be the one welcomed.

If he could get them there in time.

Up ahead, just outside of Hunswick, a lone dark man was approaching the gatehouse. Ranulf urged Pertinax into a faster gait, catching the designated first visitor just in time. "Tory!"

The solitary figure stopped and looked around, moving into the moonlight. Seeing Ranulf riding toward him with Bronwyn sitting across his lap, the young soldier's jaw dropped open. Bronwyn couldn't help but chuckle at Tory's openly shocked expression and the tinkling sound of her laughter filled the air.

Ranulf pulled Pertinax beside Tory. "Sorry to disrupt your plans, but I have a different visitor in mind."

Tory's face broke into a huge grin and he reached into his bag to pull out the log, salt, drink, and bread Lily had given him earlier. Handing them to Bronwyn, he said, "I'll go and spread the word. I have a feeling that everyone is going to want to greet Hunswick's first visitor this year."

Bronwyn accepted the items, tears filling her eyes with joy. She looked up at Ranulf. "That's why you didn't want to stop and take a break," she breathed, her voice barely audible. Then, she gave him a blinding smile and mouthed the words "Thank you."

Ranulf laughed silently down at her, glorying in the shared moment. "Ready, love? There are two people on the other side of that gate eager to start this celebration."

Bronwyn brushed her tears aside and, with mounting excitement bubbling inside her, said, "I think it's time for another feast." And with no more delay, Ranulf moved them through the narrow gatehouse and into the inner bailey.

The awaiting small crowd had gathered mostly to respect the wishes of Edythe and Lily, who had insisted the New Year tradition be followed. All knew it had been Lady Bronwyn's favorite and that she had always insisted on following the Scottish customs just as her mother had. The jubilant occasion was one of the most popular among the people of Hunswick with only Twelfth Night as its rival. This year, however, many had elected to stay away. Edythe and Lily were busy trying to pump the spirits of the ones who had come when Constance gave a piercing shriek that got everyone's attention. Unable to speak, she extended a wrinkled finger.

Lily went to help the distressed nursemaid as Edythe maneuvered her way through the gasping crowd, cursing her short nature. Had Lily selected someone else besides Tory to be first visitor? Seeing a large warhorse, Edythe marched up to the rider and was about to extend a welcome when familiar misty blue eyes came into view.

Edythe took a step back and started shaking violently. She would have fallen if it hadn't been for Tyr, who instinctively swung her into his arms as she crumpled out of shock. "Am I seeing a ghost?"

Tyr kissed her hair and shook his head, his own eyes tearing at the joyous surprise. "No, love. She's not a ghost. I see her, too."

Leaving Constance in the care of others, Lily stood back up. Upon seeing Bronwyn, the juniper she had been holding went flying into the air. She ran toward the couple, repeating Bronwyn's name over and over again. Reaching her sister's side, Lily started shouting the questions all were thinking. "You're alive! Ranulf found you! How? Are you hurt? Where have you been? Did Luc have you?"

At the last question, Ranulf sent her a silencing look that, for once, Lily heeded. He dismounted, slid Bronwyn into his arms, and then proceeded to carry her toward the Great Hall. "All questions will be answered in due time, but go find everyone and let them know to come to the Hall for food and drink. I believe this is my wife's favorite of the Twelfthtide holidays and she would like it to be a grand one!"

Immediately the crowd dispersed and the buzz of their excitement could be heard everywhere. Their lady was alive and it was she who would be bringing in the prosperity of the New Year.

Chapter Fourteen

The Feast of the Circumcision of Our Lord is held on the first day of the New Year, celebrating the circumcision of Jesus Christ eight days after his birth. The first shedding of blood is said to show his descent from Abraham, proving Jesus was a human man and under Jewish law. Just as significant, the act also is believed to have initiated the process of redeeming man of his sins. Also on this day, the child of God was given his name, Jesus, the Hebrew word for salvation or savior. Through the Middle Ages, the two feasts—the Circumcision of Our Lord and the Holy Name of Jesus—were celebrated together. In some countries, custom dictates that nothing be removed from the home—not even garbage—to retain the prosperity and good fortune brought by the First Footer.

Ranulf held Bronwyn in his lap as she clapped along to the music. He couldn't believe someone who had endured such an ordeal could be filled with so much joy. By the time she had bathed and gotten something more substantial to eat, all of Hunswick had arrived to greet their mistress. It mattered little that it was the middle of the night. Even Father Morrell had joined in the festivities, performing a fast jig in time with the music.

Ranulf wished that Bronwyn could join them, knowing her passion for dancing, but he made sure that she was otherwise entertained. If she thought he was being overly protective, she never said a word. Slowly, her strength was returning. She could move her arms freely and put weight on her legs, though for only short periods of time. Nevertheless, each time she tried, they became sturdier under the pressure.

Stretching his arm out behind her back, Ranulf plucked another piece of meat off one of the passing trays of food. After people learned of Bronwyn's nearly starved state, the kitchen hearths were fired up and soon started spilling out her favorite foods.

Bronwyn, spying the piece of juicy lamb Ranulf was dangling in front of her, pushed his arm out of her view. "No more!" she pleaded. "And tell those still working in the kitchens to come out and join us. They should not be forced to labor while the rest of us enjoy the night."

Ranulf extended a finger to the large arched windows. Bright light was poking over the horizon. "Night's over. It's nearly dawn," he murmured as he bent his head to nibble on her neck.

"Father Morrell will be quite annoyed if everyone falls asleep during today's sermon. Perhaps we should all retire."

Almost too eagerly, Ranulf jumped to his feet. "Well, I think it is time to end the night—or morning."

Bronwyn had just managed to thank everyone profusely and ensure them all that she would see them shortly before Ranulf decided she had been on her feet long enough. He swept her back into his arms and was about to proceed toward the door when she snuggled closer to his chest and purred into his ear, "Take me to bed."

"Are you tired?"

Bronwyn bit her bottom lip and gave a quick shake of her head. "I should be, but I am not. All I could do for the past couple of days was sleep in that hole. I need you. My legs and arms need to feel you around them. Prove to me I am alive."

A need unlike anything Ranulf had ever known surged through him. He hadn't believed he could feel such conflicting emotions simultaneously. Ecstatic and desperate. Fulfilled yet barren with longing. The only coherent thought in his head was that the path from the Hall to the solar was too far and definitely too long and instead changed direction, heading for Bronwyn's old bedchambers above the Hall.

Once inside her room, he kicked the door closed and walked over to place her carefully on the bed. Bronwyn immediately started to remove her clothes, but he stopped her and instead took over the task.

With each inch of skin he exposed, he placed a soft lingering kiss. He had intended to take his time and savor every minute of knowing she was alive and in his life, but the moment her shoulders were bare, his need for her became all consuming. Her own writhing form proved she, too, was unwilling to wait.

Briefly stepping from her side, he ripped off his own clothes before removing the rest of hers. Falling into her arms, she opened up to him, and unable to stop himself, he slammed inside her. Her body took control. She wrapped herself around him and met each thrust. He knew then that he was still alive. That God had not forsaken him. He was in truth blessed beyond comprehension.

He loved and was loved in return.

The noise of clattering pans and constant squabbling had been growing for the past hour and was now too loud to be ignored. Bronwyn had once told him that these bedchambers were not ones to be coveted and now he knew why. His solar was practically silent in comparison.

"Are you awake?" Bronwyn asked. She was nestled against his side with her arm strewn across his chest and was looking at him.

Ranulf grimaced. "How could I not be with all that racket? What *could* they be doing?"

Bronwyn flipped over to her back. "Preparing for the next feast, of course."

"I had forgotten."

Bronwyn gave him a playful nudge with her elbow. "Forgotten the Naming of Our Lord?"

"Yes. I along with everyone else, I might add. This place became a tomb without you here. No feasts, no activity. Without you, no one seemed to know what to do."

"You did," Bronwyn said quietly, fondling the covers. "I saw the battle, or at least enough to know you had one. How did you know it was Luc who trapped me?"

The tension in Ranulf instantly returned. "It was the only thing that made sense. But I wasn't positive until I confronted him. Afterward I had no doubts. I saw the look in his eyes. There was pride in my grief, pride knowing he was the cause."

"So you fought."

"I fought and killed, and in the end, I realized it wouldn't bring you back to me. You were gone and nothing—not even revenge—seemed worthwhile."

Bronwyn swallowed. "Did Luc say anything before he died? Was he sorry? Or did he hate until the end?" she rambled, not wanting to ask, but needing to know.

"I didn't kill him. He got away."

Bronwyn pushed herself to a sitting position and looked down at Ranulf, her blue eyes intense. "Where did he go?"

"My guess is London."

"But what about the truce? The king? What is going to happen to you?"

Ranulf threw his arm casually behind his head and replied, "Henry will definitely be angry. He takes loyalty seriously and has no qualms about razing castles of those who go against him."

Ranulf's lax attitude worried Bronwyn. "But the king knows you are not against him, that you are loyal."

"Yes, but it doesn't appear that way. I had no proof Craven tried to kill you when I attacked. And since I didn't kill him, he is most likely on his way to tell Henry just how I acted outside of the law."

Bronwyn's shoulders sagged. "So Luc is going to

get away with everything. When he locked me in that room, he had told me he was trapping you. Only later, after the fire and when I saw the battle, did I realize that my death was part of that trap. This was his intention all along. He needed me dead to force you into taking action. I wonder what Luc will do when he finds out that his plan didn't work," Bronwyn said, murmuring her thoughts aloud. Then looking down at Ranulf, she pointedly asked, "Since I am still alive, could King Henry give Syndlear to Luc?"

Ranulf returned her stare for several seconds before rising and donning his chainse and tunic nearly simultaneously. Surprised, Bronwyn just sat and watched. Ranulf's mind had just leaped somewhere else and she wondered for a moment if he was even aware she was in the room.

Grabbing his leather belt, Ranulf looped it across his waist and strode toward the door. Just before he opened it, he pivoted, and asked, "Do you think your legs are strong enough to ride a horse?"

Bronwyn blinked at the unexpected request. "I think so."

"It doesn't matter. Pertinax can handle both of us on him if necessary. I'll send someone to help you dress, and pack. We're leaving immediately."

As he swung the door open and proceeded out, Bronwyn realized he was serious. "But where are we going?"

Glancing back at her, he smiled a wicked smile. "Westminster."

"Westminster! Now? What about the Feast of the Circumcision of Our Lord? I'm the First Footer! I can't just leave."

Ranulf came back in and gave her a comforting kiss on the forehead before placing a softer one on her lips.

"Unfortunately, that is one tradition we must break. So pack only what is necessary and don your warmest gown."

Bronwyn's heart started pounding as she realized just who Ranulf intended to see and confront. "What are you planning to do to Luc?"

But the question was issued to an empty corridor. Ranulf was gone, and the next time she was to see him, they would be riding out of Hunswick at a speed she wouldn't understand for another three days.

Chapter Fifteen

Traditionally performed at the beginning of the New Year, wassailing is the ritual of pouring cider on the roots of apple trees with a ceremonial verse promising a good harvest. In the early Middle Ages, wassailing was associated with a spiced wine, Renwein, typically enjoyed only by the wealthy as it required the importation of spices, such as ginger, cinnamon, cloves, allspice, and nutmeg. However, as ales improved, the wine was replaced and the wassail became a drink indicative to the means of the family. The wassail bowl, used to dip cakes and bread, also originated in the Middle Ages and is where the word "toast" comes from as a drinking salutation.

Ranulf stared blankly into the campfire, trying to ignore Lily.

"White horses always look dirty," Lily told the young smitten soldier sitting beside her. "That's why

I refuse to ride them. Brown ones may be just as filthy, but at least I cannot see the dirt. Black ones, less so, but I have found that in general dark horses suit me better."

"You just think you look better on them," Edythe protested before succumbing to several seconds of coughing.

Bronwyn studied her redheaded sister for a moment. Tyr put another blanket around Edythe's shoulders and eventually the coughs quieted. Turning her attention to Ranulf, Bronwyn promised him softly, "You'll learn to ignore them."

Ranulf grimaced and sent a reproving look to his youngest sister-in-law. It, just like the others he had sent Lily throughout the day, changed nothing. "I just find it hard to reconcile the child I hear now with the woman who appeared after your death. With you gone, she had to grow up. Now that you are back . . ."

Bronwyn snuggled up against his side with a sigh. "I admit I encourage it. Life will force Lily to grow up soon enough and I am glad it was not my death that thrust it upon her. In the meantime, you ignore her prattle and I'll just be amused by it," she advised before planting a gentle kiss on his arm.

Ranulf, with his free hand, raked his fingers through his short hair. How had he gotten into this predicament? But it took only one look at the huddled form next to him to remember exactly how. Bronwyn. He had wanted to make her happy. After thinking her lost to him forever, he would have promised her anything, even the moon.

Before Bronwyn, he had known peace and quiet, but not contentment. Now, he possessed an inner serenity he had never imagined to exist, but the calm tranquility that once surrounded him had vanished from his life.

Yesterday morning, Bronwyn—though inadvertently—had reminded Ranulf that for Baron Craven's plan to succeed, he needed her to be dead. Not alive. And certainly not in London. That gave Ranulf three, at most four, days to get to Westminster. Barely enough time if they rode light and hard.

The moment Ranulf realized what had to be done, he had started shouting orders and making preparations to leave within the hour. But that hour turned into three by the time they left, his intended small party of him, Bronwyn, and three guards had turned into a much larger—and slower—group moving its way out of the hills in the middle of winter.

He should have said no to her sisters accompanying them right at the start. And he absolutely would have if it had been Edythe or Lily who had asked, but it had been Bronwyn who had extended the invitation to her sisters and he could not deny any request of hers right now. He did not want to see disappointment of any kind on her face and certainly not as a result from something he had said or done.

Now he was paying the price.

Just getting out of Hunswick should have been a warning to the speed and tone of the journey. Fur hides for warmth had to be secured for everyone, which should have been easy, but no one could remember the last time the previous lord had traveled anywhere. And when he did, it was always in much warmer weather requiring few of the provisions Ranulf had demanded.

Tents, which everyone agreed were somewhere, took the most time locating. Ranulf had been about to forfeit the canvas protection when Tyr had asked if he expected Bronwyn to sleep in the open, with nothing to protect her from the elements.

Finally, the canvas shelters were located and Ranulf thought they were on the verge of leaving when came the debacle of the horses. All three of Laon's daughters were accomplished horsewomen, a rare skill, though not surprising as they often had traveled between Syndlear and Hunswick. But neither Lily's nor Edythe's horse was equal to the journey in front of them. Finding others that suited both women had been a painful process that eventually required Bronwyn's firm hand.

Preparing to leave had been arduous, but it was nothing compared to the journey once it had started.

Traveling with men, in the winter, was hard. Traveling with women was difficult, but trekking through the winter mountains with females who had never journeyed anywhere was straining Ranulf's every last nerve.

Even food became a problem when Lily had declared dried beef and bread not agreeable. She was cold and needed something hot. Bronwyn unfortunately supported the idea. Probably less out of a need to appease Lily and more to support Edythe, who had caught a harsh and constant cough, but the result was the same. Another hour was lost as Ranulf found himself ordering his men to hunt for the evening's meal.

Then exhaustion followed, and by the time they had finished eating, all three women had passed out cold, including his wife. Today had fared a little better, but still they had stopped earlier and traveled less than he had desired.

If they did not pick up the pace, the journey would mean little, for it would be too late.

Bronwyn hugged her husband's arm, wishing she could take back her request to have her sisters travel with them. When Lily had caught her packing, she had asked where they were going and Bronwyn answered, "Westminster," not considering just how her little sister would react.

Immediately, Lily had begged to come, chattering nonstop about court, the new king and queen, and all the festivities that would be incomparable to anything she had ever had a chance to see. Bronwyn instinctively refused but Lily could not be persuaded to accept the decision. Then Edythe had entered the room and heard about the idea. Quickly, she decided that if Lily was to go, so would she. Both reminded her of their limited chances to travel beyond Hunswick, let alone outside Cumbria. Without a legitimate reason to deny her sisters' request, Bronwyn eventually acquiesced.

So she had asked Ranulf, explaining how after her ordeal, she felt uncomfortable being separated from her sisters. Soon afterward she had regretted it.

Yesterday, Lily's excitement had monopolized the conversation, wearing everyone out. By the time they had stopped to camp, all the events over the past few days had caught up with Bronwyn. She had barely been able to remain awake during the evening meal.

Typically an early riser, she was still fighting fatigue in the morning when Ranulf tapped her cheek and said they had to be leaving. He felt so bad about it, and she wanted to ask just what was driving this insane push south, but Lily had popped in and once again the opportunity had been lost.

Tonight, however, Bronwyn vowed to stay awake until she understood exactly what was driving Ranulf's crazed reaction. She reached up and stroked his cheek to get his attention. He glanced down and she pointed toward the tent he had set up for them when she and her sisters helped prepare the evening meal. His eyebrows shot up, high and rounded, and then rose to his feet. He outstretched his hand and helped her to stand.

Bronwyn welcomed the support. By and large, her legs had recovered from their ordeal, but having to ride for two days immediately following such abuse had definitely strained them. They stiffened every time she sat for any length of time, but at least she could walk now with limited assistance.

Ranulf pushed aside the opening and followed Bronwyn inside. Dropping the flap, he moved in behind her and slowly started to loosen the ties of her bliaut. Bronwyn reached back and tugged at the snood holding her hair and let the dark tawny locks fall down. Immediately, Ranulf's hands paused and then tangled his fingers in the thick soft mass, pulling her back against him.

He let go a sigh and pressed a kiss on top of her head. Bronwyn could feel the tension in him lessening. She closed her eyes and let his warmth envelop her. "I'm sorry this trip has been so difficult."

"It could be worse. We could be enduring Father Morrell's celebration of the Eucharist."

Bronwyn's jaw dropped and she turned in his arms to see if Ranulf was serious. He was.

Ranulf framed her face in his hands and placed a soft kiss on her lips. He then stepped aside and pulled his tunic over his head. Seeing her still stunned, sea blue eyes follow his movements, he said, "Don't look at me that way. The aggravating priest confronted me when you were packing, telling me that I was damning all of our souls by taking you away on such an auspicious day."

Bronwyn bit her bottom lip to keep from laughing. "Father Morrell's just concerned. He believes that all should be given Holy Communion at least once a year and—"

"He has chosen the last Sunday of the Twelfthtide to be that day. I understand. But just as I told him, I've missed so many of what he considers critical celebrations in my lifetime, another won't matter. And since you've attended almost every one, forgoing one or two this year is just as trivial."

Bronwyn took a deep breath, exhaled, and followed his lead, freeing the restraints of her bliaut. "I've married a heathen."

Helping her pull the thick material over her head, Ranulf agreed, "I think that is exactly what Father Morrell concluded as well."

Free from the bulky winter garment, Bronwyn felt a surge of arousal and twisted around to kiss him full on the lips. "Then maybe I'll just have to reform you."

"Sounds tempting," Ranulf murmured against her lips, "but what if it is I who corrupt you?" he asked as he slowly edged her shift up over her hips, breasts, and then head.

Bronwyn smiled and twined her arms around his neck. She felt no awkwardness for her lack of clothing. She had nothing to hide from this man. He thought her perfect. "You've already tried."

"And it's working. Just who is seducing whom, angel?"

"Oh, I am definitely seducing you, my lord."

Tomorrow she would ask him about his reasons for their impromptu journey south. She suddenly had other plans.

Chapter Sixteen

Held on January 2, unless a Sunday, the Feast of Saint Macarius the Younger honors the patron saint of pastry cooks and confectioners and is a day celebrated by making or eating sugarplums or candied fruits. Saint Macarius the Younger was a monk and a hermit known for his kindness to animals, but in his early life he was a cake maker and a sugarplum merchant in Alexandria, Egypt. Then in 335 A.D., he fled to the Nitrian Desert, where tales of his life vary. It is said that he once killed a fly and as a result lived in marshes—some say naked—for six months, letting mosquitoes and African gnats, whose sting can pierce the hide of a wild boar, bite him until he was unrecognizable. He lived meagerly on uncooked beans and cabbage leaves, indulging in bread crumbs on days of celebration. Accounts of miracles, such as basket weaving for forty days while standing, never sleeping or eating, led some monks to claim he was

not human, but others to believe he exemplified
monasticism with his austerities.

Hearing Ranulf's low voice, Bronwyn peeked her
fingers out from underneath the furs in search of his
warmth. Finding herself alone but still hearing him,
she opened her eyes and surveyed the tent, confirming what her sense of touch had told her. Ranulf was
gone. Knowing he was nearby, she was on the verge
of calling out to him when the clipped tone of Tyr's
voice stopped her.

"It's still dark outside. It might be dangerous for
the women to ride."

"Then they will ride with one of us," Ranulf replied
with suppressed frustration. "We aren't moving fast
enough and today we must make up for ground
we should have covered already."

Bronwyn turned her head toward the voices and
saw two shadows forming silhouettes on the rippling
canvas wall.

"Just when do you intend to reach London?" Tyr's
question surprised Bronwyn for it meant even
Ranulf's best friend was not aware of the overarching plan.

"Bronwyn and I need to be at Westminster in less
than three days."

"By Twelfth Night? For the celebrations?" Tyr
asked doubtfully, unbelieving Ranulf wanted to
attend an event he had always avoided.

"Sooner. I am hoping to arrive by morning, but
no later than the afternoon if my plan is to work,"
Ranulf replied with a strained grunt. Then his broad
shadow moved and Bronwyn could tell that he was
working on something while he was speaking.

Tyr let go a long sigh and Bronwyn could envision the mystified look on his face as he searched for explanations that Ranulf wasn't volunteering. "You aren't trying to beat the baron there, are you? He's had at least a full day's start and undoubtedly traveling with a smaller group."

"I don't want to beat him there," Ranulf clarified. The tenor of his voice had changed to one of anticipation laced with revenge. "I want him to get there way before us. In fact, I am counting on it."

"But if he gets there first and relates what happened, the king isn't going to welcome our arrival."

Bronwyn thought she saw Ranulf give a small shake to his head. "Any other time of the year, maybe. But you know Her Grace and her penchants, especially for celebrations and for Twelfthtide. This being the first season after her being crowned queen, I highly doubt she—or Henry, for that matter—is going to meet with a small northern baron until Epiphany."

"True . . . the duke's not likely to appreciate any business demands that are not crown-threatening."

"So I'm going to prevent the opportunity for Baron Craven to speak his mind."

The taller of the two shadows suddenly straightened. "Good God, I understand now," Tyr hummed with admiration. "Tricky. And you'll have to get to a certain baker in time . . . and pray that our good queen and king refused to leave without him."

"They wouldn't have," Ranulf asserted strongly.

"Well, just in case . . . do you have another plan?"

The tension in Ranulf's shadowed stance returned. "I do and it is ready and in place, but it lacks the imagination and intellect our king and queen would appreciate."

"The baron has no idea who he had taken on. If you pull this off, the king will be so amused, he will forgive you of anything," Tyr replied with a chuckle, obviously not worried, and clapped Ranulf on the back. "I'll see to the horses. We should be ready to leave by the time the sun rises."

Ranulf grunted and both shadows walked away, each in a different direction.

Bronwyn let go the breath she had been holding and digested what she had heard. In the end, she had learned very little. The few parts she had understood only confirmed what she suspected. Luc was the reason behind Ranulf's mad dash to the heart of England. Speed of their travel was essential, not just because Ranulf was in a hurry to confront the man, but he needed to do it on a specific day— Twelfth Night.

They had only two more days to travel, and from Ranulf's urgency, that left barely enough time, and in winter, any number of things could happen.

Bronwyn whipped off the fur blankets and quickly started to dress. As soon as she was done, she was going to see to her sisters and ensure they rose and were prepared to leave when Ranulf was ready. Neither she nor her sisters were going to be the reason he couldn't execute his plan and fell out of favor with the king. What that plan was exactly, she would ask later, but for right now, it was more important that she be a help and not a hindrance.

Bronwyn was just pulling her bliaut over her head when the canvas flap opened and someone stepped inside. Thinking it Ranulf, she tugged the garment down and beamed the incomer a smile. The smile changed to one of shock at seeing her sisters—both up and already dressed.

Seeing her initial jubilant welcome, Edythe snorted and rubbed her arms vigorously in an attempt to get warmer. Lily, on the other hand, laughed. "Sorry. You obviously hoped we were someone else," she mumbled, not meaning it at all.

Tyr poked his head in and, looking at Edythe, said, "We are to be leaving soon. Be ready."

Edythe issued him a scowl and rubbed her very red nose. "I heard you the first five times," she moaned. "The man does not believe in sleep and cannot seem to get it through his head that some do," she added, speaking to Bronwyn but keeping her gaze on him.

Tyr arched a single brow and stepped inside. "I sleep, just not all day."

Edythe sniffed. She wasn't feeling her best, but she was not about to let Tyr chide her without consequences. "You may have been the one standing beside me at the altar, but that doesn't give you permission to act like my husband."

"I know your husband well, and Garik's going to feel the same way," Tyr responded, crossing his arms.

Edythe lifted her chin and several locks of her red hair fell around her shoulders. "Not after I'm done with him. He'll be glad to have a wife. And the fact that I like to sleep *in bed*, he's going to consider a bonus." Then with a manufactured flair, she stepped around him and plopped down on the fur blankets with enough force that her hastily made braid came totally undone. Few outside of family had ever seen Edythe's auburn tresses completely free, but those who did were blessed with a sight that denied description.

Tyr just stared at her for several seconds. Every muscle in his body had gone tight and he looked as if he were struggling just to breathe. A second later, he pivoted and abruptly exited the tent, stomping off with no effort to hide his displeasure.

Edythe, who had refused to look at him, could no longer pretend to be ignorant of Tyr's mood. "The man is a menace," she mumbled as she once again rubbed her nose.

Both Bronwyn and Lily's eyebrows rose, but neither said a word. Instead Bronwyn finished lacing her bliaut. "Ready for another long day of riding?" she asked.

Lily snorted. "More than you are. We had to sleep in our clothes last night."

Bronwyn sent her a reproving look and began to work on her hair. She was concerned about Edythe, who looked like she wanted to crawl back in bed and sleep. Bronwyn pulled one of the furs around her sister's shoulders and asked, "Are you sure you are up to this, Edythe?"

Edythe sniveled, evidence that she was not only physically ailing, but not able to emotionally deflect her heated exchanges with Tyr. "Why? Are you saying that you could persuade your husband to return north?"

"I . . . no. He would not," Bronwyn answered truthfully.

"Then the question is pointless. I shall be fine. Miserable, but I refuse to let that oaf out there know it. So get dressed and let's go. The sooner we get to Westminster, the better," Edythe announced, tightening the fur blanket around her.

The speed of their travel quickened significantly. Ranulf had set the pace and refused to ease or stop unless absolutely necessary. It helped that they were finally out of the Cumbria Hills, but they were now exposed to the cold winds blowing across the rolling lands, whipping at them.

Everyone had huddled inside their clothing or blankets, keeping their faces covered as much as possible. Talking was difficult and the hours of riding in silence became tedious. Bronwyn almost preferred the trickier mountain riding in the colder temperatures where at least the wind was not clawing at her cloak constantly. But if she was miserable, Edythe looked and felt much worse.

Bronwyn and Lily had been riding on either side of her for most of the day's journey. Yet despite Edythe's declining health, she had managed to keep pace with the group. Ranulf once inclined his head, gesturing for Bronwyn to ride with him, but she shook her head no, reluctant to leave her sister's side.

Bronwyn had decided to say something when they stopped briefly for the noon meal, but Edythe must have realized her intentions and told her not to say a word. "I am cold, that's all. So is everyone." Then she set her jaw firmly, letting Bronwyn know that if she spoke in her defense, it would be a wasted effort. Unable to do anything more, Bronwyn rode closely beside her, trying wherever she could to keep Edythe focused.

By midafternoon, Edythe's strength had left her and she was teetering unsafely on her saddle. Bronwyn reached out to pull on the reins and force the group to stop when her horse was nudged aside. Tyr rode up between her and Edythe and, in an effortless move, lifted her sister out of her seat and onto his lap. Bronwyn held her breath as he pulled Edythe close to him and wrapped the blankets closely around her huddled frame, waiting for her sister to demand to be set free. Edythe only snuggled closer, proof she was ailing more than she had let anyone believe.

Knowing her sister was now safe, Bronwyn spurred her horse forward and came alongside Ranulf. It was the first time she had been alone with him since the previous night. She wanted to ask him questions—inquire about his plans, about Luc and what would happen if they didn't reach their destination in time—but the wind made it too painful to speak.

So they rode in silence, maintaining their accelerated pace over the treeless, practically deserted terrain. Every once in a while they would pass a distant farm, but they saw no one. All were either recovering from a feast or preparing for one. Most likely the latter.

Since yesterday had been Sunday, the Feast of Saint Macarius would be celebrated today. It was the most delicious feast of Twelfthtide. All day the most delectable things would come out of the kitchen. This year, with the unusually long weather, there would have been berries to make fruit tarts, nuts, and sweetmeats of all sorts. Bronwyn closed her eyes and inhaled, pretending to smell the warm pies and pastries.

Shivering, she pushed the thoughts aside and concentrated once again on the terrain, which finally had some variety. To the west, an unusual clump of trees formed the shape of a heart where two rivers came together. When she had been a child, her father once told her of such a place after being pummeled with questions about where he had been and just how he had known where to go.

Bronwyn took a second look at the thicket. Maybe, they might all get to enjoy the Feast of Saint Macarius after all.

Pulling down the blanket covering her face, she nudged her mount closer to Ranulf's. "My lord?"

"I wish you didn't have to ride in such weather."

"It's necessary," she said aloud, so he would know she understood. The air was frigid and burned when she breathed it in. "But is it also necessary for my sisters to endure the journey?"

"I should never have agreed to let them come," he replied, not really answering her question. He had not been thinking and the weather had been so deceiving lately, he had forgotten just how cruel England winters could be.

"I'm worried about my sister."

Ranulf glanced back. "Lily is doing far better than I expected."

Bronwyn nodded in agreement. "She has always been the best rider of the three of us, and it is not Lily who I was talking about. I'm worried about Edythe."

Ranulf twisted around again, this time seeing Edythe's riderless horse and the huddled mass in Tyr's arms. Ranulf, too, had seen Edythe's failing health and was powerless to do anything about it. He had considered having Tyr turn back, but they were beyond the halfway mark and the way forward was easier than the return. They had no choice but to keep going, though Tyr might decide to slow the pace for Edythe.

"Tyr will see that she makes it."

Bronwyn licked her lips and instantly regretted the action. The cold wind whipped at the wet surface, chapping the soft skin. "My father had a friend he used to go and visit, a Baron Alfred. He said it was almost a three-day ride south. And I thought maybe if we could reach his place, then Edythe could stay there. We could get a good meal—"

"I don't know a Baron Alfred," he said, cutting her off. Then regretting his snappish answer, he added, "I wish we could, but we don't have the time to search for him, even if we are close."

Bronwyn sighed. "I understand. I just saw that cluster of trees and realized how near to his place we were."

Ranulf had to turn his head severely to the left to see to what she was referring. "How close?"

Her brows shot up at his sudden interest. "If I remember right, my father said he lived a few miles down where the river converged and made a heart."

Ranulf glanced up. Clouds had covered the sky the entire day so it was difficult to tell just how much time they had left, but he suspected it was an hour. Two at most before night was upon then.

Bronwyn hadn't complained and didn't appear to be getting ill, but he knew she was cold and uncomfortable. Warmth, hot food and a restful night of sleep would do a lot to ensure everyone could keep up the pace for the rest of the trip. Not to mention, he could insist her sisters remain behind, leaving only Bronwyn to look after as an inexperienced traveler.

Aiming his horse toward the group of trees, he said, "We'll travel a few miles along the river. If we haven't seen it by dark, then we move on."

Bronwyn nodded her head enthusiastically and shifted the blankets back up to cover her exposed cheeks.

An hour later a large tower keep came into view approximately six miles east from where they were headed. Without hesitation, Ranulf tugged his reins to his left and headed for the stone structure. It wasn't far off course and the benefits far outweighed any inconvenience.

Bronwyn trotted up next to him and beamed him a glorious smile that sent his pulse racing.

"Baron Alfred, you say?" he asked rhetorically. "Well, let's hope you are right and that he still considers you a friend."

"He was a very good friend to my father, and while I have never been to his home, he should remember me from his visits to our home. Do you think that's his keep?"

"If your memory is accurate."

"I'm going to tell Lily and Edythe," she told him. "I love you very much, you know."

A grin overtook Ranulf's features. That was the best benefit of all.

Chapter Seventeen

TUESDAY, JANUARY 4, 1154
LORD OF MISRULE

The Lord of Misrule is one of the lost treasures of the Medieval Christmas celebration. Either selected by chance or appointed by the noble in charge, an ordinary citizen was crowned Lord of Misrule, responsible for directing Twelfthtide or winter festival entertainment. The extent of his powers and responsibilities depended on the length of his reign, which could last anywhere from three months to the twelve days of Christmas or even just one night. Given full license to find enjoyment however he desired, the purpose of his reign was to provide comic relief by changing rules and laws in such a way to bring merriment and delight to all. The tradition extends back to Roman times, though ironically became less barbaric during the Middle Ages, taking a more humorous slant.

Bright morning light crested over the hills. The clouds had passed, taking with them the cold wind and leaving everyone feeling much warmer. Less Edythe and Tyr, who had volunteered to stay behind and ensure her safety, the group had left early in the morning loaded with food, fresh horses, and improved moods. Baron Alfred had been more than a little surprised by their arrival, but after his astonishment diminished, he had welcomed them all warmly. They had feasted and rested and Ranulf felt himself relax and enjoy the baron's hospitality.

"I cannot remember when I have had such good food," Ranulf said, with a smile of satisfaction bending his usually firm mouth.

"I'll be sure not to mention that to our own cooks."

"Hunswick has fine cooks and a better than decent baker, but if our king ever learned of the delicacies Baron Alfred enjoys on a daily basis, your friend would suddenly find himself not nearly as well fed."

"I think after last night, you can consider the baron your friend now as well. He did promise to come and visit in the spring."

"Aye, but he won't bring his cooks," Ranulf sighed, licking his lips in memory.

Bronwyn rolled her eyes, secretly enjoying her husband's levity. "I must admit that I was amazed at how quickly you were at ease with him."

"I was surprised myself," Ranulf replied.

He only felt truly comfortable with a handful of people, and for most of those on that short list, the trust had been cultivated over time. Bronwyn and her father had been exceptions, and Baron Alfred was an unanticipated addition to Ranulf's rapidly growing group of unsought, but strangely desired, friends.

The baron was in many ways a rounder, shorter, red-haired version of Laon—generous, but far from trusting. Lily had been the first to venture forward, but it was not until Alfred saw Bronwyn did his wary demeanor thaw. Ranulf had never been prouder than when she had introduced him as the new Lord Anscombe . . . and her husband. The instant need to shut off his emotions and shun people's reactions vanished. Some did visibly retreat, but Ranulf no longer cared. Amazingly, the less he shrank from people and gatherings, the less they were concerned about his appearance. They were too interested in having fun and eating . . . pleasures he, too, found himself to be enjoying. Even the knowledge of what was to occur in London could not dampen his feelings.

Bronwyn tossed her head back and let go a long sigh that spoke volumes. "I'm glad Edythe agreed to stay, but I'm surprised Lily did not also jump at the chance when Tyr volunteered to remain behind."

"Your sister's innocent, but not nearly as naïve as she wants all to believe. She sees the attraction between Tyr and Edythe. Nothing will ever come of it, but at least Lily is smart enough to know that if Tyr were inclined toward a woman, it would not be her. Not to mention that, for Baron Alfred's sake, it was a good thing she agreed to continue with the journey. She is much better behaved when Edythe is not around."

"I have to admit she and Edythe do enjoy annoying the other. Still, Lily is handling herself much better than I anticipated."

"Yes. She hasn't complained once this morning

although the *real* reason your sister's enduring this trip is quite apparent."

Bronwyn bit the inside of her cheek and murmured, "Court."

Ranulf grunted in agreement. "I've never seen someone so eager to meet a rather pompous and boring group of individuals."

Bronwyn pasted on a shocked expression and openly stared at her husband. "Why, this is the first time I think I have ever heard you speak negatively of the king."

"I'm not talking about the duke or his wife. Just those that like to cling to them and the comforts they surround themselves with."

"And you think Lily is just like those people."

"She is. Unfortunately, she will be more successful. By the time she's done, she'll have charmed half of King Henry's nobles and I will have double to answer for then."

Bronwyn furrowed her brow and studied Ranulf to see if he was serious. And he was. His mind was in the immediate future and it concerned him. She was just about to ask him to explain his plan when Lily suddenly appeared by her side. "Did I hear you say court?"

The innocent question jerked Ranulf back to the present and he gave a short laugh before urging his horse into an ever-faster lope. Good food, new horses, and a good night's sleep had enabled them to easily make up any time loss by the deviation to the baron's home, but there was still significant ground to cover.

It was paramount that they arrive at Westminster

in time to meet with a certain baker before a certain cake was put in the oven.

Bronwyn listened impatiently as those around her sat riveted. The tale Lily was spinning was a good one, mostly because every word of it was true. Still, Bronwyn had been waiting for a chance to speak with Ranulf about the specifics of his plan all day. Only one never came. Someone either interrupted them just before she was going to ask or was riding too near to be assured of privacy. By the time they stopped to make camp, she had decided that if an opportunity didn't arrive by the end of their meal, she would make one.

Unfortunately, Lily once again had everyone engaged in conversation. Even though Ranulf wasn't necessarily participating, he was actively listening to her tales about Laon teaching her how to ride a horse. The tale conveyed her younger sister's naiveté, willfulness, and sheer determination so that by its conclusion one wondered if she was immature or just a little inexperienced. Regardless, all were charmed into admiring her as she openly exposed her flaws. If Ranulf worried about men of court instantly desiring her, then he was right to do so.

The story finally done, Bronwyn reached over and clasped her fingers within Ranulf's, but before she could lean over and whisper in his ear, one of his men asked Lily an ensuing question. Her face broke into a sparkling grin and Bronwyn knew the answer was going to be another entertaining story.

Pasting on her most endearing smile, Bronwyn stood up and interrupted, "I must beg everyone's pardon for retiring early. I have been needing to speak with my husband all day. So, we will see you in the morning." She then looked down at Ranulf to ensure he understood that she was serious.

He arched a single brow, but said nothing as he rose to join her, ignoring the short coughs and snorts of laughter of his men. Bronwyn instantly froze as she realized what the small group—including her husband—believed she had meant. Mustering up the remnants of her pride, she forced herself to march on.

"It's nice to know you've been wanting me all day, but if you desire for us to be alone, there are more discreet ways of letting me know," Ranulf teased as he lifted the flap of their tent.

Bronwyn knew her already red face was turning an even more brilliant color, but she refused to let Ranulf believe he had totally won. "You, husband, are far more in need of a modesty lesson than I."

Ranulf let go the heavy material and then crossed his arms with a smug look of satisfaction Bronwyn wanted to both remove and indulge. "Don't believe in modesty. Never have. Kind of liking the fact that you don't either," he said, hinting at what he thought was about to come next.

Bronwyn took a step back and waved a finger. "I said I wanted to *speak* with you alone . . . about tomorrow." The grin spread across Ranulf's face vanished and was immediately replaced with a sour grimace. He said nothing.

Bronwyn bit the inside of her lip in frustration. "All this while I thought there just hadn't been time for us to talk, for you to explain. I'm now realizing that you have been avoiding this conversation."

"Not avoiding. But eager to have it? No."

"Why? Do you think I might be worried, unable to handle it?"

Ranulf rubbed his temples. "More like disappointed . . . in me."

"First the king and now me? You must know by now that nothing will change my feelings for you, and as for the king, I thought he considered you a friend."

"The duke doesn't seek friendship, just loyalty," Ranulf scoffed and started to unhook his belt, needing something to do in the close quarters.

"But you are loyal, are you not?"

"I am, but some could claim otherwise," Ranulf cautioned, tossing the leather strap aside. Then he looked directly at her and added, "And they would be right."

Bronwyn suddenly felt ill as understanding hit her full force. Ranulf's loyalty, which had never wavered before, had become divided. She had become his priority and the battle she had seen waged in the distance had proven just whom Ranulf would choose whenever the two came in conflict. "But surely the king will understand—"

Ranulf shrugged and sank down onto the soft furs lining their makeshift bed. His mouth twisted into a frown as he became lost in deep thought. "England's new king is many things. Henry has the capacity for great generosity, proven by my own purse size, and he cares about his men, often riding out with me and other commanders in the morning rather than staying inside in comfort."

Bronwyn sat down beside Ranulf and gathered one of his hands into her own and listened.

"As you know, I first met Henry when he came to Bristol as a boy to study, but his interest was not thrust upon him as some would think. He loved to learn. Years later, when our paths crossed again, he was still studying a variety of topics and no doubt still does. As a result, he has an unusual understanding of the law and is a great believer in its power to bring justice."

Ranulf paused and stared at their intertwined fingers as he gathered his thoughts. "He is also quite intolerant of those who act in such ways that might be considered unlawful or—disloyal. And I, in the span of less than two weeks upon arrival, have committed three such acts."

"Three?" Bronwyn mouthed as her brow puckered with incredulity.

Ranulf pursed his lips before nodding. "When your father lay dying, he pleaded for me to protect you and your sisters and thought my marrying Lily would ensure this promise for life. I obliged him to ease his mind as he passed, but I had believed the duke would revoke the vow. I was wrong.

"I soon discovered that your father charmed not only our king, but our queen, and neither could be persuaded to my desires. Her Grace had deemed it time I marry, knowing I would never initiate the state myself. So I went north armed with Laon's descriptions of you and your sisters—"

"Which is how you knew from the start that I was not Lillabet."

"Yes, but it takes only a few minutes in your company to determine just who is the eldest and who is the youngest. I would have discovered the ruse soon enough."

Bronwyn closed her eyes as her thoughts filtered back to the day Lily bounded into her room declaring her intentions of marrying Ranulf. Bronwyn gave her head a quick shake, realizing she had been diverted by his last comment. "Maybe eventually, but go back to where you left off—unhappy about being forced north to wed the most beautiful girl of Cumbria. Something every unattached man in the Hills dreams about, but you dreaded."

In a deft move, Ranulf gave Bronwyn's elbow a sharp tug, swiftly yanking her over his knee. After swatting her playfully on her behind, he flipped her over and kissed her long and hard. "*You* are the most beautiful woman I have ever seen. I have always thought so and you know it. Now, interrupt again and I shall assume you are no longer interested in tomorrow but in other more entertaining things."

Bronwyn narrowed her eyes, but their mischievous twinkle countered the feigned glare. She pressed her lips together in a mocking attempt to show him that she intended to say nothing more.

"In response to the other part of your comment, I did journey to Hunswick with orders to marry Lillabet, but I had decided prior to my arrival that I would delay the inevitable for as long as possible. At the time, I did not consider sending you three away from Hunswick and back to your family estate a forfeiture of either promise—the one to protect or the one to marry. Then fortune brought you to my side."

Bronwyn reached over and laid a hand on the wound that had brought them together. Ranulf clasped his fingers over hers and took a deep breath. "I knew almost from the beginning you were the only one I would marry, despite my promise to your father or my king's wishes."

"Surely that wouldn't raise the king's ire, since what he truly wanted was for you to be married."

"That is what I believed and most likely would have been correct if I hadn't intentionally broke a certain promise made by King Henry's predecessor."

Bronwyn scrunched her forehead, then a second later, her expression went grim with understanding. "You mean King Stephen's promise to Luc."

"Marrying you when you were pledged to the baron and I was promised to Lillabet could have been explained, but my interference in assuring Edythe and Lily were also protected is not as defensible. If there had been more time, I could have journeyed to London, met with the king, who most likely would have negated King Stephen's promise. Instead, I had us all wed under the eyes of God and law, something both the baron and the king will have to honor."

"But I thought you said King Henry valued justice. Surely he will realize it was the right thing to do."

Ranulf winced and halfway nodded before shaking his head. "I expect Henry would have appreciated the sentiment behind my decision, but he is a pragmatist. And in this matter I agree. If my men began determining which orders to obey and which to overrule, people would die. Same with noblemen. When one noble interferes with another's rights, chaos ensues and countries fall."

"But even the king must realize there are exceptions."

"So early in his reign? No. He must establish his

authority. And my long-standing allegiance doesn't help my cause, it hurts it. For out of all his commanders, *I* knew what I was doing when I attacked the baron's land and dwelling and how Henry would react."

Bronwyn stood up and began to pace in front of Ranulf, whose soft voice frightened her more than anything he had yet said. "I don't understand. How is retaliating against a man who tried to kill your wife not justified?"

Ranulf bunched some of the furs together, leaned back against them, and watched Bronwyn walk back and forth in the small enclosure. "I started the battle—and I ended it—but the king's overarching charge when he sent me north was to *preserve the peace*. He desired England to grow and be united and stop hurting itself with ceaseless battles. But mostly he had other plans for his armies. My men and I slaughtered a fair number of men. And while even now I cannot feel guilty about ending a man's life who willingly followed Craven's cowardice and malice, they were able-bodied soldiers who could have, and would have, fought for the king."

Bronwyn remembered watching the flames and billows of smoke in the distance as the battle waged. "King Henry should be glad to be rid of such men who would fight and support someone like the baron."

"It's not their deaths that will anger Henry," Ranulf clarified, "but something far more significant in his eyes." He waited until Bronwyn paused and had her full attention. "I had no proof that Baron Craven was behind your supposed death. And anyone who was there knew I was not doling out unquestionable justice. I was engaged in revenge. The king cannot allow it to be known that he condoned one of his trusted commanders and newly titled nobles to place his own desire above that of him."

"But now you know that Luc *did* try to kill me. Will that not negate any wrongdoing?"

Ranulf reached out his hand, and when she placed hers in his, he gave it a gentle tug, causing her to collapse once again beside him. He tucked back a loose lock of hair. "To a degree. At least that is what I am hoping. But know this, King Henry has to make an example out of at least one of us—the baron or me."

Bronwyn's expression stilled and turned serious. "It will be the baron, of course. So tell me, what is your plan? And make sure you tell me just how I can help."

"My plan is actually quite simple. We need to get to London and speak with the king before the baron can relate the situation in a far different and far more damning way."

Bronwyn's back stiffened. "But Luc left a few days ago. Hasn't he met the king already?"

"Doubtful," Ranulf replied, twisting a long piece of her honey gold hair around his finger. He gave her a slight smile of merciless glee. "Oh, I assume he has tried to request an immediate audience with the king, but the baron won't get one. Queen Eleanor prefers all matters of state that are not considered an emergency to be put aside until after Twelfth Night and our young smitten king obliges her. So I doubt the baron is going to get within a stone's throw of Westminster until tomorrow night during the festivities."

"But you can since you have known—"

Ranulf placed his finger lightly against her lips, preventing her from finishing. "No. King Henry is fair and he wouldn't show preference in such a way, especially so early in his reign when he is trying to gain his people's trust."

Bronwyn brushed his hand aside and sat back, seeing the lustful sparkle in his eye. The conversation was soon going to end and she still wasn't sure what Ranulf was planning. "Then how?"

"I am going to cheat," Ranulf sighed.

"Cheat?"

"No man is above it in battle and this, angel, is a battle, just with different weapons," Ranulf replied with a matter-of-fact shrug. "I happen to know the king's favorite baker and he owes me several favors. I was going to arrange to be named the King of the Bean, and in this way I would be able to decree a meeting with Henry and have a chance to plead my case. You," Ranulf began and then paused as he reached over to pull her up against him, "can corroborate my claims, but mostly you are there to charm our good king and queen."

Ranulf pressed his lips against hers, their soft touch sparking to life every nerve in her body. She welcomed his tongue into her mouth and returned the invasion, touching every corner, tasting him, as the sensations he was stirring took over her mind and soul. Then suddenly, as quickly as the kiss began, it stopped.

Ranulf waited until the love-filled mist cleared from her eyes before continuing. "Yes, I think the king will find it much harder to strip me of my home and title if he knows he is doing the same to you. I'm not sure what your father said or did, but it gained both King Henry's and Queen Eleanor's admiration. Maybe your father's memory will be enough to grant me leniency."

Bronwyn, now recovered, pushed against Ranulf's chest to stand up, dodging his attempt to pull her back down. "But isn't the King of the Bean already named? I thought in court the title was determined days before, at the beginning of Twelfthtide . . ."

Feigning surrender, Ranulf exhaled deeply and lay back against the pile of furs. "That was King Stephen. Henry doesn't like doling out such power and only allows the tradition begrudgingly and limitedly. In the past, he offers the bean cake only on Twelfth Night, most of the time well into the evening, giving the lucky winner only a few hours to create his mischief."

Bronwyn was about take Ranulf's extended hand and return to complete what he had started but at the last moment jerked it back and started to pace. "Your plan, while clever, involves a lot of assumptions and therefore a lot of risk. First, it all hinges on you finding this baker and convincing him of making you the Bean King."

"Maybe at Hunswick the person who finds the bean is random, but trust me, the king's baker arranges who receives the favored slice," Ranulf said, propping himself up, to yank off his tunic. "But yes, I do have to find him."

Resuming her swift back-and-forth march, Bronwyn continued, "Fine. Let's assume you do find the baker and are named this year's temporary ruler. You will still need to get an audience with the real king."

"A most likely event if I find the bean," Ranulf answered as he stood up to yank off his leggings.

Ignoring him, Bronwyn asked, "And he is going to let you explain the events and decisions of the past few days?"

Ranulf paused and shrugged his chin with a knowing grin. "I would say the duke is always interested in listening to a diverting story."

Bronwyn came to an abrupt stop and firmly poked Ranulf in the chest. "And that is where the biggest flaw in your plan lives. You are taking a defensive posture, not a very *persuasive* one. It doesn't allow the king to show you leniency without appearing weak." Bronwyn recommenced her pacing. "What you need is a way to gain sympathy by depicting your acts as responses to hostility. Demonstrate this and the king, if he is a just man as you say he is, will have to find in your favor."

Ranulf crossed his arms, curious. "Just how do you think I can accomplish this by tomorrow night?"

Bronwyn bit her bottom lip, stared at his discarded sword and arched her brows. Then with an impish smile turned back to face Ranulf. "Oh, you had the right plan, just the wrong king."

A few minutes later, Ranulf gathered her into a bear hug and then swung her around the tent. "I may be clever, but you, angel, have a devilish quality about you I believe Henry is going to enjoy."

"Really?" Bronwyn gasped, giggling in response to his excitement.

"Mm-hmm," Ranulf said, leaning in for a long-drawn-out kiss. "Henry has probably the best sense of humor among anyone I know. And the one thing he appreciates is intelligent wit—and its source could come from anyone, even a chambermaid, and its topic could be anything or anyone."

"I hope so," Bronwyn purred as Ranulf slowly wove a spell around her.

"Trust me," he said and winked at her with his good eye. Then he quickly re-dressed and pointed toward the tent's opening. "Come on. For if this new plan of yours is going to work, everyone needs to know what to do upon our arrival . . . and even more importantly, just what not to do."

Chapter Eighteen

Twelfth Night or the Eve of the Epiphany is the last celebration night of Christmastide as well as the ending of the winter festival that starts on All Hallows Eve, more commonly known as Halloween. For centuries, the merriment and festivities of Twelfth Night far surpassed the other feasts of the season, and included dancing, merrymaking, and the consumption of large amounts of food and wine. A common theme was to reverse the everyday normal order and the most prominent method included the bean cake or king's cake in which a single slice held a bean allowing anyone the chance to be crowned "king." Similar to the Lord of Misrule, the person who found the bean temporarily became royalty and had the power to rule over the Twelfth Night's festivities until midnight when his reign ended. The ensuing "bean feast" was the highlight of the medieval Christmas, in which all classes

could enjoy extravagant meals of various meats,
spices, fruits, cheeses, ales, and delicious desserts.

Bronwyn had expected London to be more
crowded than the towns littering the hills of Cumbria, but never could she have dreamed the numbers
of people living practically on top of one another.
Buildings stood side by side, some practically falling
apart while others appeared to be newly erected. The
mud and the stench, especially in the smaller alleys,
were unavoidable, but so was the sheer excitement
that oozed from everybody as the hour of Twelfth
Night advanced. Only their small solemn group
seemed impervious to the merriment.

At first, Bronwyn had assumed Ranulf's tension
stemmed from his plans for that evening, but as they
traveled farther into town and onto increasingly
crowded streets, she realized their relatively innocu-
ous party was getting more attention than it rightly
should. Either people ignored them or they openly
stared as they went by, and those that did stare
focused their attention on Ranulf.

She had forgotten just how the world viewed her
husband. Large and menacing with short hair and a
dark glare, Ranulf was unmistakably a fierce warrior.
Even if he had not possessed the ominous scar
across his cheek, a sheer look from him could make
a person quake. Pride started to fill her when she
noticed something else—some of those they passed
displayed not just fear . . . but revulsion.

At Hunswick, no one cared about a person's imper-
fections. Import was placed on how one treated their
fellow man and the contributions they produced. But
in London, among such masses of people, it would be

difficult to truly know all those encountered, leaving one to judge his neighbor primarily by their appearance. Ranulf's missing eye was not in any way frightening or even very obvious, but too many believed such a wound was akin to deformity.

The desire to demonstrably show just how much she loved and admired him was enormous, but she could not do so. So instead, Bronwyn beamed him a smile. In return, Ranulf's face hardened into a threatening grimace. Unfazed, Bronwyn sighed, resigning herself from further attempts to cheer him until they were alone.

Ranulf urged Pertinax into a much wider road. Following him, Bronwyn nudged her horse closer to his until they were again side by side and pointed back to her sister. "I cannot believe Lily's quiet demeanor now that we are here. After all her moaning about coming, she shows no signs of interest or excitement."

Continuing to look straight ahead, Ranulf agreed. "She seems to understand her role." Then with a quick but condemning look, he added, "Everyone does except you."

Ranulf paused as they passed close by several people trying to cross the street before continuing his admonition. "Lily is acting like a grieving sister while you forget just *who* you are supposed to be. Would *Edythe* be enjoying the sites?"

Appropriately scolded, Bronwyn quickly transformed her expression into one of sorrow. Her eyes, however, reflected the hostility of one with nicked pride.

Either unaware or uncaring, Ranulf nodded in approval and directed his horse along the ever narrowing and widening road that matched the twists and turns of the River Thames. They traveled in silence until Bronwyn heard a short gasp escape from Lily when Thorney Island and Westminster Abbey came into view.

The large stone structure stood apart from the other buildings and was surrounded by a beautiful garden. It was hard to believe anything so peaceful-looking could be a central part of a government that in years past had both brought and fought against war. Beside it was the Palace of Westminster, the royal residence of the king and queen. Tonight, they would be visitors in the colossal building and putting on a show no one was expecting.

Bronwyn was still studying the distant fortress when Ranulf reached over to grab her reins and halt her horse. She glanced back and realized the group was stopping in front of what looked to be an inn. Slipping off her saddle, one of Ranulf's men took her reins and those to the other mounts and headed toward the stables situated catty-cornered across the street.

She felt Ranulf's hand upon the middle of her back and let him guide her and Lily inside to a small, but clean sitting area. "Wait here," he half requested, half demanded and then turned to go back outside.

Bronwyn maneuvered around one of the empty tables and sat down by the window near the front. The shutters had been left open, so the area was cool from the winter air seeping in from small cracks along the sill. But it was the one place she and Lily could see and listen to the activity up and down the narrow street.

"Switch places with me," Bronwyn whispered and stood back up. "Ranulf's talking with the innkeeper and it doesn't look like it is going well."

Lily grimaced but did as asked. "Just what do you plan to do about it?" she remarked with unmistakable sarcasm.

Before Bronwyn could muster a like reply, the heated conversation ended and the innkeeper stomped inside and marched up the stairs. Ranulf slowly swaggered in behind him and she knew her husband had won . . . or at least he thought he had. He pressed a finger to his lips, and though difficult, Bronwyn muffled her questions. Several minutes later, the innkeeper escorted two very disgruntled people out of the building.

Lily gasped and Bronwyn blinked in surprise. She had not even considered the problem of where they were going to stay and the fact that it was the night of one of the biggest festivities of the year. Of course all the inns were full. This one looked like an especially clean one, not to mention it was almost uncomfortably close to the palace, the place where their lives would soon be set free or ruined.

Once outside, the angrier of the two ousted figures swiveled to glare at the innkeeper. Then his dark eyes darted toward the window. The sparks flying from the midnight pools were aimed directly at her, as if he knew she was the reason he had no shelter, let alone bed for the night. Then the man beside him gave the darker fellow a firm elbow in the side to get his attention. Ranulf was handing them both small bags. Bronwyn suspected each held coin as the men's anger quickly dissipated.

Less than a minute later, they were gone and

Ranulf walked brusquely into the sitting area. Still in character, Ranulf's stern face held no warmth and neither did his voice. "The innkeeper's wife is preparing your rooms and a bath." Then looking directly at Bronwyn, he stated, "I have to see someone, but I will be back in time to escort you tonight."

Before he could leave, Bronwyn gestured for him to wait and turned to close the shutters. "Lily, can you give us a moment and make sure no one comes in here?"

With a sigh, her sister nodded and moved to stand guard by the stairs, where she could also see anyone coming from the kitchen or the entrance.

When they were finally alone, Ranulf's stiff demeanor instantly thawed and he pulled Bronwyn into his arms, enveloping her in a long-needed hug.

Bronwyn pressed her cheek against his chest. "Remember to be charming."

Ranulf chuckled and nestled his chin in her hair before planting a soft kiss on top of her head. "I'm always charming."

An infectious grin crossed her lips. How he had changed. He was still rigid in public surrounded by strangers, very much aware of how others reacted to his scars, but no longer did Ranulf hold those same opinions of himself. And though the peaceful countenance that had slowly grown upon him the last few weeks had disappeared upon entering London, his affectionate embrace was not that of the wounded man who had marched into Hunswick just a few weeks ago, but her Ranulf . . . her rock and support and soul.

Lily poked her head around the corner and

stepped inside, letting go a small cough. "I think the innkeeper's coming."

"I'll be back as soon as I can," Ranulf said and immediately pulled away. After sending a quick wink to Lily and a brief, targeted smile to Bronwyn, he turned and exited the room just as a slim, older woman with strays of thin mousy brown hair coming free of her bun entered. Bronwyn reopened the shutters to watch Ranulf mount Pertinax and disappear down the street toward the palace. He never looked back.

"The bath his lordship ordered for you both will be ready shortly," the woman said with a tired voice. Bronwyn turned around and gave her what she hoped to be an understanding and undemanding smile. "Thank you. I know we were unexpected."

The small encouragement seemed to reinvigorate the woman's weary features and she stood a little straighter. "If you don't mind waiting here a little longer, my daughters are preparing your rooms. Would you like some something to drink?"

"Thank you. No, but your help is appreciated," Lily replied, picking up on Bronwyn's friendly deportment. In the hall, two waiflike young women hustled up and down the staircase carrying at first buckets of water and then linens.

Minutes passed before Lily and Bronwyn were finally directed to their rooms. Both were sparse, but clean. The first room was slightly larger, just big enough to accommodate two individuals. The second held only a bed and a small table with a basin of water.

The thinner of the two girls smoothed the few wayward strands of her brown hair back and mumbled,

"If you are looking for your things, they were put in the other room per his lordship's instructions."

Bronwyn thanked her and followed Lily into the larger of the two rooms as the young woman disappeared down the stairs. Collapsing on the bed, she turned her head to see Lily similarly sprawled in the single, wooden hearth chair. Next to her was a sprawled bathtub filled with what Bronwyn hoped to be warm water.

Minutes later, she immersed herself into the heated piece of heaven. "This is wonderful," Bronwyn gushed as she reemerged from dipping her head underneath the surface.

Lily leaned forward and tugged the larger of their two bags toward her. "I hope our gowns survived the journey."

Bronwyn closed her eyes and rested the back of her head on the tub's rim. "I'm sure they are fine."

Unconvinced, Lily rummaged through the bag and pulled out her gold gown and then Bronwyn's silver one, laying them out on the bed. "They are wrinkled, but not as much as I feared."

"Hand me the soap if you could."

Lily tossed her the scented gray mound and then searched the second bag for their brushes and ribbons. When done, Bronwyn stepped out and Lily bathed, echoing her sister's delight. Afterward, they sat silently, brushing their hair until it was dry, both minds churning on about what was to happen.

"Your *hair*," Lily ground out as she fought Bronwyn's difficult thick waves to create the fancy braiding designs she could so effortlessly fashion with her own dark locks.

"I know. Don't worry about it. I'll just put on a

snood." Almost instantly, pain shot through Bronwyn's scalp. "Ow!"

"Mention your snood again and I'll pull even harder . . . there. Perfect. Well, close at least." Then after putting in a final pin to hold the twists and braids in place, she asked, "When do you think we should prepare and dress?"

Bronwyn opened her mouth, but before she could reply, a knock on the door made them both jump. The wooden bathtub had been removed sometime earlier but it was not nearly time for dinner. Pulling a worn bliaut over her head, a sense of alarm washed over Bronwyn as she rose to the door and opened it.

On the other side was the maiden who showed them to their rooms. Bronwyn's apprehension mounted. The young woman was wringing her hands and a look of sheer panic was pasted on her face. "I'm sorry to disturb you, but . . . uh . . . you are both wanted at the palace. Immediately."

Bronwyn forced her limbs to relax, refusing to be nervous—or at least appear to be so—as she followed the newest member of England's royalty along the wooded path. Queen Eleanor's brisk stride belied her very pregnant state with her and King Henry II's second child. And yet despite her wide girth, she moved surprisingly gracefully and yet purposefully as the narrow path opened into a wider, more open view of the Westminster Abbey gardens.

Bronwyn took a deep breath and exhaled the cool, fragrant air. Impervious to winter, the Abbey gardens remained beautiful with flowers and greenery that thrived in cooler temperatures. The queen also seemed unaffected by the chilly breeze brought on by the lowering of the afternoon sun.

"Please sit here," the queen said, pointing at a large, unadorned stone bench. Her inflection had not brokered argument, only that of agreement. Unfortunately, the brevity of the instruction was not enough for Bronwyn to gauge the emotion that prompted this private conversation, let alone why she and her sister had been brought to the palace in the first place.

Once told of the king's desire for a meeting, Bronwyn hesitated, wondering just how His Grace had learned of their arrival so quickly, and more important, if he knew just why they were there. It had been Lily who had suspected the request to be a ruse and from the baron.

Both assumptions were quickly dispelled as wrong. It was not the baron or the king who had sent for them, but the queen.

Bronwyn had intended to leave a message for Ranulf, but when they descended the staircase, the queen's soldiers were in the hall ready to escort them. The innkeeper was not in sight and his overly beset wife was not mentally able to digest anything that would have been said to her even if Bronwyn had found the opportunity. Resolved that Ranulf would undoubtedly learn just who'd sent for them, Bronwyn joined her overawed sister and journeyed the short distance to the palace.

Since Bronwyn was uncomfortable with mysteries, her reaction to being welcomed into the Queen's Presence Room was far different than her sister. Lily, noticeably engrossed with all that made up Westminster, stood riveted just inside the doors, her head following her eyes, taking in all the grandeur that was around her. Bronwyn's focus, however, was on the person who brought them there.

"Ladies Edythe and Lillabet of the late Sir Laon le Breton of Syndlear, Your Grace," called out one of the men who had escorted them through the palace.

The queen was standing at the far end of the room and gestured for them to come closer. Bronwyn clasped Lily's hand in her own, forcing her younger sister to do as bid, and moved forward, never glancing away in hopes to discern just why they were there.

Unfortunately, with the exception of a brief, fleeting look of surprise, Queen Eleanor's face revealed nothing nor did she say a word. Instead, she had just stared, assessing them. Bronwyn wondered if the queen was trying to make her feel uncomfortable, show deference, or something else entirely. Unknowing which, Bronwyn followed her instincts and openly returned the assessment.

The queen was just as all the rumors Lily had gleaned from visitors over the past year had claimed— very beautiful. Ranulf had mentioned Her Grace's disdain for wimples, and whether it was true or not, she wasn't wearing one nor did the intricately braided and coiled hairstyle around her face indicate she was going to don one in the near future. Her pearl-lined gown shimmered of deep blue fitted her, despite her motherly state. The jeweled pendant around her neck spoke of wealth and accentuated her long neck. Everything about Queen Eleanor was feminine and pretty—but it was her eyes that gave Bronwyn pause. Shrewd, they had the ability to peel back layers of a person's shell to reveal the truth inside.

"I was told Sir Laon had three daughters and the youngest was married to the new Lord Anscombe." The queen's comment hinted at dangerous familiarity.

Lily's fingers tightened around Bronwyn's, and for a fleeting moment, she considered ending the ruse. Instead, Bronwyn replied without hesitation, "I apologize, Your Grace, that you did not receive word earlier. Syndlear, our family home, recently caught fire. My elder sister Lady Bronwyn was believed to be inside." And then she held her breath. It wasn't a lie, but it was deceit.

Waiting to be introduced, Bronwyn had prepared herself for the possibilities driving this impromptu meeting, but what happened next, only foresight could have prepared her.

For several uncomfortable minutes, the queen continued to engage in a staring contest, and then abruptly shifted her attention to Lily. "I understand that it would be hard to marry someone after such a tragic loss. But maybe I can do something to give you a respite from your grief." Then with a snap of her fingers, one of her ladies-in-waiting jumped from the shadows to her side. "I believe Lady Lillabet would be very interested in seeing more of the palace." Seeing Lily's enthusiastic nod, Queen Eleanor's face softened. "There are a great many fascinating rooms, much more impressive than this one. I'm sure your sister will not mind if you leave us to explore."

Bronwyn did not really blame Lily for abandoning her so quickly and without pause to consider if she should. Her sister had always been impulsive and allowed to indulge in her whims. However, after the queen's last insightful comment, it was a little unsettling. Even more so was the queen's strategy to divide and conquer. She wanted to speak to her alone. The question was why?

Seconds later, Lily vanished, and with another gesture, Queen Eleanor dismissed the rest of her staff hovering about. The queen then issued Bronwyn a direct smile that hinted of admiration. "You are smart to be wary, but let us not talk here. These open rooms do not promote conversation and I find a walk around the gardens to be refreshing in the afternoon. Would you join me?"

Bronwyn had no choice but to agree and followed Her Grace out of the chambers and into the corridor.

Waving a jeweled hand at the architecture and décor surrounding them, the queen commented, "Your sister seems to admire Westminster, but I find it lacking. Do you know why?"

Surprised by the question, Bronwyn tripped. The subject was one that had crossed her mind since their arrival. Something *was* missing, but she could not conclude what it might be. The building was massive and in many ways impressive, but what it needed, Bronwyn could not explain. Whatever it was, it prevented the palace from being the majestic structure she always imagined it to be.

Resigning, Bronwyn admitted defeat. "No, I cannot say."

Eleanor stopped abruptly and eyed Bronwyn. "But I can see that you do agree with my assessment. Interesting, considering how little you have traveled." She then issued Bronwyn another smile, this one more genuine, and then waved her hand around her. "It's art. Tapestries are beautiful, if well done, and most of these are, but woven pictures cannot be the sole spirit of a home. I suppose I should have realized that if Paris required refining, so would London. When able," she said, pausing to tap on her protruding stomach, "I shall bring culture here like they have at Palermo."

The queen turned to leave, but stopped once again. "Some believe me to be pompous, but I am not. I assure you."

Bronwyn held the queen's steady gaze, this time less afraid. Her Grace was employing a baiting tactic her mother had perfected. She had given Bronwyn two choices. Either she could state her opinion and insult the queen by agreeing she was pompous or be like all the other minions, and placate the queen's esteem. Bronwyn chose a third route.

"I think, Your Grace, some take offense to women with strong personalities, but I do not. Assertiveness is sometimes a requirement of survival, especially if one is in a position of authority. I was taught the one who wills is the one who can."

Once again the queen's gaze turned shrewd. "And have you been a woman in such a position?"

Bronwyn cocked a single brow. "Yes."

Explanation was not needed. That it had been on a much smaller scale than that of the queen was obvious, but Bronwyn had been responsible for the welfare of many people, and they had survived—in some ways even thrived—under her direction.

"I must admit that I like you, Lady . . . Edythe." The queen paused again and her eyes started to sparkle. She shifted her jaw and then resumed their walk to the outside. "I was not sure that I would. Women must own their opinion and not shrink from it, and I respect those of our sex who do not cower when faced with awkward moments. I am fortunate my second husband understands such strength and appreciates it."

They approached an overly large wooden entryway, and with a single look from their queen, the soldiers standing guard opened the massive doors but did not follow them outside.

Bronwyn glanced at the bench the queen instructed her to occupy, feeling odd that she should sit while Her Grace remained standing. A large flock of birds flew overhead, gathering both their attentions.

"Do you hunt, Lady Edythe?" the queen mused.

"I enjoy attending a hunt, but am only skilled with a blade."

"Do you carry one now?"

Bronwyn gulped and nodded, suddenly realizing that the palace guards might not appreciate her having such an object and being alone in the company of the queen. "I carry one with me always," Bronwyn answered as she dove her hand into the small hidden pocket of her gown and unsheathed the blade.

Eleanor studied the polished metal and carved handle, unperturbed that Bronwyn had not disclosed its presence. "You surprise me and so few do," the queen said, returning the lethal item. "I assume you are good."

"I'm excellent," Bronwyn said immodestly, slipping the dagger back into her pocket.

"I do like your honesty," Eleanor laughed aloud.

"But I wonder that you are not also an archer. I find the sport exceedingly diverting as well as physically and mentally challenging."

"And are you skilled, Your Grace?" Bronwyn asked, returning the queen's earlier blunt question.

"I am or at least I was a few months ago," Eleanor sighed. "Indeed, if there had been time after my husband's coronation—and maybe if I wasn't so encumbered—I could have persuaded Henry to sponsor great tournaments just for my pleasure. It's a beneficial skill to understand one's husband enough to sway his decisions, do you not think?"

The queen's demeanor had become demonstrably more relaxed, reminding Bronwyn of her earlier advice to be wary. "If I were married, I would undoubtedly agree," Bronwyn craftily replied.

"I would have thought you to be married. But then again, the one who pledges himself to you would need to be strong in both spirit as well as body. I have only met a few such men. My husband, your father . . . and Lord Anscombe, of course." Then with a simple twist of her hand, the queen pointed to another area of the gardens. "Come, let us walk some more."

At the mention of Ranulf, Bronwyn gritted her teeth and kept silent, refusing to rise to the bait. Standing, she wished the conversation would just come to an abrupt end. She and the queen were engaged in a game of wits in which Bronwyn felt as if she were constantly playing the part of the mouse being toyed with by a very beautiful and very powerful cat. Why the queen didn't just pounce and get the deed over with, Bronwyn could not fathom.

"You are quite good at schooling your expression,

Lady Edythe, better than anyone I have met in some time, but you should know that I have been a long-time student of the practice."

Bronwyn held her breath, but remained mum.

"Your father, Sir Laon, and I had a great number of conversations. He was quite a learned man and a surprising strategist in human behavior. I am still amazed at how he was always able to get what he wanted from someone, not by force, but by making the other want it, too, including myself. I was very sorry to hear about his death and . . ." The queen stopped in midstride to reach out and clasp Bronwyn's forearm, locking gazes. "I know he would have been quite devastated to learn about the death of your sister. He spoke often of his daughters and I know he loved each of you very much."

Bronwyn turned away and squeezed her eyes shut. She had been a fool. The queen knew exactly who she was the same way Ranulf had known. Her father must have described her and her sisters and never could she be mistaken for Edythe.

Bronwyn turned to apologize and explain, but before she could say a word, Queen Eleanor continued, "Your restraint is wise, and strangely, I am glad you have refrained from opening yourself in any way. Married to the king, I have an obligation to tell him certain things."

Bronwyn's mouth dropped a little wider for a fraction of a second and then closed. The queen just announced that until she knew for sure Bronwyn was lying about her identity, she felt no compulsion to disclose such deceit to the king. Her secret was safe. The question was—why?

"I apologize, Your Grace. I believe my expression

is misleading as I grieve for many right now. My father, the late Lord Anscombe . . . and of course, my sister." Bronwyn took a deep breath and decided to take a chance. Besides, she and Ranulf needed an ally. "Tonight, however, I feel my spirits may improve during the festivities. I quite look forward to them."

The queen's brows shot up as renewed excitement brewed in her eyes. "Do you now? Hmm, then I think I do, too."

They turned back toward the castle without any more conversation, and for the first time, Bronwyn felt truly relaxed since her arrival. She continued to school her countenance, but physically, the tension began to drain from her limbs.

"I was wondering if you and your sister would like to enter with me this evening as two of my ladies-in-waiting—just for tonight, of course," Queen Eleanor half asked, half commanded as they reentered her Presence chambers.

Bronwyn hesitated. She needed to get back to Ranulf, for their plan required exact timing, but how did one decline an invitation from the queen? "I appreciate the offer, Your Grace, and I am sure that my sister Lillabet would be happy to oblige, but I was hoping to join the festivities . . . later. And Lord Anscombe, he is no doubt waiting for us at the inn. I should get back and explain all that has happened."

"Nonsense. I have decided you and your sister shall come with us. And don't worry about Ranulf. I'll send word to him that you will be attending with Henry and me tonight." Bronwyn's heart plummeted as Eleanor continued, pretending not to see Bronwyn's distress. "Come in here."

Bronwyn's eyes once again grew wide as she followed the queen into what could only be her bedchambers. "First, your gown."

The doors closed behind them and Bronwyn fought the instinct to gasp. The room was unlike any other she had seen in the castle. There were different styles of art and sculpture, and the shimmering materials on the bed and chairs begged to be touched. Next to a large chest against the wall, hanging on two pegs, was a gown that took her breath away. Ermine-lined, the tight-fitting robe of iridescent gold cloth was embroidered with leopards and fleurs-de-lys, a blending of England and France.

Eleanor followed Bronwyn's fixated gaze and smiled. "As you can see, I am more like your sister and enjoy standing out in a crowd. The gown is beautiful, is it not? I wore it to my coronation and will again tonight. And while I admit to my penchants for beautiful Byzantine clothing, this babe grows hourly and that dress is surprisingly comfortable. You, on the other hand, favor the simple."

Inclining her head, Eleanor turned to the servant who was sitting so quietly in the room, Bronwyn had not even realized she was there. "Could you bring the dark burgundy gown of Petronilla's and then tell the others to get ready. Oh, and bring me the items from last year's Twelfth Night."

The thin woman nodded and left to fetch the gown, reappearing minutes later with a vision of dark red. Placing it on one of the settees, she curtsied and left to complete the rest of the queen's request.

"As you can see, it is quite plain, but very pretty. My sister Petronilla will not miss it and it would be perfect for you. It will also endear yourself to the king. My husband is many things . . . most of them good, but he can be aggravatingly frugal. He will appreciate the simplicity of your dress. And I think tonight, anything that can endear you to Henry will be a good thing, will it not?"

Bronwyn stepped toward the lounge to finger the rich garment. "Your Grace, I cannot think why I have deserved such attention or such kindness, but—"

"But nothing. Consider it a gift for the one you are about to give me."

"But I have no—"

The queen waved her hand, cutting Bronwyn off. "Your gift will be the one of amusement, something that is often lacking from these celebrations. Oh, they are grand in size and the feasts notable, but beyond that, the entertainment is somewhat unexciting. I expect tonight you are going to change all that."

The thin servant woman returned holding several items and deposited them on a small table next to the settee before retreating back into the shadows. Queen Eleanor plucked one of the glittering items off the table and placed the gold mask lined with jewels and feathers against her face. "I had these made last year for myself and my ladies-in-waiting. Unfortunately, Henry was stuck here in London for Twelfthtide with that awful Stephen after signing the treaty. So he never got to enjoy the fun we had hiding our identities and letting those around us try to guess who we were. Should we not attempt the levity once again, just for him?"

Bronwyn stepped forward and took the mask

outstretched in the queen's palm. Her Grace was not just astute, but brilliant. "I think your invitation to be a lady-in-waiting for a single night to be divine."

"I am glad we are of accord. Do you think your sister will feel slighted if I change my mind and she does not get to join in our fun?"

Bronwyn shook her head and searched for the right words. "Lily . . . what she desires most is to turn heads."

"Enjoys attention, does she? Maybe I should offer a gown and a grand entrance."

Bronwyn could not help but beam the queen a large smile. Queen Eleanor was much more than an ally. She was a friend. Bronwyn wasn't sure whether Her Grace was helping for her sake or Ranulf's, but at the moment, Bronwyn didn't care. She just hoped Ranulf figured out what was happening and adjusted his plan accordingly. "I am sure Lily will appreciate your generosity. I know I do."

Smiling, the queen sank into an overly large padded chair and leaned back, finding enormous fun in having conversations within conversations. "And you? Is there any part of tonight's festivities you are most interested in?"

Bronwyn moved the burgundy gown aside and sat down on the settee. "Just one. The Bean King."

"The Bean King? Hmmm. Henry was considering bypassing the tradition this year. He wasn't sure how wise it was to hand over power so early in his reign, no matter how long."

"It would be a shame," Bronwyn began, searching for words that convinced but did not reveal, "for it is always entertaining. This year, I suspect it will be the high point of the night."

"Then I can promise you it shall happen. I just hope, for your sake, Henry also finds it diverting."

Bronwyn bit her bottom lip. "Me, too. I pray he does, too," she mumbled under her breath.

Ranulf never paced. The effort wasted energy and it accomplished nothing, but that was exactly what he was doing. Bronwyn and Lillabet were at the palace and they were not going to return before the festivities. He should have realized the day would not get any easier after the events of the afternoon.

The king's favorite baker had indeed come to London, but getting inside the castle to where the food was being prepared had proved to be far more difficult than Ranulf had anticipated. Henry had increased security and that included those in the kitchens. It had taken time, but eventually Ranulf was able to meet with the pastry connoisseur and ensure a certain slice of cake would be delivered to only one person. By the time Ranulf returned to the inn, the night had started to blanket the sky and the merriment in the street had already begun. Then he was told Bronwyn and Lily were gone—and had been for some time.

Realizing the farce had been discovered, he was about to leave and try to explain his actions when word came directly from the queen. Bronwyn and Lily were guests of the court and would see him soon after the Bean King was announced. The message was cryptic, but enough to let Ranulf know that the plan had not changed.

Pacing, Ranulf mentally reviewed every possibility the queen would have for meeting with Bronwyn and her sister and then requesting their continued company. He was sure Bronwyn did not reveal their plan, for Queen Eleanor could not have knowingly supported the temporary deception. But his instinct screamed that Henry's high-spirited wife was somehow involved. He just hoped it was to his advantage.

An hour later, Ranulf slowly maneuvered his way into the semicrowded Great Hall, trying to avoid attention. Most paid no heed to him, but as usual, several openly gaped as he moved by. Ignoring them, Ranulf looked for Bronwyn, his search made exceedingly difficult with his limited vision.

His frustration was mounting when a buzz overcame part of the crowd. A few seconds later, Lillabet came into view with several escorts, capturing the eye of every nearby male. As Bronwyn had foretold, she was an expert at handling the attention. Soon, Baron Craven emerged from hiding and hovered close by. Ranulf had to give his sister-in-law credit. She neither shied away nor gave any indication of her true feelings for the man. She engaged him just enough, and by his untroubled expression, Lily had done her job. Now it was time for him to do his. Ranulf moved near to the main entrance and waited.

Soon afterward, King Henry II entered, followed by Queen Eleanor and her ladies-in-waiting, all wearing masks. Even with their faces hidden, they appeared beautiful and forbidden, just as he remembered them being in Normandy. He also recalled how they treated him. How fortunate he was not to have been snared by one of them for not a lady in the room could compare to Bronwyn. But where was she?

Edging his way closer to the queen, he finally

caught her eye and she waved for him to come near. "Your Grace, may I ask—"

"Ranulf, I would like to introduce you to one of my newest ladies," Queen Eleanor said, interrupting.

Ranulf gave the woman a quick glance. Like the others, she was beautiful. Her hair was tangled with gems and gold threads, and her attire was simple and elegant. Tall, graceful, slender, she reminded him of his Bronwyn. Her eyes were downcast and the rest of the face was hidden behind a mask, but there was something about her overall composure to indicate that her beauty went much further than skin deep.

"Your Grace, I—"

Ignoring his obvious attempt to ask about Bronwyn, Queen Eleanor continued. "One of tonight's entertainments will be to guess the identity of each lady. I think it will be extremely diverting for everyone. Would you like to be the first to try?"

Ranulf gave a deferential shake of his head, his disinterest in playing unmistakable. "I must decline, Your Grace—"

Just as he was going to step back into the crowd, soft fingers curled around his forearm. The simple touch caused him to freeze. None of the ladies from court had ever been willing to touch him, sit near him, or dance with him in the past. They acted as if his scars were contagious and any simple kindness was enough to catch them. He reexamined the woman, and this time slate blue eyes gazed back. Queen Eleanor's newest lady-in-waiting was Bronwyn.

"I'm sorry we could not dance. Perhaps later will be a better time."

Before Ranulf could reply with an emphatic yes,

she had moved into the crowd without a single glance back or any other action that would have indicated he meant anything to her or was even worth remembering.

Renewed resentment flooded Ranulf's veins as men began to descend, eager to meet and charm the seemingly unattached companion of the queen. His wife was the most beautiful of the women there and she should have been at his side, for all to see, not only that she was married, and to keep their lustful looks at bay, but that she had chosen him— *him*—the man no woman had ever wanted.

Fighting to remain calm, Ranulf swung hastily around and collided into the one man for whom he had been waiting. Baron Craven.

"Eyeing a replacement wife so soon?" Luc drawled. "Then again, she is very beautiful. Though I doubt she'll be interested in anyone less than a whole man."

"Be careful, baron. I'm not above killing you here and now," Ranulf growled.

Craven swallowed but held his ground. "I see Lady Lillabet found her levity despite her sorrow. Tell me, is her sister Lady Edythe also faring as well?"

It was a deliberant attempt to provoke Ranulf's temper and prove to everyone he was unstable. The ploy was obvious, which meant the man was unwise or overconfident—it mattered little either way.

Ranulf shrugged. "I neither know nor care. Lady Lillabet will be herself, and I saw her sister only once, and quite briefly."

The slight shift in the baron's jaw was the only hint at his growing aggravation. "I do wonder why both women are here. An annulment, perhaps? A way to avoid a life's sentence of marriage you forced upon them? I wonder if Lady Bronwyn were still alive, would she also be here and for such a reason. Or would she still feel compelled to disregard a king's decree."

Just then the baker entered and Ranulf released an inward sigh of relief. The conversation was dangerous for it was designed to incite physical violence and, if left to continue, might have succeeded. But the pain Ranulf first wanted to inflict was humiliation, and that could not be achieved with fists.

It required intellect. And maybe a slight emotional push.

"I believe King Stephen is dead," Ranulf said softly. "You would be wise to remember my long relationship with our new ruler. Some even consider me one of his favorites. So, it's my turn to ask you a question. Who do you think King Henry will agree to see first tomorrow? A small, insignificant baron or a loyal commander who once saved his life?"

The baron's jaw went rigid. "And when you do meet the king, just what will you say? The truth? That you ignored his predecessor's wishes on whom to marry, lied to your new wife and failed to keep her safe, and then attacked and slaughtered my men unprovoked? I have witnesses. Who do you have to stand for you? Bronwyn's sisters? Lillabet has ignored you completely and Edythe still remains unseen, avoiding your company. Neither seem willing to support the man who forced them into marriage and then lost them their beloved sister."

Ranulf produced a knowing smile, intentionally irritating the baron further. "Just know that whenever you do get your audience with the king, I will have the upper hand. You started this war, baron, but you will not end it." As he spoke the last words, Ranulf ignored Luc's sputtered response and started toward the baker, who was thankfully standing just next to a tankard of ale.

Ranulf poured himself a drink and then, using the mug, pointed out the baron to the baker. "When?"

"Word was sent late that the queen desires to determine the hour and the king has decided to oblige her. But are you sure? That one . . . well, he is not the most welcomed noble of the court these past few days."

"That's good to hear, and yes, he definitely is the one," Ranulf answered and then swallowed a significant amount of the mug's contents. Now all he could do was wait . . . and watch Bronwyn be entertained by every man who could make his way to her side.

Once again, a deep sense of possession consumed him. Until now, he had not had to compete for her attention and no one had been foolish enough to try. But as one and then another hour passed, the intensity of his jealousy grew and it mattered little that in his heart he knew that she was his. Each time a hand touched Bronwyn's waist or someone bent to whisper in her ear or her laughter tinkled throughout the Hall, Ranulf had to repress the mounting urge to go and pummel the man. He almost lost the battle he was waging with himself when some overly ambitious young knight refused to leave her side. Only the queen and her long-awaited announcement saved the young man from a fate that would have required the attention of a healer and several weeks in bed.

Ranulf joined the throng and at long last retrieved

his slice of cake. From the corner of his eye, he watched Craven do the same . . . directly from the man who made it. As people bit into the moist sweet bread, sighs of disappointment could be heard throughout the Hall as each discovered they did not have the bean. Minutes passed and Ranulf started to wonder if the baker had made a mistake. But then a shout was heard over the crowd.

Craven had found the prize.

By the look on his face, Luc was completely surprised but also quite eager to enjoy his chance. Everyone watched as he proudly made his way to the king. Ranulf kept to the back of the crowd, secretly enjoying the veiled look of disgust on King Henry's face as he watched the baron advance.

The Bean King tradition was not one of Henry's favorites. For he was not one to follow customs; he preferred to set them. Most men wore their hair long, but Henry had always kept his red hair short, something Ranulf quickly adopted after first meeting him. He and Tyr also embraced the idea of shaving, something else inspired by Henry, though the king maintained a mustache, which in Ranulf's mind negated the benefits of a naked face. And then there was the king's state of dress. As always, his cloak was of fine cloth, but significantly shorter and less ornate. Baron Craven was the king's opposite in every way.

Ranulf held his breath as Craven swaggered up to King Henry with his extravagant long gold-and-red tunic swishing around his legs, looking altogether too eager to receive his honorary title. Henry grimaced and for a second Ranulf wondered if he was going to change his mind. Then, the queen leaned over and whispered something in his ear. Resigned, Henry stood up and proclaimed Craven to be the Bean King, until midnight, giving him license to enjoy whatever pleasures he desired—within reason.

Immediately Craven spun around and scanned the crowd, searching. Ranulf stepped forward and into view and locked gazes with his nemesis. Craven's mouth turned upward into a nasty smile and Ranulf returned his grin with one of his own, intending to infuriate him. It worked.

Craven whipped back around. "Your Grace, for my first and only act as Bean King, I ask for one thing. An audience with you about a matter of great importance. Now."

Even Ranulf was shocked. Craven's arrogance might cost him an audience and Ranulf the very meeting he had struggled to orchestrate. That King Henry was enraged was an understatement. His already ruddy face was now bright red. But once again the queen intervened.

Eleanor placed a hand over the king's and said melodically, "I think, Henry, that we should give the baron his request. He is, after all, the Bean King. And I have a feeling it will be quite enlightening if not very entertaining."

Henry fell back against his chair and slumped just slightly, eyeing his wife in disbelief. Ranulf knew why. It had always been Eleanor who was so adamant about audiences never to take place during a festivity.

Ranulf skimmed the crowd looking for Bronwyn, for it was clear the queen knew something, if not everything, about their plans and he needed reassurance that all would be well. When he located her, she was already staring at him and gave him a quick wink. Ranulf returned his attention to the king, who was shrugging in resignation. With a wave of his hand, he said, "To indulge my wife, I will agree to your request, but only this once. And only if it is of a short duration."

In a flamboyant gesture, Craven tucked part of his cloak back with one arm and outstretched the other toward the crowd. "Before I begin, I call forth Lord Anscombe."

With a somber expression, Ranulf moved unhurriedly toward the king, heedless of the quiet whispers around him. Arriving, he gave Henry a bow, who shifted to sit straighter in his chair, suddenly more interested than he had been before. The king was no fool and his intelligence was extremely quick. He was undoubtedly starting to suspect that it was no accident that Craven had received the bean. Henry was just wondering who orchestrated the event—the baron or Ranulf.

"My king," Craven began, "you have known Lord Anscombe for some time and believe him to be faithful to your rule, but tonight I must inform you that his loyalties have changed."

Henry's jaw clenched. "Just what do you accuse Ranulf of? And beware, you are still under my rule, baron, temporary Bean King or not. Do not accuse one of my nobles of disloyalty without being able to support such a claim."

Confidently, Craven continued, "I accuse him of several transgressions against Your Grace, and I can and *will* prove them." He paused and turned toward Ranulf. "Lord Anscombe, my first question to you concerns the circumstances of the death of your late wife's father. Could you not have saved Sir Laon le Breton and did you not choose instead to let him die?"

Ranulf had not thought of this argument since he didn't consider himself truly at fault. He certainly never considered Craven leading off with this particular attack. Then again, maybe the baron knew just how much Queen Eleanor admired and respected Laon. This was not good. "I didn't let him die. It was an accident and a sad loss. But I find your question odd as it was Laon who pleaded with me to take care of his daughters as he lay dying in my arms."

"You broke that promise, though, didn't you, not only to Sir le Breton, but to our king? Or are you going to deny ordering all three daughters away within hours of your arrival?"

"I did," Ranulf answered simply.

Pain and disappointment flashed in the king's eyes, causing Craven's smirk to enlarge. The baron was craftier than Ranulf originally believed, but he was still a shortsighted fool. Craven's inability to examine his attack strategy from any viewpoint other than his own would in the end be his undoing. Patience was needed for it was critical to let him continue to believe he had the upper hand.

"And tell me, as a knight of the king," Craven continued, "will you honorably and truthfully answer this? Was it you who shot an arrow at me and then ran away without showing your face?"

"I didn't know you to be a noble." Again, Ranulf did not expound his answer and kept quiet about the baron's lecherous, unwanted behavior prompting the potentially deadly response. Ranulf's skill with a bow was well known in court. If he missed, it was not by accident. But it was not yet time for the king to rally to his side.

"And what about Lady Bronwyn, one of the very women you were promised to protect? Was she not also just inches away from death? Did not that arrow strike between us?"

"My recollection was that it was slightly above your heads, not in between," Ranulf replied, reflecting what he hoped was a fair amount of boredom.

Craven's eyes glinted. "That woman was promised to me. Something you knew when you forced Lady Bronwyn into marriage only days later."

Ranulf shrugged in acknowledgment. The king and queen were now in his blind spot, so he could not see their reaction, but he could imagine it. He hoped both were more intrigued with his blasé reaction than repelled by it.

"And what about Lady Lillabet? Was she not to be your wife?"

"There was discussion about it. Neither she nor I desired the union."

"Admit that you made all three women marry, intentionally breaking not only your pledge to the king and God, but the one made to me."

Ranulf could feel the crowd pressing closer upon them, listening; he repressed a satisfactory smile. Soon. He just hoped Bronwyn was among them. Ready. "My promise was to protect and I did . . . from you."

"Me?" Craven shouted with feigned dismay. "Then where is your wife? This woman whom you claim needed shelter," Craven demanded. Then to the crowd he announced, "Within a week of being under Lord Anscombe's 'protection,' she turned into ashes in her own home. Alone."

Ranulf just stared, rage flickering in his dark gaze.

Craven whirled back around. "Then to alleviate his guilt, his lordship blamed me and slaughtered all my men without cause or warning."

Fully aware of his tightly leashed anger, Ranulf forced himself to speak slowly and deliberately so that no one could misunderstand. "You set fire to Syndlear with Bronwyn inside."

"You killed an army of men loyal to the king over a woman! You, the bringer of peace to the northern borders, have brought us nothing but death and lies."

Ahh, there it was. The ultimate transgression. "I killed an army of mercenaries faithful to no one but a purse held by a man who has no loyalty for anyone but himself."

Craven's demeanor instantly changed. His eyes blazed and his voice became low and menacing. "And I say you are lying. You're lying to the king just as you lied to compel Bronwyn and her sisters into false marriages. Do you really think anyone here believes that a beautiful woman would marry you?" Craven laughed cruelly. Gesturing toward Ranulf's scar and missing eye, he announced to the crowd, "No one will shake his hand. Even his dead wife's sisters won't come near him."

Ranulf remained mum, arms crossed, listening to the accusations.

"They hate you, don't they?" Craven sneered. "For the same reason your wife did. When she discovered the truth about how you killed her father, she ran away. She left you to return home and so you burned it down to hide the truth. That is what you need to know, good king," Craven spat out. "Your Lord Anscombe is a traitor and a murderer, loyal only to himself."

Ranulf leveled a long, deep look, his single eye black and dazzling with fury. "The king knows I am loyal to him, just as I am loyal to my people, and my wife's family. I am here not for myself, but them. I promised to protect them against you. And while due to distance, I have been unable to keep my king informed and ask for his counsel as I would have preferred, I kept my word. You were the reasons behind all my actions."

Craven crossed his arms, feeling victory was near. "You admit your failings, and claim I am the reason, but you can prove nothing."

"No, but I can," came a soft voice.

Suddenly the room parted and Bronwyn joined Ranulf by his side.

Craven studied the masked figure, but his confidence still did not waiver. "You? How can a lady of the court know any of what I speak?"

Bronwyn raised her hand and carefully lifted the mask to reveal her identity. "But I am not a lady of the court," she countered and then curtsied in front of the king, who waved for her to continue. "Her Grace offered the privilege of coming in disguise along with her other ladies-in-waiting and I accepted, but I am Lady Anscombe, Ranulf's wife, sister to Lady Edythe and Lady Lillabet." Then facing Craven, she added, "And the woman you tried to murder."

Craven blanched. "You're supposed to be dead! No one could have lived thought that. No one!"

Bronwyn stepped forward and in a low voice, taut with anger said, "So you admit you were there."

Craven's mouth clamped shut as his chiseled features twisted in anger. "It changes nothing," he seethed. "Your husband still lied, ignored the king's wishes, and slaughtered my men. He will answer for his crimes."

"I think I shall decide on that," came a rumbling deep voice with contempt that forbade any further argument. Instantly, the king had everyone's attention. He rose to his feet and took a step closer. "You are Lady Bronwyn? Laon's daughter and, if I understood correctly, Ranulf's wife."

"I am."

"Are you here to condemn one of my nobles or to defend your husband?"

"I came only to disprove reports of my demise."

"And nothing more? That I cannot believe. Do you have nothing to add? Your husband has been accused of much, most of which he freely admitted without remorse or justification."

A flicker of apprehension coursed through Bronwyn, but she quickly collected her thoughts and nodded. "He has, Your Grace, but if I may, I would like to make one clarifying point. As I understand it, Ranulf was charged with two primary duties when he journeyed to Hunswick to assume the title and responsibilities of being Lord Anscombe. First, he was to ensure the safety of myself and my two sisters. This, he did not just once, but three times.

"The first time he came to my rescue with the well-placed arrow when Baron Craven tried to force his attentions upon me. The second came shortly after his arrival. He indeed ordered us to be safely escorted home, to Syndlear, which we love, but not out of contempt or disloyalty, but for protection—from himself. He mistakenly thought that I and my sisters would feel uncomfortable seeing his scars, not knowing that my mother and I were severely burned from a fire years ago."

The whole time she spoke, her eyes were locked with King Henry's. His misty gray pools drew her in, giving her the confidence to speak and continue. "I would have left, but an unexpected accident occurred and I stayed to tend Lord Anscombe's wounds and assist in managing Hunswick." The last part Bronwyn stated to Queen Eleanor, knowing how she had done the same for her husband when he was away.

Turning back to the king, Bronwyn raised her chin just slightly and said, "As for my untimely death, I was not running away. I was retrieving a tapestry for my sister, who felt rushed to exit her home after being confronted by Baron Craven. He threatened her with his intentions to marry one of us. Unbeknownst to me, the baron, angered by his discovery that all of us were married, followed me to Syndlear. There he locked me in a room and then set the fire believing I would be dead before night's end. And I should have been, but my husband saved me. More importantly, he saved Cumbria and its people."

Bronwyn took a small step forward and began to wrench her hands, the desire to have the king understand and believe her words evident in her features. "My husband kept his promise to you, my king. Baron Craven would have brought the strife you sent Ranulf to prevent. The people of Cumbria, of Hunswick, know and love my husband. They will come and testify if you would but ask. I also encourage you to invite the baron's people so they can describe their lives under his rule. My husband has not forsaken you. He treasures your respect as do I and my people, and we trust that you will not forsake us and remove the man whom we have all come to depend upon."

Ranulf moved in behind her and placed his hands on her shoulders. She glanced back and he knew she saw the tears brimming in his one good eye. He had never agreed to her saying so much, but to hear someone stand up for him, to announce to all that he was loved and a good leader, would be more than enough to counter any decree Henry might give. Sliding his hand down her arm, Ranulf intertwined her fingers with his own. Bronwyn beamed him a smile, gave his hand a squeeze, and returned her attention to the king.

King Henry clasped his fingers behind his back and stared at all three of them one by one. He wasn't overly tall, but his strength was undeniable. His cheeks were red, making the freckles upon them stand out all the more, and his dark gray eyes were sparkling with anger.

The room watched in silence. Never had a Twelfth Night been so filled with drama. Still, everyone present was anxious to learn of the new king's reaction to such accusations. Suddenly, nerves took hold in Bronwyn and she squeezed Ranulf's hand. Then the queen caught the corner of her eye. And Bronwyn could have sworn she saw an almost imperceptible head nod, as if to say all would be fine.

"Ranulf." At the king's harsh tone, Bronwyn's

head snapped back. "You know how I detest these types of discussions during festivities, and don't tell me that you didn't arrange for this monstrosity tonight, for I know better. I have no choice now but to rule and you may regret your rashness."

Bronwyn felt Ranulf's callused thumb caress the back of her hand, and she let go the breath she had been holding. He was reminding her that it did not matter. They would be together regardless.

Pivoting on one heel, King Henry leveled a heated gaze on Baron Craven. "You are a fool, baron, and I hate fools. Take a look at your enemy and tell me what you see."

Craven glanced at Ranulf as instructed. "I see an ugly cripple who—"

"Those scars you disdain so saved my life," Henry interrupted. Both Queen Eleanor and Bronwyn's eyes popped open wide in surprise. "I was but nine years old when I came to Bristol for further education. A fire broke out on the second floor of the abbey and Ranulf came to make sure I got out. As we rushed to escape, a beam started to crack and as a young boy I panicked. Ranulf pushed me into safety, but a beam supporting the ceiling split, swinging down and striking him. He should have died. *I* should have died, but by the grace of God, we did not. Ranulf recovered, and despite an injury that would have broken most men, he trained and became one of my most effective commanders, a hell of an archer, and without question, one of my most loyal nobles."

The king paused to see how the baron was digesting this newfound information. Bronwyn was shocked and stood there with her mouth slightly open, staring at her husband. From the corner of her eye, she could see the queen and the king's advisors were just as astonished by the admission, their eyes shifting from Henry to Ranulf and back again. Even the crowd was hushed with awe. Only Craven scowled, his hatred consuming him.

King Henry's jaw clenched with anger. "Baron Craven, I strip you of your title, lands, and wealth. Your castle is to be razed, if Ranulf hasn't done it already. Your survival is up to you, but you will have no power over others to enact my laws and ensure my will with my people. Be gone."

Sheer fright swept through Craven's features. "But . . . but . . ."

"Another word and I shall have you drawn and quartered for what you did. I am not one to show mercy often."

Stumbling backward, Craven opened and closed his mouth several more times before turning and quickly exiting, with a final unintelligible shout.

Grimacing, the king then returned his attention to Ranulf. "Ranulf, my debt to you is now paid. As far as your actions of late, I want it to be known that you acted as I would have wanted and would have supported *with the exception* of starting a battle when you should have fought Craven in single-man combat. And yet, as your wife so eloquently pointed out, I also cannot deny that peace in the north is now more likely," Henry said with a sigh, glimpsing the crumbs of the bean cake in someone's hands. "And though I do not approve of your appropriation of the Bean King tradition"—he paused to find and issue a pointed glare at his favorite baker—"your scheme to reveal Baron Craven's true character worked. But let it be known that the next time any man raises arms without proof of the reason or my approval *will answer to me.*"

King Henry moved to sit back down, but it was clear he was not done speaking. "No man or noble is to take the law in his own hands. Not even you, Ranulf, even though I know you to be fair and impartial. But as you have demonstrated—there are circumstances—or people," he said, gesturing to Bronwyn, "that can interfere with one's ability to rule without emotion. *Only this royal court* will decide cases involving the ownership of freehold property, which this certainly was about. The stability and the securing of property rights will help end the strife of the English people. It is important for everyone—especially nobles—to resort to a court of law rather than violence, trial by ordeal, or oftentimes, incorrect noble-based ruling."

Henry leaned back against his chair and realized everyone in the room had been listening to him think his thoughts aloud. With a wave of his arm, he called out, "Resume the festivities!"

Eleanor reached over and stroked his forearm.

"Was I fair?" Henry whispered.

She nodded. "Very. Besides, I think our Ranulf gave you the justification for some of the changes you have been considering. Perhaps a court of law is needed."

"He did. And besides it was all highly entertaining. I had to bite my tongue when Craven started all that nonsense about Ranulf trying to kill him with an arrow."

"So you knew from the beginning . . ." Eleanor murmured in partial disbelief and admiration.

"That Ranulf was up to something? The man would never let anyone—even me—insult his honor without response. It was hard to wait until the oaf finished everything Ranulf needed him to say . . . and come to think of it . . . it was very convenient for Lady Bronwyn to be in disguise. How is it that you did not inform me earlier of what was to happen?"

"I did not know," Eleanor rejoined quickly. "I met with his wife, who never owned to her true identity . . . but I liked her and suspected she would enjoy the night much better as one of my ladies-in-waiting. It is a great honor, you know."

"And the idea of coming in masquerade?"

"Well, it has been dull lately."

"And you never knew who she was. Never thought to tell me you suspected Lady Bronwyn was not whom she professed to be."

"I only knew for sure that I liked her and that she was Laon's daughter. And as for the masquerade, I did it for you, my king."

"Me?"

"Mmm-hmmm," Eleanor purred against his ear. "I know how very much you like to be entertained."

"And that it was. Quite diverting. Never thought to see the day where Ranulf would be at ease in a crowd—or so demonstrative," Henry said, pointing at the joined couple.

"He's in love, my king. Just like I am. Perhaps someday I'll do something about your men and their rough-mannered ways. Maybe I will convene my own court—the court of love."

"I think that babe in your womb has made you soft in the head," Henry teased.

"Maybe," Eleanor sighed as she sat back in her

chair with a smile that spoke of a mind whirling with ideas.

As soon as Ranulf reached the rear of the Hall, he swung Bronwyn behind the screened passage and closed his mouth roughly over hers, searing her lips to his. Ignoring the servants around them busily preparing food and drink, Bronwyn wrapped her arms around his neck and melted, leaning into him, kissing him back with growing eagerness.

He felt a shudder pass through her and reluctantly eased himself away before his control was completely shattered by her soft ragged moans. Another shout could be heard in the Hall as the crowd erupted again with cheers. Ranulf smiled against Bronwyn's lips and then placed a soft peck on the tip of her nose.

"Who would have thought you had so many supporters?" she whispered.

"Not mine, my love. Yours. I had not a one till you started speaking and now I am the envy of every man present."

Bronwyn laughed and the sound of her sheer joy lit him up as nothing could. A frisson of longing rippled through him and an undeniable need to taste her once more took over. Tipping her chin up with a single fingertip, he kissed her again, slower this time, letting his hand fall to the small of her back, molding her to him. He inhaled and her female scent filled his senses, drugging him until his will was no longer his own.

When their mouths eventually parted, Bronwyn placed her cheek on his chest and sighed with absolute contentment. "If you are to remain the envy of all present, we cannot remain hidden all night."

"You're right. Let's leave," he answered thickly.

Bronwyn laughed again and playfully swatted his chest, taking a step backward. "You, my lord, are going out in that throng and will enjoy yourself immensely. I do not think there is a woman in the room who would deny being your partner this eve."

"For you, I will go out, but only if you remain by my side."

Bronwyn willingly agreed and soon found herself whisked out into the crowd. Together, they danced, drank, and enjoyed the generosity of their king. Never had a Twelfth Night been more festive or enjoyable.

"Let's go."

Ranulf's husky breath tickled Bronwyn's ear. Desire surged through her and the room was suddenly confining. She wanted nothing more than to be at the inn and in his arms. "Let me find Lily."

At once, Ranulf began to pull her through the crowd, anticipation hastening his every step. After several deft moves, Bronwyn found her sister in front of her. "Lily," she started, breathing rapidly, "we would like to leave. Can you get your things?"

Licking her lips, Lily glanced back at one woman elaborately dressed in golds and greens who nodded enthusiastically. "I think I might remain here. The festivities are not close to over and Lady Tarolind said that I could stay at the palace with her."

Bronwyn studied Lily for a second, sensing her sister's unease. "Are you sure you really want to?"

Leaning in so that only Bronwyn could hear, Lily whispered, "I am quite divided. Some of the ladies are friendly while others are rather silly and childish. But . . ." She paused to wring her hands.

Understanding dawned on Bronwyn. "But it might be your only chance to stay in the palace."

Relief flooded Lily's gray eyes. "Exactly! Forever I will be able to say that I was a guest of the court! That I slept in the palace!"

Bronwyn fought back a chuckle. Lily was growing up. She was starting to recognize the shallow traits in others, but she had yet to realize that she still possessed them herself. Bronwyn leaned in and gave Lily a quick peck on the cheek. "Be ready to leave early on the morrow."

A grin spread across Lily's face. "Thank you! I will be, I promise. One night is all I need, and though you might not believe me, I am ready to go home."

Bronwyn leaned back into Ranulf and watched her sister disappear into the crowd as the lure of court's trappings once again tugged at Lily's vain heart.

Ranulf bent his head and slyly began to nibble on Bronwyn's ear. "That leaves you and me and I know of a warm little inn where we can celebrate Twelfth Night."

"In a fun way?" she asked mischievously.

"In a most delectable and fun way," Ranulf purred against her neck.

Bronwyn spun around and with a twinkle in her eye gestured toward the exit. "Then let us not tarry, my lord."

Ranulf needed no further encouragement. He led them out of the palace grounds and decided that it would take less time to walk the few blocks to the inn than to find the stable boy in the mayhem and get a horse. People were everywhere, but most were drunk, unaware or uncaring of them. Ranulf curled his arm protectively around her and they walked side by side thinking only of each other and the inviting bed only minutes away. A battle could have erupted in the streets and he would have been oblivious. His life was perfect.

Then without warning, a sharp, excruciating pain ricocheted through his skull. Someone had clubbed him.

Years of training and fighting experience took over. Instinctively, he swung around, not using his sight but his senses, and pummeled whoever had hit him, uncaring if it was an accident or intentional. His fist collided with what felt to be a jaw.

The man fell forward, causing Ranulf to misstep and lose his balance. Ranulf instinctively clenched his grip on Bronwyn's arm and she cried out, reaching for him but unable to break his fall. His right knee hit the ground hard and he heard himself grunt. The attack was no accident.

Pushing himself back up to his feet, he reached out for Bronwyn, finding her hand. Her white-knuckle grip told him that it was far from over. Cursing his limited vision, he examined his surroundings as best he could. A partial moon lit up the main street, but they were next to one of the larger buildings casting dark shadows. Just behind them was a small alley. Ranulf looked back and saw three tall dark figures emerge. They were moving toward them and they were not merrymakers.

"Run," Ranulf ordered. "The inn is just around that corner. Find my men."

Bronwyn immediately left Ranulf and darted for help, but she had not gone forty feet when a familiar silhouette appeared. Luc Craven's tall hard form was unmistakable. His smile was mocking and his ice blue eyes pierced the darkness, promising retribution. His lips twisted into a cynical smile. "Lady Bronwyn."

Bronwyn slipped her hand into the hidden slit in the front of her gown and gripped the handle of her dagger. That afternoon she had almost yielded to the seamstress's complaints and not added the small pocket. But without the familiar weight at her left side, the gown had felt awkward, despite its beauty. So she had held firm and said that if they were going to make alterations, one of them was to be a small sleeve for her dagger.

"Choose," Luc hissed. "Life or its ugly alternative."

"I choose death," Bronwyn said, clutching the dagger. She slipped it out and spun it in her hand until her thumb hit its mark. The streets that once seemed crowded were now devoid of life. Time stopped and an eternity passed as she waited for him to move out of the shadows and into the moonlight. Finally, he did and the dagger left her fingertips heading for its mark.

Bronwyn watched as the baron's form went rigid. A second later it crumpled on the ground. She held her breath. It was too dark to know if her aim had been true or if Luc was feigning so that she would come near.

Arms enclosed her, bringing life back into her numb limbs. She threw her elbow back as hard as she could but her assailant must have been ready. Before the sharp bone made contact, it was captured in a vise grip.

"It's me, love. It's me."

At the sound of Ranulf's soft reassuring voice, she collapsed in his arms. "What about the others?" she asked, even though deep down she knew the answer. Ranulf wouldn't be at her side if they were still in danger.

"Dead or fleeing."

Slowly her shakes diminished and Ranulf let her go to examine the dark unmoving form.

"Is Luc dead?"

"Yes," Ranulf replied. "Where did you aim?"

Bronwyn swallowed, remembering. "His neck. I didn't know if he would be wearing mail under his tunic."

"Then your aim was true," Ranulf said, pulling back the top of the baron's garment. "And he *was* wearing mail."

Bronwyn started shaking again.

Ranulf pushed himself up, grimacing as he leaned against his hurt knee. "Where did you learn to do that?"

Bronwyn blinked. The astonishment in his voice was enough to rally her senses. "I told you I knew how to protect myself, and that I could and would use my knife."

Ranulf pulled her into his arms, hoping never again to feel the fear of losing her. "Aye, love, you did."

Sweeping her up into his arms, he stepped over the body and avoided the crowd that was starting to reappear. Bronwyn tried to jump out of his grasp but failed. Seeing that they were headed toward the inn and not the palace, she asked, "Shouldn't we go and tell someone?"

Ranulf shook his head. "No. The king will not

want to be disturbed by this. Tomorrow I will request an audience and tell him, but he will not care. Property is no longer an issue. Craven was just a crazed common man who attacked. As a lord, I can decide if his fate was just. And I do. The king will agree. Besides," Ranulf said with a grin, "we had other plans for celebrating Twelfth Night, did we not?"

Bronwyn bit her lip and cocked her brow impishly. "We certainly did."

Epilogue

Celebrated as early as 361 A.D., the Feast of Epiphany is the conclusion of Twelfthtide celebrations surrounding the birth of Christ. Gifts are exchanged representing the visit of the three Magi, though some believe the day originally celebrated Christ's baptism. On Epiphany, festivities come to an end, decorations are removed, and the household returns to its normal state for the coming year. This day in Christmas history was dramatically affected by King Henry II, who discovered feasts and plays and new traditions when he invaded Ireland. A country rich with customs introduced the king to new ones, including Little Christmas or Women's Christmas, in which the men assume the household duties while the women enjoy the day with their friends and family. Celebrated on Epiphany, this custom is also observed by other cultures and is becoming more popular in today's world.

Ranulf took a deep breath and exhaled. The air was chilly, and as they continued north, it would only grow colder. But no one in their group cared, just as they did not feel the need to travel faster after their hurried journey to London. In the far distance, the crowded city could still be seen, but in another hour it would be out of sight and so would the afternoon sun.

They had left later than planned, mostly because of Luc Craven's deadly end. Ranulf had visited the king early in the morning and it had gone much as he had expected. Meanwhile, Bronwyn had visited once more with the queen and was asked to prolong their visit one more day, but she had wanted to go home.

"I'm surprised you didn't want to stay longer. Didn't you like court, Lily?" Bronwyn finally asked, having wondered what happened last night after they had left, for her sister had been suspiciously quiet and contemplative.

"I loved court," Lily sighed, "but I always dreamed it would be different."

"There were several beautiful women. Were you a little jealous?"

"No . . . yes . . . I mean at first I was, but in the end, I realized that I don't want to be like them. And worse, I realized that most believed I *was*. I've just been so sheltered, by Father, you—even Edythe."

"Maybe we shouldn't have—"

"No," Lily interrupted, "but do you know what I most enjoyed about last night?"

"What?"

"Announcing to them all that I am married and

just who my husband is. You would not believe how many men and women of the court know Rolande."

Lily turned to address Ranulf, who was riding silently, but listening, on the other side of Bronwyn. "And how good-looking. Many of the women were quite envious. You should have seen their faces," Lily added with pride, sounding more like the little sister Bronwyn loved and endured. "I cannot wait until spring. I just know that Rolande and I will be happy like you and Ranulf."

"I truly hope that you are," Bronwyn said.

"Oh, we will be. I want it to be so, and I will defy anyone to let it be any other way," Lily replied emphatically and then kicked her horse to ride up ahead.

Bronwyn sighed and shook her head. "I thought for a moment she had matured, at least a little."

Ranulf laughed and said, "She has. She wants to go home!"

"And are you ready to go home?"

"Home," Ranulf murmured, rolling the foreign word around in his mouth. "Always thought the idea implausible. A place cannot make you feel safe, happy—"

"And loved," Bronwyn added.

"Or loved," Ranulf repeated. "Then I met you. Wherever you are is my home."

"So if I wanted to live in Normandy?"

Ranulf cocked his head in surprise and turned so that he could see her whole face. Seeing the mirth in her eyes, he responded in kind. "Or Scotland with your grandmother . . . even London."

Bronwyn shivered. "I choose Hunswick," she said, conceding.

Ranulf leaned over, picked up her hand, and kissed its back. "Then it is time to go home. Our home."

The joy Bronwyn felt inside lit up her face. "Who knows, by next Christmas, we just might have someone else to share it with."